TOTAL IMMUNITY

TOTAL
IMMUNITY

ROBERT WARD

[*An* OTTO PENZLER *Book*]

HOUGHTON MIFFLIN HARCOURT

BOSTON • NEW YORK

2009

For information about permission to reproduce selections from this book,
write to Permissions, Houghton Mifflin Harcourt Publishing Company,
6277 Sea Harbor Drive, Orlando, Florida 32887-6777.

www.hmhbooks.com

Library of Congress Cataloging-in-Publication Data
Ward, Robert, date.
Total immunity / Robert Ward.
p. cm.
ISBN 978-0-15-101480-4
1. United States. Federal Bureau of Investigation—Fiction.
2. Diamond smugglers—Fiction. 3. Diamond smuggling—Fiction.
4. Los Angeles (Calif.)—Fiction. I. Title.
PS3573.A735T67 2009
813'.54—dc22   2008049499

Book design by Brian Moore

Printed in the United States of America

DOC 10 9 8 7 6 5 4 3 2 1

For Jed Dietz and his wonderful family.

His wife, Julia McMillan, and awesome kids,

Edith, Robert, and Elihu

PART I
THE EVIL EYE

THE SILVER CESSNA glided down from the clouds and landed without a hitch at the private J. T. Hodges Airport in West Covina. Only seconds after it rolled to a stop, the side door slid open, portable steps dropped to the ground, and the blond female flight attendant stood by the top step and said good-bye to the muscular Arab, Kafi, dressed in his black silk tracksuit. The wiry bodyguard's head swiveled left and right as he traced the airport for signs of danger. When he was certain the coast was clear, he turned and nodded to a figure who waited just inside the plane's exit door. A few seconds later, stocky, burr-headed South African Karl Steinbach, whose parents had moved the family from Germany, dressed impeccably in his $10,000 silk Prada suit and his $5,000 bespoke Lobb shoes, walked down the silver steps. Just behind him was the second bodyguard, the apelike Welshman, Colin Draper. Like Kafi, Draper scoured the horizon for signs . . . a metallic glimmer, any evidence of an FBI agent hidden behind the eucalyptus trees to the north.

He saw nothing, no one.

Still, the two bodyguards didn't rest easy until they'd crossed the steaming tarmac and deposited their charge, Steinbach, into the black Cadillac Escalade which waited just about twenty yards away from the silver plane. Within five seconds, both of them had joined Steinbach in the backseat and shut the doors. The uniformed chauffeur locked the doors from his control panel, turned up the AC, and the elegant limo pulled away. Inside, Karl Steinbach clicked on his favorite movie, *House of Games*. He'd seen the David Mamet written and directed movie six times but never tired of it. The low elegance of the machine-gun dialogue and the endless twists of the plot pleased him in a way that no mere action thriller ever could.

But today he couldn't lose himself in it. Indeed, the things on his mind were of such a serious nature that he had trouble watching at all. This deal—and its myriad complications—had to work. It had to, and it would . . .

(But what if it didn't? What if something went wrong?)

Nonsense. He wouldn't allow himself to think about that. Everything was under control, and it was going to work just the way he'd set it up.

He watched as Lindsay Crouse shot Joe Mantegna at LAX. Usually that was the high point of the picture for him . . . but now he glowered out at the window, feeling a roiling in his belly, a tension in his neck.

He squeezed the leather armrest with his right hand.

Relax. Chill.

The flight in, the landing, and the subsequent drive-away were a total success. It was all running like proverbial clock-work. It was all going to work out. It had to and it would.

But in any human endeavor, there are plans and plans.

Take FBI Agent Michael Perry. As Steinbach and his little crew headed into Silver Lake, Perry was sitting on an old and battered projectionist's chair on the roof of the white stucco snack bar in an abandoned drive-in called The Floodlight. The dusty parking lot was covered with blowing newspapers and ancient popcorn boxes. It was all very American Gothic, but Perry wasn't concerned with the atmospherics of the place. Perry had been watching the Steinbach landing through his high-powered Canon 10 × 30 binoculars. He had seen the whole efficient event: the plane coming in, the landing, and the drive-away. And as soon as Steinbach's car had left the runway and headed into town, Perry took a bite of his cold burrito and hit the speed dial on his cell phone.

The phone had barely rung once before a voice on the other end answered. The man receiving the call was Oscar Hidalgo, a Mexican FBI agent who was thirty-four years old. He sat across the seat from his partner, Agent Jack Harper, thirty-five. The two men were diametrically opposite. Hidalgo was five foot six inches tall and weighed nearly 200 pounds. He was the strongest man at FBI Headquarters in Westwood, California. On a good day, he could dead-lift 359 pounds. Harper was thin and looked almost brittle, belying the fact that he was the champion boxer and karate man in the unit. Harper had also been an all-American college lacrosse player at the University of Maryland, where he'd been known as the quickest and toughest midfielder in the United States. He could run all day, and seemed impervious to hits from hulking defensemen. His lacrosse nickname was Scary.

Now Hidalgo spoke:

"Chef H. Here. What's happening, baby?"

"The enchilada is on the fire," Perry said.

"How high's the flame?"

"Smoking, man," Perry said. "So if you don't want supper to burn, you guys should get a move on."

"We're rolling, baby," Hidalgo said. "'Cause we're some hungry dudes. How about Moyer and Rosenberg?"

"They're inside the diner and ready to eat," Perry said.

"Good," Hidalgo said.

There was a small silence from Perry. Most people wouldn't have noticed it but Hidalgo had worked with Perry before and knew that if the voluminous talker hesitated there must be a reason for it.

"What's up?" Hidalgo said.

"I'm afraid we have two dinner cancellations," Perry said.

"Snyder and Bond?" Hidalgo used two other agents' code names.

"'Fraid so. Seems they're dining with other people."

"Who?" Hidalgo looked over at Harper, who was frowning as he weaved seamlessly in and out of traffic.

"They're out with the new clients in town. They're all going to Disneyland to see the fireworks."

"I see," Hidalgo said in a controlled way, which belied the sudden bolt of anger he felt inside.

He put the phone on hold and looked over at Jack.

"Snyder and Bond aren't going to be there. They got called away by Homeland Defense. There's an orange alert at Disneyland."

Harper punched the steering wheel.

"Oh that's nice," he said. "They got you and me walking into a warehouse full of villains, and our backups are down in Ana-fuckingheim saving Goofy."

"We could abort if you think it's too risky, Jackie."

"And let the Kraut run all the way back to his castle somewhere in the Black Forest? No fucking way! We finally got him here, and we're not letting him go."

"Then we're going in?"

"What the fuck else?" Jack said. "When it's time for dinner, a man's gotta eat."

Hidalgo clicked back on the phone.

"Mikie?"

"Yeah?"

"We're going to go get us our dinner now."

Perry started to laugh.

"What's so funny?" Hidalgo demanded.

"Like there was ever any question. You guys like it better this way? Makes for a bigger rush."

"Like my old grandmother said, *'El futuro es una nube que uno no puede ver. Osea que el sabio hijo de puta dispara hoy y no se acompleja como una nena cuando lo hace.'*"

"Which means?"

"That, my friend," Hidalgo said, "is an old *dicho*. A saying filled with wisdom. It means: 'The future is a cloud that no one can see. So the wise mutherfucker takes his shot today. And doesn't whine like a pussy when he does it, either.'"

"Some mouth on your grandmother," Perry laughed. Then he clicked off the phone.

The limo maneuvered down the 101 Freeway, turned off at the Echo Park exit, and drove north to Sunset Boulevard. Steinbach worked over the plan once again in his head, missing the street action, the blondes, redheads, and stunning Latina women of Silver Lake. He hated Los Angeles with a passion anyway, the cars, the loudmouth entertainment people . . . they reminded him of hyenas in suits. He didn't like doing business here either, but circumstances dictated that he do so from time to time.

Like now . . . He felt a tightening of his chest muscles, and casually wondered to himself if he might be suffering the beginnings of a stroke.

Ridiculous, of course, but the tension was thick inside of him, like congealed grease in his aorta.

A few seconds later, Steinbach's Escalade turned left into a potholed parking lot behind a gray stucco building, Ace Billiards

7

and Pool Supplies. The driver stopped at the back door, and the three men got out. Kafi told the driver to wait across the street at Jed's Big Star Diner.

The driver nodded and pulled away, and Kafi walked past the other two and unlocked the padlock on the warehouse's back door.

A few minutes later, Harper turned down a narrow alley and took a quick right into the same warehouse parking lot. Oscar checked to make sure his Glock .22 was fully chambered and took a deep breath.

"Here we go, Jackie," he said.

Harper smiled and reached in the backseat for the briefcase.

"It's time to play that nifty game, Fuck the Scum," he said.

Hidalgo laughed, but it came out more like a gag.

"Stomach's acting up," he said.

"You eat your breakfast this morning?" Harper said.

"Yeah, I ate it . . . a little. Two eggs, refritos, and a corn tortilla."

They were out of the car now and walking toward the warehouse door.

"Yeah, well, that's real healthy," Jack said. "You should add lard and maybe cement in there, too. Plus, did you chew? You gotta chew."

"I chewed," Oscar said. "Trust me, I fucking chewed."

"I doubt you did." Harper smiled. "You're a weak chewer, thus Hoovering indigestible bullshit down into your sensitive Latino stomach."

"Fuck you, Jack," Oscar said. "I don't fucking Hoove."

"He who hooves shall heave. Or so it is writ," Jack said.

A lame joke, Jack thought. Just chattering away to ward off the fear he felt every time he walked into a room full of animals with high-powered weapons.

8

They came to the back door, but before Jack could ring the bell, the buzzer rang them in.

"Isn't that nice," Jack said. "They're eager to see us. They love us, they really do."

They walked inside. Oscar felt his stomach turn, and suddenly couldn't remember if he'd chewed or not. All that he knew was that his stomach felt as if someone had turned up a welding torch inside his lower bowel. Maybe he had another fucking ulcer. Sweat trickled down his forehead. He took another deep breath. And the air seemed to whistle through the imagined hole in his gut.

Next life, maybe he'd be a teacher or something. But given the L.A. school system, maybe that would be worse.

He looked over at Jack who seemed as cool as a pitcher of sangria. The fucking guy . . . when it came to danger, affable Jackie seemed to disappear, and something blank and icy took over his body. He knew nothing of the way his partner actually felt. Neither of them ever talked about their fears.

They walked through a narrow hallway with a calendar of a topless Asian girl wearing a short plaid miniskirt and riding a Harley in front of a neon-lit bowling alley called JAY'S SPOTLIGHT LANES. From there they went through two more doors, then walked into a large, dimly lit warehouse, which was stacked with boxes inside which were pool tables.

Waiting for them in the middle of the room were not only Kafi, Draper, and Karl Steinbach, but two more goons, a blond boy with a birthmark on his jaw and a freckle-faced goof with a twisted mouth and a shaved head. Huckleberry Finn on crack. All of them were fully armed. Steinbach nodded to Jack, picked up a pool cue, and cleanly knocked in a bank shot.

"My friends," he said. "I trust you had a good trip."

"Right as rain," Harper said, setting the briefcase down on the edge of the table.

"That's good to know," Steinbach said. He lined up another shot, and then in quick succession knocked in the five, six, and seven balls. His hand didn't shake, and the worries, which had obsessed him only a few minutes ago, were dissolved in the small ecstasies of performance. Karl loved the game and had often wished he could be filmed.

"You look like you know what you're doing," Oscar said.

"Yes, in my wasted youth, I spent a lot of time in pool halls. They say it's a relaxing game, but that's untrue. Pool takes intense discipline and concentration. Like any game you play to win."

Harper smiled and picked up the second cue, which was leaning against the table.

"I don't think so," he said. "I think it just takes a modicum of talent and a little luck."

Jack turned around backward, whipped the cue behind his back, and lined up the cue ball.

"Eight ball in the far left pocket," he said.

He hit the cue with a high topspin, which sent it around the three ball, and hit the eight, right into the far left pocket.

"Bravo, Jackie," Steinbach said. "But that took a lot of practice and a lot of skill."

"Nah, Karl, just luck," Jack said. "But then I've always been a lucky guy."

"Maybe so," Steinbach laughed. "Look how lucky you got when you met me."

Jack smiled and put down the cue.

"Speaking of which . . . though your charming company is all anyone could hope for, my friend Luis and I have a plane to catch, so maybe we should get down to business."

"Of course," Steinbach said.

He looked at Kafi who handed him a black felt box, about as big as Jack's palm.

"More pool balls?" Hidalgo said.

"Yes, but these are special."

Steinbach snapped open the box and showed the balls to Jack.

"Hand carved, Jack. Each ball made to exact specifications and real ivory. The finest in the world."

Steinbach handed the ball to Jack.

"Push the number, Jackie."

Jack pushed it with his thumb; there was a slight click and the ball slid open.

"Just like an Easter egg," Oscar said. "You got chocolate bunnies in there?"

"Something far more delicious than that," Steinbach said.

Jack reached inside the pool ball and found a small perfect diamond surrounded by crushed velvet to keep it from rattling around. Next to it was a second diamond. Within seconds, he'd discovered a third and a fourth.

"Hey, now, this is a game I could start to like," Jack said.

"Every one of these balls is filled with prizes, my friend. Directly from Sierra Leone. Now, perhaps, I could see the briefcase?"

"Of course." Oscar handed the case to the big German. Steinbach swept the pool balls into their pockets, sat the case on the green felt, and snapped it open. It was filled with banded packets of hundred-dollar bills.

"Beautiful!" Steinbach snapped shut the case.

Jack smiled. "You don't want to count it, Karl?"

"No, Jack," Steinbach said. "I trust you implicitly."

Jack smiled wider and reached into his coat.

"That's your misfortune, Karl, 'cause you're under arrest. FBI."

He pulled his .38 out of his holster, as did Oscar.

"Drop your weapons, *pendejos*," Oscar said.

There was a brief second as Steinbach's face registered the shock of Jack's betrayal. Jack had seen this before. In any human interchange, trust is the glue that holds things together. Now, Jack thought, Karl was not only mad that he was going to jail but had hurt feelings.

Tough luck, Jack thought. The only feeling he had for Karl Steinbach was contempt.

Steinbach looked around the room, his face a panicky pale white. Behind the piles of stacked pool tables to his left, two more Feds appeared: Agents Zac Blakely and Ron Hughes, both carrying submachine guns. Both had been there, in place, well in advance of Steinbach's arrival.

"Drop your guns now, assholes!" Blakely said.

"Fuck you," the Arab said, turning on Blakely, letting go with a blast from his gun. The bullets sprayed the pool tables next to Blakely, who dove to the floor for cover.

Steinbach quickly pulled his own .45 from his shoulder holster and aimed it at Oscar Hidalgo. He was about to pull the trigger when Jack threw the diamond-filled pool ball into his face. Steinbach yelled and fell backward, holding his bleeding nose.

Jack turned quickly and saw the big Welshman, Draper, raise his gun to shoot Oscar. He picked up the pool cue and smacked him in the mouth, knocking three bloodied teeth to the floor.

One of the other goons aimed at Blakely, but Oscar cut him in half with two bullets from his pistol.

Jack watched as Kafi dove behind a cardboard box. Jack aimed dead center at the slogan HAVE FUN WITH POOL and fired. The bullet tore through the box and hit Kafi in the throat. The Arab fell to the floor, flopping like a dying fish.

Jack watched as Hughes shot Draper in the back of the leg. The Welshman fell to one knee, dropped his gun, and threw up his hands.

The bald-headed goon was caught between the crossfire and he went down in a hail of bullets. The freckle-faced boy dropped his gun and held up his arms. "No more, man," he said. "*No más.*" Hughes quickly cuffed him. Now Jack turned to arrest the German, but Steinbach was already half across the warehouse floor, headed for the far exit door.

Jack took off after him, firing as he ran, but missed and watched Steinbach disappear from the warehouse into the bright sunlight of Sunset Boulevard.

They ran down the teeming street past shoppers who were lined up for the new iPod sales from Best Buy. Jack slammed into a blonde with a pierced tongue who screamed as she fell to the pavement. Ahead of him, Steinbach turned and aimed his gun.

"Down!" Jack screamed. "FBI!"

The people on the street fell to the hot pavement as Steinbach fired at Jack. The bullet veered off to the right and smashed into a Porsche Boxster's windshield. It shattered into a thousand pieces. The car alarm went off, screaming through the smogged-out air.

Jack aimed and fired back at Steinbach, but missed as the bullet hit a patio chair outside a furniture store, spinning it around.

Steinbach ran on, turned left, heading for the lake at Echo Park. He disappeared behind a little stand of palm trees. Jack dodged around a Mister Softee truck, moved toward the lake, keeping low, behind parked cars.

Then it happened. Steinbach made a move toward the muddy beach right near the pedal-boat rental pier. Jack fired and hit him in the right leg. Steinbach fell to his knee but turned around firing, and Jack felt the bullet whistle by his right ear.

He crouched and fired again, and saw Steinbach fall backward into the muddy lake.

He splashed around, flailing like a beached walrus. Jack heard footsteps behind him and turned to see Oscar and Ron Hughes just behind him, their guns drawn.

"The mutherfucker looks like Shamu," Oscar said.

Jack ran forward, holding his gun on Steinbach who was up now, throwing his gun onto the beach, holding his hands above his drenched, muddy head.

"Come on outta there now," Jack said. "And don't try anything original or you're gonna look like a paper target at a rifle range."

Though wet and bleeding, Steinbach wasn't cowed.

"That's what you'd like, hey, Jack? Blow me up, say it was self-defense. But I'm not going to play your game. No, my friend, *you're* going to play *mine*."

Steinbach walked forward, hands still in the air, and a smile on his fat face.

"I love games, Karl. What's the rules?"

"Simple. You . . . him, and the other two cops are never going to testify against me. Because, my friends, you are all going to die."

Jack looked at his partner and laughed.

"You hear that, Oscar? We're all dead men walking."

"Yeah," Oscar said. "Scary."

But Ron Hughes wasn't laughing. He looked at the German with contempt.

"Hey, fuck you, fatboy. You scare nobody."

"You'll see," Steinbach said. "You're all going to find out. My reach is longer than any prison cell you assholes can throw me in."

"Creepy," Jack said. "Now shut the fuck up, turn around, and put your hands behind your back. You're under arrest for smuggling, and anything else you're dumb enough to say can and will be used against you in a court of law."

Before Jack could cuff him, Hughes stepped forward, knee deep in water.

"Jack, you got his name wrong. It's not Karl, it's Fuckface."

He punched the German in the head and watched as he fell

14

back in the filthy water. Then he waded out a little farther, raising his right fist to give him another little shot.

But Jack grabbed Hughes from behind and pushed him back toward the beach.

"Take it easy, Ronnie."

"That was for my old partner, Terry Masters, who this germ shot over in Munich. We got your ass now, Karl. You're never gonna get out."

Jack clicked the cuffs on Steinbach and pulled him out of the water. Behind the three cops, Zac Blakely came with the remaining two live smugglers, both of them cuffed from behind. In the distance they could hear sirens, and a paddy wagon was rolling in at the corner.

Jack pushed Steinbach down the street as a crowd gathered, mumbling and chattering.

"You guys will all pay with your lives," Steinbach said. "All of you are going to fucking die. I promise you."

"You're repeating yourself, Karl," Jack said. "Sign of an inferior mind."

"I'll take him from here," Blakely said, as the wagon pulled up.

Jack pushed the smuggler toward Blakely as the paddy-wagon door opened.

Steinbach turned and looked at Jack with intense hatred.

"Remember what I said, Jackie," he said, then turned again and stepped inside the wagon.

"He's not a very good sport, is he?" Jack said to Oscar.

"Very bad loser," Oscar said. "But that's how the Germans are. My grandfather used to say, '*Los mama huevos son en sus rodillas o tu garganta.*' Which means, 'The cocksuckers are either at your knees or at your throat.'"

Jack laughed.

"I hope to meet your grandfather when I die," Jack said.

15

"I'll see to it," Oscar said. "But don't make it anytime soon, okay?"

Jack laughed.

"You kidding? And give up all this? What say we stop into Charlie's and get us a couple of nice cold drinks on the way home? We speed a little, we can hit there just around the end of happy hour."

"Excellent suggestion," Oscar said. "You're buying, of course."

"Well, of course."

The two men turned to break through the little crowd, when both of them simultaneously saw an old Mexican Indian woman, dressed in a bright orange-and-black dress. She wore a scarf with orange parrots painted on it. She looked at them and shook her head mournfully.

"Qué pasa, señora?" Jack said.

The old woman stared intently at both of them, then turned and looked at the now-receding paddy wagon.

"Nada bueno," she said. *"El es malo. Señor* give you the evil eye, mister. *El se ve muy malo."*

"Yeah, right," Jack said. He was going to tell her that he wasn't afraid of such superstitious crap, but somehow the words got caught in his throat.

He looked at Oscar, who sighed.

"You go home now, *señora,*" Oscar said. "And thanks for the warning."

She turned and shook her head in a concerned way.

"No es bueno, señores, es malo. Es muy malo."

She pointed ominously to her own eye, then turned and limped away.

"Crazy old lady," Ron Hughes said.

"Yeah," Jack said. "A whack job."

But as they headed back to the warehouse to gather evidence, Jack felt something like an icy finger travel up his spine.

2

THE SCENE AT Charlie Breen's Deckhouse Restaurant was always rocking at happy hour. Bikers, surfers, beach bunnies, local businessmen, and cops all hung out there in rough harmony. And all of them were always greeted with the same laughter and pat on the back from Charlie himself. Now in his late fifties, Charlie was a living legend in Santa Monica. After a nomadic life of doing business and traveling in Europe, South America, and China, Charlie had come home and taken a ramshackle, falling-down druggie hangout, bought it twenty years ago for a comparative song and largely on the force of his personality—open, friendly, and caring—and made it into one of the most successful beach bars in Los Angeles. Jack had known him for close to ten years, and whenever he and Oscar finished working a case, Charlie's was the first place they headed.

This night was special, however. Jack and Oscar had been working the Karl Steinbach case for close to a year. There had been many times when the two partners despaired of ever catching him. So tonight was party time, drinking, laughing, and sitting around the big circular bar, looking out on the lights of Santa Monica Bay. The two backup cops, Zac Blakely and Ron Hughes, were with them, as was big, silver-haired Charlie Breen himself, who kept the laughs and liquor flowing.

In front and above them was Charlie's new fifty-inch plasma screen television set, with its endless games, CNN, and the local news feeds. Jack was feeling no pain as he downed his third Wild Turkey, with Hefeweizen and lemon back. Next to him, Oscar tossed back a shot of Herradura Gold Tequila. He couldn't remember which shot it was, but he was pretty sure that number five had been some time ago.

"Hey, hey, hey, wait . . . there it is," Ron Hughes said.

He pointed at the TV, where newscaster Trisha Toyota began her nightly news report.

"In Hollywood," she chirped, "we're used to seeing shoot-outs and robberies on the city streets, most of them staged for the studio cameras. But today in the Echo Park neighborhood, local residents were horrified to see the real thing unfold. In a sting operation, four FBI undercover agents took down a vicious gang of diamond smugglers."

The whole bar had stopped talking now as Charlie signaled for them to check out the TV.

"Oh, yeah!" Blakely said.

He was referring to Jack, who was now being interviewed by Toyota, his facial features digitally blacked out.

There was a loud hoot from the denizens of the bar.

"Quiet, people," Charlie said. "Our star is going to speak!"

Trisha Toyota smiled and turned to Jack:

"I have with me here the leader of the FBI operation, a man we'll call Bill Kelley. I understand you chased the suspect all the way to Echo Lake."

"That's right, Trish," Jack said.

"And all the while he was shooting at you," she said in her breathless way.

"Yeah, but the only thing he hit was Mister Softee," Jack said.

That got a big laugh at the bar.

"And he ended up in the lake," Trish said.

"Yeah, but he was a little too late for the pedal boats, so he ended up getting all wet."

Another roar from the drunken eager bar mates.

"But I understand that the suspect threatened to kill all of you. Doesn't that worry you?"

There was a brief hesitation, and then Jack gave her the line:

"Yeah, Trish, my partners and I are flat-out terrified. I doubt any of us will sleep a wink tonight."

Toyota cracked up, as did the patrons of Charlie Breen's bar. Charlie reached over, grabbed Jack's right arm, and held it above his head.

"The winner and still champion, Agent Jack Harper! Though I gotta tell you, you look a lot better with your face blacked out."

There were cheers and laughs throughout the bar. Oscar held up his tequila and toasted Jack.

"To Karl Steinbach, may his punk ass rot in prison for the rest of his life!"

Hughes and his partner, a tired and curiously quiet Zac Blakely, joined in the toast. Jack felt a shot of warmth zap through him. It was great being here . . . with Charlie, with his guys . . . successful on a case. One good one made up for all the ones that got away, and during the last few years, there had more than a few of those. Ever since 9/11 there had been just about nothing but bad news for the Bureau. Leaks to the press, moles like the traitor, Robert Hansen, a guy with whom Jack had played on the Agency basketball team for three years. A guy he thought he knew. So tonight was a bit more than an arrest party, it was a comeback celebration for Jack, his guys, and the Bureau.

"Hey, Jackie," Oscar said. "I gotta go . . . tomorrow's another bitch of a day, huh?"

"Yeah," Hughes said. "Getting late."

"Come on, O," Jack said. "Don't wimp out on us."

He reached over and hugged his partner of ten years. And added a kiss on the forehead.

"Jesus, Jackie," Oscar said. "Cut that shit out, *maricón*."

Jack laughed and kissed him again. Oscar pretended to fight back, then kissed Jack, too.

"Hey, Oscar," Ron Hughes said. "You be careful on the way home, babe. Steinbach's boys might be waiting for you."

"Fuck him," Oscar said. "As my old grandmother used to say, '*El dia de las brujas en Hollywood asusta más que ese malparido tonto.*' Which means, 'Halloween in Hollywood is scarier than that fucking mope.'"

"You got it, Osc," Jack said. "See you in the A.M."

The partners slapped five, and Oscar gave a quick hug to Charlie as he headed out to the parking lot.

A second later, as Jack downed his next beer, Zac Blakely signaled to him with his eyes: He wanted to have a private talk. The two men drifted over to the corner and sat down in a vacant booth.

"Forrester is starting again," Blakely said as he sipped his beer. He rolled his brown eyes in disgust.

Forrester was Supervisory Agent William Forrester, the bane of both Jack's and Blakely's existence. Their immediate supervisor, Forrester was a Harvard graduate, who never tired of saying, "When I was back at Cambridge, we did things this way . . ." In addition to being a first-class snob, Forrester was also convinced that Blakely and Hughes and maybe even Jack himself were rogue agents who had their eye on stealing valuable evidence, whether it be money or jewels. It didn't help that the last bust Blakely and Hughes had led (and in which Jack and Oscar had served as *their* backups), a major robbery at City National Bank in North Hollywood, had ended up with $200,000 of unaccounted-for money.

"Guy has some kind of major hard-on for you," Jack said.

"I know," Blakely said. "But Ron and I didn't take the money. We caught Miller and his crew at the track, where they were going to lay the money off. Nailed them and brought the money to the office, processed it with Garrett in Evidence. And never saw it again. Then, when we're going to re-count it for Miller's trial, we find that two hundred grand is gone."

Jack nodded his head, then sipped his drink.

"I know, Zac. You don't have to convince me. What's Forrester saying to you now?"

"He's not saying anything," Blakely said. "But he's got guys tailing us night and day. And he's intimated a couple of times, Jackie, that you were probably involved as a criminal accessory."

"I know. He's tried to rattle my cage a few times. But fuck him," Jack said. "He's got nothing on any of us."

"Yeah," Blakely said. "But it gets a little old being tailed all the time."

He indicated a bearded man with a scar under his right eye across the room.

"Check out that fuck."

Jack casually turned and looked over the guy, who was pretending to be looking at one of the ski bunnies who'd just rolled in.

"That guy was sent by Forrester?" Jack said. "You sure?"

"No, I'm not sure. But he's been watching us all night."

Jack looked over at the big man's hollow eyes, which seemed to stare right through him.

"This the first time you've seen him?"

"Yeah, I think so. But there have been other guys, too. You recognize him, Jack?"

"No," Jack said. "I don't. But I did notice him about a half hour ago, and it occurred to me that he could have been sent by Steinbach."

"But we just arrested him," Blakely said. "How could Steinbach move that fast?"

"Marvels of technology," Jack said. "With an instant message, he can set up an instant tail. The guy has that kind of operation. He could have done it while he was running for the lake."

"That sounds a little paranoid to me, Jack," Blakely countered.

"Yeah, well, it probably is," Jack said. "But maybe we're both being a little crazy. Look, I know and you know you that Ron and I didn't steal the City National dough. Forrester is worried about how the Director sees him. He's going to hassle you for a while, then, when we make another good bust, he'll give it up."

Blakely looked tired. "He threatened my pension, Jack. I swear, if he does anything to fuck that up, I'm going to bull-whip his ass down Wilshire Boulevard, then torch him."

Jack laughed. It was good to hear the Blakely of old, the angry, funny badass who had taught him much of what he knew.

"He's not going to touch your pension, Zac. He's got nothing."

"I know that and you know that," Zac said. "But to cover his own ass, he could invent a few facts. After all, in a few months, I'm retired. Might serve him very well to pin something on me."

Jack shook his head. "He's not *that* nuts. He tried anything like that, we'd nail him to the cross."

Zac nodded and managed a tired smile.

"Glad you're with me, Jack."

"Always. You're my main man."

They smiled and headed back to the bar. The bearded man watched them go, then slipped out the front door.

22

Jack, Blakely, and Hughes watched him go.

"Heading back to make his report to Forrester?" Hughes said.

Jack laughed. "Forget that germ," he said. "Could just be watching us because he thinks we're movie stars."

"Yeah," Hughes said. "The Three Fucking Stooges."

A few minutes later, a DEA agent named Tommy Wilson came in. Jack and Tommy had some bad blood between them over a shared case a few years back, so Jack tried to ignore him, but red-faced Wilson, already half in the bag, greeted him effusively anyway.

"Ah," he said. "Look who it is. The highly sung heroes of the Federal Bureau of Investigation. Heard you brought in the Kraut."

Jack didn't bother to reply, still hoping he could avoid talking to Tommy but, on his left, Blakely took the bait.

"Whoa, Fast Tommy of the DEA. We're looking forward to the day when we can wrap your humble little agency up with ours."

"Yeah," Hughes said. "Then we can teach you how to be *real* police."

Tommy waited until the three Feds had stopped laughing at him, then sprang his surprise.

"You boys are a little behind the curve. This humble servant of the people is now working for the new superstar agency, the Department of Homeland Security."

"Jumped ship, huh, Tommy?" Hughes said.

Wilson laughed and looked at Jack.

"Just went where my services are needed by my country. And the way I hear it, we might roll *you* guys up into *our* agency, given all the tragic mistakes you've made of late."

Hughes started to get off the bar stool, but Blakely held him back.

"Not funny, Tommy."

"Then why am I laughing so hard?" Wilson smiled wickedly at the three FBI agents and walked around to the other side of the bar, where three other agents greeted him.

"I oughta kick that arrogant dickhead's ass," Hughes said.

"Aw, fuck him," Blakely said. "They're still the new kids on the block."

Hughes shook his head, said, "I just hope Congress doesn't give them the *whole* block."

"Yeah," Jack said. "They grabbed off eight of our agents in the last six months. Man, it's getting thin out there."

"Fuck 'em and the horse they rode in on," Blakely said.

"Eloquently put, Zac," Jack said. "You are a master of the English language."

"Fuckin' A, I am," a somewhat renewed Blakely said. "I am the king of wit and hyperbole. And I taught you all you know, young Jackie."

"That you did," Jack said. "The man was my first partner, Charlie."

"Really?" Charlie said. "And you didn't shoot him for insubordination?"

"Tried to several times," Blakely said. "But he moved too fast. He doesn't need my help anymore. He's his own man out there. That was good work today, Jackie. I never knew you could run like that."

"Always been fast," Jack said. "Speed of foot makes up for my slow mental capacities."

"I'll drink to that," Hughes said.

Hughes and Blakely clicked glasses, said their good-byes, and headed for the door.

"Keep what I told you in mind," Blakely said. "Slick Billy would like to bring us all down."

"Got it," Jack said.

"Drive safe," Charlie said. "They got traffic cops out there."

The two Feds waved as they headed out the door. Jack looked out at the Pacific, saw the moon gleaming off the waves. Seeing and hearing the roar of the surf settled him, made his blood pressure drop, and took away the violent images and feelings that warred inside of him.

He thought of the bearded man, wondered if he was a spy and, if so, was he working for Forrester or Karl Steinbach? Or if he was just some poor beach bum who they'd only imagined was part of their little paranoid party?

Jack sighed, tried to clear his mind. He looked at Charlie, his gray swept-back hair, his broad football player's chest . . . There was something solid about Charlie, he thought, something stable, unlike himself. He was mercurial, always had been. Which was why he was attracted to undercover work. There were times when he came down off being one of the bad guys when he didn't know who he was anymore. There would be a two- or three-day period when he would look at his son, Kevin, or his girlfriend, Julie, and feel emotionally dead to them. It was like they were strangers, yet worse than that, because with a stranger he might want to make an effort to impress or at least be civil. With his own friends and family, even Kevin, he would feel as though he had blown down to zero, maybe beyond. What was real and what was false had become so twisted in his mind that his ordinary human affections seemed to go into hiding. And he secretly feared that one day they might not return.

"Hey," Charlie said, "how about one for the road?"

"Yeah," Jack said. "Why not?"

Charlie motioned to Sam, the Italian barmaid, and she picked up the shot glass and filled it with Jack Daniel's.

"You and Julie doing good, Jackie?"

"Sure," Jack said. "Pretty good, anyway."

"Wedding bells?"

"Nah, not yet, Charlie. You know how it is. I'm already zero for one on that score. 'Sides, I haven't known her long enough."

"She living with you now?"

"Part-time," Jack said. "She's keeping her own apartment until . . . you know, we're sure."

"Know what you mean," Charlie said. "Hey, you gonna bring your son up to the Brentwood League this year?"

"I don't know," Jack said. "He's got so many things going already. Plays guitar in his rock group, and he's taking AP classes."

What he didn't say was that Kevin had been rebellious lately. Just a couple of weeks ago, he'd lied about going to the library, and stayed out late, behavior which sent Julie into a panic. Jack had done much the same kinds of things as a kid, so he wasn't that worried. Not yet, anyway.

"Yeah, sure," Charlie said. "But you gotta get the kid outdoors a little. We're talking baseball, the greatest sport of all time."

"I'm a little busy right now, Charlie. I don't know if I can coach."

"Who says you gotta? I'm up there. Kev can play on my team. The mighty Brentwood Dodgers."

Charlie assumed a catcher's pose, and Jack laughed and punched him in the arm.

"All right. Maybe. When's sign-up?"

"Saturday at eleven," Charlie said. "Bring him up. I remember he can really pound the ball."

"Yeah, no doubt about it. He's got a good eye and real good bat speed. I'll talk to him about it."

Charlie smiled happily and nodded his head.

"Man," Jack said. "The way you are . . . you shoulda had kids, Charlie."

Charlie sighed and shook his head.

"Tried, man. Wasn't in the cards. Tried the normal way, and then we did the in vitro thing. Now lemme tell you, Jackie, that's a lot of fun. You go into some little room and they got porno DVDs in there and some lesbian mags, and you jerk off into a cup, and have to come out into the hallway afterward carrying the fucking thing and you run into all these other cats who are also carrying their cups around. Oh, man, it's Loser Land."

Charlie limped around with an imaginary cup in his hand as Jack smiled sympathetically.

"And after all that, and the ten grand it costs you, the shit doesn't even work. It's 12 percent or something. We did it three times, too . . . and that was enough 'cause not only did I not have the kid, but I lost my wife. You try fucking on schedule for two and a half years . . . giving her injections at night, waking up at three A.M. to crying jags. No, man, that was the end for me. But it's okay. This way I get to coach the kids when they're sweet and young. Later, when they become car thieves and teenage crackheads, I don't have to be involved."

"I'm sorry, Charlie. That must have been rough."

"Yeah," Charlie said. "It sucked. But that's long ago and far away, my friend. Look at that ocean, listen to that surf. That's what we're living for nowadays. Let the past go, Jackie. That's what you gotta learn."

Jack looked at him and smiled.

"Get out there with your kid," Charlie said. "'Cause in a few years he'll have a girlfriend, and then it'll be bye-bye, Daddy."

"I hear you, Charlie," Jack said. "Thanks for the drink. See you tomorrow, coach."

Charlie smiled and hugged Jack and Jack felt a bolt of affection for him. Something surprising and tender that he had rarely felt for his own dad.

He was glad he could feel something for his friend, glad he wasn't just a shadow self, faking it here, faking it there, as he lured scumbags like Steinbach into his trap.

· · ·

27

The Santa Monica Freeway was lit with a strange neon glow, and there was only one other car on the road. A black sedan somewhere behind him . . . maybe a hundred yards away. What was it, a Lincoln Town Car? A Caddy? He couldn't tell.

Ah, what the hell, why should he worry?

It was just some other guy like him, heading home after too many drinks. Nothing to get buzzed about.

Still, when he thought of the old woman, the way she looked at him. The evil eye. He give you the evil eye, *señor.* Like something out of a werewolf movie from long ago. What was that woman's name? Maria Ouspenskaya. When the wolfbane blooms and the moon is full . . . Christ, that was just a lot of Hollywood bullshit.

Just the same, it had scared the living shit out of him when he was nine or ten.

And now the car was getting closer . . . really speeding up, and just to be safe, Jack reached into his coat . . . felt the grip of his .38.

Not that he was worried or anything . . .

Now the other car was really closing on him.

It was a Lincoln.

Jack squinted into the rearview. Jesus, it *was* the bearded guy, no doubt about it. He *was* following him. But who had sent him: Forrester or Steinbach?

Up ahead was Jack's exit . . . five or ten more feet.

He had to slow down a little to make the turn. The Lincoln pulled alongside him. Jack turned and looked at the guy. The scar seemed to glow off his face.

He looked directly at Jack and gave him a superior little sneer as the Lincoln rushed by.

Jack headed down the ramp, his heart beating so hard he could hear it in his ears.

Maybe Blakely was right, after all. Forrester was trying to build some kind of case against all of them.

Ever since the Hansen betrayal, the service had become wired, as if they'd ingested a ton of meth and were all having multiple hallucinations and massive paranoia.

Looking for moles, criminals, bad agents . . .

Forrester, like some kind of Stalinist enforcer trying to find the mole.

Jack felt his skin crawl. What had started out as a celebration had turned into something creepy, another bad vibe.

The thought infuriated him.

Being spied on by Forrester. If it *was* Forrester.

Once again, he thought of the old woman. "*Malo, señor.* He give you the evil eye." And a chill ran down his back.

A few minutes later, Jack pulled into the driveway of his modest bungalow in Culver City. He walked up the path and saw his son's lacrosse stick lying in a bush. When he reached down to pick it up, he felt a twinge in his left knee. A sharp little pain that caught him up short.

Maybe from running today . . . he thought . . . maybe for that and from all his own years of lacrosse at the University of Maryland. Maybe in a few years he'd have to get it scoped out . . . and if it didn't work, they'd move him to a desk job.

Fuck that . . . he'd quit the Agency first.

He stuck the key in the door and went inside.

Walked through the living-room shadows and down the hallway to Kevin's room. He looked inside, put the lacrosse stick gently up against the wall, and walked over to his sleeping fourteen-year-old son.

How he loved him. The overwhelming emotions he felt for him were like nothing he had ever experienced before. A feeling of awe swept over him. His son, his flesh and blood . . . he would do anything in the world to protect him. Give his own life in a flash. He sat on the edge of the bed and stroked his son's brown hair, looked down at his long lashes, his beautiful mouth . . . He leaned down and kissed him on the head. Kevin stirred slightly and Jack cradled his head with his arms. But a second later, Kevin awakened and looked up at him angrily.

"Dad, what are you doing?"

"Sneaked in a hug. Sorry," Jack said, remembering the days when he had snuggled with his son. There were no happier moments.

"Come on, Dad. I'm not a kid anymore."

"I know," Jack said, looking at his perfect skin, his bright brown eyes. "You okay?"

"Yeah, I'm fine," Kevin said. "Just fine. Dad, look, I gotta get back to sleep."

"Right," Jack said. The coldness in his son's voice was like a knife through his chest. He patted him on the arm and then slid out of the room as Kevin turned over and went back to sleep.

As he walked softly in the hallway, he had a thought . . . that if Steinbach really wanted to get him he might come after Kevin. The thought was so grave—so unsettling—that he couldn't bear it.

What the fuck was wrong with him? Late-night jitters, that was all. Fucking Steinbach wasn't going to come after anybody. He was in the can and would be for a long time. All the bad guys made those kinds of threats, but Jack had never known even one of them to carry them out.

Nah, he was just tired, a little drunk . . . stressed.

Still, who was the bearded man, and how come he'd followed Jack on the freeway? Or was that, too, just coincidence?

He opened the bedroom door and saw Julie sleeping in the barred moonlight.

She was young, beautiful. In bed they were so right for one another. But they hadn't known each other all that long. Eight months. They'd met online: Match.com . . . Oscar had talked him into joining. Jesus, he'd had some weird dates at first. A woman who had an amazing picture in a bikini, but who, when she showed up, was twenty-five years older, and so drunk Jack was tempted to arrest her for DUI. Instead, he had one drink with her, drove her home himself, then took a thirty-dollar cab ride back to his car. Another woman, who looked fine, but had Tourette's syndrome, and cursed him under her breath as they had lattes at Starbucks. Then there was the woman who had said she was "curvy" in her online profile and weighed in at about three-ten. She had a wild, cackling laugh, and talked all about "changing her meds," the mere thought of which made her want to eat an entire pizza at lunch.

Jack was about to give up the whole thing when he met Julie Wade. A teacher, beautiful, kind, and in touch with both him and his son . . . she seemed too good to be true.

They had clicked from the first night . . . though they didn't sleep together until the fourth date.

Now, eight months later, Julie slept at Jack's a couple of nights a week . . . using the excuse that she had to get to work early in the morning and her own apartment was closer to her school, The Willows, in Culver City.

But Jack knew that wasn't the whole story. Julie said her last boyfriend, a Marine who'd come back from Iraq, had burned her and gone nuts with stress syndrome. She was gun-shy, something Jack understood only too well. He didn't want to get caught up with another wrong choice, either. His divorce was tough on him, but really murder on Kevin, who still couldn't understand why his mother, Linda, had left him and moved back East to Baltimore. Jack didn't want to tell him that his mother had turned out to be an alcoholic, failed actress, the kind of beautiful girl

31

who gets off the bus in Hollywood filled with hopes and dreams of stardom, only to end up working as an assistant to a guy who makes low-budget thrillers for a while, until the day he gives that up, and starts doing porno movies down in the San Fernando Valley. Linda hadn't made that trek, the last stop for a flunked-out actress . . . but couldn't find any legitimate work, and soon lost her agent.

When Jack met her, she was waitressing at Dantana's. They had a whirlwind love affair. She was still beautiful and fun, and at the restaurant she was a star. Jack wanted her more than anyone he'd ever met . . . and when they'd fallen in love there was no doubt about it. He was whacked out on love.

He wanted her so much that he'd barely noticed her drinking being out of control. After all, that was another time, a time when everyone he knew drank a little too much, partied a little too hard.

Then came the marriage—and her downfall . . . having a child. She was an erratic mother. A week of loving their son more than the earth and moon would be followed by a week when she "had to get out," she was "being smothered" by Jack's late hours, staying at home by herself . . . She hated her life . . . began to drink all day and night, and on top of it started hitting the Vicodin.

Two years into the marriage, it was all over. The fight, the screaming matches, the furniture throwing.

And then one night, when he got home, Jack found Kevin asleep in an empty house and a note on the kitchen table. She'd cleaned out the checking account and left for Baltimore.

Jack stared down at Julie. She looked . . . what was the word . . . beatific? Yeah, that was it. He knew that any attractive woman could look like an angel when sleeping, but in this case he felt that maybe this time . . . he really had gotten lucky.

But even so . . . even now he felt that there was something waiting, something that could come and wipe out his dreams. And the worst thing was that maybe it was Kevin. Kevin, who didn't trust any woman right now. Kevin, who disappeared until four in the morning, two weeks ago, a feat which nearly sent Julie around the bend.

Maybe Julie wasn't ready to handle a volatile teenager.

Jack felt his head bursting with negative thoughts.

He had to get some sleep. Clear his mind. Things were okay. He'd nailed Steinbach . . . everything was good.

Even so, after he finally took a quick shower and hopped into bed, he couldn't sleep, but watched and waited for something to happen . . . something really bad. He could almost feel it as it edged toward his house.

3

HE WISHED HE'D BROUGHT his shades. The sun was in his eyes as he tried shielding them with his left hand. Kevin, dressed in his new uniform, was walking toward the plate, and Jack felt a lump in his stomach.

Jesus, he was so overprotective, worried all the time. He hadn't really been all that freaked when he was undercover with Steinbach, where one false move could have put a bullet through his head, but out here, in the sunlight with all the other moms and dads, he was supernervous for Kevin.

He looked down at third base, at Charlie, who was flashing Kevin the signs now. Jack watched as the pitcher threw in the last of his warm-up pitches. He was a big guy, with a Cardinals uniform. A lot bigger than Kevin, and Jack had seen on the radar gun that he was throwing about 73 miles an hour. But Kevin was fine . . . knocking the dirt out of his cleats, waving his bat slowly back and forth.

Jack sucked in his breath.

Looked across the field at the old Pacific Park and thought for a second that he wouldn't watch the first pitch; he would just pretend to watch, and instead keep his eyes on the old gym . . . The new one was over the other side of the hill, it was going to be something . . . he'd think about that, and . . .

But who was he kidding? He was going to watch. And his kid was going to be just fine.

He looked down at Charlie, who was keeping up a steady stream of chatter.

"Come on, Kev. You can do it, boy. Get a hold of one, Kev."

The big pitcher went into his windup, lifted his front foot, and fired the ball toward Kevin.

A fastball, and right away . . . the split second it left his hand, Jack could see that it was going right toward Kevin's head.

And worse, Kevin was slow to react . . . frozen in fear.

And now Jack was up off his seat as the ball hit Kevin's batting helmet with a sickening thud, and his son went down as though he'd been hit by a sniper's bullet.

And Jack was up, his mouth opening but no noise coming out and he was leaping down off the stands, and running toward home plate, and Charlie was running alongside them and Charlie was saying, "Oh, Jesus!"

Jack was running but the plate seemed to be receding into a kind of sickening yellow mist . . . and no matter how much faster he ran he couldn't seem to get any closer. And his son lay there, blood gushing from his nose and ears.

Jack woke up, screaming.

"Kevin . . . Kevin!"

He sat bolt upright in bed, and Julie was up with him, saying, "What . . . what is it?"

And Jack heard his heart beating in his ears, his breath coming hard, as he fell back on his pillow.

"Nothing," he said, still gasping for breath. "Just a bad dream. It was nothing at all. Go back to sleep."

"Nothing at all? Going undercover for months at a time trying to catch that scum Steinbach? By, the way, baby, I heard you got him. It was on the news."

"Yeah, we got him," Jack said.

Julie rubbed his back.

"I wish you'd have called me, Jack," she said.

Jack shook his head, then hugged her. "Sorry, we had to do the paperwork, then hustled down to Charlie's for a couple of drinks."

"I understand," she said. "But I was worried about you."

"I know," Jack said. "I'm sorry . . . I should have called you right away. Guess I'm still not quite used to having to think of anyone else."

Julie smiled and kissed Jack's neck. "It's okay, baby. Just try and remember next time. I want to be in on every part of your life."

Jack managed a smile.

"You will be," he said. "From now on. I promise."

She smiled and slid back down under the quilt.

"You need a serious vacation," she said.

"Vacation?" Jack said. "Never heard that word before. What's it mean?"

Julie squeezed his bicep.

"It's when you go to a beach and you relax, and the water comes rolling in and the sand is warm . . . and there's no cell phones at all."

"Really?" Jack said. "Tell me more."

"Tomorrow," Julie said. "I'll tell you all about it. And then you'll go in and request one of your vacation days, and we'll take a long weekend down in Todos Santos."

Jack smiled.

"Now you're talking, professor," he said.

He kissed her cheek softly and fell back in bed.

Soon he heard Julie's soft regular breathing. She was back asleep. But Jack lay there, tense, until dawn.

4

MOST OF THE FBI offices at 11000 Wilshire Boulevard were purely functional, with only a few homey touches—a picture of an agent's family, a baseball signed by the Dodgers at a special game—thrown in. But Supervising Agent William Forrester's office was filled with photographs of Hollywood stars. As Jack and Oscar sat in his office waiting while Forrester droned on and on with a call to Washington, Jack looked at the pictures behind Forrester's desk. There was Supervising Agent Forrester with Arnold Schwarzenegger back in his superhero days. And there was Supervising Agent Forrester with Clint Eastwood, on the *Line of Fire* set, and there he was again, in all his glory, with Harrison Ford on some Tom Clancy project. His arm around the leading men, his phony smile plastered on. It occurred to Jack that Forrester might actually think he was a leading man and that all the other agents at 11,000 Wilshire were just small, supporting players. There to support the one-and-only Forrester, the most dedicated, the most brilliant, the most photogenic agent anywhere.

Finally Forrester slammed down his phone and looked across his perfectly neat teakwood desk at Jack.

"Good morning. Perhaps you know why I've called you two in for this little talk."

"Let me guess," Jack said. "You want to congratulate us for catching Karl Steinbach."

Oscar scrunched up in his chair a little. He didn't believe in provoking assholes. Especially when the asshole in question was your boss.

"Afraid not," Forrester said. "I brought you two in here to tell you that a full investigation into the City National Bank robbery is proceeding apace."

"Hmmm . . . Proceeding apace," Jack said, turning to look at Oscar.

Not able to help himself, Oscar let a jagged smile break across his wide face.

"Keep it up, you two," Forrester said, getting up, walking to the wall and straightening out a picture of himself with his arm wrapped around Rambo.

"Keep it up. But one day—and that day will not be long in coming—you both will take the fall, along with your partners Zac Blakely and Ron Hughes. That I swear to you."

"Bullshit," Jack said. "You know we never touched that money. We were only backup in that case, anyway. We wouldn't have been there at all if we weren't down so many agents."

"So you say." Forrester dusted off a picture of himself holding Julia Roberts in an awkward embrace. The look on Julia's face was that she would have rather been hanging off the rack in an Inquisition prison than be in a clinch with Forrester.

"But," Forrester went on, "I know how you people think. Like Robert Hansen did. The Bureau is old hat, has lost its powers, and you are here to turn it into your private investment firm. But that will never happen. I've called you in here today to give you one more chance. Blakely and Hughes are going to be indicted for stealing $200,000 and you will go down with them, unless you maker a deal before they do. You know how this works, Jack. You and Oscar can still save your own butts and I would strongly advise you to do so, before it's too late. Turn in the money now and you will be doing yourselves a huge favor."

Jack felt his temperature rising.

"Let me ask you this, Forrester: If you're so sure we stole that money, how come you haven't stripped us of our badges, taken our guns, and put us on suspension. That's what usually happens when bad agents are discovered. They disappear."

"Well, maybe we *will* do that," Forrester said. "I mean, if you're so anxious for it to happen. Then why not?"

"Okay, do it," Oscar said. "You play that game and we'll open a civil suit against you personally and the Bureau that will be so freaking big that——"

Oscar was so exasperated, he couldn't even finish the sentence.

Forrester cleared his throat a little but, other than that, seemed unmoved.

"We are gathering evidence. It's my job to rid the Bureau of any and all subterfuge, and I intend to do exactly that. There are over fifty agents in this building, and only a handful of them have compromised the integrity of the Bureau. I'm going to root them all out, starting with you two and your criminal mentors."

"Criminal mentors," Jack repeated.

"Man's got a really extensive vocabulary," Oscar said.

"Very impressive," Jack said. "You mind if we go back to work now, boss?"

"You're both excused. But the investigation is ongoing. If you have anything to tell me, you better do it before it's too late."

He turned and dusted off a picture of himself with Daniel Craig, sighed, and then answered his phone.

40

"Yes? . . . Who is it? . . . Oh, Steven Spielberg . . . well, please put him on."

Jack and Oscar walked out of the room, past Forrester's secretary, Sue, an older dumpy woman who dressed in funereal black.

"Why does he think Blakely and Hughes took the money?" Oscar asked.

"I don't know," Jack said. "But we've got to distinguish the man from his job."

"What do you mean?"

"Look, just because the asshole is a buffoon and a starfucker doesn't mean he isn't dangerous to us. Lesser assholes than him have ruined people's careers before. He really thinks that Blakely and Hughes took the dough. He really thinks we might have helped them. He's a maniac when it comes to internal affairs, and he's coming after *us*. We have to find out why."

"You think they really could have taken the money?" Oscar said.

Jack thought of all the ways Blakely had schooled him when he was new in the department.

"I don't like to think it," Jack said. "Man, I really don't. But we got to ask around."

"Okay," Oscar said. "I'm going to get into it. But personally, I would totally vouch for both those guys. I just don't believe it."

Jack nodded his head. "I read all the reports. They logged in the money, but two days later, when the evidence steward looked for it, it was gone."

"And nobody had checked it out?"

"Nope. But somebody said they'd seen Blakely down there near the locker."

"So why wasn't he busted?" Oscar said.

"Because . . . because he passed a lie-detector test, and there was no evidence against him. I got another question, though."

"What's that?"

"Why is Forrester so anxious to pin the stealing of the evidence on Zac and Ron?"

Oscar gave a low whistle.

"Funny, I was thinking the same thing. You know, when I was in training, they always taught us that when somebody went bad, they almost always got caught by living the high life. Cars, secret bank accounts . . . hanging out with a fast crowd."

"Yeah," Jack said. "And who likes to do that more than Supervising Agent William Forrester?"

"Maybe we ought to have a look at Billy-Boy's bank accounts," Oscar said.

"Uh-huh," Jack said. "Maybe we should. But I got a feeling he's defended them with some serious firewalls."

"Yeah," Oscar said. "But we'll figure out a way around that, because we are superagents who brook no shit from *pendejos* with pictures of movie stars in their office."

"This is true," Jack said. "There's no denying it. We fucking rule."

5

THE ROOM WAS BLACK, and the air smelled of oil, musk, urine, and death. Kyle felt as if something was cutting into his chest, and when he opened his eyes and looked down, he saw the ropes. Christ, he was tied up. He wanted to call out, scream for help, but it seemed he was gagged, too. He looked through the dark gloom, and saw a lump a few feet away. What the hell was *that*? He couldn't really tell. He tried to blink away the cobwebs over his eyes. Jesus, what the hell? They weren't real cobwebs, but there they were nonetheless, like spider legs crossing his eyeballs.

He looked over at the inert ball a few feet away from him, but still couldn't quite make out what it was. The blackness was deeper in the corner there, even than it was where Kyle had been dumped.

He tried to move his legs, but of course they were tied, too.

How could this have happened? What the hell were he and . . . that other person (if it was a person and not a dead animal or something) doing in this shithole, anyway?

The last thing he remembered was that he was at school, and that the driver had come for him . . . a little early, it seemed, and he'd climbed in the back and started talking on the cell phone to one of his friends, Sam, and they were driving . . .

The pirate standing in front of him suddenly broke off Kyle's musing about what happened. The guy was about six feet three and he had on a freaking pirate hat, and an eye patch, and he wore one of those old coats—what did they call them . . . great-coats, with fancy turned-up collars, all made of leather—and the guy had a beard, and when he smiled, he was missing a few teeth.

Kyle couldn't breathe.

The guy was smiling at him, and waving to him, and Kyle felt as though his bowels were going to loosen. And the guy, who now seemed to have a huge cutlass in his right hand, was walking toward him, laughing and pointing at him, though utterly silent.

And Kyle was scared shitless.

But then the pirate, all six foot three of him with giant gleaming sword . . . was freaking gone.

Like that. Bingo. Gone.

Kyle fell back against the wall, terrified.

Not only was he kidnapped, but he was losing his mind, too . . .

He was . . . had to be . . .

And then he thought of drugs.

No, he wasn't exactly losing his mind. Though he was out of it.

Drugs. It had to be drugs. Someone was drugging him—had drugged him—and the pirate was just a hallucination.

But so detailed, though. And so huge, hovering over him . . .

And what of the ball over in the corner?

Was that a hallucination, too?

He looked over at it . . . tried to whisper, but all that came out was a muffled sound.

Hey, who you? Hey . . .

Hard to even make it out as speech.

But the ball moved a little (or did he?) . . .

Yes, it seemed to. Moved a little.

Heeeehhhh!

The ball scraped around on the cold stone floor.

Kyle saw the ball sit up. Turned out not so ball-like after all.

Even with the gag, and the scratches on the cheeks, even with the dark cutting into his eyes, it was a face Kyle knew very well.

It was his younger brother, Michael.

He looked over at him and tried to shuffle across the floor.

Got maybe three inches—and then something pulled him back. He looked down at his feet, and realized the rope was tied to an old heating unit.

Somehow that detail made Kyle want to cry. Chained like a dog, or an animal.

Both he and his brother.

Now he felt the fear descend down on him like a lead sheet.

He looked over at his brother. He could see him a little better now. Guess his eyes were getting used to the dark.

He could see Mike's eyes, and he wished he couldn't. Because there was such terrible fear in them. Worse than himself. Far worse.

And there was something else, too.

Anger, fury. As though it was somehow Kyle's fault that they were in this horrible situation.

Like he had anything to do with all of this. For Christ's sake!

But it would be just like his younger brother to hold him responsible for . . .

Now he heard a noise. Coming from the back of the room.

A door creaked, footsteps, oh, Jesus Christ . . .

This wasn't any icy hallucination. This was a real person heading toward them.

He looked up and saw this huge bearded guy hovering over him. A guy with deep black eyes and a balding head. And a scar under his eye.

A guy with huge, powerful hands who grabbed Kyle and ripped off his shirtsleeve with one swipe.

And then Kyle saw the needle in the guy's hand. He tried to pull away, but there was no escaping . . . and he felt the needle burn into his arm, felt something oozing out of it and into him, like a snake going through his innards.

He wanted to cry and he wanted to scream. But he could do neither.

All he could do was fall back against the wall. He was sleepy, so very sleepy, and then . . . he was gone.

No dreams, no sounds, no brother, nothing. Nothing at all.

The bearded man did the same thing to Mike, and watched as he fell over on his side.

Then the bearded men checked the two boys' bonds and, finding them satisfactory, he went back the way he'd come, back into the light of Pier Two at the docks in San Pedro.

6

LATER THAT AFTERNOON, Jack waited at the parking lot of the United International Terminal at LAX with an attractive young Chilean woman who this week was using the name Maria Vasquez. Today she had dyed blond hair, which she wore in a knot at the back of her head. She dressed simply, in a plain blue shift, so as not to call attention to herself, and unless she was looking around for spies or for Karl Steinbach's people, she mostly kept her head buried in a mystery novel. But right now she was reading Joseph Campbell's *The Hero with a Thousand Faces*, a book that fascinated her and seemed to have everything to do with her current life.

"You're sure you're going to be all right, Maria?" Jack said.

She nodded and looked at him with her soulful brown eyes. "I'm fine."

Jack took her hand and felt a surge of affection and admiration for her.

"Before you go inside, I want you to know that I can still

get you into Witness Protection, if you want to reconsider. New name, new face. Whole new life."

She smiled and shook her head.

"No," she said. "Like I've told you before, Jack, I know of other people who did that and it didn't work out well at all. They had to live in places they hated, where they had no family . . . and the jobs they had to take were not anything at all like what they were used to."

"True," Jack said. "The Program's not perfect. But as long as people have gone along with our rules, we've never lost anybody yet. What happens if Karl decides to come after you? You know he has the money and funds to track you down."

Maria sighed. "Then I will defend myself, with the help of my friends and family in Chile. They will watch out for me, Jack."

Jack felt a twinge of fear for her.

"Listen, Maria," Jack said. "Steinbach said it the day we busted him. He has a long reach. He's got people under contract to hunt you. Now that he knows you helped me set him up, he won't give up."

"I know," Maria said. "But he doesn't know my new name. He doesn't know which country I'm going to, and he doesn't know my friends, either. Where I am going is a small town in Chile. Controlled and run by my cousin Tito. We know everyone who works there, who drinks in the bar, stays in the hotel. It's kind of like your Old West, Jack. Anyone new who comes into that town is big news in about five minutes. If they are at all threatening, I will know about it immediately. And the threat will be . . . eliminated."

Jack shook his head.

"I hope so." He laughed ruefully. "You are such a goddamned stubborn woman."

She smiled and patted his hand, as though she was comforting him.

"Yes, I am, Jack. That's the one thing Karl never counted on."

Jack laughed and nodded in agreement.

"You're right," he said. "He had no idea who he was playing with."

Suddenly she looked sad. Her beautiful smooth face nearly caved in.

"When I worked for him as his assistant, I could take everything. His abusive ways, the fact that he hit me once in a while if a shipment was late . . . or if we had trouble with the officials, but when he . . . when he struck out at Hector, that was the end."

Jack nodded and remembered the circumstances. Maria Vasquez was a secretary/assistant to Karl Steinbach. She knew whom he paid off to get his blood diamonds. She also knew whom he wanted to deal with, and if she liked you, she could get you right into Karl's inner circle. Jack had been working undercover for six months, trying to set up deals with Steinbach. But he got nowhere until he managed to get close to Maria Vasquez at the El Tropical Restaurante in Sierra Leone. It was there that he met her, and there that she confided in him that she wanted to strike back at Karl Steinbach for killing her cousin, Hector Rodriguez. She had no proof of the murder. Steinbach was always careful to give himself plausible deniability when he had someone "disappeared." But Maria knew. Hector had a wild streak, talked too much, and made the mistake of taking one of Karl's women away from him. That was enough for Karl. One day Hector had been taken into the jungle, tied to a tree, and devoured by wild animals.

That was how Karl dealt with traitors. It wasn't enough merely to kill them, you had to make them suffer, serve as an example to any other fools who might want to set themselves against him. He and his kind specialized in revenge.

Jack had cultivated Maria, listened to her growing hatred of Steinbach, and when the time was right, had turned her, made a deal for her that she wouldn't be prosecuted for her part in earlier diamond capers.

It was Maria who had vouched for him, Maria who got him in tight with Karl. And if Karl found her, it would be Maria who would be tied to a tree somewhere, covered with honey, her entrails hanging out . . .

But it was also her choice. If she didn't want to go into the Witness Protection Program, there was nothing Jack could do about it.

Besides, Jack could understand it. She'd been used to a life in South Africa and, before that, Peru and Chile. She wouldn't be happy living as a saleswoman in some godforsaken Midwestern town or down south in Fort Smith, Arkansas, where the latest members of the Witness Protection Program were planted.

She was a gambler, not unlike Jack himself, and she liked to live life close to the bone.

Maybe she'd be fine down there. With a new name, and maybe after a year or so, with a new face (Maria was considering having plastic surgery), she'd be untraceable.

Jack hoped so, anyway.

Just then they heard the announcement over the speaker. "United International Flight to Santiago, Chile, will now begin preboarding."

Maria Vasquez looked up at Jack and smiled, but there was sadness in her eyes.

"You know, Jack?" she said. "There was a time when I thought . . . really thought we could have made it together."

Jack kissed her on the cheek.

"Yeah," he said. "I know what you mean. But, in the end, we're too much alike."

"You think?" she said.

"Oh, yeah," Jack said. "You and me . . . we're both addicted to life in the fast lane. That doesn't make for much of a marriage.

In fact, that's the one thing I'm still a little worried about with you."

"What?" she said, standing and gathering up her leather handbag.

"This town you're going to down there. Zato? I wonder if it'll be big enough for you?"

She smiled. Touched his cheek with her hand.

"That's where we're different, Jack. This whole thing with Karl, losing Hector, seeing all the hatred and killing and ugliness in the diamond business . . . that's cured me. I mean it. Maybe it's made me old before my time, but I can't think of anything I'd rather do now than go back there to my small town. Perhaps I'll marry and have children. That sounds like something real. You know, real friends, real family. People you can always count on. And they can count on you. After the lies and hustle of the diamond-smuggling business, *that* sounds exciting to me."

Jack smiled and hugged Maria tight. "You know that if ever you need me, I'm right here for you."

"Yes. I know that."

He let her go and looked into her tearful eyes.

"Anything," Jack said. "Anything you need. Don't hesitate to ask. You have my numbers."

"I do." She wiped away the tears from her cheeks. "I am going to miss you, Jack."

"Me, too," he said. "But who knows? Maybe we'll meet again."

"If it's fated," Maria said with a sad smile.

Then she kissed him on the cheek, turned, and got out of his car. He watched her go through the shadows of the parking garage, out into the light, and her new life in Chile.

As Jack started his car, he silently wished her well.

But somehow, he doubted that her future would be a happy one.

7

KEVIN WALKED DOWN Venice Boulevard alone. He looked down
at the watch Jack had given him for his fourteenth birthday and
smiled to himself. It was such a kick to walk away from school.
To just go out for lunch, grab a burger at In and Out, and then,
instead of walking back to the playground, just keep on stroll-
ing away.

What was weird, he thought, was the way things looked when
you were free. Like if you were in a school bus or being driven
around by freaking Julie, his dad's so-called new girlfriend (What
the hell was wrong with Mom? He'd never found out an answer
to that.) who was always talking to him about spiritual shit . . .
"Oh, look at that tree; it's so spiritual." What a moron . . . Anyway, if you were in a car with an adult, you just drove by junky
old Lincoln Avenue and you didn't actually look at the cool places
that were out there . . . or you kind of looked but you didn't really see stuff. For example, you might see the Exxon station right
here, but you would never notice the guy sleeping on the side of

it, with a bag over his head, like some kind of dude waiting to be executed by the chopper . . . And that wouldn't remind you of the great old AC/DC song, "Dirty Deeds Done Dirt Cheap". . . like your brain was exploding with connections right and left when you walked along . . . *away from freaking school,* and away from freaking Julie who would come to pick him up and like have her mind blown when he wasn't there . . .

He felt a little shot of guilt when he thought of that.

Julie would be worried as hell, probably thinking that he was going to end up on a milk carton or something . . .

LAST SEEN IN VENICE, CALIFORNIA. If you see, please call 310-876-1167.

Yeah, she'd be freaked, but so the fuck what? Dad would be able to handle it, and it wasn't like he was around much anymore, anyway. Since Mom left for Baltimore (which proved she was nuts—who would leave L.A. for freaking Baltimore?), Dad had been out every night chasing down bad guys; Christ, Charlie was more of a dad than Jack was. Charlie picked him up for practice, and Charlie made him dinner and got him home on time . . . so Julie could tell him some spiritual discovery she'd had today . . . "Oh Kevin, I saw a pod, and I knew all life came from pods." Which was because she was a freaking pod herself. A pod from Podsville!

She'd never look at the dead cat in the gutter, which was right in front of him, dead-as-a-doornail orange tabby cat with a slightly crushed head, where some truck had run over it, no doubt . . . nor would she look at the sixty-four-year-old bum with a three-foot beard as gray and gnarly as steel wool, who was skateboarding by, turning up the street toward the boardwalk and the beach, where all the free people lived.

He could already smell and hear the ocean lapping in on the sand, and he saw a kid break dancing to some rap thing . . . Bow Wow, he thought it was . . . yeah . . . and there was a guy with a bright pink Mohawk, and tats all over his arms, and Kevin wished he could get a tat, but his dad would kill him . . .

But he might just do it anyway . . . not today but soon . . . 'cause walking away from school made you feel free, and once you had a little bite of freedom, you didn't really want to go back and see things like a freaking slave.

Okay, slave was a little melodramatic, but it was practically true. Walking around down here in Venice, watching the kids rocking around the boardwalk, people going in and out of Small World Books, stopping at the Wishing Well Tavern, drinking and eating in the middle of the day, laughing, being alive.

Not wandering around talking about spirit, whatever the fuck that was, or worrying every minute about terrorists blowing the entire world up (and those dreams he'd had for the past three months of all of L.A. blowing into a billion fragments of blood and human flesh and concrete, and palm trees ripped from the ground, and hurtling like guided missiles through human bodies . . . oh, man, he couldn't use those dreams anymore, no thank you) . . . that wasn't the way life should be. It should be like this . . .

Walking away from dead school to have an adventure on the streets and boardwalks, to find other adventurers like himself who would understand his need to get to the heart of the real world, to fathom everything at once, as he remembered some poet saying . . .

Or maybe it was Jack Kerouac in *On the Road,* which he had already read three times, and certain parts, ten or twelve . . .

That was what he needed, wanted, and . . .

"Hey, dude, you got any pot?"

Kevin turned around and saw a kid with blue hair, which looked like it had been chopped off with an ax. He wore camouflage pants, Doc Martens, and a sleeveless black T-shirt, which revealed scrawny, pale white arms.

"You deaf, man?"

"No way," Kevin said. "But no, I ain't got any."

(And he felt silly saying "ain't," trying to sound street black, which was so pretentious and dumb, but he kind of wanted to impress the kid, couldn't help himself . . .)

"Got any money?" Blue-hair said.

"A few bucks," Kevin said.

"I know where we can get some. Rainey's place just down on the canal."

Kevin had not only never smoked pot, he had never seen it. The very idea of an FBI agent's son taking drugs was almost inconceivable. Totally taboo, utterly wrong.

And thus, suddenly, now, this second, irresistible.

Why should he not experience everything? Wasn't he a free man now? On his own? Out there at the crossroads.

He smiled and looked at the blue-haired kid.

"Kevin. Who are you?"

"Flyboy," the kid said. "How much money you got?"

"Fifteen dollars," Kevin said. That was a lie. He actually had almost fifty dollars in his pockets, money he had been stealing from Julie's purse for the last month.

"That'll get us a couple of joints," Flyboy said. "C'mon, man."

They headed down the boardwalk past a flame-throwing clown who was scorching the air in front of the Sidewalk Café, and just beyond him on the beach there was a sand sculptor who was making what looked like a giant giraffe out of sand. People gathered around, enjoying the sun.

"You live down here, K?" Flyboy said.

"No," Kevin said. "I crash over in the marina. Live with my big brother."

As he said it—invented it—Kevin started to believe it.

"How about you?"

"I stay here and there," Flyboy said. "No home too long. Man, you stay somewhere too long, they might come creeping up on ya."

"Yeah," Kevin said. "That's how I feel. I might drift on down to Mexico in a couple of months."

"Cool," Flyboy said. "Before you make that little jaunt, let me know. I know people down there."

"Cool," Kevin said. He felt such a wonderful sense of freedom. Talking about living with his brother, cruising on down to Mexico, made him feel that such things were possible. A whole new way to live, a life of freedom, danger, adventures.

His old man wouldn't approve, but what did he know?

All he saw were scumbags, and germs. He didn't understand people like Flyboy (and himself?) who were free, who didn't worry about the straight world.

They wandered up and down the streets, and ended up off Dell, and suddenly there was one of the canals. It was beautiful, but had this strange odor coming off it.

"Wow, what's that smell?" Kevin said.

"You don't know?" Flyboy said. "That's the ducks. They land here and shit here . . . gets pretty bad sometimes."

"Oh, yeah," Kevin said. Trying to act like he had known that, but somehow forgotten it. "Hey, is this where we get the pot?"

"Yep, just around this corner. Guy lives in a guesthouse along here."

Flyboy gestured with his left arm that Kevin should go by the small hedge, which turned into an alley. Kevin was eager to do as his new partner said, to prove to him that he wasn't afraid at all. He was ready . . . soooo ready for a new life.

He took a step around the hedge and came to a small red house with blue trim. It looked like something he might have read about in a fantasy novel. *The Hobbit Visits Venice* . . . or something like that.

He started to make a comment about how quaint the place was (without using the word "quaint," which would mark him as some kind of fag) . . . when suddenly a blow struck the back of his head.

For the first time in his life he understood people saying a blow to the head made them see stars.

Because there they were, stars up above him and stars on his shoulders. It was so strange, he felt like laughing, and would have if his head didn't throb so badly.

He wanted to tell Flyboy, though. He wanted to tell him how stars seemed to be whizzing by his nose, his lips. He could almost reach out his hand and catch them . . .

But then there was another slam on the back of his head, and when he turned, he saw a very different Flyboy . . . a much older guy who was looking at him in what could only be described as a look of repulsion and disgust.

In the guy's hand was a steel bar, like a crowbar or something.

As Kevin fell to his knees, he still wanted to explain to Flyboy that none of this was the way things had to go.

They were both beggars on the street, weren't they? Brothers, friends . . . Didn't Flyboy know that? He should.

What the hell? Wasn't it obvious?

Kevin fell over on his side and felt blood running down his face. It was hot and ran in streams.

Polite streams, he thought as he fell asleep. The second and third streams of blood seemed to wait until the first stream had worn itself out, rolling down Kevin's cheeks, over his chin and down into his shirtfront before they started on their short journey.

"Polite blood," he thought. The words seemed funny, and he started to giggle a bit.

Then he was down on the ground, like a dumb animal . . . Down but not quite out.

He could still feel it as the guy rifled his pockets. (Was it Flyboy? His hands felt too big for Flyboy.)

"Wait," he intended to say. "Wait a minute. We're friends, we're on a quest or some shit like that . . . I mean it."

But it was too late. In a few seconds, both his money and Flyboy (and the other, bigger guy, if he even existed) were long gone. As he passed out Kevin heard the honking of the ducks.

He awakened two hours later, a spotlight burning his eyes.

"Hey. There you go, kiddo. You're coming around."

He looked up at an LAPD officer, a huge man with a walrus mustache.

"What's your name, son?"

"Kevin Harper. Where am I?"

"About two feet away from falling into the canal," the officer said.

Kevin looked over at the black water, smelled the stinking ducks again. His head throbbed, and it was all he could do not to burst into tears.

"Well, your father will be mighty relieved to find you," the cop said. "There's been an all-points bulletin out on you. FBI agent's son gone. People thought it was everything from child porno to terrorists."

Kevin shook his head, unable to speak.

Now it came back to him. Flyboy, the great quest to score pot, the steel pole in his head.

"You're gonna need some stitches up there," the officer said.

Behind him a red light was blinking on and off, and a siren was screaming.

"I don't need to go to the hospital," Kevin said. "Really."

"Oh, yeah, you do," the kindly cop said. "You stay right there. You are gonna take a nice fun ride on a stretcher."

Kevin felt the tears rolling down his eyes now. Not from the pain, but from the shame of it all. He'd thought he could take care of himself, and that kid . . . Flyboy . . . had just suckered him right into it.

What a joke.

And his father . . . oh, man, Dad was going to kill him.

That fucking kid . . . Kevin felt something coil inside of him. He'd come back here and he'd get that kid. He would. The bastard!

The light was hideous in the emergency room of Santa Monica Hospital. Kevin lay there motionless as a Dr. Wahrabi sewed up his head.

Jack and Julie stood above him, looking down at him. They looked harried, exhausted.

"He's going to be fine," the doctor said. "Lucky boy. I don't think you even have a concussion."

"Hard head," Jack said. An attempt to make a small joke, but Kevin could tell there was not much humor behind it.

The doctor gave him some prescriptions for pain medicine and said he wanted to see him again in four days.

When he had gone, Jack sat down on the bed next to his son.

"How did this happen?"

Kevin looked down at his sheets. He could lie to his father, but not if he had to look him in the eye.

"I don't know. I was exploring around the canals. I'd always wanted to see them and somebody came up from behind me and hit me over the head. Stole my money."

"You didn't see the guy who did this?"

"No," Kevin said. "How could I?"

Jack looked down at him with such intensity that Kevin felt sick.

"You were climbing around the canals all by yourself?"

"Right."

"Kevin," Julie said. "Do you have any idea how much you worried us? Walking away from school, disappearing, practically getting your brains knocked out of your skull?"

"I'm sorry," Kevin said.

Julie shook her head and sighed deeply. It had obviously been rough on her.

"We didn't know where you were. What happened to you."

"C'mon, we're going home," Jack said. "We'll deal with this tomorrow. Needless to say, you're grounded for a month. No visits from friends, no trips to the mall, nothing. You come home, you study, and you go to bed."

Kevin didn't say a word. It was not going to be fun. But it could have been worse. Much worse.

His father looked down at him. Patted his cheek and then handed him a clean shirt he'd brought from the house.

"Let's get home, kiddo," he said.

Kevin felt Jack's strong, firm hand, and suddenly wanted to cry again. But then he thought of Flyboy, and what he would do to him when he caught him.

That son of a bitch was going to pay. He'd get all his money back and more. Just wait and see. Wait and see.

8

JACK'S MENTOR ZAC BLAKELY had served with the FBI for over thirty years, and was due for retirement in less than six months. He and his wife, sculptor Val Lewis, lived on Hollywood Hills Road in leafy Laurel Canyon, in a classic canyon glass-and-steel deckhouse, which was surrounded by a canopy of green and fragrant eucalyptus trees. On their back deck they had a hot tub, which Blakely liked to tell guests had "won the Academy Award." When people looked surprised he laughed and told them that the ancient tub had first been a water tower in the great Billy Wilder movie *Stalag 17*. Near the movie's end, when William Holden tries to sneak out of the camp, he hides in the old water tower and later manages to get away to neutral Switzerland. After the movie was shot, Zac Blakely's uncle, Steve, who worked as a carpenter on the set, put the "tower" on the back of his truck, and drove it directly from the studio, up the steep and winding roads of the canyon, and attached it to his deck, where it had stayed ever since. Later, Zac bought his uncle's house and so had his own little piece of Hollywood history: a hot tub that had won the Academy Award.

Blakely and his younger wife Val had two grown kids now, and as he approached sixty, he spent more and more time relaxing in the tub. He looked forward to the day when he wouldn't have to go in at all . . . the whole deal, going undercover, tracking down bad guys, had become too much for him. He was tired, and ready to hand over the rigors of being an agent to a younger man . . . a man like Jack Harper.

During the past few years it had been especially tough being an agent. The scandals, the reorganization of the Bureau, and the rise of the Homeland Security Department, the endless war in Iraq, made Blakely's job all the more difficult.

He was glad he didn't have to learn Arabic, and he knew damned well that it would be near impossible for a white, older agent like himself to go undercover in the Muslim world.

The glory days of WASP agents were now just about as outdated as Hoover's evening gowns.

Lon was glad to retire and, unlike a lot of guys, he didn't think he was going to have much trouble finding things to keep him occupied in retirement. Between working on his deck, fixing up the house, fishing, and deep-sea diving, he was pretty sure he was going to like having his days to himself. He didn't have any great desire to top off his life with expensive trips, boats, or cars. He was a relaxed kind of guy most of the time, happy doing things around the house, or watching a movie.

Unfortunately, his wife Val, twenty years his junior, didn't really feel that way. She had given up her free Venice beat kind of life when she married Zac, and though she loved him fiercely, she didn't really want to spend the rest of her life playing tennis and going to Costco.

She dreamed of traveling to Rome, going on safari in Africa, maybe even climbing mountains like some of her Mulholland Tennis Club friends had. Unfortunately, all that cost money. Money they wouldn't get on Zac's modest pension.

The thought of spending her waning years just lazing around the house worried her, made her bitter. She was already lonely enough . . . hanging out at the nearby tennis club was fun for a while, but the people were mostly bores, Republicans whose idea of an exciting night out was going to the Hollywood Bowl and seeing Barbra Streisand. She was sick of the club. The only thing she did there was play tennis twice a week and drink the rest of the time.

She had denied her drinking to Zac, but he knew it anyway. The way she slurred her words, the way she'd let her appearance go to hell.

He knew she was beginning to fall apart.

He worried that if he didn't supply her with the things she wanted in retirement, if he didn't make up to her all the lonely nights she'd spent while he was away on endless cases . . . that she might even leave him.

Blakely was famous for his bravery in action. He'd survived street gun battles in São Paulo, and a jungle shoot-out with AK-47s blasting at close range in Brazil.

But when he thought of losing Val, the most interesting and glamorous person he'd ever known . . . he actually got scared. He could see her walking out, still attractive enough to snare a show-business exec . . . some older guy who wanted a woman like her around as a trophy. The thought of losing her made him ill.

Without Val, his retirement would mean nothing.

Money . . . money was always at the root of everything. You could say you'd done your duty, you'd lived an exemplary life, but if you didn't have the money you were finished. People like Val had expectations, and they could put them on hold for only so long.

That was what Zac Blakely was thinking about as he got into his old BMW (a car he'd bought secondhand and which, in truth, didn't run that well, but gave the appearance that he and Val were wealthier than they were) and headed down the hill to work.

He took the first curve easily, and thought about the work he had to do today. There was a bank robber loose down in Orange County; maybe it was the same guy who had knocked over three Wells Fargo branches in Studio City six months ago. He had to drive down to Newport to talk to Agent in Charge Cabot Newsome.

But first, of course, he reminded himself he had to drop off the laundry at the Laurel Canyon Country Store.

Blakely saw the steep left-hand turn at Wonderland Avenue coming up and eased his right foot down on the brakes.

But there was a problem, a rather serious one.

When he applied the brake pedal, it went all the way to the floor.

Blakely didn't panic. Could have just been a fluke. Slowly, he hit them again, trying to pump them, so that the hydraulic would kick in.

But it didn't matter how he did it, hard or soft, the results were the same. There were no brakes. Nothing.

Wonderland Avenue is a steep hill, and usually there is a long slick patch of water, which runs off from a stream, which is situated at the very top of Lookout Mountain. When you hit the water, your tires sometimes skid right and left, and you have to gently pump the brakes again to keep from skidding. Since Blakely didn't have any brakes, he tried steering his way through the little flood, but his effort was useless.

He was already going too fast to keep control of the car.

Now he found himself headed down the street sideways. He swung the steering wheel into the turn, a hard left, so that he could compensate for his right drift.

The effort seemed to help a little. He managed to straighten out the tires as he headed down the hill. But once the car straightened out, he had another problem. He quickly began to pick up speed.

Time for the emergency brake. He tried pulling it, but it, too, was detached. Then he knew for sure: This was no accident. Both his brakes were cut.

He was screaming downhill faster now, and sixty feet in front of him was the stop sign at Laurel Pass. Sitting at the stop sign was a yellow school bus headed for the Wonderland Elementary School. Blakely could see the kids in the school looking out the window, laughing, and daydreaming their kids' dreams. They had no idea that a ton and a half of metal death was hurtling toward them at 80 miles per hour.

Frantically, Blakely thought about going through the stop sign straight ahead, but that wasn't an option, either. For in front of him, walking across the street, was a whole group of kids with their mothers, walking, chatting with the chubby crossing guard dressed in her yellow vest.

He couldn't turn left and he couldn't go forward without hitting the kids. There was only one other option.

To the right was a parking lot . . . a small one in which the Los Angeles public-school buses parked for a few minutes, so they could let the kids out.

If he could make a hard right, maybe he could find a parking space available, and just possibly he could slide into it, and if maybe he'd hit the wire mesh fence which surrounded the lot maybe—just maybe—the fence would help break his speed before he crashed into the school's cafeteria wall.

That he was going to hit the wall there was no doubt. But maybe, with the mesh fence and his air bag, he'd somehow survive . . .

Then he thought of something else . . . If this had been Steinbach's work . . . well, they wouldn't miss the air bag, either. No, they'd make certain that it couldn't be deployed.

Up until he had that last thought, Zac Blakely hadn't started to panic. But now he knew . . . knew for certain that he was going to die. Steinbach must have carried out his threat. Even as his car screamed down the hill, Zac Blakely thought of his fellow agents. Hughes and Jack Harper. If only he could warn them somehow . . .

He saw the bus getting close, closer. He saw the kids and their moms walking across the street. He heard a scream and he saw a mother throw herself over her child, and he turned the wheel hard right.

The BMW screeched into a right turn, went up on two wheels, and somehow slid right by a parked yellow school bus before it hit the wire fence . . . but by now it was going nearly 90 miles an hour, too fast for the fence to make much of a difference. The fence snapped open, and Zac Blakely's BMW smashed into the north wall of the Wonderland Elementary School cafeteria at slightly over 98 miles per hour.

The car engine exploded on impact, and the cafeteria walls exploded with it, sending a shower of bricks and stucco and steel girders showering out into the parking lot. They rained down on the school bus, barely missing the driver, who had thrown himself on the floor.

Blakely was right about the air bag. Whoever had worked on his car had gotten rid of the bag, too, and so seconds before the car exploded, he was sent sailing through the windshield, his throat cut by jagged shards of glass, his body broken in twelve places by the impact with the steel-reinforced school walls.

In the end, Agent Zac Blakely lay on the hood of his BMW, like a broken doll.

The mothers and teachers and children panicked, thinking that this surely must be a terrorist attack. They screamed and ran around looking furtively for the next wave of al-Qaeda terrorists.

But nothing else happened. No one else came.

Except one person. One person, whom no one else saw, because he was perched high up in the thick branches of a ficus tree. In his hand was a Panasonic DVX 100 digital video recorder. It was mounted neatly on his left shoulder, and he carefully recorded the entire crash. Now, with his powerful new lens, he zoomed in on the broken body of Zac Blakely, and then jumped over to the screaming, terrified children and their mothers and fathers.

Staring at the havoc below, he felt a complex mélange of terror, horror, and an obscene ecstasy. The feelings were so strong that he nearly lost his balance and fell out of the tree.

Which wouldn't have done at all.

Now he heard the police sirens coming. This presented the filmmaker with a problem. He would have loved to get the cops on film, too . . . the screeching of brakes, the LAPD leaping out, seeing the chaos and ruin for the first time . . . but what if, by happenstance, one of them looked across the playground, and saw him up there filming. That would be the end of everything, of all they were trying to accomplish.

He knew he ought to run for it now, while there was almost no chance anyone would see him come down, walk up the hill to his car.

But still . . . what good was the scene without the cops and then the Agency's appearance? No good at all . . .

Nah, he had to stay for a little of it.

Besides, when he showed it to Jimmy tonight . . . Oh, man, now that was going to be worth any risk he had to take.

So he stayed, waited, got the shots when the LAPD arrived. Saw the horror on their faces and got it all . . .

And got Harper and Hidalgo, too, when they arrived. Got the look of total disbelief and shock on Harper's face as he looked down at Zac Blakely's broken body.

Oh, yeah, hanging out was a risk, but in the end, it was more than worth it.

He had it all, and he couldn't wait for Jimmy to see it.

And after he had all he needed, he climbed down the tree, walked up to his car, and shot out of the canyon, the back way.

No one had even a glimpse of him.

Jack watched as the ME took away the broken body of his oldest friend. He talked to Ed Charles, the medic at the scene, and learned that Zac Blakely had been killed on impact. He felt a rage so deep inside of him that he had to turn away from the scene for a minute before he could do his job.

Jack walked over to a uniformed officer who was talking with one of the women who was walking across the street when Blakely had come roaring down the hill.

"He couldn't stop. I saw his face. He was straining to turn the wheel. If he hadn't . . . we would have all been dead for sure."

The woman began to break down, and the officer put his arm around her.

Oscar tapped Jack gently on the back.

"They got a tow truck here. You want to go over the car first?"

"Yeah," Jack said.

They walked across the parking lot, which was strewn with chunks of concrete from the cafeteria wall, and scraps of the burned vehicle. Jack looked down at a red mass, thinking for a second that it was his old boss's intestines. But when he knelt down to take a closer look, he realized that it was stewed tomatoes, one of the items on the lunch menu for the day.

He started to walk away when he noticed something else lying there, just a few feet from the mangled car.

He reached down and picked it up.

It was a torn piece of a photograph, looked to be the bottom corner of an old Polaroid. It looked as if it had been taken long ago, but the image on it couldn't have been old at all.

He was staring at a picture of a gravestone with the name Zac Blakely on it. The birth date was October 5, 1946, which, Jack was pretty sure, was his old friend's real birth date. The date of death was today.

"What the fuck is this?" Jack muttered to himself.

Jack called Oscar over and showed him the torn photo. Oscar's eyes grew wide as he stared at the scrap of photo.

"Jesus, Jackie, somebody already bought Blakely's gravestone!"

"I don't think so," Jack said. "My guess is this thing has been PhotoShopped, and was left here by the perps just to play with our minds."

Oscar shook his head.

"Don't take a genius to figure out what the next part of the photograph is going to be. Headstones with Hughes, you, and me on them."

"That would be my guess, too," Jack said. "Somebody is playing with us."

"You mean Steinbach's playing with us?"

"I don't know," Jack said. "It seems a bit melodramatic, even for him."

"But who else, then?"

"I don't know that either," Jack said.

He put the partial photo in a plastic evidence bag and handed it to a technician.

Jack signaled to the driver of the tow truck to hoist the trashed frame of the car, then ducked underneath.

He looked at the rear brake casing and saw exactly what he expected to find—a filing job.

He looked out at Oscar.

"Electric file. Could do this in twenty to thirty minutes."

"But on the street?"

"Zac lives right up the top of Hollywood Hills Road. In a cul de sac. His neighbor up there is one of those young movie stars. He told me she's over in Europe shooting a movie right now. The perp could get under his car and do the whole job in the dark last night."

"Still, he had to drive up there. Maybe somebody saw him," Oscar said.

"Right. We have to get a timetable from his wife."

Jack felt a wave of exhaustion almost buckle him at the knees. The thought of driving up to the house and telling Val . . . Jesus, that was the worst.

"No air bag either," Oscar said.

"Yeah, and the emergency brake had been disconnected."

"Zac was just gonna retire, too," Oscar said.

Jack felt a stab of pain in his chest, took a deep breath, and headed for his car.

PART II
THE MAZE

9

THEY PARKED DOWN the street from the cul de sac where, until an hour ago, Zac Blakely and Val Lewis had lived.

"Nice up here," Oscar said. "Feels like you're in the country."

"Zac always parked facing downhill so he wouldn't have to turn around every day."

"Trees and bushes obscure his car. Guy could come up here at night and not be noticed at all," Oscar said.

"Yeah," Jack said. "But how did whoever did this get Zac's home address? He was totally secretive about it."

"These days there are a million ways," Oscar said. "You heard about the guys in D.C. who put 'Federal Agents' Home Addresses' in Google and got a list of fifty of them?"

"So much for Internet security!" Jack said.

"I feel so much safer since we started the war, too," Oscar said. "'Cause my President tells me so."

"You keep talking like that, and the guys at HQ will be investigating you and me, bro," Jack said.

. . .

They walked down the street to the door, but before they could knock, Val came from around back. She was holding a planter in her hand. She had on white gardening gloves and a straw sunhat. She looked relaxed, happy, gardening on the deck.

"Zac's already left," she said, smiling.

Then she looked at Jack, and her lips began to twitch. She let out a terrible small sigh.

"The sirens, I heard the sirens. I thought it was a fire. Tell me it's not Zac!"

Jack bit his lower lip and slowly took the planter out of her hand. He handed it to Oscar, who took it just as she collapsed into Jack's arms.

They stayed with Val for an hour. Jack told her that she didn't need to answer questions right away . . . but she wanted to, anyway.

Jack nodded and asked her about Zac's timetable during the last twenty-four hours. It turned out he'd been right. Zac had gone up to the Mulholland Tennis Club, at the top of the mountain above them, just last night. He'd played tennis for two hours and then hung out at the bar with his doubles partner, a doctor, until ten.

Jack had played tennis there with Zac once, and remembered that the parking lot was separate from the club itself. Not only that, but the club hadn't bothered to light the lot very well, either. It would have been easy for someone to come up there and then follow him home. That was one possible explanation for how the bastard knew where he lived.

"Do you think it's that guy you busted? Steinbach?" Val said.

"I don't know," Jack said. "But it doesn't matter. Whoever it is, we're going to get him. I promise you that."

She sighed and shook her head. As if it didn't matter anymore.

Jack and Oscar shut their notebooks and got up to leave.

"I can't believe any of this," she said. "Do I have to go to the morgue?"

"I'm afraid so," Jack said. "Tomorrow. I'll take you down there if you want."

"Okay," she said. "That would be good, Jackie. 'Cause I don't think I could stand it alone. The thing is, Zac was always so good. So devoted. You like to think that a guy is going to get some kind of reward for being that good."

Jack looked at her, shook his head.

Val nodded and let out another small sigh, as if she knew that she had only so many sighs left and she was rationing them.

"You know, it's wrong to let Zac die this way," Val said. "We all die, Jack, but this is wrong. To die at the hands of that bastard, Karl Steinbach."

Her voice was small, distant, as if someone had cut her vocal cords.

"I know," he said. "And I'm going to get whoever did it. Trust me, Val."

"Good," Val said. "'Cause there's no one Zac trusted more than you, Jack. No one."

"You see anyone up here that didn't belong?" Oscar said.

"No," Val said. Then she managed a tired smile.

Jack put it out of his mind. Right now they had nothing. It was important to get out and canvass the neighborhood. He hugged Val to his chest. Silently, he promised his old boss that he'd get who did this to him.

No matter how long it took.

Suddenly he had a thought. What if Blakely had stolen the bank money? What if the cutting of his brakes wasn't about Steinbach at all, but about the money? Maybe Zac had partners who thought he was holding out on them. Maybe one of them got tired of waiting.

And what if—just as an idea—what if that partner was Forrester? Forrester who was hell-bent on making it look like Jack and Oscar were in league with Blakely and Hughes?

Aah, it was all conjecture. But somebody had cut Blakely's brakes. And Steinbach and maybe Forrester were the only possible suspects.

But to believe that Steinbach didn't engineer this crime meant that he had to accept the fact that Blakely was dirty. And he just couldn't believe that. And yet, Jack knew it was possible. The best thieves were the guys who did it only once or twice, whose records were spotless.

That would be Zac . . .

He sighed deeply. And hoped it wasn't that way.

During the next two hours, Jack and Oscar rapped on doors in Laurel Canyon along with the city cops and two state troopers.

Up the hill on the top of the cul de sac lived a buxom blonde named Lily Carswell. Jack had seen her on an exercise tape. She wore a black leotard and a pink flower in her hair. She invited them in for bran muffins and tea, which they turned down. Lily Carswell knew and had heard nothing. She smiled and told them she wasn't really the neighborly type. As they left, Lily reminded them that her show on the Health Channel had been changed from eight on Thursday morning to seven thirty.

"Never miss it," Jack said.

"Drink green tea," she said, as she shut the door. "Destroys all the toxins."

"Right," Jack said. "Got it."

It was the same with a tattooed rapper who lived a couple of doors down from the Blakelys. His name was RX Murder and he said he'd been away at a rave in San Diego for the last few days. He said he never talked to Blakely because the guy was

76

"some kind of a cop." Then he shut the door in their faces. Jack had a sudden urge to take out his gun and put a few rounds through RX's window, but managed to control himself.

They interviewed a retired woman named Ida with fifty cats. She said she was deaf. The catshit odor, which came from her house, doubled Oscar over. "Guess she doesn't have a sense of smell either," Oscar said.

Next were two gay real-estate people whose married name was Herb and Rodd Coy. They knew nothing about what had happened, but wondered if Mrs. Blakely would want to sell her house now that her husband was dead.

"After all," Rodd said as he ushered them out of the house, "a widow doesn't need as much square footage as a married woman."

Jack advised them that now might not be the time to bring that up to Val, since her husband had died only two hours ago. Rodd and Herb looked offended.

"I didn't mean today," Rodd said. "I'm thinking of a decent waiting period . . . like you know, the day after tomorrow. Do you know where he's going to be laid out, Agent Harper? I find the funeral home is usually a good place to mention these practical considerations."

"Check the paper," Oscar said, pushing Jack out the door.

They rapped on a few more doors where there was no one home, then found themselves up on Skyline, the block just above Hollywood Hills, at the home of Fred Feeney, a small, bald man with a black mustache.

Feeney opened the door a couple of inches. He had eyes like a nervous gerbil.

"Jehovah's Witnesses, right? Well, I got to tell you I tried *The Watchtower* last year and I was very disappointed. I mean, the world has not yet ended. I only *feel* like it has."

He started to shut the door, but Jack got a hand in before it was closed.

"Couldn't agree more," he said. "Lousy magazine."

"Well, then, what *are* you selling?" Feeney said.

"I'm Agent Jack Harper of the FBI and this is my partner, Agent Oscar Hidalgo. We'd like to talk to you a minute Mr. . . ."

"Feeney. Like you don't know my name already. Listen, you two, if this is about that Greenpeace demonstration I attended two years ago, I can fully explain. See, I'm a photographer, and I was paid to document the protest. Purely a professional acquaintance and . . ."

"It's not about Greenpeace, Mr. Feeney. Mind if we come in a minute?"

Feeney blinked and let the door open a crack more.

"Listen, all right, I know what it is, and the so-called pornographic pictures certain so-called friends of mine say I downloaded. Okay, maybe I did, but it was for purely compositional reasons. They were very artistic and . . ."

"If you'd just open the door, sir," Oscar said, putting his weight on it and driving the deeply freaked Feeney back into his living room.

"Listen," Feeney said, sputtering like a broken radiator. "How can an artist be expected to grow if he isn't allowed to immerse himself in all kinds of visual stimuli . . . even some that the average person might find morally repugnant?"

The little man's voice had risen to a near falsetto. He ran into a ratty brown couch and fell backward onto a cushion. As soon as he hit the seat, a little brown terrier came out from behind a nearby La-Z-Boy chair and jumped into his lap. The dog was wearing a red plaid bikini bottom.

Jack looked at Oscar and tried not to smile.

"Sir . . ."

"Freddy," Feeney said. "Fred J. Feeney. Photographer."

"Yeah, well, Fred," Jack said. "A neighbor of yours down on Hollywood Hills Road, a Mr. Zac Blakely, was killed today, right here in the canyon, down next to the Wonderland School."

"That's right," Oscar said. "And we don't think it was an accident."

"Terrorists!" Feeney held his dog tightly to his chest. "Did you hear that, Toodles? Terrorists have hit the canyon. Well, I knew it would happen. Everyone around here is so weird, they can blend right in!"

Jack moved a dog sweater off a chair and sat down. Oscar looked at another chair, which was covered with dog hair, and remained standing.

"We wondered if you'd seen anyone last night . . . someone you didn't know from the canyon?"

Feeney stroked Toodles and rolled his eyes like an actor doing a bad impression of thinking.

"Well . . . let me ponder that . . . Hmmm . . . yes, no, maybe . . . it's possible. No, yes . . . *Yes!* Yes, indeed. There was a big black man. He drove up and down my block looking around, like he was lost, you know? Then I saw him go down and turn left on Hollywood Hills. He was headed up to the cul de sac."

"What time was this?" Oscar asked.

"Well, let me think. I was watching TV Land. They have on all the old *Miami Vice*s. There's the one where David Andrews plays Crockett's cousin. It's so funny. I really thought David was going to be a big star, and back then I wrote Brandon Tartikoff all about it . . . do you remember Brandon? He was the head of NBC, died tragically young and anyway . . ."

"The guy outside," Jack reminded him. "If you could focus on him? It could be very important. *You* could help us break the case, Fred."

79

"Really?" Feeney said. "Fred Feeney, Crimefighter? Did you hear that, Toodles?"

"So . . . the black man?" Oscar said. "What time was it?"

"Well, let's see, I watched *Miami Vice*, and then I started to watch an infomercial . . . I was hoping it was a new one, but it was only the same old Ron Popeil and his Roaster Oven . . . I've seen it about five hundred times. Anyway, that means it was about two thirty in the morning, because as soon as the oven commercial came on, I decided to step outside for some air. So I walked over to the curtain and looked out the window, and I saw this guy coming by. Big black man. Now, I don't have anything against black people. I mean, I hate rap, but when I was younger I used to adore Sam and Dave. Which one was it that sang the high parts on 'Hold On'? Was it Sam or Dave?"

"Sam," Jack said.

"Right, of course. Did you know they hated each other? Very sad. The Soul Men hated each other. That makes me sick to my stomach. Doesn't it make you sick, Mr. Toodles?"

The dog gave a sharp little bark and licked Fred J. Feeney, Crimefighter, on the chin.

"Anyway, I looked out, and this big black man was driving by in one of those big cars . . . what do they call them?"

"Pimpmobiles?" Oscar suggested.

"Yes, that's it. A great big pimpmobile. Not very 'canyon' at all. I mean, we have weirdos, but pimps are sooo South Central. At least that kind of pimp. If we had a pimp, it would be more like a canyon pimp, a guy who wears Levi's and T-shirts and eats veggies, and does all his pimping on a cell phone, and his car would be a hybrid. Hybrid pimps, I love that. Do you love that, Mr. Toodles?"

"Yeah," Jack said. "He loves it. Did you get a look at the guy's face?"

"Yes, I did. Very scary. Big and pimp-ugly. Though I am not saying that because he is black. People up here in the canyon are not racist. But just the same, he was ugly as homemade sin. But not because he was black . . . you know what I mean?"

"Yeah," Jack said. "I got it. Hey, listen, Freddy, you think you could recognize this guy again if we showed you a picture of him?"

Suddenly Fred J. Feeney went from his speed-rapping self back into the scared little guy who'd answered the door.

"But that would mean getting involved," he said. "That might put Mr. Toodles and myself at risk. I don't know about that."

"You want to help solve the case, though, don't you?" Oscar said.

"Yes, of course," Feeney said, squeezing Mr. Toodles like a child squeezing her doll. "But what if that guy found out I identified him. I remember an episode of *The Shield* where a guy sees a murder and gang members stick his head on an electric stove! Oh, awwwwful!"

"Don't worry," Jack lied. "The guy will have no idea who identified him."

"You're sure?"

"Sure I'm sure," Jack said.

"Well, when would we go over the . . . what are they called . . . mug shots?"

"How about right now?" Jack said.

"Now? Right now? This second? Well, how do we feel about that, Mr. Toodles?"

He put his ear down next to the terrier's mouth. Mr. Toodles licked his lobe. Feeney looked up, smiling.

"Mr. Toodles says he's up for it. So, I guess so. But before we go, he reminded me that I have to feed him."

He patted the dog and smiled. Toodles licked him again.

"No problem," Jack said. "You go right ahead and feed Mr. Toodles, then we'll all go down to headquarters together. Hey, one question though: What's with Mr. T's bikini?"

Feeney smiled as if he was awaiting that very question.

"Well, the thing is, Toodles loves to swim, but naked doesn't work for him. He's a very modest animal. Hence the suit."

"Makes sense to me," Oscar said.

"Yeah, got it," Jack said.

"I'll be right back," Feeney said. "I just gotta grind up his filet mignon."

As Jack and Oscar drove up to the crowded parking lot of the FBI Building, Fred J. Feeney kept up a consistent chatter with his dog, Toodles.

"Look at the building, Toodles," he said. "Look at all the people. Some are agents and some are criminals. Isn't that right, Mr. Toodles?"

And some are raving fucking maniacs who talk to their fucking dog as if he was a hand puppet, Jack thought.

He quickly parked the car in a space about five hundred yards away from the back entrance, and then had to wait while Feeney commented on every single person who came by.

"Look at that funny man," Feeney said as a huge man with a tattoo of a devil walked by them. "He's all dressed up like the devil, isn't he, Mr. T. He'll be going to hell pretty soon, and then he won't think it's so funny."

Jack looked at Oscar, who whispered: "Being with this guy is *already* like being in hell."

They rode the elevator up to the sixth floor to Jack's and Oscar's cramped offices. Toodles began to bark in a panicky fashion.

Feeney petted him solemnly and said, "Mr. Toodles thinks

he's going to jail, don't you, Mr. Toodles? Mr. Toodles thinks he's headed to the gas chamber!"

Jack felt a terrific urge to laugh and had to restrain himself.

At Jack's crowded cubicle on the sixth floor, Fred J. Feeney looked through the mug shots while holding Toodles on his lap.

"No . . . no, no," Feeney said, rapidly turning the pages. "We didn't see any of these bad men, did we, Mr. Toodles?"

Jack stood by, drinking some water from the cooler, trying to keep his patience.

"No, wait . . . oh, look here," Feeney said, looking up at Jack with a half smile on his face.

"That the guy?" Oscar said, moving in behind Feeney to get a better look.

"No, that's not him. It's just that he's so ug. Mr. Toodles thinks so . . ."

"Hey, Fred," Oscar said, "you think you could limit your comments to the matter at hand?"

Feeney sighed, then looked again at the man's picture.

"Well, if that one there . . . isn't a criminal, he damned well should be!"

He sighed and looked through a few more pages. Then:

"Oh, look here," he said.

"More ugliness?" Jack said.

"No sirree bob," Feeney said. "This is the guy. You remember him, don't you, Toodles?"

The dog gazed at the picture, but made no comment.

"You sure?" Oscar said.

"Oh, yes," Feeney said. "I never forget a face. Now, names I'm not that good at. Like I sometimes get Melvin all mixed up with Don. And Le Roy all mixed up with Lester. Don't ask me why, but my mother was the same way."

83

Jack looked down at the picture Feeney had pointed out.

It showed a picture of a large black man, forty-two years of age. His name was Edward T. Rollins.

"Arrested for car theft, interstate flight. Been a member of a chop-shop gang in Reno, Nevada, and Tijuana, Mexico."

"Car nut," Oscar said. "That's gotta be our boy."

"No known address," Jack said. "I'm thinking we oughta ask Michelle Wu about this."

Oscar nodded. "Yeah, if anyone knows about it, she would."

Feeney looked up and smiled in his goofy way.

"Did I do good, guys?"

Jack smiled down at him and even felt a little shot of warmth for Fred and his dog.

"You did real good, Fred. I think we might even have a crime-fighter's badge for Toodles here."

He reached into his desk and found a toy agent's badge that agents routinely gave out to school kids who toured the building.

"Oh, wow! Thanks, fellas. Say, look at that, Toodles. We're agents. Yes, we are, aren't we, Toodles. Agents of the FBI."

Oscar shook his head again, and Jack thought of how funny Zac Blakely would have found all of this. That was the thing about Zac; he knew where to find a saving laugh. He always said that one thing he knew for sure: He'd never die from stress. Not with his sense of humor.

10

MICHELLE WU LIVED in Koreatown, but nobody knew exactly where. Jack had a cell-phone number for her and she agreed to meet him at a place called General Wang's Noodle Factory, a stucco building near Western, where nobody had made noodles for thirty years. She made it clear that she didn't want to see Oscar or anyone else, and if they showed, she wouldn't appear.

So at eight that night, Jack found himself parking behind General Wang's Noodles on Eighth Avenue, and walking into a dark alley, where he looked for a long flight of rotted steps which led to the third-floor door that still had a picture of General Wang himself, a bespectacled Korean who held a steaming plate of noodles.

Jack rang a bell and a Korean the size of Goliath came to the door. Jack explained to him who he was, leaving out the fact that he was a federal agent, and followed him inside. Once inside the door, the giant frisked him professionally and, satisfied that

Jack wasn't carrying a weapon, grunted and pointed to the back of the building.

They walked through hallways strewn with trash, and then entered a freight elevator that took them to the top floor.

The man never spoke at all. When they arrived, he opened the old hand-cage door and grunted again. Jack took this to mean he should get out, and did.

He looked to his left and saw a car sitting under klieg lights. Jack walked toward the racer, a Honda EG hatchback tuner car, a twelve-second car, the model street racers used in pink-slip contests.

Jack saw a pair of shapely legs sticking out from under the engine block and walked toward them.

"Hey, white boy," Michelle Wu said.

"Hey, yourself," Jack said. "You tricking this baby out all by yourself?"

"Oh, yeah," Michelle said. "I'm getting the fuel injections put in. Pink baby. This little car gonna bring home a lot of other cars for Mama. All perfectly legal, of course."

"Of course," Jack said. "We know that a woman of your ilk would never traffic in anything illegal."

There was a chuckle from underneath the car, and then Michelle Wu slid out on her dolly and looked up at Jack.

Jack smiled at her. She was so strikingly beautiful that it sometimes hurt his face to look at her. He couldn't simply stare at her, though that was his initial instinct. Her black eyes seemed to reflect moon and starlight even in a room as dark as this one. Her body was trim, her breasts small but perfectly shaped. Her flat stomach, her stunningly shaped legs . . . the whole package was devastating.

"You come to arrest me again, white boy?" she said, slipping off the dolly and effortlessly standing by his side.

"Not unless you're stealing cars again and breaking interstate-flight laws," Jack said, smiling.

She leaned into him, purposely rubbing her breasts on his chest, and kissed his cheek. Her lips were full, and yet soft. Jack felt the immediate stirrings of desire and pulled himself away. The truth was, even now, as involved as he was with Julie, he didn't trust himself around Michelle, and he sure as hell didn't trust her. She was beautiful, brilliant, and an amazing mechanic and driver . . . but there was something constitutionally wrong with her. She would rather invent a lie even if it was easier to tell the truth. She lived for action and excitement and, as fast as she could turn you on, she could also become bored and truculent.

She didn't merely live in the fast lane, she *was* the fast lane.

Now she was all charm, leaning against Jack as she put on a high-heeled shoe, which emphasized her perfect calves.

"I never stole cars," she said, pouting and playing the hurt little girl for Jack. "You had it all wrong about that."

"I know," Jack said. "You had no idea that the cars you were running down to Mexico to the Encinitas chop shop were illegal, right?"

"Right," Michelle said, fiddling with her other shoe. "I drove down there to race them. How could I know they were hot? Baby, have a little faith in me."

"That's exactly what I *do* have," Jack said. "A *little* faith. Very little, but more than I did this time last year."

Michelle rolled her amazing dark eyes and picked up a wrench.

"I gotta fix the timing mechanism. So are you still going out with that little white angel-girl, Julie?"

"Yeah," Jack said. "I am."

"Such a waste," Michelle said. "She's no good for you. She's mental."

"No," Jack said. "She's sensitive, that's all."

"No, weak," Michelle said. "When you want a strong woman, call me. You and me are meant to be together."

"Oh, yeah," Jack said. "It's our destiny."

"Well, of course, silly," she said. "So if you're not here to sweep me off my feet, then why?"

She gave Jack her best "what can a little thing like me do for a big cop like you" look.

"There's a guy hangs out in the car scene . . . Eddie Rollins. You know him?"

As she slid back under the hood, she said, "Maybe. What'd he do?"

"Maybe he murdered one of our agents. Zac Blakely. My old partner. You know anything about him, you tell me now."

She slid back up and looked up at him.

"Zac Blakely." She frowned, looked as though she was turning the name over in her mind.

"That name sound familiar to you?"

"Yeah," she said. "It does. I think I heard you talking about him. But maybe somewhere else, too. I can't quite recall it."

"His death was on the TV news last night."

"Yeah," Michelle said. "I guess that's how I know it. You think this guy Rollins did it?"

"Maybe," Jack said. "You know him, Michelle?"

"You got a picture?"

Jack reached into his coat and handed her the mug shot.

Michelle looked at it, and then back up at Jack.

"You want to come under here with me?" she said. "I've got some pipe work I have to do."

Jack managed a small smile. "You recognize him?"

"What do I get if I say yes? A date?"

"You get another day outta jail," Jack said. "Come on, Michelle. I'm not in the mood to fuck around. Blakely was a great agent and one of my oldest friends."

She smiled and pointed one perfect leg up at him.

"I know him," she said. "He lives with his sister out in Monterey Park. He's always hitting on me, trying to get me to come over. To discuss rods, ya know?"

"You know the address?"

"It's written down somewhere. Maybe in my bedroom. Maybe you'd like to help me find it?"

"Maybe you'll go get it right now, Michelle."

"Maybe I will," she said. "After all, anything for my Jackie."

She slid back out and got up again, and when she walked away, she put a little spin in her hips that made Jack crazy. Who would know if he had a little thing with her? What man could resist her? Then he thought of Julie waiting for him at home, taking care of Kevin, and told himself he was just tired, weak, and how it was totally against policy. But as she walked back, smiling at him, he felt desire sweep over him all over again.

11

AS JACK AND OSCAR headed out the Hollywood Freeway south toward El Monte, Oscar looked up from the road for a second at the giant TERMINATOR PEST CONTROL sign, which hovered over the traffic. The sign featured a man dressed in a top hat and pince-nez glasses. In his hand was a giant mallet and in front of him were a couple of very dead-looking cartoon rats.

"You see that man?" Oscar said. "The Pest-Control Hombre?"

"What about him?"

"When I came to this country from Salvador with my parents in the summer of 1966, we stayed at the motel right down there. The first thing I saw when I woke up that morning was that sign. Man, it was scary. That funny-looking dude and those rats. See, when I was a boy in Salvador, my papa always talked about America and especially Los Angeles as the land of movie stars, Rolls-Royces, and swimming pools in every backyard, but when I wake up and see that sign, I think to myself, 'No, Papí must have it all wrong. There must be many rats here, and they need somebody to kill them all.'"

Jack smiled and looked across the seat at his partner.

"I have often thought maybe that was the day I decided to become a cop.

"I kept staring at that sign, and I felt like I was learning something I didn't want to know. But I could never forget it. And then we stayed with my uncle Felipe, and he had rats in his basement. And no swimming pool . . . and he didn't drive a Rolls-Royce, neither, but a Tijuana taxi . . . a broken-down old pickup that shot black smoke out of its pipes and fouled up the air."

"So you were a force for good," Jack said as they headed by the brightly lit downtown, the huge glass buildings where deals were made in which neither of them would ever be included.

"Yeah. That was me," Oscar said. "Captain Pest Control. Funny, isn't it, how a sign you see when you are ten can send you down a path for your whole life."

"Yeah," Jack said. "Funny as hell."

They drove from the Hollywood Freeway to Indian Avenue, then crossed the park and turned left at Serrano Street.

Behind them the park was supernaturally bright with soccer players, shouting, laughing, running under the neon. Ahead of them there was a Salvadoran restaurant called Sylvia's.

"Just a block down there," Jack said. "Cienfuego Gardens."

"Yeah," Oscar said. "Don't you love how they always call the projects 'gardens'? The only thing that grows down here is marijuana."

"Let's park down here a block. Just in case . . . our boy is making a little guest appearance."

Oscar pulled over to the side behind a rusted-out Taurus. They checked their weapons, got out, and shut the doors softly, then started down the street. They'd walked only about three feet when a huge rat ran across the street not ten feet from where they were.

"You bring your mallet, Pest Man?" Jack laughed.

"Got it right in my holster," Oscar said.

The house was a run-down Tudor, with a sharp-edged roof that looked to Jack like an elf's castle from a children's book he'd used to read to Kevin. But any elves in this castle would all be crack-smoking fiends. They made it up to a side entrance and looked at the mailbox. It read Rollins, Edith.

"Upstairs," Jack said.

They looked up and saw a light on in the window.

"Look like she's home," Jack said. "I'm going point."

Oscar nodded as they headed up the steps.

On the small porch Jack rapped on the door. Oscar stood one step below him, revolver out.

Inside there was a woman's voice.

"Who is it?"

"Edith Rollins?"

"Who wants to know?"

"FBI, ma'am. We need to talk to you. Please open the door."

There was a frozen silence, and then the sound of feet scurrying away from the door.

Jack looked at Oscar, then nodded.

"I'll ask you one more time, ma'am. Then we're coming in."

There was no reply.

But inside Jack heard something crash to the floor.

"Sounded like a lamp."

"Yeah, somebody's in a big hurry."

"Kick the muther down!"

Jack nodded and yelled one last time.

"FBI! We're coming in!"

He lifted his right leg and, with one powerful shot, kicked in the front door.

They ran into the small, crowded room, guns out, standing back to back as they 360'd the room. Then from the back of the apartment they heard the sound of scraping furniture.

"Back window," Jack said.

They ran down the hallway toward the back bedroom, but were met halfway by a small, red-eyed woman wearing a ragged pink bathrobe and shoes with frog faces on the toes.

"There's nobody here, officers," she said, bracing herself in the hallway.

"Ma'am," Jack said, "move out of the way. Now!"

She didn't budge, but stood there with her two arms pushed against the walls.

"Are you going to shoot an unarmed old woman?" she said in an even, almost amused tone.

"No," Jack said. "We're not."

He walked up to her and gave her a stiff arm to the right shoulder. She fell backward in a heap, screaming.

"Help, help! Police brutality!"

Jack and Oscar tried not to step on her as they jumped across her body and ran into the bedroom. The back window was open, and Jack jumped over a pile of dirty clothes on the floor and quickly looked out on the park and street.

At first Jack saw nothing but the soccer game down below played under the surreal neon lights. Then he turned and looked up at the roof above him. A pair of legs was scrambling up a drainpipe.

"On the roof," Jack said.

They ran back out through the hallway. When they got into the living room, they saw Edith Rollins sitting on her couch. She screamed at them as they flew by and out the door.

"Both of you are going to fucking die!"

Jack gave Oscar a funny look.

"You're gonna have to wait in line, bitch," he said.

They hit the steps and flew up to the roof.

The stars shone above them, the cries of the soccer game were below. Jack pointed to the big air-conditioning unit in the middle of the roof.

Jack took the left way around, Oscar the right.

Jack hugged the wall and came around quickly. There was nobody.

Oscar slid around the edge of the unit, and as he did, Rollins appeared from behind a chimney to his right.

Oscar turned, but not quickly enough, and Rollins shot him in the chest. He fell backward, grunting as he hit the tar roof.

Jack came running around, but by the time he arrived, Rollins had turned and made a dead run for the rooftop edge. He soared in the air and landed on the nearby roof, tumbled, rolled to his feet, and disappeared down the steps.

Jack knelt down to help Oscar.

"Where'd he hit you?"

"It's okay. I'm fine. Go."

He ripped open his shirt and showed Jack his Kevlar vest. Smoke billowed out of two bullet holes.

"Go!" Oscar said. "I'm right behind you."

Jack turned and ran down the steps by Rollins's apartment, where Rollins's sister stood by the door.

"You eat dog, you fuckface!"

The absurdity of her curse struck Jack funny, and as he ran, he began to laugh.

On the street, he looked across at the park, and in the middle of one of the games he saw a big black man running across the field. He heard the crowd scream, and as he took off after him,

Jack saw Rollins head for the sidelines toward a crowd of mothers and fathers who were watching their kids play.

He heard screams, and as he got closer, he made out the words: "*Mira!* He's got a gun!"

"Look out. *Vámonos!*"

Jack hit the edge of the park and watched as Rollins knocked people down and headed for the freeway.

The nighttime traffic was dense. He'd never get across the freeway. On the other hand, Jack couldn't risk a shot if he somehow managed to get out there among the cars. He ran across the field, his own gun out, and headed for the sidelines.

As he came closer to the terrified crowd, he screamed: "Get down! FBI!"

The crowd on the sidelines dove for cover. Jack knelt, aimed, but there was still a group of people between himself and Rollins, who was now on the freeway curb.

Rollins turned now and saw him through the mob. He pushed a woman out of the way and fired at Jack. The bullet sizzled by his head.

On the ground near him, all hell broke loose, the parents terrified for their children. Some of them got up, ran out onto the soccer field, grabbed their kids, and started running in the opposite direction. Rollins fired again and hit a woman nearby. Jack saw her fall as if she had been hit by lightning. The crowd screamed again. There was no other choice. Jack had to take a shot of his own, before Rollins hit someone else.

He knelt by a picnic bench and then fired at Rollins's right side.

The bullet hit him dead on and Jack saw a red spurt blow out of his ribs.

Jack fired again, and a red mist came from his left knee.

Rollins turned now and limped directly out into the freeway.

A huge moving van with the words STARVING STUDENTS on it bore down on him. Rollins rolled out of the way, but was hit by a truck that said Ding Dong Ice Cream. His body flew up over its roof and was left out on the freeway.

Jack got up and began to run toward the freeway, his gun still out, ready to fire.

Standing on an adjacent corner, only a half block away, was a man with his digital video camera filming the whole sequence. A man with a beard and a scar under his eye. He had been following Jack and Oscar for three days, and now—spectacularly—he had his big payoff.

The film was going fine. Everyone was going to be very, very happy.

Even that worrywart Jim.

He knew that the other cops were going to come now, and that he was vulnerable standing here. So, time to book out. Time to get back and see how this great action sequence came out.

The cars drove slowly around Rollins, who lay in the passing lane. He was bleeding from his ribs. His leg and his right side looked smashed. Amazingly, though, he was conscious and seemed to be alert. His SIG Sauer was lying nearby on the ground and Jack kicked it away quickly.

Behind him he heard Oscar's voice.

"I'll take that."

He put on plastic gloves and picked up the pistol.

"You okay?"

"Yeah, I think."

Jack got out his cell phone and punched in a code.

"Medic needed Serrano Park and the 110. Now. Several people shot. Hurry."

As Oscar walked out and began to reroute the traffic, Jack walked over to the fallen Rollins.

"You're hit bad, man," he said.

Rollins looked dazed, obviously in shock.

"Think I'm gonna buy the farm?"

"I'll tell you straight up, bro. It doesn't look good. You got something to tell me—what you did at Wonderland Avenue the other night—get it off your chest?"

Rollins looked confused. He rubbed his broad blood-splattered forehead.

"Wonderland? How you know 'bout that?"

"Don't matter how I know," Jack said. "You ain't got time to worry about that. Just tell me."

"I didn't do nothing," Rollins said.

"Cut the shit, Rollins. I know you were up there."

Rollins spit out a gob of blood. Part of it hit Jack's shoes. In the distance Jack could hear sirens wail. Rubberneckers drifted by staring at the fallen man, and one creep took a picture of him.

"I was up there," Rollins said. "'Cause a guy called me 'bout a car for sale."

"Yeah, right. What happened then?"

"I couldn't find the address."

Jack reached down and grabbed Rollins by the collar.

"Listen, Edward. You're on your last legs, man. You gonna die with a man's murder on your immortal soul? That what you want?"

"Murder?" Rollins said. "No way, my friend. I looked up and down the streets up there, couldn't find the address, and went home. End of story."

Jack looked into his eyes and shook his head.

"You didn't cut a guy's brakes so when he started his car going down the hill, he couldn't stop?"

Rollins shook his head.

"Man, you whack," he said. "I din't do nothing like that."

Jack felt a rage boiling through him. He wanted to smash Rollins's face in, see how he told it after that.

But suddenly there was a woman med tech standing next to him.

"Sir, this man is wounded."

"No shit," Jack said. "Jack Harper, FBI."

"Get out of the way, Agent Harper. You know better than to interrogate a wounded man."

She pushed past Jack and began to attend to Rollins.

"You lying fuck," Jack said. "I *know* you did it."

The tech looked at him and shook her head in disbelief.

"You get out of here, Harper, before I write you up," she said.

"Yeah," Rollins said. "I might jest get me a civil suit outta this. Breaking and entering into my sister's pad, shooting up the 'hood. You a menace, Harper. One of them Mark Fuhrman mutherfuckers."

He laughed and spat up another gob of blood and aimed it at Jack. It hit the cuff of Jack's pants as he turned and walked away.

12

BACK HOME, JACK REACHED into his fridge for a bottle of Rolling Rock. He popped the top, shut the door, and then sat wearily down at the kitchen table. His right leg ached, and his shoulder was bothering him. He shut his eyes but that didn't help. He kept picturing Zac Blakely's terrified face as he turned and smashed into the cafeteria wall.

He'd sacrificed his life to save the kids, and Jack was going to get the bastard who did it . . . he swore it to himself.

Then the phone rang. Jack reached over, took it off the hook. "Hello."

"Hello. Is this my friend Agent Harper?"

Jack felt the shock hit his chest.

"Who is this?"

"I'm sure you know."

Jack let out a breath.

"Steinbach. How'd you get my number?"

There was a mocking laugh on the other end of the line.

"Well, you can hardly expect me to tell you that, Harper. Remember what I told you? My reach is long."

"You call me at home again, asshole, and you'll find out how long *mine* is."

There was another laugh. It was clear Steinbach was enjoying this.

"So violent. So defensive. I just called to say that I was terribly sorry to hear about the death of your old partner and mentor, Zac Blakely. They just aren't making cars the way they used to."

Jack felt a wave of rage passing over him and struggled not to reveal it to Steinbach.

"You're right, Karl, they're not," he said. "And they're not making hit men the way they used to, either."

"Meaning what?"

"Meaning your boy Eddie Rollins won't be doing any more work for you anytime soon."

There was a brief silence on the other end. Then:

"I have no idea what you're talking about, Jack. Eddie Rollins? I've never had the pleasure."

"Yeah, right," Jack said.

"No, really," Steinbach said. "I merely called to commiserate with you. Yours is such a dangerous line of work. Why, anything can happen to a guardian of the public trust at any given time."

Jack felt his jaw tense up. He wanted to reach through the phone and squeeze Steinbach's Adam's apple until it turned to pulp.

"Listen, you fat fuck, if anything . . . anything at all happens to either my partner or Hughes I'm going to come up there and take it out on you, personally. You hear me?"

There was another little chuckle from the South African's end.

"Jack, Jack . . . Listen to you raving on. One would never know that you were an agent of reason and the law."

"What would you know about the law or reason, Steinbach?"

"Quite a bit actually," Steinbach said. "I passed the bar in 1989. Do you realize that in my home in Capetown, I was one of the few lawyers who stood up for repatriation?"

Jack wanted to hang up, but there was something irresistible about talking with Steinbach in this way.

"So what are you saying, Karl? You used to be a good guy?"

"Yes, Jack. I was very good. But the powers that be didn't appreciate my idealism. They set me up for smuggling. Sent me away. I lost my wife, my son, my home . . ."

"So you had no choice but to become a scumbag, is that it?"

"None whatsoever. After my five years in jail, I got them all. Every one of them who had sent me up. They paid for violating my honesty."

"Bullshit!" Jack said. "You were always a germ, just waiting to infect somebody."

Steinbach laughed again.

"You're so simpleminded, Jack. Do you really believe there's any difference between you and me?"

"All the difference in the world, Karl."

He slammed the receiver down.

"That fuck!"

Julie appeared in the kitchen doorway. She looked shocked.

"Jack, is something wrong?"

"No," Jack said. "Just a little mix-up at work. It's cool."

From the other room, Kevin called, "Will everybody chill out a little? I'm trying to watch *Ghost in the Shell*."

Jack gritted his teeth. He wanted to talk to his son about skipping school, but he hadn't had a moment.

"How's Kev doing?" he said to Julie.

"Not so great," she said. "He won't talk about the school thing. But I talked to the principal today, and if he does it again, he could be thrown out. When I mentioned that to him, he got very defensive and wouldn't talk to me at all."

Jack sat down at the kitchen table.

Julie looked harried, worried.

"He said I wasn't his mother and that I had no right to ask him anything. It's so funny, Jack. When I first started going out with you, he seemed like any other kid. I had no idea how angry he was about your divorce."

Jack nodded and tried to stroke Julie's hair, but she pulled her head away.

"I'm sorry," Jack said.

"I think he needs a therapist, Jack. Could do him a world of good."

Jack shook his head. "I don't think so."

"Why not?"

"Why not? Because my ex and I went to therapy sessions for two years and all that happened is that we got angrier and angrier at one another. The therapist would say, 'This room is a safe place to get out your feelings,' so we did. Man, did we ever! But it turned out it wasn't a good place for that at all. We couldn't leave the stuff we'd said to one another in the room, and when we got home, things really got twisted. You know what I believe in now? You got bad feelings, you work harder, you get a girlfriend, you change your life. You don't need to indulge them all the time."

"Great," Julie said. "Well, they're coming out anyway, Jack. Maybe not at you. But at me. I spend the whole day teaching fifth graders, then I come home to a furious teenager and a boyfriend who gets home around two A.M. four nights a week. And where the hell were you all night?"

Jack laughed harshly.

"Oh, I was at a party. Yeah, at the Playboy Mansion. Me and Hef and the Bunnies. Yeah, it was a lot of fun. Oscar almost got killed, and I ended up shooting a guy in the middle of the freeway. Yeah, you shoulda been there. It was a real gas."

Julie shook her head and looked at the floor.

"I'm tired," she said. "And tomorrow's a long day. Good night, Jack."

She got up and walked out of the kitchen toward the bedroom. Jack wanted to stop her, take her in his arms, but something held him back. The something that stopped him from going into the front room, switching off the tube, and dealing with his son.

He felt a mental and physical exhaustion, and he knew that he wouldn't have the words to make things better.

He'd have to deal with it all tomorrow.

Christ . . . the list of things was endless.

And then, just as he had gotten up to head into the shower, the phone rang again.

If it was Steinbach, he was going to take his head off.

But it wasn't. The phone said F. Feeney.

"Hello."

"Hi, Agent Harper?"

"Yeah?" Jack said.

"I know it's late and I'm sorry, but you said if I thought of anything else, I should call you."

"That's okay," Jack said. "What's up?"

"Well, I've thought about it and thought about it, and gone over it with Mr. Toodles, and we both agreed I should call you at once."

"That right?" Jack said. "And what is this vital information, Fred."

"Well, I'd forgotten this. Guess I didn't think it was top-notch important but the thing is, there was another guy I saw wandering around the canyon the day before the agent got killed."

"Really, you saw him in the mug-shot book at the office?"

"Noooo," Fred Feeney said. "That's the amazing thing. The person I saw wasn't in the book. He was . . . He was an agent. A guy who was right in the next office while we were in there looking at pictures."

Now Jack was fully awake.

"What? You sure, Fred?"

"Trust me," Feeney said. "Fred and Toodles never forget faces. As in absolutely never, ever. I saw his door. I remember the man's nameplate. Kind of gold. And he had movie stars' pictures all over the walls. Trouble is, I'm not as good with names as I am with faces. I've asked Toodles, but he draws a blank, too."

"Forrester? That ring a bell?"

"Yes, that's it. Forrester. Supervising Agent William Forrester. Mr. Toodles and I were out for a walk and we saw him drive up to the turnaround, park his car, get out, and walk around. I didn't think anything of it. Maybe you should ask him about it, hey?"

"Yeah, maybe I should," Jack said. "You've done a good job, Fred. But I don't want you mentioning this to anyone else. Except Toodles, of course."

"Toodles should get some of the credit. Without him, I might never have seen him at all. Well, hope I'm helpful. I *like* being a secret agent, Jack."

"You're a hell of a good one," Jack said. "Good night, Fred."

"Good night, Agent Harper," Feeney said.

From behind him there was a sharp bark. As if Special Agent Toodles was signing off, too.

Jack sat at the kitchen table, head in his hands.

Forrester up at the Blakely house? The night before?

What the hell was he up to?

Could it have been Forrester who cut the brakes? Using the Steinbach threat as a cover?

Was he up there, intending to break into Blakely's, and trying to find the stolen bank loot?

Whatever it was, he had to keep his eye on both Steinbach and his boys *and* Forrester. And he wondered how long it would be before whoever the hell it was would be coming after him.

13

"WAIT UNTIL YOU SEE this, Jim," he said.

"You really think so?" James said, sitting in the leather seat at the projection room they'd set up in the old bedroom at the back of the house.

"Oh, yeah." He switched off the lights. "I don't think anyone is ready for this. Amazing stuff."

He switched off the light and took the seat next to Jim. He was getting all nervous in his stomach, tingly in the arms, just like he'd felt up in the tree. Couldn't decide if he was excited out of his mind or sickened by the whole thing.

Only one way to find out. He hit the remote, and the movie started on the screen in front of them.

There was Blakely in his green BMW heading down the hill.

There were the school buses and the kids down there.

There was a ZOOM IN on Blakely's face, at the exact moment he realized that his brakes had failed.

Pull back and see the larger view. The mother screaming, then close in on her face, a scream like something out of *Potemkin*.

Then back to Blakely, as he realized what his choices were.

Suddenly he hit the PAUSE button, and the image froze right there on Blakely's face.

Jim turned and looked at him, his face agitated.

"Why'd you stop it?"

"See, Zac Blakely has a choice here. He can either save the kids and their mothers, or he can hit the wall. He can think of himself, his career, his retirement party, which is coming up soon, his wife, a very beautiful woman, or he can hit the wall and die a hero."

"Yes," Jim said. "I see that. And he chose . . ."

"The wall," he said. "That's right. Funny about that, isn't it? He chose the wall. And died a hero."

"The hero," Jim said. Then he laughed, but it wasn't a happy laugh at all. There was a deep bitterness in it.

"Yeah, the big FBI hero," he said.

"Let's see how the hero looks when he hits the wall," Jimmy said.

"Right," he said.

Then he clicked the button again, and together they watched Zac Blakely turn into the Wonderland cafeteria wall.

They watched the car explode, the bricks flying through the air. Blakely launched through the windshield.

"Great shot!" Jim said. "Great goddamned shot!"

"Thanks," the older man said. "I would have never gotten it all if you hadn't shown me how to use the camera."

They turned and looked at one another, fondly. A mutual-admiration society.

"Who do we hit for Act Two?" Jim said.

"We need to talk about that," the man said. "I got some sensational stuff with Rollins running through the soccer game. That stuff is golden."

"Good," Jim said. "But that's more transitional stuff. We need a solid Act Two. Something that'll top Blakely."

"Don't worry about that," the man said. "I've got some great ideas. You want to eat first?"

"Nah, I'm not hungry," Jimmy said. "And I gotta go soon. So let's get down to the nitty-gritty, okay?"

"You gotta run, huh?" the man said.

"Yeah," Jimmy said. "So let's get started. Who is the next lucky asshole?"

He laughed wildly this time, and it gave the other man the creeps. But he didn't say so, and they soon got right down to work.

14

KYLE WAS DREAMING that he was floating in a pond while his father sat on the riverbank, dozing. Kyle saw him there, so close by he could almost touch him. And there was Michael nearby, too. Floating on his back just a few feet away. The sun was shining, the frogs were croaking. It was . . . what was that word . . . in the dream Kyle tried to find it . . . oh yeah, idyllic. That was the word.

But there was one tiny thing that was a little amiss. There was a purple membrane of some kind floating on the pond, just a few feet away from them. It was really kind of amazing looking, bright purple, and sort of curled up at the edges. It looked like . . . a giant jellyfish, but it seemed harmless.

Kyle found it interesting, fascinating . . . because it seemed to be growing . . . getting longer, and now it was turning into something else. Kind of like a giant clam . . .

Only now it was moving toward them, and in a second it had kind of oozed all over Michael, and then devoured him.

Kyle started to scream. He really couldn't believe what he was seeing.

He turned and looked at his father, screaming, "Dad! Dad! It's taking us. It's coming to kill us!"

But his father was still dozing on the pond bank, a pleasant grin on his face, as if he was having a really good dream.

Kyle turned back and looked at the thing, and he could see Michael's head, pushing against the purple membrane, screaming in horror. And now the thing was oozing all over Kyle as well, and he couldn't breathe . . . the thing forced itself down his throat, squirted itself into his ears, and up his nose.

He was drowning in ooze—and his father wouldn't wake up.

And he was beating at the membrane, but it just gave with every punch he threw.

And he felt it turning hot and sticky and he knew without a doubt that in a few more seconds . . . he was going to die.

He awoke, screaming, and tried to flail about, but he was still tied tight. The membrane was a blanket the bearded man had put over him. And the lack of breath . . . that had to be caused by the gag, which was tied even tighter.

Why didn't someone come for them?

Why was his father dozing on the riverbank somewhere?

Who the fuck had done this?

Why?

He looked over at his brother, who was out cold.

The kid looked so peaceful, he hated to do it. But there had to be a way out, and they had to find it before the kidnapper came back and killed them both.

Because that's what he was going to do. Kyle was sure of it. After all, they had seen his face.

He couldn't afford to let them go now.

Kyle looked at his ropes. Saw how they were tied to the pipes, which came out of the old boiler.

If he could only untie his hands, get over there. Maybe he could smash the pipes, and then slide the ropes off.

He tried to move, but he could barely get an inch before the ropes dug into his wrists.

"Fuck!" he said. "Mike . . . wake the hell up. C'mon. We gotta get out of here. Mike, do you hear me? Do you?"

And then Kyle felt a terrible emptiness invade his soul.

Mike wasn't moving. Wasn't hearing him at all. Mike wasn't . . . Couldn't be dead . . .

He saw an old can of Coke on the floor. Took careful aim with his right foot and kicked it at his brother.

Bull's-eye!

The can hit his sleeping brother right on his forehead.

Still silence . . . Kyle felt sick . . .

And then there was movement. An eye opened, and his brother looked up at him.

"What the fuck was that?" he said. Only it came out through the gag like "Whatfargcat?

He sounded pissed off, like an angry little kid. Kyle smiled.

Nodded. And looked up at the ancient pipes. It took his battered, scared, younger brother a few minutes, but finally he nodded.

Good, Kyle thought. Because the only way they would escape this shithole is if they worked together.

15

JACK WAS MORE THAN a little relieved to get to work. He had serious plans for Karl Steinbach and wanted to get started right away.

In his sixth-floor office, he addressed Hughes and Oscar, who sat on the other side of his desk, coffee and doughnuts in their hands.

"Thanks for coming in early, guys," he said. "We're taking a little trip to visit our friend Karl Steinbach today. The creep called my house and practically admitted he'd killed Zac."

He'd thought that this information would make them both want to get moving, but Oscar looked at Hughes in a troubled way.

"What?" Jack said.

"It's Steinbach, Jack. He's not locked up anymore."

"What-the-fuck-are-you-talking-about?"

Hughes shook his head. "He cut a deal with Homeland Security. Our old pal, Tommy Wilson."

Jack felt the fury building in his temples.

"No way!"

Oscar opened his palms in a gesture of helplessness.

"The fucking guy said he knows all about terrorists out in Africa. Claims he met them in the diamond market, which is how they finance their network."

"Gimme a fucking break," Jack said. "Tommy went for that?"

"'Fraid so."

"Mutherfucker!" Jack said. "Don't they know he killed Blakely? He even left a goddamned picture of his tombstone at the crime scene."

"I talked to Tommy about it this morning. On the cell on the way in. He said we got no proof he did it. He also said that Steinbach says he knows of something big these guys are going to pull off in the next few months. At LAX. That's gotta take priority."

Jack slammed his fist down on the desk.

"He's playing these guys. Christ, has everybody in this country lost their minds?"

"Yeah, you're probably right, Jack," Hughes said. "But what if you're wrong? That's the thing. Five thousand people could die. The airport could be fucked for a year. We're the second team, man. And that's how it's gonna be from now on."

Jack slumped down in his chair, thoroughly deflated.

"It sucks," Hughes said. "Man, I gotta couple days' vacation coming, and I sure as hell am gonna need 'em."

Oscar looked at Jack, who said nothing but stared moodily down at his desk.

16

LATER THAT NIGHT, Ron Hughes kicked back at his trailer on the beach at Ventura. The ocean smashed up against the beach below and Hughes sat by his fire, remembering his friend and partner Zac Blakely. He had Chet Baker on his CD player, and drank a Negro Modelo. Usually, coming up here to his trailer, one that he'd inherited from his uncle Herb ten years ago, put him in a perfect state of mind. He'd always been the kind of agent who could turn off the frustrations of the job with music, a good beer, and the roar of the ocean. But tonight that was impossible. The idea that the thieving rotten bastard had killed Blakely was like a stake in his heart. All the years they had worked together, doing things their own way and making it work, and the son of a bitch cuts his brakes. He wanted to get his gun and go after Steinbach on his own.

And besides, when he looked at the evidence, he wasn't really sure if it had been Steinbach at all.

Possibly there were other people who wanted to kill Blakely . . . Blakely and himself, too. It wasn't as though they had a shortage of enemies.

Maybe he'd look into them as well.

Hughes poured himself a cognac to go with his beer, and downed the shot in one gulp. He looked at his watch and a small smile lit up his lined face.

It was 10:50, only ten more minutes until the train came by. The Northern Pacific. All the way from San Diego, through Los Angeles, then up to Santa Barbara, Monterey, San Francisco, and back again.

When he'd first started coming up here from L.A., the train coming through at night had bugged him. The little trailer shook and rattled as the big train rumbled close by on the tracks. But after a while he'd grown to love the sight and the sound of the gleaming train streaming through the moonlight. It had become one of the natural sounds of the area, as familiar and welcome as the surf pounding the beach, the seagulls crying as they circled his home. It was a high, lonesome sound, and the boy in Hughes responded to it eagerly.

Now he picked up his beer, slipped on his loafers, and walked out the side door toward the beach. The night was mysterious, foggy, and the beach looked hazy in the mist and moonlight. A magic place, made even more so by the fact that Hughes knew the train was speeding toward him . . . He walked east toward the tracks, taking another sip of the rich Mexican beer. It was good and cold, and it reminded him again of Blakely, the beer aficionado. It was Blakely who had gotten him to drink good beers, rather than working-class Pabst. Hughes wasn't sure that moving up in life wasn't somehow a betrayal of his working-class roots. But Blakely had teased him for worrying about such stuff.

Called him "peasant man." Zac had shown him the way. He owed Zac so much, and now he'd never be able to repay him.

Hughes arrived at the tracks around 10:58. He stood there sipping the last of his beer, and waited for the first sound of the train roaring up from the south. In the wind and the moonlight and with the surf still pounding, it was always an amazing moment for him. Sometimes he'd take off his shirt and let the sea mist cover his chest, and when he heard the train whistle, and the sound of the engine rumbling down the tracks, he'd shut his eyes and imagine that he was a boy again and that he could hop the train and go . . . go anywhere. Anywhere in the world he wanted, start over, maybe live a whole other kind of life . . .

Yeah, it was silly, and sometimes later, when he thought about it, he'd get embarrassed and red-faced thinking about his little fantasy. But what was wrong with it, after all? Didn't everyone wish they could live multiple lives, start over and maybe be a different kind of person? A better person. Hell, maybe he wouldn't have become an agent at all.

Tonight was just such a night. The mist, the moonlight, the ocean, and now the train itself. He could hear it coming up the line, and he smiled and took off his shirt and felt the cool air clinging to him. He took one last long chug of beer and waited, a foot or two from the tracks, where he could feel the draft the train made swirling all over him, and there in the moonlight for a few seconds he'd be transformed . . . transformed into the kind of guy he used to dream of being when he was a kid in Reseda.

And then he heard it getting closer to him, speeding out of the electric night, the rush of speed, the sound of the whistle, the roar of the ocean, the sound of the circling and crying birds . . . all of it was inside him as well as outside on the beach. He felt a huge happiness, a transcendent moment, of pure, clear sensation . . . felt it right up until someone stepped up behind him. Someone who seemed to come from nowhere, and who waited until the train was barreling down upon him, someone who thrust Ron Hughes onto the tracks. The whistle screamed, and as Hughes looked up, he saw the engine coming down on him like a screaming silver torpedo. And then—briefly—he felt another sensation . . . as the torpedo exploded into his chest, squashed his ribs, chest, and lungs, all in one brutal motion.

Like the snap of one's fingers, Ron Hughes's life ended.

The person who had pushed him stood there for a second, silently, filming every piece of the action. Actually, it had been a little awkward sneaking up with the camera on his shoulder. For a second or two, he felt a little resentment toward Jim, who wanted all this to happen, who thought it all up, but who left him to do the dirty work. He was too sensitive to actually see bodies flying into school walls, or people being ripped apart by machines.

But just the same, it had been exciting to pull it off. And there was a bonus tonight. He felt as though he could actually feel the precise second Ron Hughes's soul had left his body. That was the kind of thrill you could never get just sitting on the side-lines.

You had to be out here, on the front lines, to feel that kind of thing.

He was a player. Blakely, Hughes, Harper, and Hidalgo thought *they* were the players, but they had no fucking clue.

Compared to himself and Jim, they were *nada*. Nothing at all.

17

JACK AND OSCAR watched as the mangled body of Ron Hughes was placed on a gurney and carried to the coroner's van.

Oscar kicked at the train tracks, shook his head:

"I don't get it," he said. "How did Steinbach even know Ron had this place?"

"Inside information?" Jack's voice was as flat as his mood.

"Yeah, but who? I'd stake my life on our guys."

Jack picked up a rock and threw it down to the beach. Some gulls cried and scattered away.

"That's what I used to say, too. Until the starting guard on our basketball team, Bobby Hansen, turned out to be a traitor. And talking about Hansen reminds me of our old pal, Super Agent William Forrester."

"I don't know," Oscar said. "I know he had it in for those guys, but killing them?"

"You think it's a long shot? But what about what Feeney told us? He saw Forrester up at Blakely's house the night before Zac was killed. What was he looking for?"

"Money?" Oscar said. "The City National Bank money."

"Exactly," Jack said. "Here's the way it could have gone down. Zac and Ron pull the robbery, which maybe Forrester fingered and planned for them. Then they split up the money three ways, only Forrester's third is a lot less than theirs is."

"They screwed him? Why? Why would they do that?"

"'Cause they could," Jack said. "And because Forrester is a jerk. They figure he has no way of really knowing how big the take was, so they give him a smaller piece of the pie. But though Forrester is an asshole, he's anything but a moron. He finds out from the bank that the cash haul was a lot more than what Zac and Ron told him. He threatens them both, and finally knocks them off."

"Yeah, but does he have the money?" Oscar said.

"I don't know. Maybe he searched Blakely's house, didn't find it, and knocked him off. Then he comes out here, looking for the money, but runs into Hughes. Why does he do it now? One, he's afraid they're going to do it to him. Two, he's seen the Steinbach threat on the tube and thinks that's the perfect cover for his crimes. Three, he can pin the thing on us if he wants to."

"Yeah, but does he really think we were in on it?"

"I don't know. Maybe. He knows we were tight with them. And if he didn't find the money here at Hughes's place, he is sure as hell going to come looking at us. And remember, he can still pin the whole thing on Steinbach if he wants to."

Oscar rubbed his neck, picked up a rock, and threw it down the beach.

"Man, this is really one fucked-up case."

"*Two* cases," Jack said. "That's what we have here. Two cases intertwined. Or maybe even something more."

"Let's check Hughes's photo albums, and Blakely's, too."

"Okay," Jack said. "I'll call Val and set up a meet."

At three in the morning, back at FBI headquarters, Harper and Hidalgo were still going over personnel records, looking through endless employment files, bank and tax records of their fellow agents. By five A.M., Jack was nearly at the breaking point.

"Not a goddamn thing here," he said. "From these records, everybody at the Bureau is squeaky clean. I don't even see any requests for information by Forrester."

"Yeah," Oscar said. "But he could disguise his searches. Slick Billy's capable of anything."

"I know it," Jack said. "We have to find a way to check his bank records, loans, and mortgages."

"That's going to be tough," Oscar said.

"Yeah," Jack said. "All right. We'll table that for now. But let's think: Who else who works here can get all the personal information on any agent?"

Oscar sighed and opened his palms in a show of helplessness.

"Nobody but the Director, without permission."

"Yeah, but forget permission. Nobody who is selling information is going to ask."

"Somebody who works here. Somebody who has access to the information . . . somebody who knows all the codes, passwords. Not even Forrester has all that stuff, or the clearance to use it."

Suddenly Jack smiled and sat down quickly in front of the computer.

"You and I need brain transplants. There are only a few guys who can access all that stuff. And they aren't agents."

He typed in the number 45-T.

Oscar looked at it and whistled through his teeth.

"*Mira!* Tech support. The invisible men."

"That's right," Jack said. "Look here. There are currently seven of them employed by us. We need to go through all their records. I'll take the first four."

"I'm on it, dawg," Oscar said.

It took less than an hour before Jack found the record he was looking for.

"It's right here," he said. "Philip Marshall, tech support, grade-eight. Got access to his TRB, and he's run up a very sizable debt. Took out an $800,000 mortgage to buy a house in the hills."

"Any inherited wealth?"

"Not much. His father was a construction worker, mother was a housewife. Grew up in Northridge, went to Cal Northridge."

"How about fancy cars? Other investments?"

"Nothing under his credit, but according to a security scan of his computer, he's been looking at ads for Jaguars."

"Very interesting."

They leaned into the bright yellow light of the screen and Jack typed in the password which enabled them to access Philip Marshall's entire record. The word was Stealth.

18

AT TEN THAT NIGHT they arrived at Marshall's bungalow in the Valley. An unassuming place in Studio Village on Lemp and Moorpark. There was a white picket fence outside and a '50s retro glider on the little front porch.

"Wonder if Beaver Cleaver lives here?" Oscar said.

"More like Eddie Haskell all grown up," Jack said.

They got out of the car and walked toward the house.

Jack rang the bell, and both of them waited, their guns still holstered but unflapped.

In a minute there was a voice from the other side of the door.

"Excuse me, do you have any idea what time it is?"

The door opened a crack, and Jack flashed his badge.

"Yeah, we do, Phil. Time for you to come clean. FBI. Open the door. Now."

There was a brief hesitation, then Marshall slid the chain off the lock and let them in.

. . .

Philip Marshall was a slender, nerdy-looking guy, who had once had a bad case of acne. He wore a bathrobe with pineapples on it. His hair was short, befitting an agent. He said nothing, but sat down. Got up and sat down again.

"You seem a little nervous, Phil," Jack said.

"Not at all, I'm merely tired. It's been a long couple of days, and I fell asleep early."

Oscar nodded and looked sympathetic.

"Relax, man, we're all on the same side, right?"

"Yeah," Marshall said. He reached into his pocket, took out a cigarette, and then—rather than light it—put it back.

"How can I help you guys?"

"Nice house, Phil."

"Thanks. It's kind of beat up, but I'm selling it soon, anyway."

"I don't mean this one," Jack said. "I'm talking about the one you've been looking at up in the Hollywood Hills."

"No harm in looking, is there? Besides, I planned on flipping it," he said. "I might do a deal on it with my cousin. He'd be the main financier. I'd do the work on the place. Then we split the profit. Say, what are you guys getting at, anyway?"

"Been looking into Jaguars, too, huh, Phil?"

"Yeah, so what? I look at a new Jag just for the pricing, then I get my car for about half that on the Web. Big deal."

Jack walked over to him and got in his face.

"You're right, Phil. It's not much. But murder is. We want to know why you accessed the addresses of two federal agents who were murdered a couple of weeks later."

Marshall's sallow face turned red. He shook his head.

"This is bullshit," he said. "I'm not talking to you guys anymore. I'm calling my lawyer."

"I wouldn't advise that, Phil," Jack said. "'Cause if you make us wait around all day, we're gonna arrest you as an accomplice in both these killings."

Phil Marshall swallowed hard and rubbed his nose.

"That's crazy," he said. "What are you guys trying to pin on—?"

"Two murdered agents," Oscar said. "Forget the outrage. We know you're the guy."

Marshall swallowed again and felt as though his mouth was turning to sand.

"If you're talking about Zac Blakely, I heard his brakes gave out up in the canyon and . . ."

Oscar said, "Cut the shit, Phil. Blakely was murdered, and now Ron Hughes. If I was the guy who had supplied organized crime with their names, I'd be very concerned for my health. Since you're the only one who can pin the killers to the victims . . . how long you think you're going to remain breathing, Phil?"

Marshall ran his hand over his chin. Jack saw tiny drops of sweat coming off his upper lip.

"I didn't know what they wanted. I had no idea."

"Sure you didn't, Phil," Jack said. "But you know how those guys are . . . they find out you've been talking to us . . . they're gonna come by and take you for a ride out into the desert."

Marshall sat down in a bamboo chair, and then got up again.

"Okay, then . . . look . . . I tell you about this you'll cut me some slack, right? And give me some protection?"

Oscar nodded and said, "You talk to us and yeah, maybe we talk to somebody for you."

Marshall gasped for air, rubbed his forehead. As he talked, he couldn't meet either of their eyes.

"Okay . . . well, a while back, this guy I know in Hollywood . . . comes over to me and tells me he wants some information on two agents. Blakely and Hughes."

"What's this guy's name?" Oscar said, taking out his notebook.

"Nicki . . . Nicki Sadler."

Jack got up from his chair and walked across the room.

"Sadler? The lawyer? I know that creep. He used to be a bagman for the boys at the Tropicana Club. He say why he wanted the names?"

Marshall shook his head.

"No. Something about old debts."

"He ask for only two names, Phil?"

Marshall gave a weak little laugh and sat back down on the bamboo chair again.

"I had no idea what he wanted to do with them. I swear it."

Jack walked over close to Marshall and looked down at him.

"How many other names, Phil?"

Marshall looked up and then showed Jack his palms.

"Two more. The other day. I didn't want to give them to him, but he said the people he represented wouldn't like it if I didn't come through. I was afraid."

"Who were they?" Jack said.

"I didn't know what he was gonna—"

Jack reached down and picked Marshall up by his hair. Marshall made a high keening sound, like a dying bird.

"Stop."

"Names," Jack said.

Marshall began to cry.

"It was yours . . . yours and his . . . Hidalgo. He asked for your families' names and addresses, too. I'm so sorry. I never did anything like this before. It was like a game at first, and there was so much money in it . . . I've never had any money and . . ."

"You gave him our names and our families' addresses . . ." Jack felt a cold rage. He punched Marshall hard in the stomach. Marshall fell backward into his chair, weeping.

Jack looked at Oscar.

"We gotta call Judge Schur and get his okay for a wiretap."

"Yeah," Oscar said. "C'mon, Phil, you gotta slip outta that bath-robe and into some prison stripes. Move your sorry little ass!"

He reached down and pulled the weeping Marshall to his feet.

"I am so sorry," Marshall said. "Isn't there any way I can help you? C'mon. Give me a break."

Jack wanted to break Phil's face for him, but then he had an idea.

"All right, Phil. I'll tell you what. You're going to go back in there tomorrow, do your job, and meanwhile I want you to look up any and all information on another agent, William Forrester?"

"Forrester? You think he's involved in all of this?"

"I do," Jack said. "You gonna do it or not?"

"Well, I don't know about that. Forrester is a nasty guy. If he found out about me looking up his records, I can't imagine what he'd do to me."

Jack slapped Marshall's face so hard he knocked his glasses off.

"You don't have any idea what I'm going to do if you *don't* do it, Phil."

Marshall's face turned bright red.

"All right. I'll get all his financials. But it might take a couple of days."

"You got two is all," Oscar said. "And you better come through, pal. 'Cause starting right now, we own your ass, *amigo*."

Jack got home late that night. After checking on Kevin, he took off his shoes and tiptoed toward his bed, not wanting to wake Julie. But he was barely under the covers when she turned and glowered at him.

"Where have you been?" she demanded.

Jack felt a tightening in his stomach. Julie had been extremely tense lately and short with Kevin, too.

"Working the case," Jack said. "Think we might have caught a break."

Suddenly Jack was overwhelmed with exhaustion and hoped Julie wasn't in a talkative mood.

"Is *that* right?" Julie said. "Out this late working the case?"

He hated her tone and felt some bile come up in this throat.

"Yeah, as a matter of fact. It took this long."

She gritted her teeth and turned away from him.

Jack looked at the soft curve in her neck, at the wisps of hair around her ears. She was so delicate, so beautiful. Suddenly he wanted to take care of her, make her feel safe, loved.

"Look, honey," he said. "It just took a while, that's all. No ulterior motives. No parties or cop groupies involved. Honest. That's not my style."

"Great!" Julie cut him off. "That's fine. Can we just go to sleep now?"

Jack felt a certain measure of panic inside his chest. Things were so new between them, yet she already seemed to be un-happy. No . . . not just that, either. It was something scarier than that. It was as though he didn't even know her anymore.

Oh, man, he'd done this before. Fallen in love with an illu-sion of a person and found out, only after it was too late and his heart was entangled, that the woman he thought he was in love with was a figment of his own overactive and somewhat desper-ate imagination.

"Look, Julie." He tried to use his most soothing and convinc-ing voice. "I know you've been left alone a lot lately, and I'm sorry about it. But since the Bureau murders, I've really had to be out there all the time."

She turned her head toward him. Jack had the weird feeling that he had no idea what her reaction might be. Would she take his head off? Understand? He wasn't sure. In fact, he thought, maybe he wasn't sure who Julie was at all.

Aside from the fact that she was great in bed and a teacher, what did he really know about her? And maybe some of this anger she was displaying was really about Kevin, too.

"You and Kev get along okay?" he said.

She turned over, away from him, curled herself into a ball.

"Fine, if you like hostile silences for hours. Great, if you like asking someone for help with cleaning up dinner, and he mumbles curse words under his breath. Yeah, things are just great around here!"

Jack tried to put his hand on her shoulder but she jerked away as though he were a rattlesnake.

But then she turned over and looked at him again.

"I might as well tell you now, Jack. I'm going home tomorrow for a while. I just . . . need my space."

Jack felt a bolt of anger.

"That's it?" he said. "Things get a little rough, and you just walk?"

"A *little* rough? Kevin is headed for a breakdown. I'm not ready for this . . . taking on the job of being a stepmother to an angry, confused child who could even become . . . violent."

Jack sat straight up, glowered at her.

"Violent? Did he ever hit you, even threaten you?"

"Not in so many words, but if looks could kill, I'd be stone dead."

"C'mon, Julie. You know that's not true. He wouldn't ever hurt you. He *loves* you. He's told me so."

She looked down at the blanket, afraid to meet his gaze.

"I know. He can be very sweet. But there's something there that really scares me, Jack. And your work. This guy threatening to kill you. You see, it's all part of the same thing. Violence on the outside, threats, and then your wife leaving . . . you told me how upsetting that was, and now Kevin acting out all over the place. I can't . . . I can't do it, Jack, I just can't."

128

She began to cry, and Jack tried to put his arm around her again, but again she pulled away.

"Julie, I love you," Jack said.

"I know. I love you, too. But I'm not as strong as all this. I can't live in a place where violence and fear . . ."

She burst into tears, as Jack stood by helplessly.

Finally she looked up and shook her head.

"Jack, I think I'm going to go now."

"You sure?" he said. "It's so late."

"I'm sorry," she said.

And then she was out of bed, grabbing her already-packed suitcase from the closet.

In a half hour, she was gone. Jack sat on the front-porch steps, looking out at the night. He tried telling himself it was going to be okay, that he could handle it, that after his marriage had cracked open and he'd nearly fallen apart, he'd been fine.

But somehow he didn't believe it anymore.

He wasn't going to be fine, and neither was Kevin.

He tried again, and then asked himself what a mature man would do in his position.

But he came up with nothing.

Then he asked himself what he'd really like to do now. That was easy. Take off, go down to Charlie's place, and tie one on.

But he couldn't leave Kevin here.

Fortunately, he had the next-best answer close at hand. Jack walked inside, went to the pantry, and cracked open a bottle of Jack Daniel's.

This was the immature and wrong thing to do. No doubt.

But the first shot went down smoothly, as did the second, and the third.

Soon he was back on the front porch looking up at the lunatic moon, feeling total immunity from all the pain.

19

JIMMY SEEMED TIRED tonight, kind of listless.

"You okay?"

"Yeah, I'm fine. Just got a cold or something."

"Well, I've got something that's going to cheer you right up."

They sat down in the comfortable padded chairs again and stared at the dark screen.

"Here we go," he said.

"Wait a minute," Jimmy said. "I think we need to talk about this."

"No, wait . . . I've got some sensational stuff here, Jim."

"I know . . . I'm sure you have. But I've been thinking about this. Is it really the movie we want to make?"

"Of course it is. We talked about this for years. C'mon, for God's sake."

"Yeah, I know. But that's my point. When we were talking about it, it was like one thing. You know, a concept. But now that we're actually seeing the raw footage, is this the movie we really want to make?"

He was up out of his chair now. Feeling hot.

He knew he shouldn't lose it. Not after what they'd been through.

But what the hell? The risk he'd taken—that they'd both taken—and now Jimmy wants to back out. That wasn't right. No way.

"Look, Jimmy, if you get out there with me, if you experience the thing with me, then you'll see. That's the part of the process you're missing. If you were there . . . if you saw the looks on their faces . . ."

Jimmy shook his head.

"No, I can't . . . on this one I'm more of a conceptual guy. A producer."

"Which is very handy for you. So you don't have to dirty your hands."

Jimmy stood up and stared at him. It was surprising how thin he was.

"I think I've suffered plenty so far. I don't think I have to justify my position."

That got to him. He sat back down.

"Look, we're so close to home now, and this is great stuff. Take a look at it, will you? I know you're going to like it."

Jimmy smiled then, and it was like the room had been lit up.

"Okay," he said. "I will. It's okay. I just get a little hinky sometimes about the project."

"Yeah, sure. I know. But we're doing this together, Jimmy. That's the important part."

"I know," Jimmy said softly. "Roll the tape. Let's see just what you got."

20

FAT NICKI SADLER took a long hit off his bottle of Absolut Mandarin, then wiped his pudgy moist lips with the sleeve of his shirt. He reached into his bowl of Doritos chips and slammed six or seven of them into his mouth. Then, while grinding them down, he finished his denunciation into his office phone.

"Lemme try and fucking clarify what I'm telling you, Lansing. Here's the deal. I already gave you two extensions of the loan, and you aren't getting any more, that clear?"

On the other end, the out-of-work actor who supported himself by dealing cocaine to the studios in his ragged old Porsche began to whine:

"But Nicki, you know I'm good for it. I just got a little behind 'cause I was in Vegas, and the fucking Chiefs tanked, and then the Dolphins fucked me when they missed a goddamned fifteen-yard field goal. How often is that gonna happen? Like never. So if you could just front me, say, 10 Gs until . . ."

In his office, Nicki readjusted his big belly and opened his pants a little. He'd just eaten a massive pizza from Rainforest and nine rolls drenched in butter and garlic. Now all that dough and cheese was clogging up his pipes.

"Lemme say this again to you, Jerry. Here's the answer. N.O. spells NO. That's NO written in fucking italics. It's not like a conditional NO, which really means yes. It's a big, heavy, body rush of a NO. Maybe it would help if you would think of it as the Hollywood sign of fucking NO."

There was a long silence, and then Jerry Lansing tried one last time.

"They say they're gonna hurt me, Nicki. I gotta get that money."

"Pray," Nicki said, taking another drink of the hot vodka. "Pray, and God'll give you everything that's coming to you."

"You prick!" Lansing said. "All the dough I made you and now, when I need it, you . . ."

Nicki didn't bother listening to the rest. He slammed down the phone and laughed to himself. Fucking losers! He was sick of them all. Anytime you got into business with a skell like Lansing . . . well, what could you expect?

He pushed his chair away from the desk and, with great effort, ambled over to his mini-fridge.

He opened it and was pleased by the cone of yellow light, which came out and made a pleasant pattern on his dingy office.

Inside the fridge were bottles of beer and another ice-cold Absolut. Only this one was lime flavored.

He leaned down, felt a crick in his back, and then pulled out the bottle and a box of La Roca chocolates. His doctor, hip Lon Huizenga of Beverly Hills, had told him to chill out on candy and booze, but he found it difficult to heed his doctor's warnings. It was the class of people who drove him to excessive eating, he told himself as he hobbled back to his desk. So many losers, so many hustlers and creeps. It was killing him inside.

And the women he knew . . . skanks, all of them skanks. Jesus Christ, the only real pleasure a guy got living in fucking L.A. was from food.

He ripped off the top of the vodka and took a hit. Cold and limey. Now that was good. After he knocked back a few and ate a few chocolates, he figured he'd get the car and head out Sunset to grab a little Thai.

In the basement of Nicki Sadler's building, Harper and Hidalgo sat in the janitor's closet equipped with headphones and digital recorder. Oscar had deep bags under his eyes; he had not slept for more than two hours a night for the last three days.

"Nicki's a warm and lovable guy, huh?" he said.

"Yeah," Jack said. "A real sweetie. Hey, man, you all right?"

"I'm fine," Oscar said. "Okay, I walked into a wall today, but outside of that, I'm terrific."

"Glad to hear it, 'cause I'm not hanging out with no Mexican slackers."

Oscar laughed and shook his head.

"'Tween you and Nicki Sadler, I'm just *surrounded* by compassion and kindness."

"Yeah," Jack said. "That makes you a lucky man."

Through his headphone, Jack heard Sadler dialing again.

"Here we go again."

After two rings, a woman picked up and said hello.

"Miss Heyward, I have those photos you contracted for."

On the other end was Doris Heyward, a worn-out-looking blonde. She was wearing a midriff-revealing shirt, but her midriff had quit standing up about four years ago. Now it sagged over her hip-hugging pants. As she talked, she looked into a cracked mirror in her trashy bedroom and plucked her eyebrows.

"Save me another heartbreak, Nicki. Tell me about what you got."

On Sadler's end of the phone there was a dismissive sigh.

"Hey, Miss Heyward . . ."

"Call me Doris, sweetie."

"All right, then, Doris, listen up. I'm not some phone-sex worker, okay? I don't wish to regale you with the gory details."

"Gee!" Doris Heyward said as she plucked out a vagrant brow hair and dropped it on her fake Indian rug. "I never realized how delicate you were, Nicki."

Jack and Oscar exchanged a smile.

"Like a flower, Miss Heyward. If I have to do verbal, it'll be a hundred bucks more."

"You fucking vampire!" Doris Heyward said. "Go."

"Okay, Miss Heyward," Sadler said. "You asked for it. Let's see here. The first shot we have here is a very candid picture of your husband and the woman in question. She's kneeling down in front of him and taking his engorged member into her open mouth and . . ."

"That's enough. The son of a bitch!"

Now Nicki Sadler was starting to get into his verbal shtick.

"You're still paying the hundred, Doris, so you might as well hear the second picture. In a way, it's much more charming than the first. In this one, the woman in question is leaning over a desk and your husband Brett is giving it to her up her asshole, which is causing a look of extreme pain-slash-happiness to be elicited from her very reddened face."

"Fuck you!" Doris Heyward said. "You send me the pictures and forget the hundred. You already got your fun out of this, you sadistic bastard."

She slammed the phone down and Nicki Sadler cackled like a madman.

In the basement Jack and Oscar did as well.

"That's the thing I love about this job," Jack said. "We get to see the crème de la crème of society every single fucking day."

"Yeah," Oscar said. "Like my madre used to say, 'The world is a beautiful place if we could just eliminate all the humans.'"

Jack fell asleep on the moldy old couch, bedbugs chewing on his arm. Oscar manned the phones, but from eight to ten there was not one call. He curled up in a battered armchair and read *The Charm of Quarks: Mysteries of Particle Physics*. At eleven there was another call, in which a voice said, "The bitch said she was gonna deliver, and since she din't, she's gonna be delivered to the fucking morgue." The caller hung up immediately after delivering this happy bit of information, but his caller ID was blocked. A few minutes later, there was a call to Nicki in which a woman said she was "gonna shoot her sister in both her heads." Sadler laughed out loud at that one. Oscar looked over at Jack, who snored mightily from the couch.

Oscar waded through the book, only on the edge of understanding it, but liking it, anyway. There was something clean and refreshing about science . . . just reading about string theory and the way the universe was put together made him feel better about everyday life. And the fact that men could understand it . . . well, some men, that was amazing. Maybe when he retired from the force, he would go back to school and get a master's in physics. Then again, maybe he'd go down to Baja and disappear like his favorite author, B. Traven.

Finally, at 12:10 A.M., Sadler made a call, which caught Oscar's full attention. The voice was male, muffled.

"Hello."

"What a great pleasure it is to talk to you," Sadler said.

"Fuck off!"

"My, you've become crude," Sadler said.

"It's late. What the hell do you want?"

Sadler laughed and began his spiel:

"What do I want? I want Osama bin Ladin's head on a pike in front of the Pantages. I want happiness and eternal youth in a bottle. And I'd like Angelina Jolie to dump Brad Pitt for me. But I'd settle for a one-time payment of $300,000."

In the basement, Oscar kicked Jack's foot and in a second Harper was wide awake and had on his headphones.

There was a long silence before the muffled voice spoke again. This time he was furious.

"You want to keep on living? You kinda left that out."

But Sadler didn't seem shaken by the threat.

"Very much so," he said. "But given my classy tastes, I want to live *well*. I'm sure you, of all people, understand."

There was another brief pause. Then the muffled voice said, "And if I refuse to make this payment?"

Sadler gave a nasty little laugh.

"You won't. May I remind you I got you all the information, and I know what you've done with it. That makes me an accomplice, which means you didn't give me the correct job description when you employed me. By paying me, you're only acknowledging the true value of my work."

Jack looked at Oscar and shook his head. This is what they'd been waiting for. It had to be.

"You're a clever boy, Nicki," the other man said. "Meet me tomorrow at Musso's. Four o' clock. At the bar. I want all the information, including any copies you made. Oh, and if you ever try this kind of play again, you won't be able to talk so slick anymore, 'cause I'm gonna cut out your tongue."

Sadler didn't miss a beat.

"I knew you'd be reasonable," he laughed. Then he hung up.

Jack looked at Oscar and smiled.

"That was fucking Steinbach. I'm pretty sure."

Oscar shook his head.

"I don't think so. Came from a cell phone, but not his. And that voice. It sounded sort of like Forrester to me."

"Whoever it is, we're gonna find out tomorrow," Jack said. "Maybe we can wrap this thing up. Meanwhile, you hear from Marshall today?"

"Yeah, he called me today. Looks like Forrester has a little bank account in the Cayman Islands. But, of course, it's untouchable."

"Not if it turns out to be the result of a criminal activity."

"Very hard to prove that, Jack."

"Just the same, I'd like to find out how much dough he has in there, and the dates the deposits were made."

"I already got Marshall working on that."

"Good man!"

"Man, that's it for me tonight, bro. I'm wasted. Heading home."

"You go ahead," Jack said. "I'm so wired, I need a drink."

"See you tomorrow, bro," Oscar said.

He shambled out . . . Jack watched him go and felt a surge of camaraderie for his partner. Having never said a word about it, he knew that Oscar would lay down his life for him, and Jack would do the same.

It was an amazing bond, one neither of them ever had to mention. And yet it was more real than any other bond in his life, with the exception of his son.

The way things were right now, Jack realized that Oscar was the only sure thing he had in his life.

21

FROM THE MIRACLE MILE stakeout Jack drove his Mustang down Fairfax, hit the 10, and, speeding all the way, made it to Charlie's bar by 1:30 and was surprised to find it still packed.

He gave his car to Sergio, the valet, and went inside. Charlie was standing right by the door, pouring salt into his hand. Two good-looking women in their thirties, wearing hip-huggers and skimpy tank tops, looked on as Charlie made the salt disappear, then reappear.

The girls laughed and hugged Charlie, who turned and smiled at Jack.

"Hey, Jackie," he said. "Just in time. I get you something?"

"How about a Harp?" Jack said.

Charlie nodded and waved to the bartender. The two girls smiled at Jack and then turned to talk to two surfer guys. Jack envied them their youthful freedom.

Charlie got the mug of beer and handed it to Jack.

"Here you go, Jackie," he said. "Man, I haven't had a chance to talk to you about Zac and Ron. It just doesn't seem possible. I keep expecting them to walk through the door."

"Yeah," Jack said, not wanting to talk about it. "Hell of a thing."

Charlie nodded, then drank his ginger ale.

"Hey, we got our first big game tomorrow night with the Palisades Angels," he said.

Jack sighed.

"Oh, man, I'm sorry, Charlie. I'm going to be working tomorrow night."

"Maybe Julie can bring him."

Jack quickly looked down at the floor. Charlie, who never missed a thing, put a friendly hand on Jack's shoulder.

"What's going on, Jack?"

"Julie and me . . . we're taking a break from each other."

"Oh, man, what happened?"

"It's a long, sad story, Charlie, and to tell you the truth, I'm too wasted to tell it right now."

"That's tough," Charlie said. "If you want to talk about it, I'm here for you."

"Sure," Jack said.

Charlie managed a smile.

"Look, we gotta get Kevin up there," Charlie said. "He's turning into my best hitter. We need him out there. Tell you what: I'll pick him up and take care of him until you get back. I can let Bobby, the night manager, run the place for a few hours."

"That's great," Jack said, taking a swig of his Harp.

"Sure," Charlie said. "Anything to accommodate my slugger."

Jack smiled and slapped five with Charlie. This was a good thing . . . his son living a normal life. Baseball, surfing, school . . . like any other kid. Maybe he'd come around . . . maybe they'd seen the last of the teenage rebellions. If so, the bump on the head was a good thing.

Jack took another swig and set the mug down half filled. Time was he would have knocked back two or three, but he suddenly felt tired; it was all he could do to stand up. Charlie smiled and talked to two customers who were leaving, and Jack chatted briefly with a trooper he knew from a murder case in Solvang. He was about to call it a night when he saw him. The same scarred and bearded man he'd seen at the Little League field. This time there was no doubt. The guy was over in the corner, looking directly at him. Jack watched as the man picked up a shot glass, knocked back what looked like whiskey, and then walked toward him. Jack felt for his shoulder holster and steadied himself. But there was no need. The scarred man walked right by him, out the front door.

Jack ran his hand through his hair. Maybe he was just jumpy after what had happened to Zac and Ron. Maybe the guy wasn't looking at him at all. But why was he both here and at the ballpark?

Jack thought about asking Charlie, but he bagged the idea because he already knew what Charlie was going to say: "Hey, the guy likes baseball and hanging out at the beach, like a million other guys. He looks scary because of the scar, but you can't hold that against him."

Yeah, Charlie would think Jack was losing it, and maybe he was right. Seeing ghosts, hearing voices. Now his head felt like hell, and he decided that he'd had enough. Time to pack it in and go home.

Jack walked by the little cluster of smokers who huddled together like lepers outside the bar. He took the keys from Sergio and walked toward his car. It was going to be good to get home now . . . fall asleep for six hours, then deal with Sadler, maybe nail Steinbach for good.

He was about five feet away from his car when it happened.

A car with its headlights turned off roared toward him. Jack was unable to move. He saw the car bearing down on him, and then—as quickly as it happened—it was over. Someone had tackled him from the side, and both of them were rolling over the hood of his car to safety.

Jack's head smashed into his fender, and he fell headfirst into the hard gravel of the parking lot.

He saw little blue lights, and then the world went black.

Three minutes later, he came to and saw Charlie looking down at him with concern.

"Jackie, you okay?"

Jack tried to push himself off the ground, but he was groggy and there was a searing pain in his forehead.

"I'm fine, except I'm gonna look like a unicorn tomorrow morning." Jack gently touched the bump in the middle of his head. "Thanks, Charlie. Where'd he come from?"

"I don't know. I was just saying good night to two other people and I saw you. You were walking toward your car, and then he just came from back there . . . He musta been out of it. Man, I just went into linebacker mode."

"Thank Christ you did, or I'd be with Zac and Ronnie."

Sergio came running back from the curb.

"Mr. Jack, are you all right?"

"Yeah, Serg. You see which way he went?"

"Yessir, he turned left, headed south."

"You know the car?"

"Yessir. It was a silver Porsche."

"Either of you know who it was?"

Sergio nodded.

"Yessir, I saw him pretty good, Mr. Jack. He real ugly with scar on his face, like this."

He drew an imaginary scar down his right cheek.

142

Jack looked at Charlie and shook his head.

"That's the same guy who was at the ballpark, Charlie. We gotta find somebody around here who knows him."

"Sure thing, Jack. You really think it was from that guy you busted?"

"Yeah," Jack said, "I do."

He pulled out his cell phone and dialed for LAPD dispatch. Within thirty seconds, he had three cars headed for the 405, looking for a silver Porsche and a man with a long scar across his right cheek.

Only minutes later, Jack came out of Charlie's parking lot and headed south. Once he got down to Main Street in Santa Monica, there were any number of turnoffs the guy could have taken. Jack roared down the freeway, then made a systematic search of the side streets running into the city. But there was no sign of the silver Porsche. After an hour, he gave up. After all, the scarred man could already have parked his car in any of the countless garages around the area. Or maybe they'd find the car abandoned while the driver was already home, snug in bed.

Jack turned up Pico and headed east. He had just gone by McCabe's Guitar Store, where he'd bought Kevin his Strat, when his cell phone beeped.

He assumed it was one of the other agents who were helping in the search, but when he looked at the display, he was surprised to see Michelle Wu's number.

"Hey, Jackie . . . You still up? What are you doing, you bad boy?"

"Nothing, baby. Just defending the public from late-night predators and other scum."

Michelle laughed and Jack immediately felt aroused.

"You going to owe me some serious fun," she said. "Dinner, drinks, and maybe a night in a first-class hotel."

"Nothing I'd like more, babe," Jack said. "But it all depends on the quality of the information."

"You think I give you anything but the best, Jackie?"

"I don't doubt you one bit, baby," Jack said. "You are the info queen. Now what you got?"

"Well," she said. "I was thinking and thinking about that friend of yours, Zac Blakely. Like where I heard his name before. And then I was at the Valentine Room the other night, you know the place over on Ventura Boulevard, and it comes to me."

Now Jack was fully awake.

"*What* came to you, Michelle?"

"Where I heard the name. Your man Zac Blakely . . . I had heard his name before. He wasn't just an agent, baby. He had another side. The man was a serious player."

"What the hell are you saying?"

"I'm saying that he and his partner, Hughes, they had a thing going with Timmy Andreen. They was doing deals with him, baby."

"Bullshit!" Jack said. "Who told you this shit?"

"Nobody had to tell me, Jackie. I play around with those boys sometimes. They let me sing at their club. You should come hear me, Jackie. Anyway, I met this guy there . . . said his name was Jay Richards. After you left the other night, I looked up Blakely's obit in the *Times*. The picture there? That's the same guy I met."

"You sure, baby?" Jack felt something in his chest sag.

"I never forget nobody, baby," Michelle said. "Is why I am so successful."

"But how'd you know he was an agent?" Jack said.

"'Cause Andreen told me he was. Said he had him in his pocket. Him and his partner did favors for the boys so he could get a nice fat retirement fund."

Jack said nothing. The mere thought of it . . . Zac Blakely, his mentor and friend . . . it made him sick. A bitter taste came up in the back of his throat, like three-day-old coffee.

"Hey, Jackie, you still with me?"

"Yeah, Michelle . . . Yeah, I'm here."

Jack was no longer driving. He'd pulled his car over in front of the Apple Pan on Pico, and was staring at the green letters in a daze. They looked too bright, as if they were exploding on him.

"Thanks, Michelle," he said. "I'm going to look into this."

"Sorry to tell you about your friend, Jackie," she said. "You should know better than to trust peoples."

"Yeah, I know," Jack said. "But how the fuck do you live if you can't?"

There was a long silence from Michelle Wu, and then she gave an odd little laugh.

"You don't count on them, Jackie, you just learn to be amused by them. If they amuse you, then they are good company. That is my number-one belief. Keep Miss Michelle laughing, and everything will be fine. Trust is for the dead. They got nothing to lose."

"I'll try and remember that," Jack said.

"Yeah," Michelle said. "Lighten up, Jackie. People ain't so bad. Long as you keep real low expectations. Love you, baby."

Then she hung up the phone.

Jack sat there staring at the green neon sign, his head aching and spinning. *Are Zac Blakely and Ron Hughes bad cops?* He would have bet his life against it. Jack felt dizzy, lost. He had known Blakely for . . . twenty years. It *couldn't* be true.

And yet more than one cop had wanted to pad his savings when he was staring at retirement and living on a fixed income.

But not Zac . . . not his mentor. He knew the guy like a brother. It just couldn't be . . .

The only problem was that Michelle Wu was rarely wrong about people. If she said she met him there, hanging with the Valley Boys, then it was true. But maybe there was more to the story than she knew. Blakely could have been down there setting them up for a bust . . . Maybe Jay Richards was just his cover name.

And maybe not, too. Now he had to make an audit of all of Blakely's computers. That would be easy . . . unless his wife had already cleaned them. And did she know, too? No, probably not. Zac was always secretive and would have wanted his crimes known by as few people as possible.

Jack turned the engine back on, feeling the bitter taste in his mouth and a pain in his temples. Forrester was right: the two of them were crooked. But where did that leave Forrester himself? Was he involved? Had he killed them for double-crossing him?

Jack felt like a man sinking into quicksand.

Then he remembered. Steinbach had once mentioned Timmy Andreen, too.

Was it possible that Steinbach and Andreen were in business?

How did Blakely and Hughes fit in with them?

And the bearded man who had just tried to run him down? Did he come from Steinbach, Andreen, Forrester?

Or somewhere else? Fuck it, he was wasted. He had to get home.

Get home, be with Kevin . . . Jesus, he'd forgotten. Julie wasn't there . . . He'd left Kevin alone. It wasn't the first time, but now, with all of Kevin's troubles, he should have skipped Charlie's and gotten back there sooner.

He gunned the motor and raced home, his mind reeling from the possibilities in the case and his conscience bothering him for being a neglectful dad.

22

IN THE MORNING, Jack went into his office and found an e-mail from Maria Vasquez in Peru.

Dear Jack,

Things here are better than I ever had hoped for. My cousin, Jorge, is an excellent chef and we're opening a great new restaurant in town. Think we may feature both local food and some of the great California food I learned to love and miss. The town has some money now and needs at least one good place to dine, so I think we're going to be it! Miss you and hope you're doing well. Write me and don't worry. I've got all the "security" I need.

Love,
Maria Vasquez

Jack felt a huge sigh of relief. In a world of seemingly endless fear and terror, something was going right.

He smiled, wrote her a short note back, and sent it.

As he did, he wondered if he'd ever see her again. He knew he shouldn't be thinking such things, but there was something so seductive about her . . .

Maybe someday he'd get down there to see her . . .

No, that was the wrong way to think. His dogging days were over, Jack told himself. Time to grow up for real.

Maybe Julie's insecurity was at least partially based on the mixed signals Jack was sending. You didn't really have to cheat to make your partner feel that you might. Maybe Jack looked at girls on the street for just a few seconds too long. Or maybe he mentioned women's looks too often. That was probably okay in a relationship which had stood the test of time, but he and Julie had just gotten started, and maybe he had to think of her feelings more often.

He swore to himself he would. He would call her, try to win her back. Tonight, if he had time.

Meantime, he was really happy for Maria, though that wasn't her real name. And, in fact, maybe that was part of her appeal. She and he were alike in that they played roles so often as undercover cops they sometimes didn't even know who they themselves were.

Only that they were both on the same side.

Good guys. That was one thing he was sure of.

As the rain came down on Hollywood Boulevard, Jack and Tommy Wilson from Homeland Security waited in Jack's unmarked car outside Musso & Frank's Grill. Oscar was around the other side of the venerable old restaurant, keeping watch on Musso's back parking lot.

Jack looked at two teenage girls who were wearing blouses that revealed bare midriffs as they walked by, eyeing potential clients on the street. He felt a desire to pull them into the car before something happened to them, but the blonde was hot . . .

148

and he suddenly imagined her in quite a different way. On her knees, naked, in front of him. He shook his head, as if the physical action could shake the temptation out of his brain and heart. That was the trouble with working in Hollywood. Temptation was everywhere. He had friends who worked for the Bureau in Kansas City. When they came out to L.A. to visit Jack, they couldn't believe the women. Man, you could knock them for their lack of brains, but the sheer carnality of the women in Hollywood was overwhelming. That thought led Jack to think of Zac Blakely . . . the idea of him turning, taking money . . . fuck, the thought made Jack's belly tense in pain. He grunted, let out a deep breath. He hadn't told Oscar about it yet. He knew it would make him sick.

From the shotgun seat, Tommy Wilson looked at his watch and snarled at Jack.

"It's fucking four thirty! I told you Steinbach isn't your guy."

"Let me check with Oscar."

He punched 1 on his cell phone, and Oscar picked up on the first ring.

"Any sign of Nicki or the Kraut?"

"*Nada*. You want to give 'em a couple more minutes?"

"Yeah, all right," Jack said.

He clicked off and turned to Wilson.

"Few more . . ."

Wilson laughed, shook his head.

"You're a funny guy," he said to Jack. "You got a hard-on for this Steinbach guy. He's not your boy. 'Sides, how would he get here when I got men watching him night and day?"

"He might shake 'em, Tom. Or he might send somebody else with the money. Either way, we nail him."

"That's bullshit," Wilson said. "You know your problem, Jack? You get an idea and you get attached to it. You know what I mean? You got too much pride."

149

Jack said nothing, but stared solemnly out the window.

"Anyway, the guy's a hustler and all the rest," Tommy said. "But I don't make him out to be a cop killer."

"Bullshit!" Jack said. "Aside from killing our guys, I know the kind of shit he pulled in Sierra Leone. Word is he had ten guys burned alive to get those diamonds."

"Word is," Wilson repeated. "But no proof. The guy's a scam artist, I'll grant you that. Maybe he would do what he has to do, but killing cops . . . that's out of his league."

"You're fucking naïve, Tommy. He's playing you . . . he doesn't know shit about terrorism."

"He knows a lot of people. He knows guys who we know are connected to al-Qaeda. You think I pulled him out of jail without checking? There's something driving you, Jackie. Something making you see things that aren't there."

"Hey," Jack said. "You already fucked me by taking this piece of shit out of prison. Now I gotta put up with your third-rate psychoanalysis? I don't know what went down here today, but I'm still betting Steinbach is our boy."

Wilson laughed dismissively and opened the door.

"See you later, babe. If you want me to keep you company for another stakeout, it's gonna cost you. For a hundred and fifty bucks an hour I can bring CDs, a picnic basket, and a red-checkered tablecloth."

He laughed, slammed the door, and ran down the rain-soaked street toward his car.

Jack slammed his hand on the steering wheel as he watched him go.

A few minutes later, Oscar was back in the car as the two agents drove by Frederick's of Hollywood. A six-foot-five-inch black transvestite in a shimmering bronze miniskirt and ballet shoes leaned up against the window, pressing his/her hands on the glass as if she was trying to crawl inside.

"Look at the dude," Oscar said. "Think about all the families who come out here from Iowa and the heartland just to catch a glimpse of Hollywood glamour."

"Yeah," Jack said. Ordinarily he enjoyed riffing with Oscar about Hollywood decadence. It was like water-cooler talk, familiar and even comforting in an odd way. How fucked are we? Very fucked. But now he felt like something was crawling inside of him. Like he was a freak for being taken in by Steinbach. Like his old mentor had maybe taken him in. Like everybody in the world was a fucking liar. And after all these years, that fact still hurt.

"You know why Steinbach didn't show? 'Cause fucking Tommy tipped him off."

Now Oscar looked a little shocked.

"Hey, I don't know," he said. "Tommy's competitive, but you think he'd go that far?"

"Yeah, I do. He got the guy immunity, didn't he? He thinks the guy is going to tip him about something big . . . maybe a dirty bomb in the Grove. So he's gonna try and keep him clean."

"Maybe you're right," Oscar said as they drove east past Cahuenga. "Man, that's fucked. But what about Sadler? They wouldn't tip him, too."

"Unless Sadler was dirty, too?" Jack said. "Involved with Steinbach in a way that would put him away?"

"Fucking immunity!" Oscar said. "That's the deal. You protect one bad guy, then you find yourself protecting all his skell pals. Makes you wonder which side we're on."

"Tell me about it!" Jack said. "Listen, I think it's about time we paid a little visit to Nicki. Put a little pressure on him."

"Yeah," Oscar said. "I'm down with that. Let's head down to the Magic Mile."

They pulled out of their parking place, running over a discarded Frederick's doll that had fallen off a delivery truck.

"Hey, there's something you should know," Oscar said. "I talked to our sweet little lamb Phil Marshall today. He looked up all the information on Forrester. I also had him check Blakely's and Hughes's records again."

"Come up with anything?"

"Yeah," Oscar said. "Blakely has a numbered Swiss bank account, which, of course, we can't see."

"Cute," Jack said. "Hughes?"

"He has accounts in the Caymans, under three dummy corporations. And Forrester has been buying real estate in Todos Santos, down below Baja."

"So there *is* something to what Michelle told me."

"What?"

"She called me late last night. She said Zac Blakely was hanging out with Timmy Andreen in the Valley, at his club. She said she knows Andreen was involved with Steinbach."

"Wow!" Oscar said. "This thing is like a freaking octopus."

"Yeah, that it is, Oscar. That it is."

As they stood in the rain on Wilshire Boulevard, Oscar looked at a wig in one of the endless shops on the Miracle Mile and remembered a clown he'd seen as a kid in the circus in Tijuana, a huge, muscled clown who had bright red hair, and who had eaten fire. The clown had scared Oscar so bad, he never wanted to go to the circus again. There was something about him that seemed supernatural, like the devil's clown . . . Maybe that's what they were now, a couple of the devil's clowns, trying to solve murders that were already fixed.

Jack hit the buzzer to Nicki Sadler's office for the third time, but got no answer.

"Maybe he's not in," Oscar said.

"Yeah, possibly. But then why is his Caddy sitting right there."

He pointed to Sadler's black 1995 Cadillac parked illegally at an expired meter. There was a wet ticket bleeding blue ink on the rain-spotted windshield.

Jack hit the super's buzzer, and after a few seconds a voice came over the ancient speaker.

"Yeah, what 'chu want?"

"FBI, sir. We need to speak with you."

The super was a Mexican named Ariel Rodriguez. He had one arm and wore a Dodgers shirt with Gibson written on the back.

"Police, huh?" he said, eyeing them in the smelly elevator.

"Yeah. You know Nicki Sadler."

"The attorney? Yes, I do. I want him to get my son a rap-record deal. My son Xavier is a great rapper. Eminem is zero compared to him."

"Yeah," Oscar said. "I'll bet."

"He is, man," the super said. "He's deep."

"You seen Mr. Sadler today?" Jack said.

"Yeah, I talked to him an hour ago. He was jest coming into the office. He said he's gonna get my kid . . ."

"I got it," Oscar said. "Your kid's gonna be an American Idol."

"He is," the super said. "If you two guys heard him rap . . . He makes 50 Cent sound like a quarter."

Jack looked at Oscar as they got off the elevator at the third floor.

The door to Sadler's office was closed and locked. They rang the bell three times. No one answered.

"Open it," Jack said.

"I can't do that, man," the super said. "I bother Mr. Sadler, and I don't get no rap deal for my son. You should hear him like rap. He makes Snoop Dogg sound like Lassie."

"Open the door, please," Jack said.

"Well, okay, I guess," the super said. "But I hope this doesn't make him too pissed off."

He stuck a key from his huge ring into the lock and turned it.

Jack and Oscar walked inside. The super stayed back a little, pretending he wasn't part of this obvious intrusion.

There was an outer office with an old termite-eaten desk in it, and a couple of pictures of Nicki Sadler and some forgotten blonde on the wall.

Then there was a second door, an old-fashioned glass door with Sadler's name stenciled on it.

They walked over and Jack tried it. It opened, slowly, making a groaning noise.

Inside, there was another desk—this one a lot bigger—made of steel. Behind it Nicki Sadler slumped sideways, his head resting on the high back of his chair. There was a red line on his neck, which stretched from his left ear to somewhere under his right eye. It was thin, like a red line on a map which showed a bad stretch of highway. The blood had poured down his shirt and pooled on the desktop.

His left hand was on the telephone, but he'd never picked up the receiver.

The super came in and made a terrible choking noise.

"Oh, Jesus Christ," he said. "Jesus fucking Christ. *Mira* . . . Oh, Jesus!"

He staggered back out in the anteroom, gagging.

Jack looked at Oscar who was staring at the open window and the fire escape.

"Looks like Nicki pushed the wrong guy," Oscar said.

"Yeah," Jack said. "Let's call it in."

"I wonder what Tommy Wilson would say now," Oscar said.

"Yeah," Jack said. "I was just thinking the same thing."

"You don't think that Tommy would let Steinbach kill Sadler, do you?"

"I don't like to think it," Jack said. "I wish that idea would grow legs and walk out of my mind."

23

LONG AFTER SADLER'S BODY had been taken to the morgue and the lab boys had dusted the room for prints, taken photos of the scene, and picked up hair follicles and blood samples, Jack and Oscar checked Sadler's computer for evidence which might link him to Steinbach. Also Blakely, Hughes, and Andreen. But nothing came up in any of the dead lawyer's financial records.

Jack stretched and leaned against the crumbling old wall.

"I know the guy is dirty," he said. "He's as much as admitted it to me. The cocksucker. He's laughing at us right now."

He looked down at the screen, which glowed off Oscar's face.

Then Oscar smiled and turned to him.

"Hey," he said. "Look at this name. Timmy Andreen. That's the guy who runs a place called the Valentine Room down in the Valley. Timmy-boy is into all kinds of nefarious shit. Fences stolen jewels. Used to be a hit man . . . worked with the late Jules Furth who, if you recall, was in business with Steinbach."

Jack leaned down behind Oscar and looked at the ledger, which read Payment Owed . . . 200,500 . . . S.

"S for Steinbach?"

"Could be," Oscar said. "Maybe these are our boys. Maybe they hit Zac and Hughes for Steinbach and received their blood money from Sadler."

"Yeah," Jack said. "Then maybe Sadler needs dough and decides to shake down Steinbach. Which was what the meet at Musso's was supposed to be about. But instead of collecting the money, he gets an extra mouth in his neck."

The two men looked at one another.

Jack stood up and began to pace the room, his arms folded across his chest.

"If our tarnished little researcher is right, Blakely and Hughes, and Forrester, might have been branching out from bank robberies to sales. 'Cause Andreen deals in an eclectic catalog: guns, diamonds, whores, anything they can boost, sell, or kill."

"Yeah, but Blakely and Hughes helped us bring down Steinbach," Oscar said. "How do we account for that?"

"Okay," Jack said. "But what if it went down like this: They want a bigger share of the take, so they don't tell Steinbach we're investigating him. They want to make it a little hot for him. He gets in a jackpot, and now he wants to kill them. Now think about what he said: 'I'm going to get all of you.' But he hasn't gotten us, has he? Maybe that's what it's all about. They didn't do their jobs, so he has *them* hit."

"Uses Andreen."

"Yeah, why not?"

"Andreen doesn't know us. Maybe we ought to go down to Ventura, take a little trip to the Valentine Room."

"I got a problem with that," Oscar said. "Timmy knows me. I busted him once a long time ago when I was with the staties. He might remember my face."

157

Jack smiled. Shook his head.

"All right. I'm going down there; see if I can get inside."

"Alone? I don't like that."

"I know, but it's the only way. I'll be okay."

"All right," Oscar said. "Man, this case has more twists than a corkscrew. But you know we're going to get it solved. They can't stop the Hardy fucking Boys."

Jack laughed and punched his partner on the arm. Good old Oscar, the one man he was sure he could trust.

24

THE THING WAS, it was almost fun being watched. Kevin enjoyed it when the chubby teacher, Miss Buchanan, kept an eye on him during the lunch hour. Of course he wasn't allowed to go out and hang in the playground for another two weeks. He remembered Julie (the traitor, the coward) taking him to school, talking to the principal, this supertough Irish guy, Mr. McGuire. Oh, yeah, McGuire had given him a real talking-to, and they'd made it clear that he couldn't go out with the other kids to play basketball and that whatever teachers were on cafeteria duty that day would be keeping a "special eye" on him.

Kevin almost laughed out loud when McGuire said that. A special eye?

What was that? Some kind of third eye from Zen or something?

Anyway, that was what Miss Buchanan must be doing now, as he headed toward the boys' room. She was sort of standing sideways to him and watching him, trying to look kind of cool about it all.

But fortunately for him, she couldn't follow him inside the bathroom. What could be easier? Take a quick pee, then head to the window.

Wait until the coast is clear, push up the window, and up, over, and outside in about 0.3 seconds.

And then running across the playground, dodging in and out, climbing over the fence and he's free. Only a few minutes later, down on Venice Boulevard, and headed for the boardwalk.

Yep, he thinks to himself, headed back to the scene of the crime.

Only this time he's not the same Kevin Harper. No way, Jose.

This time he's grown up about twenty-five years. Thanks to his good friend Flyboy. Yeah, the blue-haired little shit had taught Kevin well.

First thing he'd learned: Gotta watch your own ass in Venice.

Second thing he'd learned: In order to do that, you had to have your very own little weapon with you.

Which Kevin had right now, in his jacket pocket . . . a nice small weapon so nobody would know it was there.

A screwdriver's six inches of cold steel, as they say in the action movies Kevin loved.

Not as deadly as that goddamned blackjack Flyboy kept in his backpack, but in many ways, Kevin thought, more effective.

That was the thing. Nobody would see it coming, and Kevin had already practiced ripping it out of his inner pocket over and over again in front of the mirror in his bedroom.

Oh, yeah, he'd even timed it. He could get it out and jab someone in the face with it in three seconds. Maybe even under that: 2.8 seconds.

That was his little plan.

Wander down the boardwalk, find Flyboy, and let the little shit-ball take him down one of the dark little Venice streets again. Only this time, when he tried to get into his backpack, Kevin would be ready, baby.

Oh, yeah, he'd have him on the ground, and he'd jab the freaking screwdriver into his nostril. Not too hard . . . (though he did have a cool fantasy about driving it all the way up into his frontal lobe. Lobotomy time!) . . . Just hard enough to maybe rip open his nose a little bit, which would cause an inordinate amount of blood to drip down Flyboy's face.

Then maybe a little jab to the ear to top things off, and then he'd take all the kid's money, and book right out of there. Bye-bye . . .

Oh, yeah, Kev was a different boy now.

Hey, his dad always told him to learn from his mistakes, and he had. Oh, yeah, that was for sure.

Kevin wandered down the boardwalk, checking out the usual show, the artists who painted pictures of dead rockers. Who was that one guy? Oh, yeah, Jim Morrison of The Doors. Everybody painted him because he'd lived in Venice in the old days . . . the fabulous '60s, when it was cool to be alive.

Just seeing pictures of that time made Kevin envious.

People looked really wild and crazy, and even though some people (like Jim himself) died, it must have been cool.

Though he knew he shouldn't think so. Being a cop's son.

He saw the sand-sculpture guy again; this time he was making what looked like a giant dinosaur. Cool. Kevin watched for a few minutes, and the man looked up at him and smiled.

"Hey, man, you like him?"

"Yeah," Kevin said. "Very cool."

The sculptor smiled and nodded his head, and Kevin felt a rush of happiness. The last trip hadn't been so bad after all. This guy was pretty famous. Kevin had seen his pictures in books about Los Angeles and on TV once on that show, with that guy Huell Somebody-or-other . . . the guy that ran around California telling people how lucky they were to live here. Kevin had heard that the guy was a fag, but he didn't care. It was kind of a cool show, and now he was part of one of the coolest places. Venice, California.

He walked on down the boardwalk, almost forgetting for a time that he was here for vengeance.

He had to pump himself up by talking to himself: "Don't forget what they did to you."

"You're not a chickenshit, are you?"

"What are you doing? Don't lose focus, asshole!"

Talking to himself like a drill sergeant on some TV show . . .

But the charm of the beach, the pleasant ocean breeze which cooled his brow, and the girls in tight shorts on roller skates . . . all of it was too much for him to resist.

He felt as though he was in a dream, floating along, happy just to be part of it all.

And he thought maybe it wouldn't be so bad to live down here, to hang out every day. Of course his dad would miss him some . . . or would he?

Maybe for a while, a couple of days, but then after that, maybe this was what his dad wanted: for him to just disappear.

Like Mom disappeared.

Like Julie disappeared.

That was what adults did, he thought. Talked a lot of stuff about responsibility and loyalty, and then one day just walked away from it all.

So maybe he'd beat Dad to the punch.

Maybe this time he wouldn't come back at all . . .

Maybe this time he'd be like the hoboes he'd read about in school: hop a train going down to Mexico.

Maybe . . .

And then—right there in front of him—there he was . . .

Flyboy standing over by the lemonade stand, eating a big pretzel, carrying his backpack . . . but this time without his skateboard.

Kevin walked toward him. Flyboy looked up and for a second there was a hint of fear in his face.

"Hey, man," Flyboy said. "How's your head?"

"Better, no thanks to you."

Flyboy assumed a look of injured innocence.

"You're not blaming me, are you? I had nothing to do with it."

"Is *that* right!" Kevin said.

"Yeah, that's right," Flyboy said. "What happened was you were climbing up around that house on the canal, and this guy comes out of the bushes and whacks you from behind. I woulda stayed to help you, but he was waving this pole at me, too. So I din't have no choice. I hadda get outta there, right away. Man, I am so glad to see you! I thought you was dead for sure."

"You expect me to believe that?" Kevin said in a tough tone (which he'd practiced over and over in front of his mirror the night before).

"Look," Flyboy said, "I know it sounds bad, but it's true. I even know who the guy was. His name is White, Johnny White. He's a runaway from Chicago. Badass. He musta followed us down there and robbed you."

Kevin wanted to come back with something like "Bullshit, Flyboy. You took my money. Now give it back or I'm gonna kick your ass." The problem was he kind of believed the kid. Maybe it had gone down the way Flyboy said it had.

After all, he'd never actually seen Flyboy take out a sap. He'd just assumed it.

"Look, here's the thing," Flyboy said. "I know where White lives. In a house not far from here. And I also know when he works and when he doesn't work. And right now he's working. Just down the boardwalk at the Ocean House, where he tends bar a couple times a week. He gets off in a few hours, which gives us plenty of time to go over to his place, break in, and see if we can find your money. If not, we can rip off the place and sell the stuff to a fence I know lives over in Ocean Park. Guy named Director."

Kevin felt a little dizzy. This wasn't the way it was supposed to have gone at all. He was supposed to have walked up to Flyboy and scared the living shit out of him, then worked on him a little bit with the screwdriver until he got the punk to tell him where his money was. Then he'd get the cash, and the whole case was closed.

Only he kind of believed Flyboy. The kid didn't seem the slightest bit afraid, and he also seemed genuinely glad to see Kevin again. On top of that, Kevin really wanted to find a friend, a partner he could hang with . . . and he kind of admired Flyboy for being out there on his own.

And so, somehow, he couldn't get the tough-guy words out of his mouth, and instead he felt a kind of warmth for Flyboy, like the last thing was just some kind of test and he'd passed and now he was a part-time street kid. Flyboy must have gained some respect for him or else he wouldn't have been walking down the narrow little Venice streets with him, until they got to the run-down Victorian boardinghouse.

And there they were creeping up to the porch, and then up to the front window.

"Look, it's half open," Flyboy said.

"Yeah," Kevin said, feeling kind of sick to his stomach, thinking now what Dad would say if he got caught breaking and entering. Or doing a B and E, as the cops put it.

Kevin the criminal. That was fucked up, really.

But it was exciting, too. It was better than sitting around being a victim, wasn't it? Besides, he wasn't really stealing anything, just getting his own money back. I mean, how bad was that?

Of course, Flyboy might take some stuff from the guy, but that wasn't Kevin's responsibility, was it? Plus, the guy deserved it, didn't he? He was a criminal himself, wasn't he?

"You coming?" Flyboy said as he climbed all the way in.

"I don't know," Kevin said. "How do we know he did it?"

"'Cause I saw him do it," Flyboy said. "Now c'mon."

Kevin felt sick. He didn't want to go in the window. He didn't want to get revenge on Flyboy anymore.

He just wanted to go back to school. Until Charlie picked him up.

If he wasn't there, Charlie would go nuts and call Dad, and then, oh, man, he'd really be in trouble.

But now that the window was up and Flyboy was inside, he had to go in or . . . or . . . no, there wasn't any "or." He had to go in. Now.

And then the monologue in his head stopped. He was in, inside White's house.

And they were opening drawers in the little dining room, looking for money.

And they were looking in the drawers underneath the telephone, and they were looking all around, but they hadn't found anything.

"Upstairs," Flyboy said. "He must keep it in the bedroom."

"Aww, forget it," Kevin said. "I don't want to go up there."

"C'mon," Flyboy said. "We gotta at least look."

Kevin felt suddenly like crying. Which made him feel like a punk. No, there was no question. He had to go upstairs, too, and so he started walking, feeling more and more like a fool, and a criminal, walking softly, though that made no sense since it was obvious no one was home.

It would all be over in a second, he thought.

All over, in a second . . .

They crept down the hall, past a weird-looking picture of a clown on the wall, a clown that looked like it was made from one of those velvet materials which Kevin always associated with horror movies.

Killer clowns, he thought.

Flyboy was just ahead of him, walking into the master bedroom. Kevin was looking at his back . . . and then he heard a gasp.

"What?" Kevin said.

Flyboy moved out of the way so that Kevin could see what was in front of him.

What it was, was a man. A big man with cold white hair and what looked like an old .38 revolver in his hand.

"Hey," the man said. "Look what we got here, thieves. Or possibly killers. Were you two going to kill me in my sleep?"

"I thought you worked on Thursday," Flyboy said.

"Used to," White said. "But I got laid off for knocking down on the cash register. So here I am asleep in my own house, and trash such as you see fit to rob and maybe maim me."

"Hey, no, Johnny," Flyboy said. "It's not like that. We were just screwing around. I rang the doorbell and nobody answered, so I seen the window was up, and we just did it."

"An impulsive act of friendship?" Johnny said. "Should we chalk it up to that?"

"Yeah," Flyboy said. "Like that."

"An impulsive act," Kevin said.

"Fuck you!" Johnny White said. "I'm going to kill both of you little fags and plaster your bodies up in the wall I'm putting in for the owners downstairs in the basement. Now get over here."

Terrified and shaking, Flyboy shuffled around the side of the bed.

"Before I kill you both, though, I'm going to make sure you butt-fuck each other and lick me off," Johnny White said. "Isn't that nice of me? I see it as honoring your last request. I'm generous of spirit that way."

That was all Kevin needed. He reached into his pocket, pulled out the screwdriver, and hurled it across the room at White. The tool struck White in the cheek, leaving a hole, out of which blood surged.

White looked at the screwdriver, then leaped up from the bed, howling like a wounded animal.

Kevin turned and ran down the steps, raced to the front door, and realized it was still locked.

He ran to the still-open window and dove through to the porch.

In seconds he was down on the street, racing for Venice Boulevard. He turned and saw the crazed, screaming Johnny White behind him.

"You cocksucker! I'm gonna fuck you to death now. You don't deserve a bullet!"

Kevin pumped his legs in a sheer fear-based adrenaline rush, but as he turned to look again, he could see that it wasn't enough. The madman was gaining on him with every step.

He turned up a street he didn't know and looked to see if there was a place to hide, but the block was short, with only an empty lot and a torn-down old home.

No good place to get out of sight. He felt bile come up in his throat. He was through.

He heard the lunatic's heavy footsteps racing toward him, and he felt a strange sensation of deflation. Not only a mental deflation, but also a very real sense that he was a balloon and that someone had punctured him, and he was going to soon be this piece of rubber which lay there useless on the ground, with the grotesque remains of a human shape.

And then he heard a voice. A voice he knew.

"Kevin?"

He turned and saw . . . it was impossible, ridiculous, but true . . . he saw Charlie Breen right there looking at him. Charlie, in his comfortable plaid shirt, baggy Levi's, and work boots, dear Charlie staring at him.

"Charlie!" Kevin said. "We've got to get out of here. There's this guy . . . This guy who wants to kill—"

"Where?" Charlie said.

"Right around the corner," Kevin said.

He took a step and peered around the corner. White was about fifty feet away.

Charlie saw the huge man steaming toward him.

Kevin grimaced and felt terrified both for himself and now for Charlie, whom he'd gotten into this impossible mess.

But then Charlie did something Kevin couldn't believe. He turned his body, bent down, and delivered a perfect cross-body block to the bigger man. The guy went down like a collapsed building and rolled into the gutter.

Charlie got up and dusted himself off. Then he leaned over and whispered something into the huge man's ear.

All the anger and bravado in White's face crumbled, and as he got to his knees, he nodded slowly.

He started to say something else, but Charlie shook his head, then kicked him in the ribs.

The man groaned and fell back into the street. Kevin could

barely believe it had happened, and seconds later Charlie was walking him toward his car, with his arm around him. As they left the scene, Kevin peered back one last time and could see Flyboy disappearing into a copse of trees, apparently a back way to the beach.

Charlie smiled down at him. "Everything's fine now, Kev," he said.

"Yeah. Man, what did you say to him, Charlie?"

"I told him I was with the FBI," Charlie said. "That my name was Agent Jack Harper, and that if he had a problem with you, we could take it up at headquarters."

Kevin broke out into a wild laugh.

"You did?"

"I did," Charlie said. "I also said that if he bothered you anymore, I was going to come back and kill him twice."

"Oh, man!"

"Now let's go get in the car. You were a very lucky young man today. I just happened to be down the street at the antique store looking for some chairs for the Deckhouse."

Kevin smiled and suddenly hugged Charlie. He felt a radiant warmth spread through him. Like the love he used to feel for Jack.

"What the hell are you doing wandering around here on a school day?"

"I, ah . . . It's a long story, Charlie."

Charlie laughed and gave him a little hug.

"Well, I've got all afternoon," Charlie said. "Since I've become your fairy godfather, I think we should go back to my place, have a burger, and you can tell me all about it."

"That sounds good, Charlie," Kevin said.

Once again he felt like bursting into tears. Charlie had saved his life.

Amazing! It was like a minor miracle.

"Thanks, Charlie," he said. "I don't know what would have happened if you hadn't been there just then. I still can't believe it."

Charlie looked at him then and grinned.

"Forget it. You're like my own son, buddy. Old Charlie will take care of you. Don't worry about a thing, kid. Now's let get you on home."

25

THE VALENTINE CLUB was located in a mini-mall between a Korean doughnut shop called US Very Good Doughnuts and a sushi restaurant called the Yellowtail Palace. If you blinked, you'd never notice the Valentine at all. It didn't have a sign, but instead featured a small red valentine on the outside of the wall. The average person might think of the place as an obscure blood bank, which was, in a way, what it was. If you hung out there long enough, you would end up giving your life savings and maybe even your blood to Timmy Andreen, con man, dope dealer, and contract killer.

Jack parked and went in through the heavy black door into a room that was painted red. There were little lamps on the tables like the kind you saw in Warner Bros. movies from the '30s. Jack laughed to himself, remembering watching those movies with his old man, thinking that somehow hanging in speakeasies with the little lamps on them would be the height of sophistication. What a joke . . . This place, with its hellish red walls, its cheap black plastic tables, and its little lamps—probably stolen from the loading dock outside Costco—would pass as sophisticated only in the Valley. What it really was was an imitation of a movie set, itself a bad imitation of a '30s speakeasy. Gangsters, it seemed, were as nostalgic and sentimental about the past as clubwomen or the DAR.

The waitresses wore French maids' outfits and had their hair puffed up in '60s bouffants.

Jack walked over to the bar, a massive oaken structure that didn't go with the rest of the place. Andreen probably picked it up for nothing from a Western movie set. Now Jack remembered that he had been a porno producer for a while back in the '80s and had even made a couple of Westerns, which went straight to video.

Jack talked to the bartender, a blonde with a ponytail, and breasts that looked as hard as cue balls. Her name tag said RAE.

"What can I getcha?"

"Vodka, straight," Jack said. "Ketel One. And I need to see Timmy Andreen."

"Timmy might be in the back," Rae said. "Who do I say you are?"

"Bobby Hopps," Jack said. The real Bobby Hopps was a kid he'd played lacrosse with who had been killed in Desert Storm, but there was no way they would know that.

"And why would he want to talk to the aforementioned Bobby Hopps?" the blonde said.

"'Cause Mickey Benz told me to look him up."

Mickey Benz was a con Jack had put in prison for robbing a military armory in Arizona. Looking at a thirty-year bit, he'd decided to play ball. Jack was pretty certain that security had been tight enough that Timmy Andreen didn't know he'd ratted out people in the L.A. dope world. At least he hoped so, because Andreen and Benz had worked together a couple of times.

172

Jack might have scooped up Andreen back then, but they didn't have anything major enough to warrant busting him. Maybe that would work for him now. Andreen would probably think of Benz as a stand-up guy. That was the plan, anyway. And God help Jack if it didn't work.

Rae picked up her cell phone and mumbled something into it, then set it down and gave Jack a wry smile.

"He said you could come in the back. He'll talk to you for five."

"My gratitude knows no bounds." Jack dropped five bucks on the bar.

"Yeah, well, you shoulda tipped me a dime instead, cheapskate," Rae said. But she was smiling when she said it.

Jack walked through another black door. He was getting tired of the red-and-black color scheme. He felt a sudden urge to simply blow the cover, take Andreen out in the back alley, and kick the shit out of him. But that would have been wrong. Very unprofessional. And totally against policy.

The back room had more red walls but there was a big desk sitting in the middle of the room. On a couch on the side sprawled a guy in a pink silk shirt who looked like he was stuffed with bowling balls. Over his left eye he wore a black leather eye patch. He was dressed in shiny leather pants that were so tight they looked as though they might burst at the seams. His massive head was flat on top, and his eyes were slits and set about two feet apart. His nose was about a yard wide, and his nostrils looked like two caves that were big enough for bats to fly in. His lips were big and meaty, and when he smiled, there was a gap between his teeth that you could have used for a mail slot.

• • •

He grinned at Jack and nodded his head up and down in a rhythmic way to a tune which only he could hear. Jack guessed it might be a moronic nursery rhyme he liked to play while eating human intestines.

The man behind the desk, on the other hand, was small and wizened. Had a head like a bulbous raisin. His face was all wrinkles and angles, and his eyes were hidden in the folds of his leathery skin. His nose was like a pug's, and his mouth was as thin as a staple.

"So, *Mister* Bobby Hopps," Raisinhead said, standing and waving to Jack with his thumb up, as if he was Roger Ebert endorsing a movie. "You come from an old friend of mine . . . *Mister* Mickey 'The Quick' Benz. Mister Quick and I go way back to the days when we were hustling pony rides on the parking lot at the new and highly touted Happyland. Thing was, we didn't have an 'animal license,' and they turned us over to their very own little fascist park police. I assume a world traveler like yourself would know that they house a whole little mafia down there . . . Took us into these stucco buildings . . . and by the way don't you just hate the fucking word 'stucco' . . . a lot of what's happened with Western civilization—I mean the decline thereof—could be related to the use of the word and substance 'stucco.' Shoddy shit, stucco. Anyway, they take us into stucco land, and they sweat our asses and threaten to call the state troopers on us, mere striplings. Lads. Eventually they let us go but kept our pony as evidence. I heard tell that the man himself straddled the horse, putting its giant member into his mouth . . ."

The giant on the couch began to laugh at that one. Well, Jack was pretty sure it was laughter. It was something like "A harhar-har har . . ." a sound which seemed to be an imitation of a cartoon pirate laugh. The laugh was shortly followed by a gagging cough, and Jack watched as the great flat-headed giant tried to right his shaking muscle groups.

"Well, how can I assist you, Bobby Hopps?" Timmy Andreen said. "Any friend of The Quick's is a friend of mine . . . Et cetera. Et cetera."

"I don't know, exactly," Jack said. "I just got out of Soledad and I need a gig. Mick said if I mentioned his name, you'd get all soft in the middle and offer me a truckload of money."

Andreen raised an eyebrow, and five or six hundred wrinkles rose with it.

"I like your exceptional banter," he said. "But what is your specialty, Mr. Hopps? Driver, safe expert, perhaps gemologist?"

"I lean more toward the security department." Jack smiled and looked over at the massive one-eyed hulk on the couch.

"Yes, I see," Andreen said. "But that's one area where I'm pretty much up to snuff. I mean, Winkie over there has never met a man he couldn't best."

For the first time, Winkie opened his twisted, flabby lips and spoke. Jack expected a deep, guttural sound befitting a giant idiot, but was surprised to learn that Winkie's voice was high and light, with a kind of Oklahoma twang. Like Mickey Mantle's on ether.

"I fuck up whoever messes with Tim," Mr. Winkie said, then gave his pirate cough/laugh.

"Yes, Winkles, that you do," Mr. Tim said. "Just the other night, we had a small skirmish out there in the Valentine Room. A fellow accused me of sexually abusing his date, the remarkably endowed Sunny. Of course there were no witnesses to my said affront, but the fellow insisted on making an issue out of it, and Winkie had to severely discipline him. Choked him right down to bare carpet and tossed him out on the macadam. Ugly, but deeply efficient, and he left not one scar."

"You can't have my job," the giant said sadly.

"Well, certainly not," Jack said. "But I thought I might assist you. 'Cause sometimes you might get double-teamed."

"Winkie works alone," the giant said.

He stood up and Jack saw the giant's shadow block out the light from the wall lamp. It was as though an office building had suddenly been erected in the room. Jack felt an appealing fear glowing inside of him.

"Listen, man," Jack said, opening his palms in a gesture of conciliation. "No offense."

Winkie took a quick step forward. His hands were not opened. Indeed, they had been turned into fists, which looked like dumb-bells. And there was now a kind of sweet smell coming off him, a joyous and murderous lather.

Jack moved forward quickly, before the giant could raise his mountainous arms. His own hands were now clenched lightly, all except his pointer finger, which he now swiftly jammed into the soft flesh just below the giant's Adam's apple. The effect was immediate and extreme. Mr. Winkie gave a screeching choke sound, then fell to his knees making horrible sucking noises. The floor shook, and sentimental paperweights of vacations past fell from Andreen's desk.

Before the behemoth could recover, Jack kneed him in the face, knocking him over on his side. Blood squirted from his massive nose and sprayed all over Jack's shoes.

Winkie lay there quivering and gagging for some time.

Tim Andreen made a face and shook his head, as if to say "tsk-tsk." He walked around to the other side of the desk, stepped over the gagging giant's body, and offered Jack his wrinkly right hand.

"That was fine work, Mr. Hopps," he said. "I think I can find a place for you in our organization. Would you mind terribly if we discuss your salary tomorrow? It would seem bad form, given Winkie's humbled condition."

"Not at all," Jack said. "Would you like me to move him out of here?"

"Yes, and be gentle with him," his new boss said. "Under that tough hide, Wink's very sensitive."

"I thought as much," Jack said. "Is he going to remain with your organization, or would you like him deposited in the Dumpster outside?"

"Oh, no, I could never fire the Winkster," Andreen said. "He's been with me for lo, these many years. I feel very much like his guardian. Perhaps, you could teach him that deadly move you sprang on him. Bring him up to date with the latest methods of self-defense."

"I'd be happy to," Jack said. "He seems a little rusty."

"Yes, and get him a drink," Andreen said. "He prefers vodka . . . and pineapple juice. Have one for yourself, too, Hopps. On the house."

"Thank you," Jack said. "Do you want me to start now or tomorrow?"

"You've already started," Andreen said. "Get yourself a sandwich or something. I like to treat my people well. The kind of work you do takes energy. Got to eat a balanced diet. Try our wheatgrass tequila infusion. Miss Rae will get you one."

Jack smiled as the door opened behind him.

"Ahhh, look who it is," Andreen said. "My dear, I want to introduce you to the newest member of our happy little family. Mr. Bobby Hopps."

The woman stepped out of the door's shadow and into the light.

It was all Jack could do not to gasp openly. The woman was none other than Michelle Wu. Dressed in black tights and ballet slippers, she looked as if she was there to dance the night away.

"This is Michelle," Andreen said. "She's our new singer. Michelle, this gentleman is Mr. Bobby Hopps. Our new employee in security."

"Really?" Jack said. "Well, I'll look forward to hearing you."

"I start this weekend, if you're still around," Michelle said. Her voice was cool, her Vicodin eyes bright with pinwheels.

"Oh, I will be," Jack said. "I think I'm going to find working for Tim very interesting."

Michelle bit her lower lip and looked down at the floor where Mr. Winkie's color was slowly turning from icy blue to salmon pink.

Then she moved past Jack and walked around the desk, and ran her long fingernails through Timmy Andreen's dyed black hair.

It was after three A.M. when Jack left the club. He'd hung out, met some of the club's regular patrons . . . a second-tier star named Simon Blazek from second-rate action movies, and Kitty Wedge and Gretchen Hipe, a couple of failed starlets, who were worn out playing "the girl" and thinking about becoming hookers or porn stars.

There was nothing going down; no one got out of hand. Jack's biggest fear was dealing with the grumpy Winkie, who occasionally looked over at him and offered a snarl/smile. This, Jack was certain, was only the first encounter with the great giant, who definitely desired revenge.

Now he waited a half block away, sitting in front of El Diablo, a grease-pit Mexican restaurant where married Valleyites came to rendezvous with their tennis instructors, drink margaritas, and play sex games beneath the table in the dark, moody bar.

Jack's nerves were frayed, and he felt sleep pulling him down, but he couldn't afford to sleep. Not yet.

Not until he talked to Michelle Wu.

She finally came out of the Valentine Club at four A.M., got into her Mercedes, and headed down Ventura toward the city.

178

Jack let her go by, then pulled a quick U-turn and seconds later pulled her over right outside of Terresushi.

"Jackie," she said, smiling as they pulled into the empty parking lot. "Were you surprised to see me, baby?"

"Yeah, I was. What the hell were you doing there?"

"I told you I played around with the boys sometimes. Gambling, a little fun . . . that's all. And now Tim was giving me a chance to sing. You know I've always wanted to be a star, Jackie."

"You're *already* a star, baby," he said.

"True." She leaned into him and smiled. "But I've got a great voice. Do you know I trained to be an opera singer in Hong Kong?"

"You're a girl of a million surprises," Jack said.

"Now that you're working security, you'll hear me," Michelle said. "I might start a whole new career. Do you think I'm pretty enough to be a singer, Jackie?"

She batted her eyes in a comical way, and Jack had to laugh.

"What *you* are is a piece of work," he said. "You know why I'm there, Michelle. You wouldn't give me away to Timmy-boy, would you? So maybe he'd help you in your new career?"

Michelle opened her mouth and gave a hurt little sigh.

"Jack, how can you say that?"

"Knowing you, it's easy," Jack said.

"You obviously don't know me at all," Michelle said. "You think I would ever do anything to endanger my Jackie-boy?"

She ran her finger across his lips, and Jack felt a surge of desire for her.

"You want me to do something to help you, Jackie? 'Cause I will . . . I'd do anything to help you, baby."

"Is that right?"

"It is," she said. "It's very right. Like you and me, Jackie. We're very right."

"Yeah, we're practically family," Jack said. "But don't forget,

Michelle. I've got four stolen vehicles on you, and a couple more that I think you sold for parts in Mexico."

"How could I forget that, Jackie, when you remind me of it every time I see you? Just tell me how I can help you, and maybe those old charges—all lies, anyway—could go away?"

"Yeah," Jack said. "Maybe they could."

"Then we could have the kind of relationship we are capable of," Michelle said. "I could take you to Hong Kong and show you my world."

Jack laughed. She was dead-on charming, the greatest bullshit artist he'd met in twenty years. She was so good that he wondered if she believed it . . . at least, while it was coming out of her beautiful mouth.

"All right, I'll tell you what I need. I need to get into Timmy's office and check his computer. The sooner the better. I want to find out if he hit Zac Blakely and Ron Hughes. Maybe you could also divert him for a while. Are they open every night?"

"No. They're closed on Sundays."

"He ever go in there to work then?"

"Not very often. I'm not sure, but I don't think so, Jackie. Trouble is, Winkie is on duty on Sunday."

"All right," Jack said. "This Sunday night. Think you can divert the goon?"

"Maybe I could possibly distract Winkie," Michelle said.

"That's my girl! You could leave the back window to the office unlocked and crawl inside."

"That sounds a little scary, Jackie. You get caught, they're gonna know I was in on it."

"But I won't get caught. I find his password and I check his records. There ought to be something there . . . a payment, a date, phone records. They won't even know I was in there."

She pushed her body into Jack's and kissed him on the cheek. Her lips were soft, and the kiss was as tender as a new bride's.

"Okay, baby. I do it for you. You know I love making plans with you, Jackie. I think we make a wonderful team."

"Yeah," Jack said. "There's no doubt about it. Just get Winkie out of there on Sunday."

She smiled and kissed his cheek again.

"Of course I will, master," she said.

Then she turned and walked away. Shaking her perfect little ass one more time for Jack, she slid into her blue Mercedes and drove down Ventura toward Chinatown.

26

IT WAS RAINING the day Nicki Sadler was buried, and though he was interred at one of the most famous celebrity cemeteries in the world, Forest Lawn in Glendale, the funeral didn't make the afternoon news.

The only mourners were Jack, Oscar, and a woman wearing a black veil over her face, circa 1953. There was a priest, with a bad comb-over and a melon-sized head. He worked for the cemetery. He said a few words about Nicki Sadler's various charitable donations and how Nicki worked in the land of "celluloid magic. Behind the scenes, yes, but no less of an important part of the wonderful world of Hollywood than the actors and directors."

Oscar and Jack huddled under a half-dead eucalyptus tree. Oscar wore his old Dodgers baseball cap as the cold rain ran down their faces.

"That woman looks familiar," Jack said.

"Yeah," Oscar said. "That's 'cause she used to star in horror flicks. I saw her in *Beasteaters* and *Brain from Planet Jerry*. Name's Joyce Domergue."

"Oh, yeah," Jack said. "I remember her. Something about her nostrils. She had a perfect face, but her nostrils were too big."

"Yeah," Oscar said. "And she used to flare them to show she was sexually aroused. Looked like you could drive a dune buggy in there."

"Great tits, though," Jack said.

"Yeah, but not enough to overcome the monstro nostril factor," Oscar said.

They waited until the minister had intoned "dust to dust," then walked over to the retired horror starlet.

As they got closer, Jack silently reminded himself to be polite, and not to stare at her nose.

"Hey," he said. "Excuse me, but aren't you Joyce Domergue?"

"Yes, I am," she answered. "Let me guess. You're at Nicki's funeral, so you must be creditors."

Jack laughed and shook her hand.

"No, ma'am. FBI."

"Oh," she said. "I knew Nicki was a bad boy, but not an international felon."

She laughed and lifted her veil. Her nostrils looked almost normal, Jack thought. Maybe it was bad camera work. She had a few lines in her face, but she was still beautiful.

Jack introduced Oscar, and they walked with her toward her limo.

"Loved you in *Beasteater*," Jack said. "When you killed the monster with that magic lantern . . . whoa!"

"It was actually a parking flare with some stucco bullshit on it," the actress said. "Cost about twenty cents to make."

"Yeah, but it looked like the real deal," Oscar said.

"You guys are funny," she said. "That movie was total shit. But I *was* great in it."

"Yeah," Jack said. "You were my favorite eater of beasts."

"Thanks," Joyce Domergue said. "You gonna put the cuffs on me now, boys?"

"Not yet," Jack said.

"Oh, why not?" Joyce said. "I could use some fun."

"We just want to ask you a little bit about Nicki Sadler's friends," Oscar said.

Joyce Domergue put one hand on her hip and sighed.

"Honey," she said, "that's a very short story. I mean, you're looking at 'em. Nicki was garbage. When I first got out here from Iowa, he tried hard to get me work. For a while. That is, until his various vices and unpleasant associates caught up with him."

"We're thinking of the guy who might have done this," Jack said. "Guy he collected information for. Information which led to the death of two federal agents."

Joyce Domergue looked puzzled. "I don't know . . . There was a guy that he was worried about. Guy he always met at Musso's."

Oscar looked at Jack.

"You ever meet him?"

Joyce shook her head.

"No, I didn't know him. But after one of their meetings, when Nicki and I had gotten a little sloshed on Reuben's martinis, he said the guy wanted some information that was hard to get."

"He say what it was?"

"Something weird. About the Witness Protection Program. Guy wanted to know how he could get inside it, find someone who had changed their identity. I told Nicki he started playing around with that kind of stuff, he was going to end up in a trash bag."

Jack felt a strange sensation in his temples, like a small electric current was whipping through his head.

"Witness Protection? The guy say why he wanted it?"

She shook her head.

"Nah. 'Least, Nicki didn't tell me. But he *did* say it was worth a lot of money to him if he could come up with it."

"And did he get the information?" Oscar asked.

"I don't know," she said. "Listen, boys, I'm getting all wet here and between you and me, I *hate* fucking graveyards."

"Yeah, me too," Jack said.

He handed her his Bureau card.

"You think of anything else, will you please call me?"

She looked down and read his name.

"Jack Harper," she said. "Hey, listen, Jack, I'd call you even if I couldn't think of one damned thing."

She smiled her sexiest smile and then turned and got into the drenched limo.

They watched her drive off in the rain.

"Man," Oscar said. "What the hell was that about?"

Jack felt a buzz of confusion.

"Doesn't make sense," he said. "Why would Steinbach or Forrester want a name out of Witness Protection?"

"I don't know. You want to hit Nicki's home again? We might have missed something."

"Yeah," Jack said. "Let's go."

"I thought she looked great," Oscar said as they headed to their car.

"Yeah," Jack said. "What about the nostrils?"

"Looked like she had 'em worked on," Oscar said.

"Yeah," Jack said. "That's what I thought, too. But she waited too long."

"That's the problem with her career," Oscar said. "You work in low-budget movies, you can't afford nostril work. That is, until you save up, and by that time, you're too fucking old to get eaten by the Beast anymore."

"Tough racket," Jack said. "But she was still cool."

"Yeah," Oscar said. "I always kind of dug the big nostrils, anyway."

"Yeah," Jack said. "Me, too."

Oscar laughed. "Hey, you think agents in D.C. or other parts of the country have conversations like this."

"Fuck, no," Jack said. "Nostril work. That's a Hollywood thing."

They smiled and got into their car.

27

CHARLIE AND KEVIN headed down Culver Boulevard toward Jack's place. They were cruising with the convertible top down in Charlie's 1968 Caddy Coupe de Ville, both dressed in their baseball uniforms. Sitting in the console between them were two double cheeseburgers from In and Out Burger.

Kevin took a bite of his Animal Burger and looked over at Charlie with an almost-worshipful gaze. Charlie smiled back at him.

"Oh, man," Charlie said. "I wish your dad was here. I still can't believe that throw you made."

Kevin smiled and tried not to think about the other day and what might have happened to him if Charlie hadn't appeared.

"I didn't really think I could get him," Kevin said. "He was rounding second, and I hadn't even gotten to the ball yet. When I picked it up, I was three feet from the fence, and I saw him rounding third. I just wound up and let it go!"

Charlie nodded happily at the memory of it.

"Yeah. Amazing! Of course, you missed the cutoff man!"

Kevin's face suddenly went blank. "Cutoff man? What cutoff man?"

Charlie looked stunned. Then Kevin cracked up. And Charlie joined him. Then he threw up his right arm and made a fist.

"He's *out!*" he yelled. "The man is *out at home plate!*"

He jerked his thumb in the air as they made a left on Jack's street and a few minutes later pulled into the Harpers' driveway.

As they pulled in, Kevin suddenly felt choked up.

"Charlie," he said. "Man, I owe you for what you did for me the other day. I don't know what I was thinking, going into that dude's house."

Charlie shook his head.

"The important thing is you survived it. Look, kiddo, we don't have to say a word about any of this to your dad. He's had enough troubles for a while. But promise me this: If you feel the need to do something off the wall again, you come to my house first. Before you get in trouble. Okay?"

Kevin nodded his head and smiled sheepishly.

"You got it, Charlie," he said.

"Okay, gotta get the bag," Charlie said. "We got all the gloves in here?"

"Sure," Kevin said. "I took care of 'em back at the field."

Charlie smiled and tousled Kevin's thick black hair.

Kevin laughed and hugged Charlie. It struck Kevin that he really loved Charlie like an uncle or something. It was great having him around. But somehow loving Charlie made him wish his dad was around more, too. He hated it when his dad missed games. Of course, he couldn't help it because of his work, but still . . .

Better not to think about it. Put it out of his mind. Thank God for Charlie.

• • •

Charlie carried the canvas bag with the batting helmets, gloves, balls, and catcher's gear up the front steps.

Kevin drank another sip of his milk shake and remembered the great throw he'd made again as Charlie opened the door.

Charlie called out as they went inside.

"Jack? You back there?"

Kevin looked at Charlie quizzically.

"His car's not out there, Charlie," he said.

"I know," Charlie said. "But I thought I heard . . . something from the back of the . . . there! You hear that?"

This time Kevin heard it, too. A shuffling of papers, like someone was trying to clean up something . . . fast. Then a sound like someone stumbling around.

"Kevin," Charlie said. "Get back to the car, fast."

"What are *you* going to do?"

"I'm going inside. Don't worry about me."

He set the canvas bag down by the overstuffed chair in the living room and took out a baseball bat.

"No, Charlie," Kevin said, feeling panic rising in his stomach. "You can't go back there!"

Charlie turned and grabbed Kevin's shoulders.

"You get back out there to the car," he said. "Now! I'm not letting anyone rob your house."

Kevin saw the utter seriousness in Charlie's face and headed out the door. Maybe the guy who had come after him had somehow found out where he lived.

Charlie held the bat with both hands, swinging it back and forth like a sword in front of him.

"I'm armed," he said. "You better come out now!"

He heard another scrambling noise. It seemed to be coming from Jack's second bedroom.

Charlie held his breath, heard the beating of his heart in his ears.

"I warned you!" he said. Then he dodged down the hall and quickly went into the back bedroom. The one Jack used as his study.

Charlie leaped inside, the bat in front of him. But the room was dark, and before he could see anything, something hard smashed him in his forehead. He fell to the floor, dropping the baseball bat, which rolled down the slightly inclined floor under the sofa.

Charlie felt his head swim and threw up his hands to protect himself from further blows.

But no more blows came. The intruder stepped over him and beat a hasty retreat to the back entrance of the house. Dazed, his head throbbing, Charlie heard him open the screen door and run out into the backyard.

Charlie made an effort to get up, but his head was killing him. Blood was dripping down his face, which put him in shock.

He tried to pull himself up again by using the couch as leverage, but when he got to his knees he felt a black pool collecting in his eyes. Seconds later, he lay unconscious on the floor.

"So far I got a big fat *nada*," Oscar said.

"Yeah," Jack said. "Me, too."

He walked over to Sadler's bar and stared at the crystal decanters.

"There's got to be something we aren't seeing," Jack said.

"Yeah. If *we're* the targets, then why does he need some guy's name in Witness Protection?"

Jack said, "The thing is, if Blakely and Hughes were killed because they were in bed with Steinbach, and they didn't give

190

them the protection they said they would, maybe there's another angle here. Maybe someone in Witness Protection is involved in some other part of the case."

"I don't get that," Oscar said, slumping down in a dark leather chair.

"I mean, maybe Blakely and Hughes and somebody else in Witness Protection were skimming off the top. Maybe that's why they were killed. Maybe they have money put away . . . a lot of money . . . diamond money."

Oscar nodded.

"So, according to that theory, the guy in Witness Protection had some kind of information about Steinbach. He and Blakely and Hughes were working some kind of scam. They've killed Blakely and Hughes, but they don't know how to get to the third guy 'cause he's got a new ID and a new address. So we should be looking for somebody in the program who once worked with Steinbach."

"Right," Jack said. "So think about it. Who would be looking for this guy? None other than Timmy Andreen. Still another reason I have to get into his computer."

"I guess," Oscar said.

"What's the matter? You don't like the theory?"

"No, no . . . I mean, as a theory it's all right, but, well, . . . you know how sometimes a case seems too easy. So you gotta look at it in a more complicated way?"

"This case seems too easy?" Jack laughed.

"No, *compadre,* this case is the exact opposite. It seems too damned complicated. I mean, we are breaking our asses trying to make this add up, finding connections here and there . . . but what if it was just a lot more simple?"

"Simple how?" Jack said. Oscar was starting to annoy the hell out of him. On the other hand, his partner had great instincts . . . and when he differed from Jack, there was usually a good reason for it.

"Come on, Osc, tell me a simple story. I'm all ears."

Oscar sighed and shook his head.

"That's the problem. I don't have a goddamned story. But I do know what we need to find out. And that is who these sons of bitches are looking for. If we know that, we understand the whole case. I'm sure of it."

"That makes sense," Jack said.

"Okay," Oscar said. "Let's say the whole case was about that. Let's say that everything that has happened from . . . from the day we arrested Karl-baby to Blakely and Hughes getting hit, to Sadler's death . . . Let's say all of it was really about that one thing. Some guy in Witness Protection. That somehow all of it added up to him."

Jack felt a vague stirring inside of him. The idea sounded crazy, but what if it were true? The thing was, no matter how complicated a case was, it usually was about something simple. Something like money, or revenge, or power.

If you could find the one thing it was *really* about, then all the disparate parts might fall into place.

Maybe Oscar was right. Maybe they did have to think of it that way . . . as far-out as it seemed. Because the way they were going was getting them nowhere.

"You know, Osc, I think you might be on to something," Jack said.

Just then his cell phone rang.

"Harper," he said.

It was Kevin, and he sounded panicked.

"Dad," he said. "Come quick. It's Charlie. He was attacked, right in our home."

"Jesus!" Jack said. "How bad?"

"I don't know. He's unconscious, at Cedars. I called 911."

"Good boy. Are you okay?"

"Yeah, sure. I rode over here with the ambulance drivers."

"You see who did it?"

"No, Dad. Charlie heard something from the back of the house, like in your bedroom. Looks like they took your computer."

"I'll be right there, Kev."

Jack hung up and looked at his partner.

"Whoever wants this information wants it bad. They broke into my place and attacked Charlie."

"Jesus!" Oscar said.

The two men turned and ran for the door.

28

JACK AND OSCAR PARKED in police parking at Cedars and ran into the emergency room.

Standing in the lobby with his baseball uniform still on, Kevin rushed to his father, hugging him in a way Jack hadn't felt since he was only an infant.

"How's Charlie doing?"

"He had to have twenty-four stitches in his forehead, but he's going to be okay," Kevin said.

Jacked turned to Oscar, who crossed himself.

"In my own home," Jack said. "The son of a bitch."

But even as he said it, he realized that he didn't know which "son of a bitch."

Oscar was already dialing his cell phone.

"I'm getting Tommy Wilson right now."

Jack hugged Kevin tighter and felt the rage well up inside of him.

· · ·

A few minutes later, Jack and Oscar stood by Charlie's bed-side. The nurse, a middle-aged woman named Ruth Anne with bleached blond hair, smiled at them.

"Five minutes," she said. "That's it."

Jack smiled back at her.

"You in the business?" she said.

"The cop business," Jack said.

"Oh," she said. "I thought you were a producer. I've been do-ing a little extra work."

Jack said nothing and she opened her palms, faceup.

"Hey," she said. "A girl's gotta try, huh?"

"Yeah, sure," Jack said. "You mind if I talk to my friend?"

"No problem," she said.

She walked out of the room, giving Jack a sexy parting smile, just in case he was lying about not being a producer. It never hurt to leave a good impression.

Jack looked down at Charlie, whose skin looked pale, almost gray, like a frozen haddock Jack had seen on ice in a stall at the farmers market.

"Charlie, how you doing, buddy?"

"Okay," Charlie said, grimacing as he spoke. "I shoulda never let him get the jump on me like that, Jackie."

"Cut it out," Jack said. "You get a look at him?"

Charlie shook his head a little and grimaced again.

"Nah. It was dark. Back in your extra bedroom. He had on a ski mask."

"Yeah," Oscar said. "Big guy?"

"Yeah, he used a gun butt on me. I'm just glad it was me. When I think it coulda been Kevin walking in there . . ."

Jack felt the icy shiver up his back. The mere thought of Kevin meeting one of Steinbach's crew made him feel cold and sick.

"Yeah," Jack said. "I owe you big-time, Charlie."

"Nah," Charlie said. "You don't owe me a thing. Just try and make it to the next ball game, huh? I'm sorry they took your computer, that's all."

"Don't worry about it," Jack said. "Get some rest."

He squeezed Charlie's hand and watched his battered friend close his eyes.

Outside in the hallway, Jack looked at Oscar.

"There's something they want really bad, all right. But I got nothing like that in my computer."

"No, maybe not. But they don't *know* that. Maybe we should really take a look at anything we've ever been involved with that had Witness Protection in it."

"Okay," Jack said. "I'll think about that tonight."

Jack and Oscar walked back out to the lobby, where Kevin was watching an old episode of *Family Guy*.

"This is a great one, Dad," Kevin said. "The dog goes to California to be a movie star."

"Some lucky dog," Jack said. "C'mon, kiddo. Let's go home."

At home Jack tried to act as though everything was normal but, in spite of Kevin's best efforts, Jack saw a flash of fear in his eyes. His son looked like an animal that was cornered, trapped in a hunter's gun sights.

Jack sat on the corner of the bed and patted Kevin's hair away from his eyes. It was the kind of gesture he'd done when his son was much younger. The last few times he'd tried anything so blatantly tender, Kevin had jerked away, mumbling, "Cut it out. What do you think I am, a baby?"

But now Kevin didn't flinch. He smiled at his dad in a vulnerable way, his eyes still darting around the corners of the room searching for something lurking there, something monstrous, which would emerge only when he was alone.

"You okay, buddy?" Jack said.

"Sure, Dad, fine," Kevin said. But his voice was filled with doubt.

Jack saw his eyes watching the window. Waiting for whatever might be there in the backyard, just waiting.

"Listen, pal," Jack said. "Nothing like that is going to happen again."

"Yeah, I know that," Kevin said.

"The alarm is here, and so am I," Jack said. "Anybody who comes through that door won't be walking when he leaves."

"What do you think the guy wanted, Dad?"

"Something he thought was in my computer. But I'll be damned if I know what it is."

"You think it was that guy you arrested . . . one of his guys?"

"Steinbach?" Jack said. "Could have been. But there's something that bugs me about that, too."

"What?" Kevin said. He sat up on his pillow. Jack wondered if he should talk about the case with his son. But then again, all this affected him . . . so maybe he had a right to know. Plus, he was a smart kid. Maybe he'd come up with something helpful. In any case, he seemed wide-awake now.

"You see, if Steinbach sends a guy, he's a professional. He goes in, he looks for something, and he doesn't panic if somebody walks in. More than likely, he would have been quieter and simply gone out the window. That's what bugs me. Whoever was in here panicked and got involved with armed robbery. Pros never want to do that. In a federal agent's house? Something about it doesn't add up."

Kevin's eyes gleamed.

"So maybe it wasn't Steinbach who sent him, huh?"

"Yeah," Jack said. "Maybe it wasn't."

He thought of Forrester. That made sense somehow. Forrester sending the guy to find someone in Jack's computer whom Jack had sent into Witness Protection.

Jack hugged his son good night and went back to the kitchen, where he poured himself a beer.

That was the problem. There was only one person Jack had sent into Witness Protection, a guy named Mark Reynolds. But Reynolds had died of lung cancer years ago, and the case had nothing to do with anything Forrester could be interested in.

No, that didn't make any sense.

He drank his beer and looked out the window at a green palm tree in which three wild parrots made their home. Behind them was the wonderful purple-and-orange light, a perfect L.A. sunset. Of course, the colors were created by toxic waste, but you can't have everything.

Had to be some other case, and then it seemed to him—just then—that there was another case sometime long ago.

But what *was* it? Something he couldn't quite put his finger on.

But it was there, somewhere . . .

If he could only recall it. But he was wasted, exhausted. Within a few seconds after putting his head down on the kitchen table, he was fast asleep.

29

THE NEXT MORNING at eleven, Jack stood behind his desk at FBI headquarters. He looked tense, jumpy, as he rubbed his hands together. Leaning on the wall just to his right, Oscar felt nervous himself. If things weren't handled just right, putting Jack in a room with Steinbach and Tommy Wilson, from Homeland Security, could backfire . . . and both of them could be in a world of trouble.

Now Steinbach was dressed in a khaki safari jacket and a black sport shirt. He looked like a successful Hollywood movie director, the kind of guy who made millions off action movies.

The Afrikaner smiled.

"Excuse me, Jack," he said. "Did I hear you right? Did you say I was in your house? That I attacked a friend of yours?"

"Yeah, you heard it, Karl," Jack said. His voice rose from the tension constricting his throat.

Steinbach laughed and shook his head, like a father dealing with an impudent and misbehaving child.

"You find that amusing, Karl?" Jack was bouncing on the balls of his feet now, so Oscar took a step closer to him.

"Yes, Jack, I do." Steinbach turned slightly to include Tommy Wilson in his astonished look.

"It's funny, Jackie, because last night I was with my partner here, Tommy Wilson."

"All night?" Oscar asked.

Wilson nodded. "Yes, all night. We're setting up an important operation."

"Okay," Jack said. "So it wasn't this shithead here who was actually in my house. Doesn't matter because he still set it up. Put a guy inside my home to grab my kid."

Tommy Wilson coughed as he spoke. He didn't like what was going down here. Why couldn't Harper just admit he was wrong?

"Jack, come on," he said. "You're reaching."

"Bullshit!" Jack said. "It was him. If Charlie hadn't been there . . ."

"Jack, Jack, Jack," Steinbach said. "Listen to yourself. I think you need some counseling. Maybe a prescription for some Paxil. That usually quiets patients right down."

"Fuck you, you piece of shit!" Jack said. He exploded around the desk, moving so fast that he went right by Oscar, who seemed to reach out in vain. Jack pushed Wilson aside and was all over Steinbach, punching him in the face, then again in the stomach. Steinbach hit him back, then got him in a clinch. Oscar was around the desk now and tried tackling both men at once.

A few seconds later, they were all over the floor in a tangle of arms and legs.

Tommy Wilson came up from behind Jack and pulled him off Steinbach. Jack reluctantly let himself be brought to his feet.

As Steinbach managed to scrape himself off the floor, Oscar put a small electronic bug inside Steinbach's leather brief-case.

Then he shut it quickly and scrambled to his feet.

"Jack," Oscar said. "That's not the way, babe."

Tommy Wilson was up in Jack's face.

"Harper," he said. "You're way out of line. One more time like that, and I'll put you on report. You won't leave this building for the next five years!"

Steinbach smoothed his expensive shirt.

"And I'll hit you with a civil suit. For both physical and mental damages."

"Do whatever you gotta do," Jack said. "But if you or any of the creeps who work for you come near my family, you're gonna die. You hear me?"

Steinbach looked at Tommy and laughed.

"You heard that, Tommy. Harper just threatened my life. You're my witness."

Steinbach looked at Jack with a smug twist of his lips and headed out the door. Before he left, Tommy Wilson turned and looked sadly at Jack.

"You used to be a good agent, Jack. But you're all burned out. You need help. And then you need to fucking retire. Go write your memoirs or something."

He shook his head as if Jack was a lost cause and walked out the door.

Jack waited until he was sure they were gone and then turned to Oscar.

"You get the locator in the bag?"

"Oh, yeah," Oscar said.

"You're a good man," Jack said.

"And *you're* a good actor," Oscar said. "For a while there, I thought you'd actually turned into a psycho."

"Who's acting?" Jack laughed and pounded his partner on the back.

Oscar laughed with him, but wondered. Jack had looked a little too convincing. Maybe his old partner was headed over the edge after all.

"Look," Jack said. "There's something we gotta talk about."

"What's that?"

"I want to break into Andreen's place on Sunday night."

"Jackie, you know I'll be out of town. I got my sister's wedding out in Glendale."

"I know," Jack said. "So I'll do it on my own."

"Jack, that's bullshit. You can't go in there without backup."

"Cut it out. We've both done it before."

"Yeah, but it's a freaking risk . . . we can wait until next week. We got other cases, you know: the Wilshire bank thing, the Blackstone Gang case."

Jack felt a steady, pulsating pressure in his head.

"No," he said. "The guy is killing agents. I don't think we want to wait around to see if he comes at us next. Man, he was in my fucking house, okay? We need to do it this weekend."

"That fucking vein is pulsating in your head, *compadre*," Oscar said.

Jack put his right hand up to his forehead. Oscar was right. The vein *was* pulsating. He felt clammy down in his fingertips, too. The whole goddamned case . . . the sons of bitches in his house. Thoughts of Kevin getting hit with a hail of bullets crossed his mind. He could see his son lying there, in his own bedroom, dead. Or maybe they would come after him at school, or at the baseball field. Then he remembered the scarred man. What was his part in all this?

"I'm sorry," Jack said. "I gotta do this now."

"Jack, it's my sister. I don't go to this, I'm expelled from the family. I'm serious."

"It's fine," Jack said.

"How dangerous is it going to be?"

"It'll be nothing. I already got it worked out, checked the alarm. Piece of cake."

"All right, Jack. But be fucking careful, *amigo*."

"You got it," Jack said. "Have a great time at Laura's wedding, *amigo*."

Oscar smiled. "You know you're invited, too."

"I know," Jack said. "But this thing . . . I don't think we can wait."

He tried smiling at Oscar but the pain in his head was worse. He ought to take something for it, he thought. He ought to go see the doctor, but there was no time for that right now.

He had to get this prick, and he was sure there was something in Andreen's records that was going to help him do it.

30

IT WAS SUNDAY NIGHT, and Winkie was having a hard time breathing. Whenever he sucked in air, he got a terrible burning sensation at the back of his Adam's apple . . . (which Wink thought of as "the Apple").

That dirty son of a bitch, the new guy . . . Bobby Hopps had just about smashed "the Apple," and now it was all swollen inside. Wink, as his pals called him, made horrific hacking noises all day and night, irritating everyone at the Valentine Club.

Timmy had told him to get the fuck out of his office a couple of times in the past few days. Which made Wink sore as hell. He would just love another crack at Mr. Bobby Hopps.

Even worse, Timmy seemed to be in love with the guy, telling him stories and laughing with him . . . hanging around with him in the office, like The Winkster himself used to do.

Winkie now sat on a hard-backed chair outside of the office, his throat burning and his heart half-broken.

Man-oh-man, if ever he hated a guy, it was that Mr. Bobby Hopps.

He was so angry, he had invented a new name for Mr. Bobby. It was one people had called him when he was a kid. One that royally pissed him off.

Junior! How he hated being called that. So that's what he'd do to Hopps.

Call Mr. Bobby Hopps "Junior"!

Yeah, when he could talk without hacking up blood and pus he would spring that one on Mr. Bobby, for sure.

He'd say:

"Oh, look who it is. Mr. Bobby Hopps . . . *Junior!*"

That would really bug Hopps—he was sure of it.

'Cause nobody but nobody liked to be called *Junior!*

And if it pissed Hopps off enough to come after him with the Finger Trick, Wink would be ready this time. He'd reach out and grab Hopps's forefinger, and snap it off like a freakin' No. 2 pencil.

He could already see Hopps falling to the ground in excruciating pain. Once down there Winkie would kick him in his testicles until they looked like chipped beef.

Winkie started to laugh, amused at his own witty mind, but the laugh caught in his throat . . . literally. He began to gag and cough, and felt "the Apple" bulging out of the right side of his neck . . . man, that Hopps asshole had pushed "the Apple" all sideways!

The asshole! He'd kill him the next time. No doubt about it. He was about to dream up another sadisto fantasy concerning what punishment he would lay on Hopps when his attention was diverted by the sound of footsteps down the hall.

He jumped off his chair and put his mammoth hand on his .44 millimeter cannon, which was cradled in his brand-new

Spanish leather holster, a present from none other than his boss, Mr. Tim Andreen.

Back two months ago, when Timmy still valued his friendship.

But he couldn't worry about that now. There was somebody coming down the hall on a Sunday night. Somebody was inside the Valentine Club, and this was all wrong.

People weren't supposed to be "in the structure" during off hours. Nobody but Timmy and Winkie himself were supposed to be here. That was a solid fast rule!

Wink adjusted his eye patch, unbuttoned his holster with a flick of his finger, and waited . . . to see who it was.

He hoped it would be Mr. Bobby Hopps and he would have a reason to smash him in the gonads with a swift kick . . . would that not be a great thing?

Oh, yes . . . Yes . . . indeed.

But no . . . no . . . it wasn't Hopps. Instead it was that new singer . . . the Chink chick, Michelle Wu, and she was dressed in this unbelievable midnight blue gown, with a plunging neckline . . . a neckline that revealed big ice-cream scoops of her fabulous breasts.

Winkie felt dizzy. Girls did weird stuff to him.

He tried to assume an angry posture but she was smiling at him (at him!) and he felt kind of swoony.

He managed to croak out a couple of words as he sat back down in his chair.

"Hey, Michelle. Just what the heck are you doing here?"

"I came to use the piano in the dining room, Wink. Need to practice my tunes. Think you could come in and help me?"

"Me?" Wink said. His lizard heart fluttered like a butterfly's wings inside his massive chest.

"You," Michelle said. "Come on, Wink. I heard you're musical."

Wink felt really funny now. She was standing oh so close to him, and she had on this perfume that just seemed to smother him . . . but it was a *good* kind of smother. Really good.

But still . . . He had a job to do.

"I'm afraid I can't, uh, do that," he said, immediately feeling like a dork. He'd hoped it was going to come out suave, like maybe James Bond might say it. Instead, he sounded like a constipated bullfrog.

"Why not?" Michelle said. "I just need you to turn the pages of my sheet music. Let me show you. It's easy."

"I'm sure it is," Winky croaked. "But, see, you are not supposed to be in the structure on Sunday nights. That's a hard-and-fast rule."

"Yes, well, I've already talked to Tim about it. He gave me the key."

She dangled the key in her right hand, and Wink looked up at her, astonished.

"But I don't get it," he said. "Tim has always said that no one but no one can be—"

But it was kind of hard to finish. After all, she *did* have the key, which meant that Tim must have given it to her. And she was leaning in so close to him, he could see her breasts right there in front of him . . .

And the thought of sitting there, right next to her at the piano seat, and turning the pages . . . oh, my gosh . . .

Winkie began to feel a red flame torch his cheeks.

He was blushing, for God's sake, and he was worried about standing up. She might see his . . . erection popping up against his pants.

But then the way she was staring at him, and those breasts . . . scoops of coffee ice cream . . . And what if she liked the fact that he was getting a hard-on? Was that a possibility? Why not? When it came to women, Winkie was no fool. He knew he wasn't much to look at. But it had happened to him before. Some women liked a man who had lots of muscles. Some of them liked the eye patch. And there were always the kind of girls who really went for the Beauty and the Beast routine.

The thought made him salivate a little. A bit of drool leaked out of the side of his mouth.

And then he stood up and reached out for her hand.

"Okay," Wink said. "I'll help you. Let's go."

"No problem," Michelle Wu said. "But first I have to go to the little girls' room. Just wait right here, Wink."

She hurried down to the ladies' room, while Winky sat back down, and felt his erection getting bigger and bigger. This was wild stuff! He just hoped Mr. Tim wouldn't find out.

On the back roof of the Valentine Club, Jack had just finished disarming the security system. The night was blue, and there were slashes of yellow crossing the Valley sky. Pollution was such a beautiful thing. He thought of Oscar off at Laura's wedding. Good for his partner to have a night off. The case was beating them both down.

Now his cell phone rang.

"Jack?"

"Yeah, Michelle. We ready?"

"Of course, baby. Count to, say, 200, and then come in the back window. But be careful. We're not that far away."

"Got it," Jack said. "Just keep playing that piano. And if for some reason he comes back there, call me. Remember, I won't answer. I'll just get out the way I came in."

He hung up and started counting.

Jack found the back window of Andreen's office unlocked, just as Michelle Wu had promised. He slid open the window and crawled inside.

Out in the club's big dining and dancing room, he could hear Michelle singing the old Ray Noble song, "Do Nothing Till You Hear from Me." She sounded pretty good; he could imagine her becoming the Asian Diana Krall. From whore to car thief to recording star to Hollywood actress . . . hey, it wouldn't be the first time it had happened. Joan Crawford screwed her way to the top, and Marilyn Monroe slept with everybody she ever met. Jack had heard about a couple of other stars that were supposed to be hookers, too. Back in their early days, before they bought their dignity.

Jack took out a small flashlight and trained it at the desk.

Then he walked over to Tim Andreen's computer, turned it on, and sat down in the comfortable leather chair.

Now he had to figure out Andreen's password. He'd worried about this part of the break-in for two hours. In movies it was always easy. The secret agent sat down and turned the mouse pad over, and there it was, written on the other side, just in case the villain forgot it. If it was only that easy!

Just to make certain it wasn't, Jack turned the mouse pad over. Nothing there but dust. He'd gone through a number of combinations last night. Now it was time to try them.

What the hell could it be?

From looking over his tax records, he knew Andreen's birth-date: 10/27/63.

He punched in the numbers and hit Enter, but nothing happened.

Damn . . . maybe the same numbers backward.

He punched them in again.

Nothing.

What the hell!

Jack sat at the computer. Outside, the music stopped. Jack held his breath, listened for footsteps.

. . .

"You sound so great, Michelle," Winkie said. "You have a really cool voice."

Michelle smiled at the ogre, who sat uncomfortably close to her. She was acutely aware of his monstrous body odor—kind of like the smell of rotted bananas—and it was all she could do not to start gagging.

"I'm glad you liked it, Wink," she said. "Well, I think I have that one down. Now let me try another song. We'll do 'The Lady Is a Tramp.'"

Winkie made a grumpy face and shook his huge head.

"You don't like that song?" Michelle said. The idea that he would even know the song surprised her. She figured that Wink's taste would run toward AC/DC or Slayer.

"No, it's okay," Winkie said. "I like Cole Porter, but he's old-fashioned."

Michelle was surprised by the intelligence in Wink's voice. The monster had a human side after all!

"Well, what would you suggest?" she said.

"I'm thinking something much more current. Like one of *my* songs."

Michelle's mouth dropped open in surprise. The idea that the massive muscleman wasn't a total idiot after all struck her as stupendous.

"*Your* songs?" she said. "You write music?"

"Oh, yeah," Wink said. "You know, country stuff, mainly. I like country stuff 'cause it tells a story."

"Right," Michelle said. "Some country music is really good. Who do you like, Wink?"

"I like the old-timers most of all. Lots of the new guys don't sing all that good, can't write much, either. I like Townes Van Zandt. And Merle Haggard."

"Really?" Michelle said.

"Yeah," Winkie said. "Would you like to hear a couple of my songs, Michelle?"

"Sure I would," she said. "You play the piano?"

"Not too well," Winkie said. "A little. But I'm a heck of a lot better on the guitar."

"I see," Michelle said. She envisioned Mr. Winkie on the guitar, perhaps standing on the stage in gold spandex tights. The image made her start to giggle.

Winkie frowned with his one good eye.

"I'm serious," he croaked. "You don't believe me?"

"Sure, I do," Michelle said. "There's nothing that I'd rather do than hear you sing, but I have to practice now, Wink."

Winkie snorted his disapproval, but settled in as she started "The Lady Is a Tramp."

After ten tries, Jack finally figured out Tim Andreen's password. It was simple, really. Andreen had a smug schoolboy contempt for people, the usual punk Valley irony factor. Use "Mister" in front of their names and you immediately marginalize them in your mind. Thus Bobby Hobbs was MISTER Bobby Hobbs, and Winkie was MISTER Wink. Now reverse the practice when thinking of yourself. That is, calling yourself Mister showed what a sport you were, that you weren't afraid to be the butt of your own little joke. Thus MISTER TIM. And even though he was a miserable creep, a sadist, and, when duty called, a child molester, in his own mind playing a small joke on himself proved he could be one of the guys.

Anyway, it was a theory.

Jack punched in "Mister Tim," using both capitals and lowercase letters, but alas he got nowhere.

He heard the piano begin again, and then tried another name, one that would surely prove to Timmy what a cool cat he was.

MISTER T. Just had to be.

He typed in the name of the old TV star, and instantly he was into Tim Andreen's mainframe.

Looking through the raisin-headed criminal's files, he quickly found a Payments Made column and began to search.

Jack went back a month, two months . . . looked through all the restaurant receipts, but found nothing out of the ordinary.

He searched again and found a file called Special Projects.

Once into that he began to search carefully in the double-entry ledger.

He could feel it coming. It had to be there. Sweat poured down his face, and he felt the vein throbbing again in his left temple. Blinking on and off like a stroke's friendly warning.

It *had* to be here.

In the dining room, Winkie was getting antsy. Michelle was a good singer and her breasts swelled with every breath she took, which made him more than a little excited, but in the end she lacked . . . passion.

That was it. The girl lacked passion. No soul.

Winky suddenly felt just like Simon on *American Idol*.

He had to tell her the truth. Had to.

She needed his advice. She really did.

Ever helpful, when he wasn't strangling, stabbing, or stomping people to death, Wink decided that what she needed wasn't so much criticism . . . after all he had had a life of that and what had it ever done for him . . . but a positive example.

He remembered that he had stored his guitar in the back closet, right across from Mr. Tim's office. His old Les Paul. Some nights when Mr. Tim and the customers had gone, the lonely behemoth would stand up on the little stage, where the band played four nights a week, and pretend that the guys were up there with him, lending him backing as he exhibited his serious lead-guitar chops.

Of course, if Mr. Tim had ever found him up there, he would have put Winkie's head in a vise and squeezed until his eyeballs popped out. But he had to take the chance, because after all was said and done, he really would have rather made his mark as a crooner of country tunes than a leg breaker, eye gouger, and reluctant ball crusher.

After all, no one wants HERE LIES A TOTAL HOPELESS VIOLENT ASSHOLE written on his tombstone.

And so, he thought, if he could just get to the closet and pull out the old electric guitar and play a few blistering quick country runs for dear Michelle, she might find her Asian soul and be ever so grateful. So grateful that she might fall upon her knees under the piano keys and fasten her sensuous lips on Wink's bulging manpride.

And so Wink got up from the piano stool. And started his noble walk back toward the closet where he stored his ax.

"Where are you going?" Michelle seemed perturbed, saddened by his exit. This could only be a good omen.

"Be right back," Winkie said. "Gotta surprise for you!"

"No, Winkie . . ." her eyes flashing with fear.

"What?" he said, suddenly growing suspicious. *What was her problem?*

"It's just that . . . I need you here." Her voice softened, her eyes quickly glowing again.

"Well," Winkie said. "Don't you worry. This will only take a minute."

"But—"

He decided not to listen to her anymore. Sometimes a man knows his course and can't be dissuaded from his mission. This was definitely one of those times.

He headed out of the main room, toward the darkened hallway where his trusty old ax lay in the closet behind brooms, mops, and pails.

It would be only a minute or so more, he thought, and he would show her not only his own brilliance, but also her true soul.

Things didn't get much deeper than that.

There it was! Jack had found the item he was looking for.

Fifty thousand dollars paid from Timothy Andreen to a man named Jesse Lopez.

Jesse Lopez, the mechanic at Star Motors in the Palm Desert. Fifty thousand dollars—and not for a car, either. Fifty thousand dollars for "Services Rendered."

Jack took out his BlackBerry and within seconds had looked up Jesse Lopez's criminal records.

No surprise there. Lopez had done ten years for second-degree homicide in San Quentin.

Jesse Lopez, contract killer. Jesse Lopez, dope dealer. Jesse Lopez, master mechanic. The perfect guy to sever Zac Blakely's brakes?

Jack hit the PRINT button on Andreen's printer, and waited. It was the first time he'd felt really good since Blakely and Hughes had died.

He finally had some hard evidence. What he had to do now was to get Timmy Andreen to roll over on his boss, whether it be Steinbach or Forrester.

And with this little receipt in hand, Jack didn't imagine it would be all that hard.

But he still didn't really know if Blakely and Hughes had been playing a double game. He ran through the accounts quickly and found something else. Something that made his heart sink.

A $100,000 payment to a corporation called Mason Security.

Mason . . . as in Mason City, Iowa.

Zac Blakely's birthplace. He remembered it because Blakely had always talked about what a wonderful childhood he'd had out in the Midwest, how things were so idyllic there, how it wasn't anything like L.A., where all a man was judged by was how much money he had.

There it was, Jack thought.

Now it started to make sense.

Blakely had been forced into capturing Steinbach and probably was the reason he got out. But Steinbach didn't trust him anymore, so he had both him and Hughes removed.

He had pretended that he was mad at Jack for busting him, but that was just an excuse for his real motive. Hughes and Blakely knew too much and had to go.

Think of the order in which Steinbach had killed them. First Blakely, then Hughes . . . not first Jack, then Oscar. But if he had been killing them in the order in which he'd made the threat . . . well, that would have been a different story altogether. After all, it was Jack who'd betrayed him, not Blakely or Hughes. It was Jack and Oscar to whom he'd dealt his blood diamonds, and it was them that he'd threatened. So, logically, they should have died first.

But it was Blakely and Hughes who could really put the finger on him for good. In a situation like this, it was only a matter of time before someone found out that two Feds were bent, and they would, of course, roll over on Steinbach.

So Jesse Lopez would be the one to knock them off.

Hell, Jack thought, maybe he and Oscar weren't even on Steinbach's hit list. It all made sense . . . and yet, even now, as Jack printed out the crucial records, he felt he was still missing something.

For example, if this were really about the crooked payments to Blakely and Hughes, why would Steinbach threaten to kill them all? Why not just do it?

215

The answer might be bravado. Steinbach had plenty of that.

But drawing attention to himself, defying them to catch him . . . was that the way he had operated in the past?

Not really. Jack thought of the elaborate security measures, the secret airstrips, the bodyguards, and the cleverness of the pool balls . . . All of that bespoke a smart, secretive criminal. Yes, he did have another side, a loud, playboy side that liked expensive wines, beautiful women, and fancy German cars, but Jack had never known him to be quite so verbal about his plans.

It was true that he was angry, especially at Jack, who had become something like a brother or a son to him, and that could have accounted for his threat, which is what Jack had thought at first.

But now that Jack knew for sure that Blakely and Hughes were crooked, the threat seemed somewhat out of character.

There was something wrong with the way he was looking at the case.

Was there some other reason Steinbach had threatened them all? And what was the connection with Witness Protection? How did Forrester figure into all this, or did he?

Christ, would he ever untangle it all?

But no matter. What he had to do now was grab the printed material and get the hell out of there. Then grab Jesse Lopez and see what he could tell them. With a murder rap pinned on him, Jack guessed he might get to a whole new level of the case.

As Jack waited for the first paper to slide toward his hands, Winkie was about to open the closet and grab his old guitar. He was struck by a musical dilemma. Should he play "White Line Fever" for Michelle, or some newer tune? It hardly mattered, he guessed. She probably wasn't a country fan in any case. So do the one he could deliver with the most feeling, the deepest soul. That was the point. He had to teach her how to reach down there and grab her own soul.

He was about to reach inside, past the cleaning fluids, when he heard an odd noise just behind him, across the hall, in Tim's office.

The sound of . . . of . . . the printer going off.

Winkie forgot all about his mission to get Michelle up to *American Idol* status.

He had an important mission to perform.

Someone was breaking into Mr. Tim's office, and it was up to him to stop them. Man, when he did that . . . He'd be back in Mr. Tim's good graces, for sure!

He held his .44 Magnum in his right hand, while he stuck his key into Mr. Tim's door with his left.

Then he turned and blasted through the door with all his weight.

Inside, a shaft of light from the hallway blinded Jack. He reached for his own gun, but never had a chance.

The gagging, cough-racked voice of Wink spoke volumes:

"Well, well, look who we have here! What are you up to, *Junior?*"

Junior? What the fuck was the great moron talking about?

Jack was about to come up with something clever, but he saw the barrel of the .44 in front of him, and Winkie's enraged, snarling face. Jack glanced at the window to his left. But there was no way.

When he looked back at Winkie, the giant was already on top of him. He smashed Jack hard in the forehead with his gun butt.

Jack fell quickly and heavily to the floor. The last thing he saw before he blacked out was a sneering porcine face, leering down at him with obvious glee.

31

WHEN HE AWOKE, Jack tasted sweet, hot blood—his own.

His arms were bound behind his back. There was a killer pain in his shoulders, and another one in his left temple.

He half-expected Winkie to be standing over him with a baseball bat, but instead there stood a very dapper-looking Tim Andreen, dressed in a sharp-looking silk suit and a black-and-white–patterned tie.

Jack was sitting in what seemed to be a cane chair with the back half busted out.

Where the hell was he? Certainly not at the Valentine Club anymore. The place had the look and worn smell of an old ranch somewhere in the Valley . . . the kind of place only known to the coyotes and wolves that howled outside at the besmogged stars.

As his eyes grew accustomed to the low light, he looked over at the cages just behind Andreen.

There was Winkie, leaning on one of them and smiling at him in an ugly way.

A tangle of snakes crawled up and down a piece of carved driftwood which sat in the middle of the cage.

There were pipes assembled from the cage walls, and a red-and-yellow snake crawled there and made a hissing noise which curdled Jack's soul. Jack recognized it at once. A coral snake, the most deadly in the United States.

How many snakes were in there?

It was hard to say. Ten. No, more. Fifteen, at least. More like twenty.

Jack looked up at Andreen, who had a wooden box in his own hands now.

"So, Bobby Hopps, it has come to this." Timmy smiled and showed a little gum.

"I liked you, too. That's the pisser. I guess I really have to mend my ways. I have always gone by gut instinct. Felt I could tell what was essential to know about a man on the first meeting. And, of course, your introduction to me was so spectacular. I guess I just fell in love with you a little. I don't mean in any fag way, but you know, man to man. You are a charismatic type, Hopps, if indeed that is your name at all. You have the silent-but-deadly act down cold. But unfortunately for you, from now on it's not going to be deadly, but dead. But I can make your death tolerable—even, I might add, pleasant. Through the marvelous world of chemicals, I can send you on to the next, and we all hope, happier world, in a state of advanced ecstasy. Or we can make it more like Hellsville. Now, you may ask by what manner can you make it terrifying? Fire, lead, edged steel? But sir, I must say no to all of those. What I have in mind is much, much worse. Death by Ronnie and Jerry."

He smiled and slid open the top of the wooden box.

Then he reached in and pulled out a reptile that for a second Jack couldn't name.

"This is Ronnie, a full-grown and very bad-tempered gila

monster. Picked up off the Sonoran Desert sands. Ronnie is a fierce little biter, wouldn't you say so, Wink?"

Wink had stepped up and joined his boss now. A diamondback rattlesnake slithered over his forearm and wrapped its head around Winkie's massive bicep.

"That gila can tear through sheet metal, so think what it's going to do to you, *Junior*. Now, he's not very poisonous, as you may already know. But his bite is excruciating. And what we like to do is mix it up a little. We start you off with a little gila juice, and then we add this guy, Jerry-boy, the old diamondback rattler. Trust me, when them two poisons team up, things get pretty interesting, *Junior!*"

Tim waved the gila around slowly in front of Jack's face. It had two big walleyes and a forked, flickering tongue.

"Now maybe you want to tell me just what you were hunting for in my computer?"

"Playing video games," Jack said. "I come from an impoverished family that only has television."

"That's funny," Tim said. "Listen, my friend. We have a piece of paper, which you printed out. Why you would want to see my payment to my Porsche dealer is beyond me. The man was getting me a sweet deal on a Carrera. Admittedly stolen, but I doubt you'd go to all this trouble to find a stolen car. So there must be something else. Of course we could find it if I called in the tech boys, but that might get a bit messy, because once they found it, they'd know, too, and I'd have to off them . . . so suppose you save me all that trouble and tell me what it is."

He flicked his forefinger on the back of the gila's head, setting the animal into a mad hissing fit.

Then he set it down on Jack's right arm.

Ronnie opened his hideous jaws and slowly clamped them down on Jack's forearm. Jack felt his dry lizard tongue flicking over the skin and then a pain that was beyond endurance. He opened his mouth wide as the gates of hell and screamed.

"Ooooh, that must sting a little," Andreen said. "Would you call it slashing pain or a deep solid one? I'm guessing slash."

"Fuck you!" Jack said, gasping for breath.

"Tough nut, hey, Winkster?"

"We'll see just how tough *Junior* is," Winky said.

The monster dug deeper into Jack's forearm, eating his way through Jack's skin. The sensation of being eaten alive was unpleasant in the extreme.

"Now maybe you want to tell me, and I can give you the proverbial hot shot. A nice mixture of heroin and cocaine, and I send you out with a Fourth of July rocket blast. This way you get all chawed up, and when they find you, your corpse will be embarrassed."

"Fuck you, Timmy-boy," Jack said.

"Okay, tough guy. Then it's time for Snakey."

Without another word, Winkie applied the giant diamondback to Jack's left arm. The snake sank in with two-inch fangs, and Jack screamed again.

"Hey!" Tim smiled a little. "This could be one of those reality shows. A combination of a nature show with the greatest race. World's Greatest Predators, Reptile Division. Which one of these deadly reptiles can kill the asshole the quickest? In the end we'd have a showdown and see which one could kill the other. Of course, that's long after you're dead. By the way, Hopps, I have some antivenom right here, if you want to tell me the truth."

Jack felt the venom shooting through his system, felt his stomach contracting violently, his head snapping back.

Above him, Winkie smiled and wondered if there was a song in this deal.

"Snakebit by Your Love. . . ."

Jack screamed and his head lashed backward.

"You sure are stubborn," Tim said. "Maybe we're going to have to go for the coup de grâce. That would be your coral snake. Man, once we put that one in there, there's no antivenom in the world that's going to be strong enough to bring you around. No, Mr. Bobby Hopps will have hopped his last, and since we're going to bury you right out here in the godforsaken San Fernando Valley, none will ever know the pain you have suffered and died from. Now, that is sad . . ."

Jack screamed louder. And spat venomous froth in Winkie's face. Both men leaned back and Jack was able to rock the chair back a tad and violently thrust himself forward, knocking the rattler off at Mr. Tim's feet.

That made it Mr. Tim's turn to scream and fall backward.

He fell into Winkie, and both of them went tumbling down.

As they rose, the snake bit Tim's left thigh and he screamed and grabbed the writhing serpent, flinging it wildly toward Winkie, who fell against the cage, knocking open the half-latched door. As he fell, his head went into the cage and the dozens of snakes seemed to see this as their opportunity to stake their claim on their jailer. Three of them attacked his huge head as he screamed and flailed wildly.

Jack felt the bonds grow looser on his right hand. And then he was free. He reached across and grabbed the gila, ripped it off his ravaged arm, then threw it into Andreen's pale, terrified face. The monster clung to Andreen's lower lip, hanging off his head like a reptile beard with feet.

Andreen ripped it off his face and dropped it on the floor. Jack reached to stop him from pulling his gun, but Jack suddenly began to foam at the mouth and fell to the floor on his knees, snakes heading toward him. Jack looked up, and through a haze of poison saw Tim Andreen raise his pistol and put it to Jack's head.

Though his brain was a scramble, his body feeling as though his skin was suffocating, Jack knew for sure that the game was over. One more second and the bullet would split his brain and—given the agony he was in—it would be a relief.

He heard the gun go off and waited for the split second later which would end his life.

But there was a loud popping sound and the owner of the Valentine Club fell forward on him instead. With his last ounce of strength, Jack pushed him over onto his side.

Tim landed on top of snake-laden Winkie, the two of them lying there amid a coil of vipers.

"Jesus Christ, Jackie! Let's get out of this freakin' snake house!"

Just before he fainted, Jack saw Oscar reach his short, powerful arm down to gather him up. And just behind him, coming in the door, was Michelle Wu, with a very worried look on her beautiful face.

32

TWO HOURS LATER, Oscar and Michelle Wu stood above Jack who lay writhing in his bed in the ICU at Van Nuys Hospital.

"Bad?" Oscar said.

"Only when I breathe," Jack said. "It's like having a snake coiling 'round your lungs."

Michelle Wu smiled and took his hand.

"That's my Jackie. Always good for a laugh."

"Yeah," Jack said. "I'm a laugh riot. Ohhh, man . . . Trust me, having this shit in you ain't funny."

"Yeah, I know," Oscar said. "But the doc said we got you in here in time. Just takes a while for the antivenom to work. You know what the guy told me? They used to make it out of rattlesnake venom, but now they make the stuff out of hens' eggs."

"Fascinating," Michelle said. "You ought to go on freakin' *Jeopardy* or something."

"Whatever," Jack said, writhing in pain again as his stomach cramped. "I just hope the hens' eggs do their thing soon, 'cause this is definitely not great."

Michelle held Jack's hand tighter and he looked up at her with gratitude and a certain amount of surprise.

"You saved my butt tonight," he said. "I won't forget it."

"Yeah," Michelle said. "I surprise myself sometimes."

"I wasn't going to bring that up," Jack said. "But maybe you surprised me, too."

Michelle smiled and looked slightly befuddled.

"Thing is, I blew a perfectly good gig saving you, Jackie. Now that Timmy's dead, my singing gig at the Valentine Club will go down the tubes. I mean, what's getting into me? I might be getting morals or something in my old age."

"I doubt that," Jack said. "Anyway, I want you to know that I'm grateful."

Though another wave of nausea and cramps shot through his stomach, he managed a smile at her.

She smiled back and then leaned over the bed and kissed Jack on the cheek.

Just then a voice came from the back of the room.

"Well, what do we have here, a party?"

Jack looked over Michelle's shoulder and saw Julie Wade standing in the doorway. She smiled at Oscar and glanced briefly but with maximum hostility at Michelle, then pushed past her to Jack's bedside.

"Oscar called me at home," she said.

She leaned over and gave him a kiss on his lips. Behind her, Michelle Wu suddenly seemed to find something very interesting to look at on the ceiling. In spite of their problems, Jack was overjoyed to see her. She looked stunning in a pink cashmere sweater and a short black skirt.

"Hey, baby," Jack said.

"I was going to pick up Kevin," Julie said. "But then I thought that I didn't know what kind of shape you'd be in, so I left him at Charlie's place. He's sitting in the back room playing video games on Charlie's computer."

Jack managed a smile. "That was smart, but I'm going to be okay. They tell me I need to spend the night—that's all."

"Don't worry," she said. "I'll take care of Kevin."

"Yeah," Jack said. "That's fine."

She hugged Jack again, then stood up and looked at Oscar.

"Do I have you to thank for saving Jack?"

Oscar shrugged and pointed at Michelle Wu.

"Not really. If Michelle hadn't called me, things might have turned out a lot differently."

Julie turned to Michelle and did her best to look grateful.

"Michelle Wu?" she asked.

"Yes, and you must be the fabulous Julie Wade," Michelle said. The contempt and jealousy in her voice were barely hidden.

Lying there in bed, Jack suddenly felt an intense discomfort that had nothing to do with his snake and gila bites.

"Jack tells me you're an invaluable asset," Julie said. "I want to thank you for saving his life."

"It was nothing," Michelle said. "It was a slow Sunday night, and I didn't have anything better to do."

Julie managed a small, dismissive laugh as Michelle reached down in front of her and caressed Jack's cheek.

"Oh, you're hot," she said. "Somebody better cool you down, baby."

She looked directly at Julie as she spoke, then turned and gave Oscar a kiss on the cheek.

"Take care of him," she said. "He's my favorite Fed."

Then she turned and walked swiftly across the hospital room and out the door.

Oscar laughed. "What a woman!" he said.

He looked at Jack and Julie, who were now staring into one another's eyes, as if they'd just met.

"Okay," Oscar said. "I think it's time for me to head home to *mi casa*."

Jack smiled at him warmly. "Thanks, partner, I owe you. Tomorrow we've got a lot to talk about."

Oscar smiled and squeezed Julie's arm. Then he turned and walked out of the room.

Julie sat down in the chair at Jack's bedside.

"Sorry I messed up, baby," Jack said.

Julie squeezed his arm. Touched his cheek.

"I love you, kiddo," Jack said.

"Me, too," Julie said.

"I know I've been too much into my work," Jack said. "But you're going to be number-one part of the time. From now on. 'Cause I can't afford to have you leave me, baby. No way."

He opened his arm and Julie hugged him tightly.

But inside she was filled with doubt.

33

KYLE HAD LOST all track of time. All he knew was that he and Mike had almost gotten out of their bonds—twice—only to be slapped down by the bearded man, their lives threatened.

Mike had been reduced to a ball of fear. He rolled over on his side, like he'd given up.

But Kyle wanted out.

He had been scraping his ropes against the old rusted pipes for hours. And worked his way through one of them. The problem was there were three more to go.

Still, he had no choice.

The guy had looked at them with such hatred the last time.

And then smiled his pitiless smile, which said more than any words about what he was planning for them.

They were going to be dead soon. He knew it.

Both of them with their throats slit, or bullets in their brains.

And they didn't even know why.

Who would have anything against them?

Yeah, who?

And not only that, whoever it was . . . who would have the nerve to do anything against his family?

Who would have the balls?

Not that it mattered now. He had to get out. Had to.

Tears rolled down his face as he scraped the ropes harder and harder against the old rusted boiler pipes.

The sons of bitches. They'd all pay. When they got out and told their dad, the assholes would wish they had never been born.

34

JACK STAYED IN THE hospital for two days, watching his swollen arm rise and fall as if someone had inflated it, then deflated it with an invisible bicycle pump. His stomach felt as though it had been put through a wringer, and he had dreams of snakes attacking his legs, sinking their fangs into his ankles.

By the time he was released from the hospital, he felt a serious need to hit somebody.

He had the information concerning what he thought was Blakely's Mason Security account but when he investigated it, he found that it was a Cayman Islands account and that it was protected by laws which even the federal government couldn't touch.

As for Blakely's wife, Val, she swore she knew nothing about it, and unfortunately Jack believed her. Zac had always been secretive . . . and Jack doubted that Zac would have let Val in on something that could potentially mean trouble for her.

Hughes's ex-wife, Leslie, knew nothing, either, and he had no children. Chances were he was going to use the money for his retirement in either Mexico or Portugal. Jack found travel brochures for both places on his office computer.

He remembered Forrester's Little Cayman account, too. So there they were, three dirty cops, but he still had no ideas how all of that connected to Steinbach or Witness Protection.

And he still couldn't recall the old case—if it even existed—that seemed to haunt his dreams.

It was maddening . . .

The thought that one of them might actually get away with killing federal agents, that he might walk out of the whole thing . . . that he might even become a hero if he happened to tell Homeland Security something that led them to terrorists . . . well, that was too much. If that happened, Jack thought, there was no freaking justice left in the world.

And for all his cynicism, Jack didn't want to believe that. No matter how lousy he felt, with some of the poison still in him, he had to get back out there. Do the next step, which meant finding Jesse Lopez.

So, two days after he was taken home, Jack was back at work. And ready to visit the car designer who had just gotten back from a weeklong trip to T.J.

Lopez lived out in the desert, near Borrego Springs. The place where the wildflowers bloomed.

Jack and Oscar drove there on a bright, sunny day, down Route 15 through Orange County. Jack was still in pain and half out of it on Vicodin. As they drove into the desert, Jack found himself obsessed with finding Jesse Lopez, considered maybe breaking his arm if he didn't talk.

Oscar, on the other hand, seemed to be taking the drive like a car trip, a mini-vacation.

"You been down here before, Jackie?" he said as he drove.

"No . . . to San Diego, yeah. But never Borrego Springs."

"Ahh, you gonna love it, man," Oscar said. "They got bighorn sheep down here with antlers like you wouldn't believe. And they got mule deer, and kit foxes . . . and the sunsets are amazing. Makes you feel alive, Jack."

Suddenly Jack was annoyed by Oscar.

"You know," he said. "We're going down there to get this fucking skell Lopez, a guy who is involved in killing federal agents, Osc. It ain't like we're having a freaking holiday."

Oscar smiled and shook his head. "I know that, Jack. But, just the same, this is a beautiful place. Big freakin' state park, with all kinds of animals. You know they used to have a real nightlife down here, too. Sinatra and Dean Martin and Peter Lawford and all their chicks used to party down here. Amazing, man."

"Yeah," Jack said, moodily. "Freakin' amazing. Ring a fucking ding ding."

Oscar shook his head and sighed.

"You can't let this get to you, Jack. We're gonna get the guy."

"Oh, I know that," Jack said. "You can be sure of that."

He felt the ache in his arm where the gila had sunk its teeth in deep. Oh, yeah, he was going to get them all right . . . if he could just figure out who the fuck he was after.

And he'd had another thought, just five minutes ago.

What of Tommy Wilson? Why had Tommy moved over to the DEA? He said it was just an opportunity. But that opportunity had resulted in Steinbach being taken out of their hands and put into Homeland Security. And it had resulted in him getting freaking immunity.

And why had Tommy seemed so gleeful about it? And furthermore, what kind of information had Steinbach given to his new protectors?

That might not be easy to find out, but Jack had to try. Because what if Tommy Wilson had been bought off, too? What if his happy new smile had been bought and paid for by the bad guys? Steinbach? Or someone even higher than Steinbach?

Because, the more Jack thought about it, why would Steinbach go through all this shit, unless he had to?

Maybe that was the key question. The one they hadn't asked.

Why had a millionaire diamond smuggler gotten caught, put into Witness Protection, and threatened the agents' lives if he didn't have to?

Yeah, maybe Jack and Oscar had caught him, but what if they hadn't? It was crazy, but what if *he* had *let* them catch him?

That was crazy. Where could such thinking take them?

It was like a drawing of concentric circles with no end in sight . . . and the thought of it all hurt Jack's head worse than the residue of poison still in his system.

Up ahead of them there was a fork in the road. Jack stared down at his Thomas Guide.

"Looks like we take a left. Down Frying Pan Road."

"Frying Pan Road," Oscar said, laughing. "I like that name. Very laid back."

"Yeah, real homey," Jack said. "Just the good old cozy kinda place where you could have a meth lab. Or maybe contract killers live. Hey, maybe you could buy a place down here and smell the wildflowers with them every year."

Oscar nodded his head.

"Yeah, that sounds real nice, Jack. You know, you're starting to turn into a bitter and resentful kinda cop. Those are the kind that don't appreciate their blessings and end up eating their gun. I hope that don't happen to you, Jackie."

"Yeah," Jack said. "I got so much to be happy about."

"You do. A great kid, a wonderful girlfriend."

"I'll give you the kid," Jack said. "I'm not so sure about Julie."

"Cut it out, man. She's beautiful, and she loves you and Kevin."

"I don't know," Jack said. "It was great she came to the hospital, but she's very delicate, Osc. I'm not sure she can handle being a cop's wife."

"Yeah, sure," Oscar said. "Sylvia acts that way sometimes, too. But that's because I'm getting all wired up in a case. When I start bringing that kind of stuff home with me and get all jumpy, it changes how she feels. She starts to worry I'm going to go nuts or I don't love her anymore. So she starts to . . . you know, withdraw . . ."

Jack felt his skin crawl.

"Man, you're talking just like some fucking shrink. That's what it is, right? You go to the shrink, then you attend the freaking AA meetings, and you start talking like you're some Mexican textbook."

"Fuck you," Oscar said, without raising his voice at all. "Don't lay that shit on me. You don't take any fucking responsibility for shit, Jack. A woman has got to believe you want her. You got to take care of her. They say all this shit about being independent, but that's not how they are. They need to be spoiled a little. All of 'em."

Jack started to snap back at Oscar for no reason at all. He knew his partner was right, that he hadn't taken care of Julie at all lately, that he hadn't really been there for Kevin, either. Charlie Breen was more of a dad to Kevin than he was. Just like Julie said.

But he couldn't stand hearing about it just now. He was wired, thinking about Lopez, feeling like a coiled rattler ready to strike.

He looked out at the desert, the parched landscape, and thought that once he was as tough as one of the cactuses, but not anymore. He was prickly, but somebody had chopped him off at the roots . . .

"There," Oscar said, pointing down the road. "There's our boy."

Jack shielded his eyes and looked a half block down the dirt road.

A shabby-looking, weather-beaten sign said: Borrego Springs Car Repair. Proprietor J. Lopez.

"Let's do it!" Jack felt an electric current cut through his arms and chest. Thoughts of Julie and Kevin and his home miseries faded away . . .

This is what he lived for, he thought. Moments like this, when you could take the assholes down. Something solid you could do like a man, losing yourself in pure action.

He checked his revolver under his jacket and took a deep breath as Oscar pulled into the dusty parking lot.

Jesse Lopez was working on a Lincoln Navigator SUV in his steaming tin-roof shed with a big window fan blowing on him. He was a sleek-looking man with jet black hair, somewhere in his early thirties. His shirt was open down to the third button, revealing a muscular chest. His arms were cut as well, suggesting to Jack that he'd spent a lot of time in the weight room in his four years in Chino State Prison.

He looked up from the engine and wiped his face with a greasy rag.

"Help you gentlemen?"

Jack flashed his badge.

"Jack Harper, FBI. This is my partner, Agent Oscar Hidalgo. We'd like to ask you a few questions."

Lopez blinked wearily and picked up a bottle of water. He took a long sip, then nodded to them.

"So ask."

"First of all, we want to know about a certain $50,000 check you received from a man named Andreen on April 27 of this year."

"He gave me a check to customize his car."

"Fifty grand for a customizing job?" Oscar said. "You put wings on it or what?"

"That's funny," Lopez said. "But that's what it costs to do the kind of work he was looking for."

"What kind is that?" Jack said, moving a step closer.

"Well, that isn't for me to say. See, he wanted the work done privately, which is one of the reasons he came to me."

Jack stepped around the bumper of the car until he was six inches away from Lopez.

"Let me ask you a question, Jesse. You think we would come all the way out here to talk to you in this heat if we wanted to fuck around?"

Lopez glared at Jack directly in the eyes. He didn't look the least intimidated.

"I don't know why you came out here. But what I did for Mr. Andreen is *his* business, not yours. I don't gotta tell you jack-shit what kinda work I did."

"Technically, no," Jack said.

He grabbed Lopez by the throat and kicked him in the balls. Lopez squawked and fell to his knees.

"You're gonna tell me," Jack said. "You're gonna tell me all about the shootings of the two cops, or you're gonna end up in the fucking lethal-injection chamber."

He squeezed the mechanic's Adam's apple until he fell over on his side, gasping and gagging.

Finally he looked up at Jack, his eyes bloodshot and watering.

"You're out of your mind. *What* cops?"

"The ones you got $50,000 to fucking kill," Jack said. "Feds.

You're not walking away from this, Jesse. We already looked at your record. Two ten-year bits for armed robbery. Suspect in two gang slayings. Nobody is going to get you out of this one."

Jesse Lopez pulled himself up and spat out blood on the floor.

"I didn't kill any cops. I did a job for Mr. Andreen's car. Or maybe his boss's car . . . I don't know the guy's name, but he sort of said it was for some other guy."

Oscar came up to him and straightened out his spit-mottled shirt.

"What did you do for his car?" he asked.

"I made some secret compartments for it, that's all. He said he was in a dangerous business and he had to use the car to transport valuables. So I made two secret compartments in it. One on the undercarriage and one in the roof . . . It was a convertible and I made it in the back, next to the retractable roof motor. Small compartments. I don't know what he was transporting, but unless you knew, you would never find either of them."

Jack grabbed Lopez's arm and twisted it behind his back.

"You fucking lying sack of shit! I know you took that money for killing two cops. I know it. We're going to take you to a place that makes fucking Guantánamo look like a picnic. Tell me now. The truth, shithead."

Lopez screamed in pain and cried out:

"You're nuts! I didn't do a damned thing. I fixed his car, and I sold one to some buddy of his. That's all I did."

"Who was he?" Jack said, pulling out his revolver. "Tell me now, Jesse, 'cause I'm losing it."

"Wait . . . wait," Lopez said. "I had an old Jaguar I picked up down here cheap. I sold it to him for a price . . . 'cause Andreen asked me to help him out. Guy's name was on the bill of sale. It was Wilson. Thomas Wilson."

Jack let him fall to the floor in a heap.

"Tommy Wilson," Oscar muttered.

Jack felt as if the blood was leaving his head.

"Let me see that bill of sale—now!"

Lopez staggered to his feet and walked over to a greasy-looking file cabinet in the corner. He opened it slowly and went to the back, looked under the Ws. A second later, Jack had the bill of sale in his hand, with Tommy Wilson's signature at the bottom.

"We shoulda seen it with Tommy," Oscar said. "If Zac Blakely and Hughes were bought off, then it only makes sense they'd get to Tommy, too."

"Yeah," Jack said as they drove through fields of bright yellow flowers. "Of course. How could we not see that? He's got them all paid off. But if that's the case, why did he get arrested? That's the question we haven't asked yet."

Oscar looked as though someone had hit him in the face.

"You mean he *wanted* to be arrested?"

"I don't know," Jack said. "But think about it. Two of the guys who arrested him were guys on his own payroll. So why didn't they tip him off before we arrested him?"

"Jesus, Jack, we already talked about this. You had him on the diamond thing, and Blakely and Hughes couldn't tip him or they would give away their own crimes. They *had* to let him get caught. So now Wilson gets bought, and he gets Steinbach moved to the Homeland Security side of things . . . where he can help him out."

"Okay," Jack said, as they hit a massive three lanes of traffic near Long Beach. "Then riddle me this, Batman . . . if it goes like you said it does, then why are Blakely and Hughes killed?"

"Because," Oscar said, "they didn't tip Karl off. He did it to send a message to all the other people he has on his payroll. 'Cross me and you'll get this.'"

"That's where I don't get it," Jack said. "It makes sense,

yeah . . . but to do it in the open this way, to say you're going to kill federal agents and then do it, and think you can get away with it . . . that's the work of another guy. Karl is a blowhard sometimes, but he was always very careful in his dealings. That's why it took us so long to get undercover with him, right? He had us checked and rechecked. At any time in that process, Blakely or Hughes could have tipped him that we were agents."

"But you're forgetting something, Jackie," Oscar said. "Blakely and Hughes weren't in the mix with us until the end of the case, not at the start. They didn't know what our assignment was until later in the game, when we were only a month or so away from springing the trap. Then, if they'd tipped him, it would have been obvious."

"No, Oscar. That's where you're wrong. Even that late, they could have let him know and blamed it on one of his guys."

Oscar shook his head.

"Too risky," he said. "They had to play it out."

"And then a subtle, smart operator like Karl Steinbach deals with this whole thing by telling us he'll kill us and does it, and gets away with it? I don't buy it."

Oscar looked out at the huge oil derricks which lined the 405 like rusted robots.

"There's only one thing wrong with your idea there, Jack."

"What's that?"

"He *is* getting away with it. We got nothing on him at all. Every step we've taken has just led us to another dead end."

"That's right," Jack said. "And that's why this is all starting to feel as though it's been scripted. How could he have set all this up so fast? And one more thing, Osc . . . If he hates us all so bad, how come nobody has tried to kill me or you yet? I'm telling you, Steinbach is not the guy. Not the *top* guy. He's a player in all this, yeah, but there's somebody above him. Somebody who made him play this game."

239

"I don't know, Jack. That's paranoid. Maybe you got too much snake venom roiling round inside you."

Jack laughed as they turned onto the 10 Freeway and headed toward Westwood.

"Yeah, well, look at it, Oscar. Wilson is involved. He gets Stein-bach out of it, almost instantly. It feels like a setup. So what you and me are going to do now is put our own little tail on Tommy Wilson. And dig this, old pal: I think what you said about the case really being about whomever it is they're trying to get to in Witness Protection . . . that is starting to make more sense. That's what all this is leading to, somehow. I can feel it."

"Yeah, I'm a genius for thinking that," Oscar said. "But who *is* the muther?"

Jack shook his head.

"Remember the other night when you told me to think about all the old Witness Protection cases?"

"Yeah. You come up with one?"

"Sort of. But it makes no sense. Still, there's something strange there. Thing is, it was a case so long ago, I can't really remember all the details. Did you come up with anything?"

"*Nada,*" Oscar said. "But tell me about your case."

"That's the problem. It was one of my first cases, and I don't really know how it all came out. I gotta dig deeper. Probably nothing, anyway."

"So can you remember what it was?"

"Not all of it. But there's something there—it's like a picture that hasn't quite been developed yet."

"You think it's got something to do with this case?"

"Maybe . . . Fuck, I don't know. But if it does I'll let you know. Now let's go see *Mr.* Wilson."

35

AFTER MAKING A COUPLE of quick calls, Jack and Oscar found out that Tommy Wilson was at his home, a condo in Playa Del Mar, just two blocks from the beach. A place where the rents and condo prices were pretty steep for a cop. They waited a half block down the street from the place, the salt ocean smell in the air, both of them more than a little worried.

"What do you think Tommy did with his new car?" Oscar said.

"He's got it stowed somewhere. Probably with another house and another life."

"I never figured him for a sellout," Oscar said.

"Yeah," Jack said. "I remember when we met him. Young, gung ho. Wanted to save the world."

"Yeah," Oscar said. "I wonder how it happens."

"How what happens?"

"How a guy like that goes from wanting to save the world to wanting to own it."

Jack shook his head and looked through his binoculars again.

The door to Tommy's bungalow swung open and he came out, dressed to kill.

"Check out Mr. *GQ*," Jack said. "Man, those aren't fed clothes."

He handed the glasses to Oscar, who watched Tommy walk down to his Chevy Trailblazer.

"Maybe he's going to meet the man," Oscar said.

"Yeah," Jack said. "But *which* fucking man?"

He started the car. They waited until Tommy backed out of his driveway and made the turn onto Olympic Boulevard, then, following a couple of car lengths back, they tailed him east to Fairfax.

"Heading toward the 10," Jack said.

"Yeah," Oscar said. "Going east. Downtown."

They roared out onto the Santa Monica Freeway and followed Tommy in the dense traffic. He exited on the Hollywood Freeway and quickly got off at Hill Street. Jack cursed as they were cut off by an *L.A. Times* truck.

"You see him?"

Oscar hung out of the car, trying to see around the huge truck, which blocked their view.

"Yeah, I see him. Turn at the next street. There . . . See him?"

"No, where?"

"Not on the street. He's pulling into the underground parking garage at the Mark Taper Theatre. See, to your left. He's the second . . . no, the third car in line."

"Tommy is going to a play?" Jack said, with a laugh. "Who would have thought Tom was a patron of the arts?"

"Get over, quick," Oscar said.

With a blast of his horn and a squeal of brakes, Jack cut off a Mercedes and managed to pull into the parking line.

"Wonder what we're going to see," Oscar said.

"What difference does it make?" Jack said.

"Well, I never been to a play before," Oscar said. "I just wondered if my first experience of the dramatic arts is going to be life changing."

Jack laughed, but his stomach churned. Up ahead he could barely see the Trailblazer as it turned left in an effort to find a parking space.

Having not shaved, covered in road dust, and smelling like two wildebeests from the heat, Jack and Oscar looked seriously out of place in the L.A. theater crowd. Jack waited until he saw Wilson go inside, and then flashed his FBI card to the youthful female usher, who tried to look bored.

"There's some kind of trouble here, sir?" she said.

"None at all," Jack said. "But it's high-security. We need to be in there now."

"I'm supposed to call my manager on something like this," she said.

"You do that and we lose our guy," Oscar said. "Please let us in now, and you'll be doing your country a great service."

"Yeah," the girl said, suddenly standing her ground. "Like what . . . spying on left-wingers, or . . . maybe feminists. I happen to know that Gloria Steinem is in the audience tonight. She's come with Ellen De Generes. Is that who you're hunting for? A couple of feminists you can harass?"

"Come on." Jack smiled. "If you don't move out of the way soon, I'll miss the opening act."

"If you hurt Ellen, I'm going to call *60 Minutes*," the girl said. "My uncle knows Andy Rooney."

"Yeah, well, *my* uncle is Mister Ed," Jack said. "Now please move before I have to arrest you and ship you and Ellen to a secret FBI torture camp in Iraq."

"Very funny, Fascist-police-state asshole!" she said.

But she edged away from the gate, though barely enough for Jack and Oscar to squeeze through.

They headed up the marble steps and went through the golden doors to the gleaming theater. Oscar took a playbill from an usher and examined it.

"*The Maze*," he said. "The Tony Award–winning play about a man in a labyrinth of his own making. Sounds good, huh, Jack?"

Jack was going to come back with a wisecrack, but suddenly the description of the play sent a chill through his chest. He wasn't sure why, but there it was: cold, unrelenting, and somehow familiar. Like the case he'd been involved with so many years ago. A case that was coming back to him now . . . but surely that could have had nothing to do with . . . No, it couldn't . . . That made no sense at all. And yet . . .

"Jack, come on," Oscar urged.

Jack followed his partner to their seats but he felt as though he was already in some other place, watching a private play unfolding in the dark theater behind his eyes. He told himself to calm down, using his binoculars to scan the audience for Tommy Wilson.

Oscar stood still, ostensibly doing the same, but for a few seconds he was overwhelmed by the cacophony of noises, the orchestra tuning up, the sound of muffled voices and nervous coughing. The stage looked strangely appealing and scary simultaneously.

"Wow," he said. "This is something. I gotta start getting into plays."

"Try looking for Tommy, Mister First Nighter," Jack said.

"I already found him, wise guy," Oscar said. "Third row, fourth seat in."

Jack looked through his binoculars and, sure enough, there he was, sitting by himself, clutching his Playbill in his hand.

He smiled like a happy kid going on a school trip.

Jack sat down next to Oscar at the end of the row, where he could keep an eye on Wilson.

"It's gotta be a meet of some kind," Jack said. "And when we find out who, maybe we finally get somewhere."

Jack sat back and, though he was tense, as soon as the house-lights were turned off, he shut his eyes and fell back into his own little theater.

He saw a bank being held up. Men wearing Addams Family masks racing out of the bank. He saw them turn and shoot a bank guard, point-blank. The guard fell backward, blood spattering his shirt. He saw one of the masks slip as one of the robbers tripped and fell in the street. A ferret-faced little hustler named Billy Chase . . .

As the play opened, Jack blinked, looked up at the stage. He began to feel something like panic shooting through his chest. There was something happening inside of him that made him break out in a clammy sweat.

He shut his eyes and saw another bank robbery . . . and this time there was more shooting, more deaths. Cops shot, a witness . . .

He opened his eyes, afraid to see any more. This could have nothing to do with the current case. Nothing . . . except it was the only other person he knew who had ever been put into Witness Protection.

Nah, forget it. He had to keep his eyes on Tommy Wilson.

Jack wiped the sweat off his brow and tried to keep up with the play on the stage and not the scenes which seemed to be jarred from his memory. It seemed to be about a guy who, due to his own pride, chooses the wrong son to take control of his business, an oil company in Oklahoma. There were loud speeches, and at the end of the first act, the hero had been voted out of the company he started.

Things were looking bad for the hero, who was considering suicide until he met a woman, Faye, at a flophouse, and fell in love with her.

At that point the play took on a whole new meaning for both Jack and Oscar. Not because of the writing, which was melodramatic and over the top, but because of the actress playing Faye.

The two agents turned and looked at one another, both of them speaking at once.

"That woman . . ."

"Faye . . . You know who that is?"

Jack looked down at the Playbill and saw the actress's name.

"Alison Baines plays the part of Lake."

"Alison Baines?" Jack said, stunned.

"Man," Oscar said, "I could have sworn that her name was Maria Vasquez."

Jack felt something twisting inside his gut. The e-mails from Chile, saying how well she was doing. The refusal to go into the Witness Protection Plan.

He watched her on the stage as she and the fallen hero convincingly planned their revenge on the hero's evil sons.

"She's a hell of an actress, isn't she, *mi hermano*?" Oscar smiled.

"Yeah," Jack said. "She ought to win an award. Wonder if they give any out in the Sybil Brand Pen for Women?"

He slid out of the row and walked around to the far side of the theater, then zeroed in on Tommy Wilson.

As Tommy watched the sexy, moving actress Alison Baines, his face lit up like a man in love.

. . .

The play, though hammy, was a tremendous success; the cast came back for three curtain calls.

Finally, as people poured out of the theater, Jack and Oscar followed Tommy Wilson stage right, lingering behind him as he made his way down the steps toward the dressing rooms beneath the stage.

They watched from the shadows at the end of the hall as Wilson rapped on Alison Baines's dressing-room door. A second later, he was admitted.

"Let's go," Jack said.

"Shouldn't we buy her some roses first?" Oscar said. "They always do that in the movies."

"Nah, that's a cliché gift," Jack said. "We have something a lot nicer to offer her. About fifteen by thirty in a very cozy little condo."

Jack turned the knob and found it open. He and Oscar walked inside with their guns drawn.

Alison Baines was sitting up on her dressing-room table, her long, bare legs wrapped around Wilson's waist. She was looking over his shoulder, and when she saw her latest guests, she gasped.

"You!"

Wilson turned around, in shock:

"What the hell is going on here . . . ," he said. But the rest of the sentence died in his throat.

"Tommy, and the fabulous 'Maria,'" Jack said. "How good to see you both here."

"Yeah," Oscar said. "I never been to a play before and I really liked it. You were real good, Miss Baines. But I thought you played the other role—Maria—even better."

"Yeah," Jack said. "You had Maria Vasquez down cold."

The two lovers managed to pry themselves apart.

"I can explain all this," Tommy said. "Alison was working for me undercover. We were going to tell you, but then you busted Karl Steinbach so there was no need to."

"That's right," Alison said, lighting a cigarette. "We decided we'd keep the cover alive."

"So we could use it again, if we had to. But now that Alison's acting career has taken off with the play, we obviously won't be using her anymore. The truth is, Jack, that once we started working together, we fell in love, and we're going to be married next June. So why don't you put your gun away. It's making Alison nervous."

Jack shook his head slowly.

"Isn't this a touching story, Oscar?" he said.

"Yeah, Jackie," Oscar said. "I love seeing people in love. You know who else used to be a sentimental kind of guy—though you wouldn't have known it from the way he acted?"

"Who's that?" Jack said.

"Zac Blakely," Oscar said. "He was a real sucker for romance. Ron Hughes, too. You gonna invite them to your wedding, Tommy?"

Wilson bit his lower lip and let out a deep sigh.

"I had nothing to do with any of that," Wilson said. "I was really sorry about that, but it wasn't my responsibility."

"No?" Jack said. "Well, how come you bought a Jag from Jesse Lopez down in Borrego Springs?"

"I don't know what you're talking about," Wilson said.

"No?" Jack said. "That's a pretty nice pad you have down in Playa, too. I wonder, you loan it out for parties to your pal Steinbach? Or maybe it's Forrester you're hanging with?"

"I won that money in Vegas, playing poker," Wilson blustered.

"Lucky you!" Jack said sarcastically. "Cut the shit, Tom. I already got three people working on your secret bank accounts and your other houses. You better make a deal as fast as you can, 'cause you're going to be looking at life in San Quentin for conspiring to kill two federal agents."

Wilson's eyes seemed to glaze over, as if he'd just taken a pill that had strange side effects.

"Look, Jack, you got this all wrong."

"And *I* didn't know anything about it," Alison Baines said. "I was just hired to play a part. I was just an out-of-work actress."

"Yeah," Jack said. "You fed me stuff so we could catch Karl, but you had no idea what was going on. Uh-huh. That's such patent bullshit that I don't think even O.J.'s jury would buy it."

"I didn't know anything," Alison Baines said as tears ran from her eyes. "They just fed me a script, and I delivered the lines."

"And you had no idea why Karl Steinbach might have intended to be caught."

"No. It was like . . . a role in a play or a film. Say the lines, don't stumble over the furniture."

Oscar looked at Jack and laughed.

"You're going to be starring in a reality show soon, Maria. It's going to be called *Prison Cell,* and you're going to be playing the role for a long, long time, *señorita.*"

"But I didn't know anything," she protested. "Tommy got me in with Steinbach. I thought I was working for the DEA."

"Be quiet, Alison," Tommy warned. "Don't say another word to them."

"That's right, Alison. Listen to him. It's really worked out well for you so far," Jack said. "You didn't know about Tommy getting Steinbach out of jail by getting him a fake immunity? You didn't help scam the FBI on the investigation of two dead officers? I think you're going to have a very hard time proving that, especially since we caught you here together. You're going away for twenty years, kid. I'll personally see to it."

Alison Baines began to cry.

"But I have a hit play!" she whimpered.

"Don't do that to her, Jack. She's clean," Wilson said.

"Why not?" Jack said. "Give me a reason. Tell me why Steinbach wanted to get busted. Why you got him out. I finally see this more clearly, pal. You two did this to cover up something else. Something that involves Witness Protection. Something that maybe still isn't finished. I want to know what the fuck it is, Tommy."

Sweat dripped down Tommy Wilson's neck, like a man having a heart attack.

"All right . . . Steinbach reached out to me."

"Reached out how?"

"He said he needed to get busted. But he also needed a way out of the bust. I told him the only way to get out was to get immunity, but he didn't have anything to offer. He didn't know shit about terrorist attacks. So I helped him figure a way out . . . he'd set up four Muslims, guys who we've been watching, and who might be involved with al-Qaeda. They talked a lot of revolutionary shit but weren't really going to do a fucking thing. We'd been looking for a way to bust them. They needed money to finance their plans, so we were going to put him in touch with them. He'd offer them the dough for political reasons. Then, when they tried to pull off their bombings, we'd nail them all."

Jack felt the same chill that bothered him before.

"And maybe you were going to kill a few of them, too, huh, Tom?"

"Maybe," Wilson said. "They're bad guys, Jack. We know that. What difference does it make if a couple of them catch a stray bullet or two? Everybody comes out ahead. Homeland Security is a hero, and Steinbach gets to go home with a medal."

"But why . . . why would he want to get busted in the first place?" Oscar said.

Wilson smiled and shook his head. "I don't know. Of course, I asked him about that. He said he owed a guy a favor. A big one. He had to pay the guy back."

"A favor?"

"Yeah, it sounded like bullshit to me . . . I tried to talk to him about it a couple of times. I was worried he was setting me up . . . but he wouldn't discuss it. Anyway, I know he hated Blakely and Hughes, but I don't believe he killed them."

"You *believe* he didn't kill them or you *know* he didn't?"

Wilson looked down at the ground.

"I'm not a hundred percent sure, but . . ."

"But what? It sounds like he played you for a sucker, Tommy. You gave him an out, and he killed them both. That makes both of you his accomplices."

"No, you're wrong," Wilson said. "And Alison didn't know anything."

"And how much did he pay you to give him that alibi, buddy?" Jack said.

"Nothing," Tommy said.

"Bullshit!" Oscar said. "We know Slick Tommy. He always gets paid some way."

"I'm not saying anything else until I have my lawyer," Wilson said. "Nothing."

"That's smart, Tom. Both of you are under federal arrest. Turn around. I gotta cuff you. "

"Oh, c'mon," Alison said. "You can't do this. It's opening night. There's a party I have to get to."

"Hey, you're gonna be having it, all right," Jack said. "But in a four-by-eight holding cell. And the other guests might not be from Beverly Hills, bitch. Turn around so I can cuff you."

Tommy Wilson started to turn but as Jack tried to get his handcuffs with his free hand, Wilson turned and chopped him in the neck. The Glock went off, discharging into the wall. Oscar reached for Wilson, but the actress reached out and raked his

251

face with her inch-long fingernails. Oscar fell back, blood dripping down his chin.

Wilson shoved by them both and made it to the door. In a second, he was gone. Oscar saw Alison Baines moving past him and hit her in the head with his right hand, sending her sprawling over a rattan chair and onto the floor. She moaned as she stood up, and Oscar pulled her arms behind her and clasped the cuffs.

Jack was up now and through the door. He ran down the hallway and up the stairs, but hit a wave of stagehands who were carrying a sofa down the stairs. He tried to get by them, but they stumbled and dumped the sofa down the stairs. He barely avoided it by jumping over the railing and rolling onto the floor.

By the time he'd gotten to his car, Jack saw Wilson pulling out of the gate and turning left. Headed toward the freeway, Jack thought, backing up and squealing his tires as his car roared through the gate and went up on two wheels as it screamed down the street.

Jack cut off a giant Cuervo Gold Tequila truck and nearly smashed into a local bus, but somehow reached the 101 Freeway, though he could barely see Wilson's car up ahead.

He drove like a madman, passing cars and trucks on the left and right, and several times going up on the right shoulder, almost hitting a sign which advertised NUDE NUDES. (What the hell were Nude Nudes, anyway?)

He screamed past the Echo Park exit, no sign of Wilson at all now.

"Shit!" he said. Wilson could have already gotten off the freeway. Where the hell could he be heading? Certainly not to his home, which was in the opposite direction.

· · ·

Up ahead of Jack, Tommy Wilson roared west down Sunset Boulevard, past Denny's Diner, past EAT, past the Hollywood ArcLight Theatre. He crossed Cahuenga and turned right at Schraeder, went past the Hollywood YMCA, and pulled up one block short of an ancient, battered rooming house called the Mark Twain Hotel.

Quickly getting out of his car, he hurriedly walked toward the front steps of the decrepit three-story building.

What looked like an old wino sat on the three crumbling front steps, but as Wilson started to pass him, he stood up and announced: "Sorry, sir, the hotel is being refurbished and is closed to the public."

Tommy reached into his pocket and showed the man his Homeland Security credentials.

"Sorry, sir," the man said.

"No problem. I need to see Baker right now."

"Second floor. Room 245. I'll tell them you're coming."

"Thanks," Wilson said as he swung up the steps and went through the badly warped front door.

Jack was stuck in traffic three or four feet in front of the turn-off at Sunset. Though he was frustrated, it gave him a chance to think . . . Where would Wilson go? Would he keep right on going out to the Valley? Did he have some kind of safe house out there in Studio City or Van Nuys?

It was possible. But what would be the advantage of going to ground now?

He was sure to be recognized once his picture got on the evening news and in the L.A. Times, not to mention flashed all over the Internet.

No, if Slick Tommy was going somewhere, it had to be an airport or a train station.

But LAX was in the opposite direction, and he'd passed right by the exit for Union Station.

So where was he headed?

To get money?

To see someone who could help smuggle him out of the country tonight?

Yeah, that made sense, but who might that person be?

Tommy Wilson walked up the termite-eaten steps of the Mark Twain Hotel. At the top floor there was another guard, this one an agent he knew: David Snyder, a man with a square head and an even squarer jaw.

"Tommy," Snyder said. "You want to see your boy?"

"Mmmmm-hmmm," Wilson said.

Snyder walked down the hall with him. At the end of the hall, something went squeaking across the floor.

"Rats," Snyder said. "Fitting, huh? We babysit a rat, and the other ones come by to pay their respects."

Tommy faked a laugh as Snyder rapped three times on the door, two longs and a short.

In a few seconds, the door opened, and Tommy was staring at Homeland Security Agent Booth Staller. Booth was a thin man with an even thinner rug on his head. The hair looked lifeless, like a couple of strands of damp vermicelli.

"Young Tom," Booth said.

"Boother," Tommy said, in what he hoped sounded like a collegial tone.

He looked across the room and saw a portable card table, and on it chips, playing cards, and Cokes.

At the table sat another agent, Lenny Carbon, a thin, sickly-looking agent who took endless medicines and cold remedies.

He waved in a depressed way and quickly took three green pills which were sitting out in a row next to his poker hand.

Steinbach sat at the end of the table facing Wilson. He looked rumpled, tired, and harried.

"Agent Thomas Wilson," he said. "What a rare pleasure to see you, sir."

"You ready to come through on your promises, Steinbach?"

Steinbach's face took on a quizzical look, as if to say, "But this wasn't the deal at all, Tom."

Still, he smiled and tried to assume an affable tone.

"Of course," he said. "Ready to go."

"I don't get it," Lenny Carbon said. "We're not supposed to meet with those guys until tomorrow."

"Yes, I know," Wilson said. "But there's been a slight change of plans. The Muslims want to go today. And they insisted that just Karl and I show up."

Now it was Booth Staller's turn to look doubtful.

"I've had no indications that this is so," he said. "No calls, no text messages, and no e-mails."

"Right," Tommy Wilson said. "That's how we decided to go with it. There's been some concern about the other side intercepting our messages. This is why I came to tell you the old-fashioned way—in person. The truth is, I've got to take Karl out right now. The meet is going to be at Musso's in two hours, and we need to rehearse what we're going to say."

"Take him where?" Lenny Carbon said, scratching his head.

"On a walk," Tommy Wilson said. "On a stroll around Old Hollywood, up and down the boulevard of broken dreams."

Carbon looked at Staller, and both of them frowned.

"No fucking way," Staller said. "Not unless we get it from HQ."

"But I've come from HQ," Wilson said. "Straight from the horse's ass."

"Maybe so," Carbon said. "But maybe not, too, Tom. This smells like old fish to me."

"That's good," Tommy said. "Tell you what? You make the call to HQ and see for yourself, okay?"

Carbon looked at Staller doubtfully, but took out his cell phone and began to punch in numbers.

"It's not that we don't believe you, Tom," Staller said. "But you'd think that the powers that be would have let us in on this little change of plans, ya know?"

"That is certainly true, Booth-baby," Tommy Wilson said, taking out his SIG Sauer automatic and shooting Staller in the forehead. Staller flew backward over a chair and ended up draped over the end of an old couch on the other side of the room.

Lenny Carbon dropped the phone and reached for his gun, but Karl Steinbach kicked his chair out from under him and he fell on his side. He got up quickly but not quite quickly enough, as Tommy Wilson shot him in the head as well.

He fell over on his side, blood pooling around his neck.

"Cry for help," Wilson said. "Loud."

Steinbach did as he was told and sent out a mighty yowl of pain.

"Help me!" he cried.

Tommy shook his head, but situated himself behind the door. He heard feet running toward the door, then a question:

"What's happening in there?" hissed David Snyder.

"They're all dead!" Steinbach answered.

"All of them?" Snyder said.

"Except me. They went crazy and shot each other. And I'm wounded."

Tommy heard the key put into the door.

The door opened and Snyder came in, training his gun on Steinbach, who sat in the middle of the room, cradling Lenny Carbon's bloody head in his hands.

"Jesus, Mary, and Joseph!" Snyder swore.

Then he noticed movement just behind him and turned. That was when Wilson shot him in the head.

He fell down to his knees, but his gun went off reflexively and a bullet landed in Tommy Wilson's left pec.

Tommy had spent years lifting weights to make himself have a washboard stomach and perfect pecs, and his first reaction to the terrible pain of the bullet was to think how lame he'd look in a bathing suit down at Muscle Beach this year. On the other hand, a bullet hole in his pec might draw some admiring glances from blond beach bunnies.

All of these vain thoughts took about three seconds. Suddenly Tommy was hit with a killer burning in the chest. It was as though someone had drilled a hole in him with a power drill, and for the first time he understood the term "drilling someone with a bullet." It was just like that . . .

He fell to one knee and gasped for breath.

When he looked up, he saw Karl Steinbach standing over him.

"The little fuck got me, Karl. Help me!"

Karl looked down at him and smiled curiously.

"What would you like me to do, Tommy? I mean, this is all so sudden!"

"I would like you to . . . help me up, get me out of here, then we go down to my car . . . and get to your private airplane. Then we fly the fuck out of here to South America, or wherever you can hide me."

At that moment, they heard feet running down the hallway.

"The outside guard, Karl," Tommy said.

The guard stopped, and they could hear him creeping forward to the room.

Karl almost started to laugh.

"Help, I've been shot," he said in a choked-up voice.

The guard came into the room, and Karl shot him in the stomach and then the face.

The guard fell back out into the hallway. Karl reached out and pulled him inside by his feet.

"The cops are going to be here real soon," Karl said to Tommy Wilson. "I don't think the two of us can make it. One person running, maybe . . . but two, one of them leaking blood like a bread-crumb trail . . . I don't think so."

"You're not thinking of leaving me, Karl," Tommy said. "Not with what I know."

Karl smiled, aimed his gun at Tommy. Tommy swiftly came up with his right hand and aimed as well, but then blushed as he realized he'd dropped his gun but had been too stunned to notice.

"Too bad you can't shoot anyone with your fingers," Karl laughed.

"I can *help* you," Tommy said.

"You *are* helping me," Karl said, and shot Tommy Wilson through the throat.

Tommy fell backward, then on his side like a twisted modern sculpture, blood gurgling from his neck wound like hot tomato soup on a cold winter's day.

Karl knelt down and riffled through Tommy's pockets. In a second he'd found his car keys, and a second later, his money clip. There was $200 in twenties and he took them, but left the clip. Then he stood up, looked around at the carnage for a second, stepped out into the hallway, closed the door, and ran toward the back exit, fast.

Jack had come down Sunset slowly. He'd had to make three calls before he'd been able to call in a favor and find out where the Homeland Security boys were stashing Karl Steinbach. When he heard the words "Mark Twain Hotel," he knew at once that was where Tommy was headed. Probably to grab Karl and head out to his airplane at the secret airport in Reseda.

What better bet? Then he'd have access to Karl's entire support group, could get himself a new passport, a new pile of cash, new clothes; Christ, even a new head if he wanted to.

Karl had everything Tommy needed. They'd probably both be armed and dangerous.

Except there was only one of them.

Jesus, he couldn't believe his luck!

He'd just pulled up past the Hollywood YMCA, was stuck behind a freaking Hummer with about twenty rappers inside of it playing their moronic music at decibel levels previously unknown to mankind, when he saw Karl Steinbach racing out of the side alley behind the Mark Twain Hotel, a revolver in his hand.

Steinbach ran up the street toward a car, opened it, and got in on the driver's side. For a second, Jack thought he was waiting for Tommy to come out as well, but there was no Tommy, and now the car was pulling out, headed up to Hollywood Boulevard.

Jack hit his horn, but the Hummer just stood there blocking the middle of the street.

He started to get out of the car when the driver of the Hummer, a huge black kid, got out first and walked back to Jack.

He looked in the window, a huge, beefy face with spaced-out *Dawn of the Dead* eyes.

He then rapped hard enough on the window to shake the car.

Jack opened it, and the massive rap fan stuck his face in the window.

"You got a beef with me, muthafucker?" the big man said.

"Absolutely not," Jack said. Then he whacked the man on the end of his nose with his gun butt.

The man howled and fell backward on the street. His nose was bleeding, and his dead eyes watering.

Two other men got out of the car. Their bodies were also huge and beefy, their clothes black, and Jack had the weird feeling that they were all one organism, just chopped into humongous steaks and then clothed with tents.

He flashed his badge and aimed his gun at the Hummer's tires.

"Three seconds," he announced. "That's how much time you got to get that freaking tank around the corner. Then I start shooting."

The two Beastie Guys leaped into the Hummer and quickly moved it out of the way.

Jack looked at the fat man, got back into his car, and roared up Schraeder toward Hollywood Boulevard.

He turned right at Hollywood and saw Steinbach roaring down the boulevard, passing cars on the wrong side of the street. When he got to Cahuenga, he made an impossible left turn and headed north.

Jack followed him, almost hitting a guy dressed like Spider-Man who was having his picture taken with two young girls.

The guy screamed at him and gave him the finger.

"Cocksucker!" the kid yelled. "Spider-Man hates you!"

Jack drove off the curb, back onto the street, and hit a yellow light at Cahuenga. He sped through it, his tires screaming as he followed Steinbach up past the Yo Yo Korean Doughnut Shop and Solarz's Red Noodle Heaven.

Steinbach was caught in the on-ramp at the 101 Freeway. The car in front of him was a roach coach called Pepe's Taco World. It had colorful Day of the Dead mannequins all over it, skeletons eating tacos and smiling with huge, dead-men's teeth.

The light said one car per green, and the Taco World driver was taking the light literally.

"Fucking moron Mexican asshole," Steinbach said. "Move, you asshole!"

The Mexican man stuck his head out the window, and yelled, "Eat shit, *gringo* fuckface!"

Steinbach reached for his gun. To be held back by a chubby Mexican in his death trap made him sick to his stomach. He could only imagine the roaches crawling over the three-day-old goat meat.

He thought briefly about shooting at the Mexican, but that would attract attention. Anyway, now the guy was pulling out into the traffic and giving him the finger again in the rearview.

Fifteen seconds later, Jack pulled up to the same on-ramp stoplight and completely ignored it, jammed the car into second gear, and careered crazily into the northbound 101 traffic.

He could see—anyway, he thought he could see—Steinbach up ahead of him, zigzagging through the afternoon traffic, almost hitting several other cars and causing pandemonium as he switched lanes maniacally.

Jack started after him, but after successfully maneuvering his way between two cars, he found himself stuck behind a school bus filled with raving rich kids from Harvard Westlake. They looked out the window and gave him the finger, while one boy mooned him and looked at him with his tongue out between his legs.

Jack crept along, unable to see around them.

Five miles up the road from the on-ramp is the Bruce T. Hinman Exchange. As Jack watched up ahead, he saw Steinbach bounce off a red Corvette and then bear left at the "Bruce," which is what police officers called it. That meant he was going for the 170, heading west.

Suddenly he had another idea. The name Bruce T. Hinman had dislodged something in his foggy brain. Hinman had helped him in something a long time ago. He was sure of it. The name had stuck in his memory. Bruce T. Hinman, a Valley motorcycle cop who had been killed chasing a drunken driver. Yeah, Jack remembered it all now. He'd even gone to Hinman's funeral. He knew him for sure . . . but how?

He turned left, got into the outside lane, and nearly ran into the concrete wall which divided the 101.

He saw Steinbach move up, then get cut off as he tried to get over to the left lane.

Jack stomped on the gas and cut over to the middle lane.

Bruce T. Hinman was rolling around in his mind.

Now he remembered. The Valley bank robberies. He and Hinman had run down one of the robbers.

He remembered it now.

The Adam Moore case. And there was the name he'd thought about at the play again—the little hustler Billy Chase.

He blinked, felt a panic, thought suddenly of Kevin, his son. He imagined someone stepping out of a shadow, shooting Kevin in the head.

"Bullshit," he told himself. "That's just fear talking."

And yet he couldn't get it out of his head.

Bruce T. Hinman, the officer who helped run down Chase.

Awww, Jesus, he couldn't believe it.

He saw it all in his head now.

The bank robberies, seven in a row in the Valley alone, and everyone knew it was Moore.

But how to get him? You couldn't get undercover, not with Moore. He used only guys he'd been tight with for fifteen or twenty years.

How to deal with him?

Jack looked out the window and realized that he'd almost lost sight of Steinbach. He had to get his shit together.

He saw Steinbach's car head to the far left, and for the first time, there was an empty stretch of cars between them.

Jack smiled.

Now he'd be able to take him. No trouble.

He gunned his car and, as the speedometer topped 125, he narrowed the distance between them.

He saw the next exit up ahead. Sherman Way.

Steinbach was going to try to take it, but Jack knew that he was moving much too fast. The turn there was a half circle, and steep . . .

Steinbach cursed himself for taking the 170. All the traffic on the 101 was his friend. He could keep a good line of cars between himself and Harper.

But once they went past the interchange . . . the traffic headed out to the West Valley disappeared. Eighty percent of it went to the right, out to the 101.

Yes, he could go faster on the 170, but unfortunately so could Jack.

And now the crazy bastard was gaining on him. God knew what he would do to him once he caught him.

He had to get off the freeway and onto Sherman Way, where the traffic would be heavy enough to get him lost again. Eventually he could take a side street, hide in the approaching dark, and make his escape.

It all depended on making this turn. If he could pull it off, he'd leave Agent Jack Harper far behind.

He hit the brakes and turned the car right, onto the approach road to Sherman Way Boulevard.

Jack watched Steinbach turn Tommy Wilson's Crown Vic right, onto the approach road.

He saw the car hit the turn at what must have been 100 miles per hour.

At first it looked as though he was going to make it. The car went up the ramp smoothly enough.

But then came the turn, a forty-degree angle and an upgrade which it just couldn't make.

Jack throttled down and watched in horror as Steinbach's car launched off the approach road and sailed through the air like a guided missile.

Only it was a guided missile that had turned sideways and that had never quite made it into full liftoff mode.

Instead, the car sailed over the rooftop of a warehouse which bore the words NOT TO PUBLIC on it, and then disappeared from Jack's view.

But not from his ears.

Jack heard a tremendous crash and saw a flash of light come from the other side of the warehouse.

As Jack made it around the cloverleaf, he could barely believe his own eyes.

There in front of him was an In and Out Burger Restaurant on fire, with people screaming and racing to their cars.

In the window of the In and Out was Karl Steinbach's getaway car, the hood inside the restaurant, nose down, like a fallen rocket ship.

The rest of the car was outside the restaurant, part of the trunk and back wheels resting on the hoods of two other cars parked outside while their owners went in for a burger and fries.

In the background, Jack could already hear the fire alarms and the sirens blasting.

Jack parked a half block away and started running toward the disaster. People were screaming. A woman walked away dazed, blood running down her face. A man crawled over what at first looked like frozen cigarettes to Jack. But upon closer inspection he realized they were piles of uncooked French fries. Jack made his way around the cars, over a field of broken glass, and climbed through the shattered window.

There was Karl Steinbach behind the wheel, his body mashed by an air bag. His left arm flopped out of the window.

Jack started to pull Steinbach out of the wreck, but suddenly the smuggler's eyes opened and he looked at Jack with a terrifying clarity.

He tried to speak, but a gob of blood shot from his mouth, like a melting red ball.

"Jackie, help."

"Okay," Jack said, trying to pry open the smashed door. "I gotcha."

But Steinbach shook his head slowly.

"Dead, Jack. All crushed inside."

Jack tried to open the door. But somehow Karl gathered his strength and put a finger on Jack's lips.

"Help," he said again. "Need you to . . ."

His words were interrupted by a terrible hacking cough, and more blood poured from his mouth.

"C'mon Karl. We can still get you help."

"No, no, you don't unnerstan'. You think . . . but . . . sons . . . and your kid . . ."

He looked as though he wanted to say more but his words were again cut short by a terrible, rasping cough, and then a seizing up of his body, as though it was trying to expel something inside it, but the very act itself would be his last.

He looked at Jack, tears rolling down his face, made a terrible sound from somewhere deep in his chest, and died.

Jack looked at him, at the imploring look in his eyes. Was

he trying to tell Jack something? Or was he just in shock, senseless?

Now he would never know.

Jack turned and hurried away.

When he'd made it to the end of the parking lot, Wilson's car exploded, blasting Karl Steinbach and a thousand hamburger patties throughout the purple sky, all the way across Burbank Boulevard.

PART III
TOTAL IMMUNITY

36

JACK AND OSCAR sat in the warmth of Charlie Breen's Deckhouse as the rain came down and the ocean waves crashed on
the beach.

Oscar held up his glass of Cuervo Gold.

"Well, personally, though maybe we haven't solved the case
yet, here's to the passing of Karl Steinbach, supreme creep and
all-around bad guy."

Behind the bar, Charlie Breen lifted his usual celebratory
glass of Newcastle.

"Yeah, fuck that creep . . . Steinbach . . . Here's to the good
guys!"

He clinked glasses with Oscar and both of them waited for
Jack to join them. But Jack was slow in picking up his own glass
of Sierra Nevada.

"Maybe we ought to wait a bit to toast this one," he said.

Oscar gave him a skeptical look and put his arm around Jack's
shoulders.

"I still don't know why Steinbach wanted to get arrested. And when he was dying, he said something about his kids. It was like he was trying to tell me something. And Kevin. He mentioned my son."

Oscar shook his head in disbelief.

"We'll check on his kids. But maybe he just wanted to say good-bye to them. I mean, even Karl was human enough for that."

"I guess," Jack said.

"He was desperate," Oscar said. "He was dying and he knew it. Didn't he say, 'I'm all broken up inside'?"

Jack sighed and opened his palms in a gesture of helplessness.

"Yeah, but he mentioned Kevin, too. I don't know . . ."

Behind the bar, Charlie took a swig of his Newcastle. And shook his head.

"Well, it's none of my business, but I tend to believe Oscar here. Look, the guy is dying. In shock. Probably has no idea what he's saying. And as far as Kevin goes, what the fuck can they do to him?"

"Yeah," Oscar said. "He just wanted to fuck with you one last time. And what better way than to bring up your son? 'My reach extends beyond the grave!'"

Jack laughed at Oscar's Bela Lugosi impersonation.

"All right. You're both probably right. Still . . . There are a lot of unanswered questions."

He thought to himself once again of smiling, blond-haired Billy Chase. The case from so long ago . . . but still didn't see how it could add up.

And there was still Agent William Forrester.

Though he still wasn't sure why.

"Okay," Oscar said. "I can see you're not convinced, so I'm going to give you the Oscar Hidalgo bread-and-butter fucking psychological test, used by all police headshrinkers in the known world."

Jack looked at Charlie and smiled.

"Okay, do it."

Oscar looked at him hard, his hazel eyes not wavering.

"What I am going to ask you is serious, okay? So I really want you to search your memory, and no fucking around."

"Yes, doctor," Jack said.

"Okay," Oscar said. "Is there anything—anything at all in your past, either professionally or personally—that could come back to haunt you?"

"Whoaaa!" Jack said. "You got all night?"

"No, I am serious as a heart attack," Oscar said. "Think it through."

"Personally, there's a lot of shit, of course," Jack said. "Stuff with my ex. Stuff going on right now with Julie. Maybe I didn't treat either of them right. Maybe I was too involved with my work. Maybe I am, as certain women have insisted I am, a self-ish male chauvinist pig."

"Okay," Oscar said. "Knowing that, is there anything in any of that . . . that could have somehow crossed over to your professional life. Stuff that somehow Steinbach knew so that he and anyone he works with or for could use against you?"

"Christ, I don't know."

"C'mon, Jackie. Think about it. We've been talking about something coming to get you, your son. So I figure it's gotta be something coming from your past, right? So whatever it is, somebody must carry a big fucking grudge. So think . . . Is there something that you did to somebody, wittingly or unwittingly, that is so heavy that they've set up this whole fucking thing? I mean all of it. Steinbach getting arrested, giving you the evil eye, and setting up the chick . . . what's her name, Maria?"

"Alison Baines?"

"Yeah, Alison Baines. And enlisting Tommy Wilson: the whole enchilada. In other words, somebody who is very fucking clever and hates your ass. Somebody who would like to bring you down. Plus, seriously fuck with your mind while they do it."

"Jesus!" Charlie said. "You're talking about some kind of Svengali."

"Maybe I am. Come on, Jack. If it ain't Karl Steinbach, then there's gotta be someone who has it in for you. Somebody who is smart, has the juice to collect people like this, and get them to do this whole freaking operation."

Jack looked at Oscar and nodded his head as he smiled.

"I can think of only one guy who has the brains, the juice, the opportunity," he said.

"Who's that?"

"Forrester," Jack said. "William Forrester. Who knows we are on to him, also knows that we're investigating him, and who hates my ass. Who would like me to fuck up professionally, and who would stop at nothing to bring me down, including making me worry about my son instead of doing my job. But does that really explain why Steinbach would say what he said about my son just before he died?"

"It could," Oscar said. "Maybe he was saying that Forrester was going to get your kid. Maybe he was saying that he was going to get his kids, too."

"Yeah, but why would Forrester want to hurt Kev?" Charlie said.

"Yeah, that doesn't make any sense," Jack said. "But outside of him, I don't know. There was this one case . . . a long time ago . . ."

"Really?" Oscar said.

"Yeah, but it doesn't add up. Not really. Still, if someone knew about it . . . I don't know. You think it's Forrester who is behind all this?"

"Why not? He was in the bank deal with Blakely and Hughes. He got cut out of the money, and now he thinks you and I have the dough."

"And somebody we put into Witness Protection?"

"I don't understand that part of it yet," Oscar said.

"Me either. We need to find that guy. I still think it'll all clear up once we do."

"Hey," Charlie Breen said. "Can we drink our goddamned booze now? The stuff is turning into turpentine."

Jack and Oscar laughed, lifted their glasses, and drank. Jack felt little satisfaction in it.

37

AS THE THREE GOOD friends inside Charlie Breen's Deckhouse clicked glasses and toasted the future capture of Supervising Agent William Forrester, Forrester himself sat outside in his 1992 Porsche Carrera. In his hand was his new Nikon camera, which he trained at the Deckhouse door.

He had been clicking away for the past two hours, pictures of Jack and Oscar heading into Charlie Breen's Deckhouse. And he would get more photos as they left the place. Maybe they'd even come out together. Maybe Charlie would do his man-hug thing with them all, which would be exactly what he needed to build his case.

Of course, what would be even better would be recordings, wiretaps of their conversation. The thought of that made him smile. No doubt the three of them were figuring out some way to bring him down, make him take the fall for the missing money in the First City Bank robbery. Oh, yeah, he could almost hear smug Harper's voice, probably going on about what a phony and what a jerk Supervising Agent William "Showbiz" Forrester was. How Forrester was the perfect person to take the fall, since everybody hated his ass anyway.

Well, maybe it was true. Maybe he wasn't Mr. Popularity in the Bureau, because maybe some of the other agents were freaking jealous of his connections, how he had been able to turn his FBI gig into serious-money consulting-producer gigs with Spielberg on his new cop/alien movie *The Green Home* . . . Yeah, they were all jealous of him, and why? Because they had this ancient FBI mentality . . . the Bureau against the world . . . yeah, we few, we incorruptible few, versus the sordid, compromised, and downright filthy outer world . . . an idea started back when Miss Blue Panties J. Edgar Hoover was in command. Well, Hoover had a reason to be paranoid, the dick-sucking, ass-eating, pillow-biting, ball-gown–wearing fag!

But this was a new era. Hoover was long gone, and now the whole world (outside of the monks at the Bureau) was in the multitasking, schmooze-or-lose-universe! The idea that a man was guilty of a crime just because he had more ambition than another guy was sooooo over. The idea of being good at Just One Thing was so '50s, so G-man, so black-and-white Anthony Mann movie world, when the rest of the world was running on computers and BlackBerrys.

The thing now was to be good—no, great—at a lot of things. A man could be an agent, which was still way cool, but he could also translate that position into a new top position as a consultant to only the biggest director in the world, *and* this same agent could expand that position ever outward, commanding more and more respect, garnering more and more power. Agent, consultant, yes, beautiful, and then who knew, like other great cop entrepreneurs before him, maybe series creator (he already had the title: *The Hard Guys!,* which would be the continuing adventures of two FBI agents who were not only hard-asses against scum like the Neanderthal Muslims, but also guys who got it up with Hollywood-royalty actresses as well. Thus the subconscious HARD GUY HARD-ON reference, which would get every red-blooded kid up and ready to fight (but mainly to watch every week) and fuck like the loyal and obedient Americans they were. Yessir, there was no reason he couldn't be a producer, none at all, but to get there you had to have contacts, and to have contacts you had to pay for lunch occasionally, and when you were taking Steve Spielberg or Bill Friedkin or David Milch (though he always paid) out there to lunchville, you had to have money. Yess! That was like soooo right. And if you were going to play the rich-and-cool producer guy, you had to have a decent car. Just imagine showing up to lunch with Steve S., and he's driving his freaking Lexus or supercool Jag and you're driving a Honda Accord! No, sorry, *nada*, won't work, don't play, homie!

No, you had to have your own bread, baby.

You had to show up in a car, not a piece of fucking tin.

You also had to show up in a suit—not some FBI Shop at Syms, a freaking knockoff—but a real suit, custom made, from Savile Row, buddyroo.

You had to spend the cash and get the real stitching. The buttonholes had to look right, or they would spot you as a Pretend Player and you were through.

Thus, you needed a cash outlay to move forward, to reach your own human potential, and so, well, maybe you had to break a few eggs to make an omelet, after all.

So he had taken the money and he had used it to finance his own little Liberation movement (as so many of the jerk-off movements the Left had out there in Sunni Land were called) . . .

Yep, the Liberation of William Lindsay Forrester, and now the thing was he had to protect himself from scum like Jack Harper and his Tex-Mex partner, the burrito-eating slob, Oscar Hidalgo.

Jesus, it wasn't even fair that he had to protect himself against such scuzzballs. In the old days, the Bureau wouldn't even have let in a Mexican bean-eating greaseball like Oscar.

But that was how things had fallen apart.

Nowadays, anyone could get in.

Nowadays, if you could speak the language of the freaking Iraqis or knew two facts about Islam, you were in, you were golden.

The good old boys, the guys who went back, the real American guys, were being pushed out by freaking greaseballs from the Mideast!

Which was another reason he had to play hardball with Jack and Oscar, the evil bastards.

And which was why he was watching them night and day now.

And coming up with a plan.

A plan that would get him free of their corrupt influence and let him move on up in the Bureau hierarchy and then . . . zap, right beyond it to showbiz riches.

TV and movie Producerhood, major bucks, lunch every day at The Grill, and endless A-list actress pussy . . .

But first things first.

There were things to do, and let us not get the left foot tangled up with the right, lest we fall and break our face!

Soon his enemies would be out of the way. 'Bye, 'bye, 'bye . . .

And he would be soaring above the other fucking agents and their minuscule problems, high above them, and he'd come down, so soft and perfect a landing, right in Beverly Fucking Hills!

38

PAUL WAGNER HAD FOUND the perfect retirement job, head of Security at the Huntington Gardens in San Marino. He loved working with the curator of the gardens and the other retired people who became tour guides and docents at the museum. As far as the work itself went . . . well, there wasn't that much. Occasionally a drunken teenager or two would get stoned and try to climb over the electric fence, but the small shock in the wire usually sent them scurrying back to their cars.

Really, there was little to worry about, and he'd found that after thirty years of working in the FBI it was a great thing to commune with nature every day, walk through the fantastic moonscape of the famous desert garden, appreciating the amazing variety of cacti planted there, some as long as eighty-five years ago.

His favorite was the golden barrel cactus, the yellow-spined, spring-flowering cactus, which was thorny, and yet stunningly beautiful. It was, Wagner thought, a survivor, just like himself.

And he'd had a lot to survive over the years.

More than he could remember. After all, he was in his late sixties now, and he'd been shot, stabbed, his car blown up twice (he somehow survived without a scratch both times), and he'd received a mail bomb when he worked in Tucson. That one had almost gotten him. It had blown off three of the fingers on his right hand.

But somehow God had been with him . . . and he'd survived it all.

Survived and prospered and was still married to the same good woman, Ruth Ann, whom he'd been with for thirty-one years.

They had two kids and three grandkids, and Wagner knew he was lucky.

He had a good job, and that meant he didn't have time to think a whole lot. Think about how most of his life was over, and also how maybe he hadn't always done the right thing. Not that he hadn't tried to. But sometimes you wanted a guy so bad, maybe you pushed the envelope a little too much.

Or maybe you did something even worse than that.

Maybe you'd done something, taken a calculated chance to get a guy—a real bad guy—but maybe there were things you couldn't foresee, things that, hell, nobody could foresee. They couldn't blame you for that, could they?

At least that's what you thought when you did whatever it was that you did, that you were doing something that was just a little outside policy but sometimes, if you were going to be a really great agent, you had to go that way.

And you thought that people would get it, and maybe, maybe, they would have, too, if certain things—things you couldn't know, couldn't foresee—that no one but God in Heaven (if there even was one, and after this particular case Wagner didn't really see how there could be anymore) could possibly know.

And how could they hold that against you?

. . .

Paul Wagner walked by some of the agave cacti and the terrestrial bromeliads, and looked at their amazing grotesque shapes and thought that maybe that was how his conscience looked.

Twisted and spiky and defensive, just waiting for an attack from the outer world.

But maybe it wasn't the outer world that was going to get him.

Maybe it was going to happen from inside.

Maybe on a certain month and on a certain day of that certain month, every freakin' year, memories would start to seep under the walls he'd built in his head.

(Though sometimes, truth be told, he had to add a little fortification to the wall, in the form of a few shots of Maker's Mark, and sometimes maybe more than a few.)

And maybe this one thing he'd done, maybe even the booze didn't stop it from seeping under the walls, and especially at this time of the year, which was when it had all happened. Just about now and . . .

Stop it!!!

Just stop it!!! Give it up, Paul!

But he couldn't.

Why did he feel that something was coming his way, something that was unstoppable, something like Destiny with a capital D, if you believed in such things (which rational Paul Wagner certainly didn't) . . .

But there it was, this feeling of Doom about to rain down on him.

This certain knowledge that something was coming and all the goddamned safeguards and preventive measures in the universe weren't going to be able to stop it.

Because it was Destiny.

And because he Deserved it.

He walked by the lovely weird bottle palms, and then stretched and looked up at the sky.

Check it out, Paul, he said to himself. The sky is a perfect desert blue, and there are a few cumulus clouds. And as anyone can plainly see, there are no wraithlike demons riding down to get you.

Everything is cool.

Everything is fine.

You're here at the Huntington, and the cacti are blooming and the birds are chirping and the worms are happy in their wormholes, and all is right in God's (if there is a God) Kingdom.

And there are a couple of early-morning cactus lovers walking around the curvy, beautifully laid-out garden path, and two of them are girls and one of them is a man dressed in a seersucker sports jacket and white bucks. Good Lord, those are white bucks; just proves that everything comes back.

What next, Pat Boone records?

"On a day like today, we'll pass the time away, writing love letters in the sand."

Ha-ha, those were the good old days.

And the guy seems to be walking toward you, and, oh, he's got a digital video camera, and he's filming the cactus. Something about that guy looks vaguely familiar, though he can't see all of his face because the camera is blocking the view.

And just for a second, Paul Wagner feels the cold hand of vengeance coming down for him. That this is the day all the chips are called in and it's all over.

But it's not like that at all, because the guy has taken a path away from Paul. So he's obviously not here to spell out some kind of cosmic vengeance, the same vengeance that got Blakely and Hughes.

He's not the guy, not him at all. Just a bearded tourist with a scar on his face making a little nature movie.

Except that now—suddenly—from behind Paul Wagner, the bearded filmmaker has suddenly doubled back, walked right off the path and between the barrel cacti, which means he picked up some sharp, thick needles in his legs, but he doesn't even seem to notice. Doesn't notice pain, doesn't notice the sky, the gardens. Doesn't notice anything, except he's still got the camera in one hand, and with his other he's shoving a knife into Paul Wagner's back, and—talk about multitasking—he's also still half-looking through the viewfinder to make sure he gets the camera super close up on the entry wound. The bloody tissue popping out and the agonizing little groan from Paul.

And Paul Wagner is on the ground now, lying next to his cacti, and the man is over him, getting a great shot of Paul's dying rattle/gasp.

But even as Paul takes his few final breaths, he feels a strange relief, and a thought comes into his almost-gone mind:

"I couldn't struggle any longer against it. I couldn't stand waiting. I don't even want to fight. Maybe . . . I'm glad it's finally happening."

That's all there is. All Paul Wagner (Ole Wags) can muster.

And he feels it now, flying, speeding away from him, out into the silent California blue.

And the cameraman is walking very quickly toward the entrance. His job is done.

And ex-agent Paul Wagner is lying there among the sharp green needles, bloody and very dead.

39

AN HOUR LATER, Jack and Oscar stood in the Huntington Desert Garden and searched the ground for clues as the boys from the ME's office took away Paul Wagner's body on a stretcher.

Oscar ran his massive hands through his hair and shook his head.

"Terrible thing," he said to Jack. "But I don't see how Wagner's death is even remotely connected to Blakely and Hughes. It's more likely a break-in, a robbery that went bad."

Jack sat on a bench and felt the ominous shape of a huge saguaro cactus hanging over him. Like the Grim Reaper itself.

He said nothing, but stared down blankly at his feet.

"You guys almost convinced me."

"About what?"

"Down at Charlie's the other day. We toasted. The whole thing was on Forrester, somehow. All we had to do was connect the dots."

"Come on, Jack. That case is closed. This is something else.

283

Paul Wagner was an old guy. He never worked with Blakely or Hughes or us . . ."

Jack looked up at the eerie cactus hovering over him and felt like he was on another planet, one with different physics, too many dimensions for him to fathom.

"That's where you're wrong. He *did* work with them. Wags and Blakely and Hughes and . . . and me, Oscar."

"You? When was this?"

"A long time ago, *compadre*. Before I even knew you. In fact, it was one of my very first cases."

He stopped then, too stunned to talk.

"Maybe you better tell me about it, Jack."

Jack nodded, then stood up.

"I will," Jack said. "But in the car. We have to pay someone a visit. Right now."

Jack drove out the 5 Freeway toward the deep Valley. He looked straight ahead and talked in a voice Oscar hadn't heard before. His voice sounded like that of a man who has just learned he has a terminal disease. Still technically alive, but emotionally already dead.

"All this started way before we arrested Steinbach. Now I'm sure of it. Yeah, this goes way back."

Oscar looked at him in disbelief.

"How can that be true?"

Jack bit his lower lip.

"Just listen. You'll see. On my first big case, I was teamed up with Zac Blakely and Hughes. We reported to the supervising agent, an older guy—or at least he seemed old to me. Paul Wagner."

"The same guy we just . . ."

"One and the same," Jack said, as they cut toward Montrose. "See, back then the big thing was bank robberies. Man, sometimes there were five a day. And what made it so frustrating is we knew who was the brain behind all the jobs, a guy named Adam Moore. But Moore was smart—very smart—and you couldn't get next to him. And anyone from his organization who talked found themselves chopped up into pieces and floating in the Hollywood Reservoir."

"Yeah, I remember that guy," Oscar said. "A badass. He was running four or five crews at once."

"Yeah," Jack said. "A real entrepreneur, Mr. Moore was. But finally we got a break. We busted a guy named Billy Chase, Moore's right-hand man. He had all the shit we needed on Moore: names, dates, where he invested his money, but he had a good attorney and there was no way he would talk unless we gave him total immunity from prosecution. You know that's not easy to do, but we went to the DA and we got it for him."

"Wow, they rarely do that anymore."

"Yeah, I know," Jack said, passing a Dos Equis Beer truck. "Anyway, it looked good. Chase started talking, and we were getting all ready to drop the hammer on Moore. But then Billy Chase fucked up—bad."

"What, he booked on you?"

"No, he was out on bail. In fact, no one even knew he was ar- rested. That was part of the deal. If Moore had known he was in prison, he'd have had one of the other inmates stick a shiv in Billy. So we had to leave him out. What we didn't know about him was he was a dope addict. Not heroin, but downers, co- deine pills; the guy was a pillhead from the get-go. So he pulls this dumb little robbery to get dope money. Robs a 7-Eleven. He walks in with a gun and holds it on the Pakistani guy behind the counter. Right in West Hollywood, near Barney's Beanery. The gun was all for show. I don't think he even had any bul- lets in it. Anyway, there was this boy in there, a fifteen-year-old boy, Jimmy Gregson. He was this ultrabright kid, sensitive . . .

wanted to be a movie director, we found out. You know, the kind of kid like Spielberg might have been. Supersmart, already making his own movies at age nine and ten and winning contests. He'd served an internship at Universal Pictures the summer before. Straight As in school. Just an amazing kid.

"Well, he's in there, and he freaks when he sees the gun. He tries to run, and Bill Chase panics and starts to grab him. Maybe he gets a little rough with the kid—nobody ever knew for sure. Whatever, the boy falls and hits his head on the edge of the counter, and he's knocked out. There wasn't much of a mark on his head, but he's unconscious. Didn't seem like that big of a deal at the time. He recovered after a few minutes and seemed fine. And Billy? Well, two LAPD street cops caught him a few minutes later. Looked like no big deal."

They turned into a gas station and sat there by the pumps, neither one of them getting out of the car. Behind them loomed the San Gabriel Mountains looking serene, majestic. Jack looked up at the golden butte and thought how it would have made a nice moment if his stomach wasn't tying into knots.

"Then, two weeks later, it happened," Jack said. "Jimmy went to bed one night, complaining that his head had started hurting again, on the side he'd hit it. His parents didn't think anything of it. Only when they went to wake him up for school in the morning—"

Jack couldn't finish the sentence.

"Jesus," Oscar said. "That's terrible!"

"Yeah," Jack said. "It ate me up. Man, I didn't know what to do. Jesus . . ."

"But it was your first case, right?" Oscar said. "It wasn't your call."

"That's right," Jack said. "It was Zac Blakely's call. I didn't really foresee anything bad happening from it. It sounded like we did a simple trade-up. It wasn't all that unusual back then."

"Yeah," Oscar said. "You couldn't blame yourself. Anyway, it's a bad thing, but I don't see how it has anything to do with this case."

"Well, it does, trust me. I don't know exactly how. The thing is, Osc, I knew it was going to come back someday. Even then I knew that case would never die, that someday we were all going to have to pay for what we did. We made a deal with the devil, and he still has to collect."

"Hey, now, wait a minute," Oscar said. "Look, this Chase guy: After the accident, did his information help you catch Moore and his crew?"

"Yeah," Jack said. "From what he told us, we got Moore and his gang. Locked them up for good. They're still serving time."

"That's my point," Oscar said. "Who knows how many people they might have killed or hurt if they'd been out there taking down more banks? It's not a science, Jack, it's a trade-off. You made a call, and basically it turned out for the best."

Jack laughed bitterly.

"No, don't you see? Whoever is doing this . . . he's making it seem like it's related to Steinbach. That was the deal."

"But how did he get Steinbach to go along with it?"

Jack shrugged.

"Well, I don't know for sure. But I bet when we get our answer back from our agents in South Africa, we're going to find out his kids are missing. That had to be what he was trying to tell me when he was dying. Whoever did this kidnapped his boys."

"Ah, it's fantastic," Oscar said. "After all these years."

"That doesn't mean anything," Jack said. "When some people lose their child—their only child—time stops for them. How many times have you seen it, people making shrines to their dead kid, keeping his or her room the exact way it was when they were kids, talking to them like they're still there? There are cases where people waited twenty or thirty years just to get revenge. And who knows, maybe they deserve it."

"That's bullshit," Oscar said. "You couldn't have known how it would turn out. You're an agent, a cop . . . not God."

"Trust me, I know that," Jack said. "God wouldn't have made a deal with Billy Chase. But, really, there's only one way to find out for sure. And it involves going to see someone I hoped to never have to see again."

"Who's that?" Oscar said.

"Jimmy Gregson's mother."

Jack turned the key and they shot off toward Palmdale. Sweat rolled down his cheeks, and he had a feeling that time had collapsed. The death of Jimmy Gregson hadn't happened in the past at all. In fact, there *was* no past.

Because it was still happening all these years later. Still happening right now.

40

THEY DROVE UP Daggett Way, a sunbaked, golden-dust, unpaved road with small houses, some of them with little horse runs attached to the side. Spanish knockoffs stood next to Western ranch-style houses from the '50s, and down near the end of the street there was even a small Southern-style mansion, as if somebody had seen *Gone with the Wind* one too many times and had tried to build a miniature Tara.

For a second or two, Jack managed to fool himself into thinking that he wouldn't remember the place, or that when they got there, the Gregsons would have moved away. That the whole story he had just told Oscar was too crazy to be real.

But who was he kidding?

The Gregsons would never move.

No, they'd never move away from the place where their genius filmmaker son had lived and died.

If they were still alive, they'd be there.

Which is why Jack hadn't even bothered to call.

The whole thing felt like it was out of his hands now. It was going to play out however it played out . . .

And once again, he had the feeling that if the Gregsons wanted to put a bullet through him, maybe that was okay. Maybe he deserved it.

It was a feeling he had to fight. If not for himself, then for Kevin and Julie.

The dust kicked up into the windows and Oscar coughed and pulled out a handkerchief from his suit jacket.

"There it is," Jack said. "Right over there."

They looked over at a broken-down ranch house with a wagon wheel out in the front yard. At one time, the wheel was painted robin's-egg blue, but that day was long gone. The paint had peeled off, and it looked like the last remnant of a Conestoga wagon's wheel after an Apache attack. All that was missing were a couple of feathered arrows in the spokes.

The front porch was lopsided, the old pine beams twisted and half falling over.

One more earthquake out here in the Valley, and the Gregsons' house would collapse forever.

Jack parked in front of the place and saw a battered old dog glaring at him from the broken-down steps.

He felt his tongue getting larger in his mouth. Like a toad's.

Dreading every step, Jack and Oscar headed into the dusty yard.

Oscar tried the doorbell, but there was no sound inside. He rapped on the old screen door, waited. Nothing. They rapped again, and the door opened, a half inch. A woman with good bones but deep wrinkles in her face looked out at them.

"Whatever you two are selling, I don't need any," she said.

Jack held up his badge.

"Mrs. Gregson. We're with the FBI. We need to speak with you."

Faye Gregson's head jerked back a little, as if Jack had slapped her in the face.

"FBI? I ain't got anything to say to you."

"Ma'am, it's very important," Oscar said. "Please let us in."

Faye Gregson sighed, and gave a bitter little hiccup of a laugh.

"Like I got a choice in the matter. You people do whatever the hell you want."

She stepped back and wearily held open the screen door. Jack and Oscar walked inside.

Faye Gregson's home was a place where the amenities were no longer observed. The yellowing shades were pulled down so that no one could see the old newspapers and magazines which spilled all over the battered furniture. Several soda bottles sat on chair arms, and the coffee table was covered with tabloid newspapers like *The Star* and *World Weekly News*.

The old throw rug was covered with crumbs and dust and what looked to Jack like pieces of an old ham sandwich.

There was an odor in the place, too. An odor of mold, and from the back of the house what could easily be recognized as urine. Apparently, Faye Gregson didn't bother cleaning her toilets very often.

She made a halfhearted gesture for the two agents to sit down and sat across from them on an old overstuffed couch.

"So, what little surprises you guys got for me today?" she said, as though she were trying to be casual.

"Well, Mrs. Gregson . . ." Oscar started.

"Call me Faye," she said sarcastically. "I know we're going to become great friends."

Oscar looked at Jack who began to feel impatient.

"Faye, my partner here, Agent Hidalgo, and I are investigating the deaths of three FBI agents."

Faye Gregson snorted a mocking laugh, then took out a Camel and lit it. She blew two trails of smoke across the room at them.

She looked, Jack thought, like an old, battered lizard on her last legs.

"You think maybe I did it? Well, can't say I blame you. I thought about it enough times."

"Is that right?" Oscar said.

"Yeah, that's right. You ever have a kid, mister?"

"Yeah," Oscar said. "Three of them."

"Well, then you know something about it. Wonder what you'd do if someone just came along and killed one of 'em. And you knew he did it. And the law wouldn't touch him."

"That would be rough," Oscar said. "That's what happened to you?"

"You know it is or you wouldn't be here. So why don't you cut the bullshit?"

She got up so slowly that it seemed almost like a joke, a parody of motion, then walked over to an old, scratched-up wooden cabinet, opened the top drawer, and took out a picture. Just as slowly she walked over and handed it to Oscar. Jack leaned over and looked on.

"That's him. That's Jimmy. Just the smartest kid you'd ever want to meet. Had a career all lined up for him in film. You can ask anybody. He could have been a great moviemaker. Like Spielberg or one of them. 'Cept you guys let out a little shit name of Billy Chase, who happened to drop by just to kill my boy. Shoulda been in prison. But you guys let him out."

Tears rolled down her cheeks. Jack couldn't meet her eyes.

"Listen to me. If I wanted to kill one of your agents, I would have every goddamned right to—you both hear me? But I didn't do a damned thing. 'Cept die myself."

Jack sucked in his breath, then spoke.

"Faye, I know this is hard for you. But somebody is killing agents connected to your son's case . . ."

Faye Gregson looked at Jack, and blinked as if she'd made some kind of connection.

"I know you?"

"No, ma'am," Jack lied. "What about your husband, Dick Gregson? He took it really hard, too, right?"

"Do I know you?" Faye Gregson repeated.

"Jack's been on television a lot lately about a case," Oscar said.

"Oh . . . what do you want to know about Dick?"

"How he reacted. When—"

"When Jimmy was murdered by your informant? Isn't that what you called him? That's a great fancy name for a piece of shit. How do you *think* he reacted? He was very . . . very . . . up-set. Angry."

There was something curious about her words, Jack thought. When she described Dick Gregson's anger, there was no real fury in her voice. And she seemed to be staring off into space, as though her mind were somewhere else.

"What is it, Faye?" Jack said softly.

"Nothing. See, Dick didn't have a mean bone in his body. He was a long-distance trucker, and if he got, you know . . . up-set . . . he just took on a few more loads. Used to say once he was out on the highway, his 'road self' kicked in. It was like every-thing back here was a dream to him. Didn't mean a thing."

"Where's Dick now?" Oscar said.

"Died two years ago. Had a big accident up near Eureka. Wet highway, big bend. He didn't make it."

Faye Gregson took another hit off her cigarette and glowered at them both.

"Someone is killing everyone that was involved with my Jimmy?"

"That's right," Jack said.

"Goddamn. Jesus Christ!"

She looked as though she were about to say something, then turned away and took two long drags off her cigarette.

"Look, Faye," Oscar said. "These guys who've been killed. They have families, too. Some of them have kids. So if you know something, please tell us."

She turned quickly then, filled with fury.

"Oh, really? I lose my son because of you guys, and now I should step forward and save the lives of the very people who did it to him? You take care of a kid for years and years, worrying about him at school, every time he gets sick, but you tell yourself it's all going to come out fine. But you know . . . you know somewhere deep inside you that it's been wrong from the start. That the whole thing, the father, the son . . . you know it's cursed, 'cause it was wrong . . . wrong from the start."

She broke down and sank back to the couch, her body shaking with sobs.

Oscar looked through the dust motes at Jack.

"Your husband, Dick? He wasn't Jimmy's father?"

"No," she said. "No . . . but Dick never knew."

"Then who?" Jack said.

Faye Gregson put out her cigarette in a coffee cup and lit another one.

"Thing was, Dick was gone all the time. See, I was used to having a big family. And friends. That's how I grew up back in Iowa. So when we come out here, and Dick starts going away all the time . . . I was so lonely. I could hardly stand it. So finally I joined this tennis club. Which is where I met Roy Ayres.

He was the owner of it. Supersuccessful man. He'd made millions of dollars in real estate, and he opened the club just for
something to do. His wife had died from cancer, and he was
lonely, too. Place was called The Palms, and it was beautiful.
Roy also owned this restaurant and bar called The Ranchero. It
was a great spot. Music and happy hour. It was just the gayest
spot. Roy and I were friends at first, but he was so much fun,
always ready with a story and a laugh. He paid attention to me.
Thought I was beautiful. And you know what? I was. Yeah, I
know I don't look it now, but I was back then. I was young and
beautiful, and he just lit up whenever he saw me. It was like I
was alive again."

"You got pregnant?" Oscar said.

"Yes. That's right. And I was going to get an abortion. But
Roy said not to. See, he and Dick were the same types. Dark
complexioned, and near the same age, and sort of stocky. Roy
said he'd always wanted a child, and the thought that it would
be ours . . . He couldn't bear to kill it. We figured we might get
away with it. So I did it. I had Jimmy and I never told Dick the
truth. Dick wasn't all that into having a kid, anyway. But Roy, he
was crazy for Jimmy. It was Roy who liked to take pictures and
it was Roy who brought Jimmy his first camera, and it was him
that saw that Jimmy had a natural talent for taking snapshots,
and soon he got him a movie camera. By the age of four or five,
Jimmy was making little home movies that were so clever. And
with Dick away on long trips, Roy and Jimmy and I would drive
in Roy's big old white Caddy convertible and we'd go to Beverly
Hills to Chasen's and eat Sunday dinner, and we'd have our own
little family. The *real* family, as I came to think of it."

Jack tried to say something—something that would be comforting—but there was nothing comforting to say.

"And Jimmy, he just loved Roy. I never saw two people who
loved each other so much. And he just blossomed with Roy

helping him. Know what they did? They made little movies together. They wrote them down, real scripts with speaking parts and all that, and they acted 'em out. Started out with little horror movies. *Dracula* was the first one, 'cept they did their own, and they used the club and the bar as the castle. You never saw two people take to each other like they did. See, that's when I learned what life was all about, and Roy did, too. He used to say to me that all the money he'd made in all his real-estate ventures and his club and bar, why, none of it meant anything at all besides having me and Jim. And then Jimmy got his internship at Universal—the youngest kid ever to get one since Spielberg—and you shoulda seen Roy; you shoulda seen him. He was so proud he could have busted, and I had to tell him to bring it down a little, you know, 'cause we still had Dick to deal with. That was a great summer, us going over there to see Jimmy and meeting so many of the stars and the big directors and producers. It was like all our dreams were going to come true. No, that's not exactly it. It was more like dreams we'd never even knew we had were going to come true, 'cause being poor and from the Midwest, you don't even dare to have dreams like we were having now. I mean, then . . ."

She stopped and looked around, as though she'd suddenly dropped back to the real world, her sordid little living room with its smell of piss and death.

"And then it happened. Jimmy and that Billy Chase. At first we thought he was going to be just fine. He laughed about it a little. But for two weeks he got tired at night. And he wasn't interested in his cameras and his movies. He just didn't care anymore. I knew there was something wrong. I should have taken him right into the hospital. But Roy said he was fine, said it was just me feeling guilty. I did, you know? I wasn't a swinger. I believe in loyalty and my marriage oath. I wouldn't ever have started with Roy 'cept I was so lonely. And then Jimmy went to bed that night, and when I came into his room in the morning and called him . . . 'Jimmy? Jimmy?' I said. 'Time to get up, honey. You have school today, and they're going to show your film in class. It's your big day, honey.' But he didn't move. He just lay there. It's funny, when you see a scene like that in a movie, the mother always screams. But I didn't scream. It seemed like I knew this day was coming all along and the whole thing—me and Roy and Jimmy and our happiness—was all a setup, that life was just waiting to cut us down. 'Cause it was wrong from the start, and Jimmy . . . Jimmy was the product of a deal with the devil. I know that sounds terrible, but he was. He was an angel himself, but he came from us, and we were bad. And you . . . you guys were the devil come to get his due. And maybe I shouldn't hate you, but I do. Part of me. Part of me is glad if you all die. I can't help it. I just can't."

She began to cry and make low mournful sounds, whimpering like a dog under a car wheel.

Jack felt a chill run down his back. Oscar grimaced and looked away.

"Faye, what happened to Roy?" Jack said, after she had quieted down.

"It was funny," she said. "He had such a strange reaction. When I told him, he just said he'd come over. And when he saw Jimmy lying there in his bed, turning blue, he just touched his head and looked up at the sky. And he said, 'It's all right. I can still reach him.' And I said, 'You can?' and he said, 'Yes, I can hear him. I can hear him talking to me.' And then he smiled, and he said he was going to take care of everything. That it would take a long while, but he and Jimmy had a plan. It was so strange. It gave me the chills. I asked him what he meant, and he said they were going to make a movie. It was going to be great. They had to work out the plot . . . they had to come up with a plot that would blow everybody away, but it was going to

297

happen. It was going to be the greatest work ever . . . 'cause it was going to be a movie in reality. Real people would be the actors. Then he began to touch Jimmy's lips, like he could hear the words through his fingers and he was saying, 'What's that, Jim? You what? Oh, good. That is brilliant. Jimmy.' And I told him we had to call the hospital, and he said, 'Not yet.' And he sat there with Jim, running his hands over his dead body, laughing and nodding his head. And said he had it, he got it. It would take a long time, but he would do everything Jimmy wanted. And then, after two hours of this, which made me sick . . . after two hours or so, he got up and walked out. And I called the police and the hospital, and they took my son away."

There was a long silence. Then Jack said:

"And then?"

"And then Roy disappeared. Two days later, he was gone. The club was there, the Ranchero Bar was there, but he was gone. And when I asked about him, the guys who worked for him, they'd never say anything at all. It was like he'd vanished into thin air. And I never saw him again."

"You have a picture of him, Faye?" Oscar asked.

"Yeah, sure. But better than that, I still have their old home movies. Come with me."

They walked through the kitchen, with its filthy pots and pans sitting around like an old science project, and went out into the backyard, where Jack was surprised to see a small kidney-shaped swimming pool, with only three inches of water.

The water was green, and there was a fine skin of scum on the top.

They walked to the far end, and then to a small house . . . the pool house, Oscar guessed, back when Jimmy was alive and they had lunches out here and pitchers of lemonade.

They went inside; both Jack and Oscar were shocked to find the place immaculate.

There were five rows of old theater seats and a large screen. In the back of the room there was a projector, with a film ready to play.

"It's all ready." Faye's voice was light and cheerful, as if the years and all the pain had fallen away.

"Jimmy never had a proper premiere, but in this theater his are the only movies we show. Of course there is usually a limited audience, myself . . . so today is very special. Sit down."

As she said it, she gestured graciously with her arms, as if she was welcoming royalty.

They sat in the front row and waited as the leader film counted backward from ten . . .

And then, there it was in front of them, the title *The Deal*, a Jimmy Gregson production. Written and directed by Jimmy Gregson, Produced by Roy Ayres.

There was a fake thunderclap, and a shot of the tennis club. The club coat of arms—a palm tree crossed with a tennis racquet—appeared on the screen.

The camera trailed up the driveway of the club, where a boy was tending the lawn. He was a beautiful boy, with great green eyes and thick black hair. An older man dressed in black came toward him. The scene was shot from behind the boy, who looked up at the man, a sad expression on his face.

"What's wrong?" the man said.

"I want to play tennis," the boy said. "But I'm not a member of the club."

Jack sat still. The voice was scratchy, but somehow familiar.

"You must come to see my master," the man said. "He will make it possible for you to not only join the club, but play like a champion."

"Really?" the boy said.

"Really," the man said.

On the reverse angle, Jack and Oscar saw the man's face. It was the bearded man . . . the one who had tried to run Jack over at the bar.

"It's our old friend," Jack said. "Who is he?"

"That's Roy's brother Terry," Faye Gregson said. "He and Roy were in a fire when they were young. Roy came out fine, but Terry . . . well, it was very sad. He has to wear that beard to hide the scars."

Jack suddenly felt his stomach twist inside him.

It still made no sense . . . but suddenly he saw it coming.

"Speed the film up," Jack said. "I've got to see Roy."

"No need to," Faye said. "He's in the next scene."

And indeed he was. There in the very next scene, shot at the old Ranchero Bar, late at night. A man greets young Jimmy, a man dressed in a string tie and a cowboy shirt. A man who tells him that he can not only make him a club member, not only a great player, but a boy who will be immortal.

"You will live forever," Roy Ayres, playing the mad scientist in his son's film, says, hamming it up like Lionel Atwill in an old Warner Bros. movie.

"You ride with me, Jimmy, and you will have life everlasting. Immunity to decay, to sagging muscles, to broken bones . . . to death itself. All you need to do is to come with me, now."

And the boy smiles and says, "Yes, doctor, I'll do as you say."

And Jack Harper sits there staring at the screen and feeling his heart sink in his chest.

41

JACK WALKED UP and down the road in front of Faye Gregson's place punching in Kevin's phone number, but it didn't come through.

"No service. Fuck!"

Oscar paced alongside of him.

"Come on. We've got to get our asses back there now. We'll call the playground when we get closer."

Faye Gregson stood on the porch, smoking and looking at them as if they were people from another planet.

Jack looked at her standing there, all hollowed out.

And knew, just then, without a shadow of a doubt, how she felt.

Like him.

Like he would keep right on feeling if anything happened to Kevin.

They got in the car, turned on the motor, and took off, leaving a cloud of dust in their wake.

. . .

At Brentwood Little League, the afternoon practice was breaking up. Kevin Harper, dressed in his jeans and Angels T-shirt, was walking off the field next to Charlie. As they headed toward the car, middle-aged mom Peggy Dent came walking toward Charlie with her daughter Kathy in tow.

"Coach," she said. "I just wanted to thank you for the year we've had so far. And the way you've watched out for Kathy this year."

Ordinarily, funny and genial Charlie Breen would stop and chat, but today he barely slowed down.

"Yeah, thanks," he said. "I try to give all the kids time on the field. Kathy was great."

"Thanks, coach," Kathy said.

"You know, when I was a young girl, we never got a chance to develop that side of our personalities. The left side of our brain," Peggy continued.

She smiled and blocked Charlie's way, thinking he was going to stop. But Charlie moved around her, and when she moved with him, she found herself being not so gently pushed out of the way.

"Excuse me," she said with a shock. "You almost knocked me down."

"I know," Charlie said. "Sorry. I'm in a kind of hurry."

He grabbed Kevin's hand and headed for the car.

"Well, thanks a lot!" Peggy Dent yelled. "You fat bastard!"

Her face contorted into a mask of rage. Charlie ignored her and pulled Kevin along with him to his car.

Charlie took a left at Ohio, right by the junior high school, and then a left into a little park adjacent to the school. He pulled over by a Dumpster and gave Kevin a worried look.

"I think there's something wrong with the back tire on your side. Can you look back there for me? We might have a flat."

"Really, Charlie?" Kevin said, smiling generously at his coach. "I didn't notice anything."

"Just check it, will you?" Charlie said.

Kevin was surprised by the anger and impatience in his voice. He nodded and got out of the car.

He knelt down next to the rear tire and felt it with his hands. It felt as solid as a rock.

"I don't know, Charlie. It's seems fine. It's definitely not flat."

Behind him, Charlie put his huge hand around Kevin's neck and pressed the ether-soaked rag against his nose. The boy twisted and turned, his eyes rolling wildly back in his head, but there was no escape. Within ten seconds, Kevin Harper was unconscious. Charlie picked up his limp body and pressed a button on his car key.

The trunk door popped open and he dropped Kevin inside, then slammed the trunk closed.

Then Roy Ayres went around to the driver's side, got in, gunned the engine, and drove away.

He turned on his new iPod and happily sang along with "Sgt. Pepper's Lonely Hearts Club Band."

He loved the Beatles. They'd helped him get over Jimmy's death, and now they were here for him as he avenged his son.

Think positive, Ayres thought. All good things come to those who wait.

42

JACK FLOORED THE ACCELERATOR and fishtailed through the traffic, almost causing a major accident with an ice-cream truck on the 405.

Oscar thought about saying something, but he could see there was no point to it. Jack was obsessed.

"Try Julie," Jack said. "I want to see if Kevin has come home."

Oscar punched in the buttons, waited as they headed south, past the Getty Museum.

The phone rang, once, twice, a third time. Then Julie picked it up.

"She's here," Oscar said, handing the phone to Jack.

"Hello, Julie."

"Hey, baby."

"Where are you right now?"

"At your place. Sitting in the dining room, grading papers."

"You heard from Kevin?"

"Not yet. They're a little late. Guess he and Charlie stopped at 7-Eleven to get a Slushy."

"Jesus!" Jack felt electric anxiety shooting through his arms and legs.

"Julie, listen, if Kevin *does* show up, you get him out of there. Right away. And if Charlie is with him, don't tell him where you're going."

"What? Jack, what are you saying?"

"Go to your sister's place, and don't tell anyone. But especially, don't tell Charlie."

Julie gnawed the end of her eraser.

"Jack, what is this all about?"

Jack felt a wave of nausea pass over him. There was no use hiding the facts any longer.

"It's Charlie Breen, Julie. He's our guy."

"Jack," she said. "C'mon. That's crazy. Why, if Charlie would have wanted to hurt Kevin or any of us, he could have done it three times over by now. And he was beaten up by whoever is the real bad guy."

"That was a ploy," Jack said. "His brother Terry stole our computer while we were out and Charlie was at the baseball game with Kevin. But he didn't find what he needed because it was on my *old* computer, which is stored up in the closet."

"Jack, you're sure?" she said. "Charlie? Good God!"

"I know," Jack said. "It's a shock. But trust me, this is how it is. I'll tell you the rest later. Just make sure you get Kevin away from him."

"Jack, they must be together right now."

"I know," Jack said, feeling like he was going to puke. "If he *does* have Kevin, he's going to call me. If he *does* call home, switch him here at once. And try to sound normal. We can't spook him."

"Okay, Jack," Julie said. "I love you."

305

"Me, too," Jack said.

They both hung up and Jack tore down the freeway.

"Where the hell would he go, Osc? Christ, he wouldn't take Kevin if he didn't have a hiding place all picked out. But where the fuck *is* it?"

Oscar said nothing, only stared straight ahead, lost in thought.

43

THE OLD WAREHOUSE in San Pedro was a ramshackle dump, with tiles falling off the roof, and rats and mice scampering around the nearby docks. Ayres had owned it for years. Originally, he'd thought of building Charlie Breen's Deckhouse right here in funky old working-class San Pedro. But certain business transactions in the diamond trade during his years in South Africa had left him a wealthy and wise man.

So he was able to "convince" a real-estate mogul in Malibu —who had owed a tremendous amount of money to Roy in gambling debts—to let him have the Malibu property for a song. So that was where The Deckhouse ended up being built.

Roy had planned to sell the San Pedro place, but for some reason he wasn't even aware of—not back then, anyway—he knew that he had to hang on to it.

Now, of course, he knew why he needed it.

Jimmy had filled him in.

Jimmy always told him what to do—not always right away (which was sometimes more than a little frustrating!), but eventually he'd let Roy know by calling him on his cell phone.

Take now, for example. It had just been a little over two years ago when Jimmy had contacted him on his cell phone to let him know what his plans were. Charlie hadn't expected to hear from him, was in fact at a Dodgers game with the very boy he had in the trunk right now. Kevin Harper.

Then the call came on his phone and he looked down at the screen and saw it, just like a trailer for a movie.

Exactly like that.

The trailer for Jimmy's great, unmade movie. Of course, he didn't tell anyone how the movie flickered to life on the screen, how only he, Roy Ayres, could see it.

If people had heard about such a thing, they would have thought he was stone nuts.

But they were wrong. Very wrong.

They didn't know shit about the movie. No, not at all. They didn't know how it had come about, exactly two weeks after he'd buried his son. Buried brilliant, soon-to-be-great movie director Jimmy in the ground, up near the Angeles Crest.

What they didn't know was that two weeks after he'd been buried there, among the pine trees and the great boulder—exactly two weeks later—Roy had received his first motion picture on his cell phone.

At first it was just a kind of blur of images: a tree, a rock, something with claws that scurried across a parking lot.

And some sounds, which again the uninitiated would have thought were nothing more than some kind of random chatter. Things that sounded like static, or some kind of rebel radio signal sent through the phone.

Hell, at first Roy/Charlie (sometimes he forgot which one was his real name and which his fictional one) had sort of written it off as some kind of fugitive bullshit, or maybe some kind of hideous grief aftertaste.

But then the weird sounds and weirder pictures kept coming, and strange voices could be heard like a voice locked in an iron box somewhere, and speaking through a megaphone with maybe the artificial larynx of a throat-cancer victim.

Roy thought for a week or so that he was cracking up. Thought about putting a gun to his head.

But then the voices and the pictures got clearer.

Someone was making nervous little movies in there and sending them to him.

Little movies with strange hissing sound bites that only he could understand. And what he could finally understand from the little pictures and the snake sounds was that—well, of course it seemed nuts, insane, goofy—but that it was Jimmy, still making movies from beyond the grave.

They say talent is like a force. Like energy, which can neither be created nor destroyed. They say it seems to live independently of the people it inhabits. How many times had he read about ordinary people who didn't even have much of an education, somehow being able to paint masterpieces, or pick up a guitar and play something amazing, or, in Jimmy's case, start to make movies at three years of age.

It was almost as if—no not "almost"—it was really as though Jimmy's talent had existed before his birth, and could live after his death, as well.

Yes, that was it.

Jimmy was mortal, but his talent was immortal. That's what the messages were telling Roy/Charlie. (And who was he to have had such a kid? A businessman, talented, of course, in his own way but merely clever, far from a genius.)

And then it started to happen.

Jimmy's dead genius seemed to coalesce. Yes, that was the word, wasn't it? Whatever. It came together, and he saw an image of a dead man on his phone; yes, he did. The man was Agent Zac Blakely, and he was lying near a school bus, a big yellow school bus that said Wonderland Elementary School on its side. And Blakely had sailed through his own windshield and was lying half on the fence and half among the bricks of the ruined school cafeteria.

Yes, he was. Jimmy had made the movie of Blakely's death before it even happened.

And then Ron Hughes. That was even better. On his phone he saw a picture of a railroad train, and he knew. He knew . . .

And Paul Wagner as well. Wagner lying in a cactus garden with a barbed-wire garotte slicing into his throat.

And now there was a picture of Kevin Harper, hanging from a pipe in a filthy room somewhere. A room with little lights shining in between the slats from the streets.

And then Roy saw that his role was now a starring one. Yes, he was the star of the picture while his dead son (or not-so-dead son) was the director.

Yes, that was how it would be.

And so it was Jimmy who led him to Tommy Wilson, who drank every night at The Deckhouse and threw all his money away on hookers and blow. It was Jimmy who told Charlie/Roy/Dad to kidnap both of Steinbach's kids and threaten to kill them unless Steinbach played along.

And it was Jimmy and Roy who had acted like such good friends, a couple of lightweights Karl didn't have to worry about at all. In fact, he was such a "good guy," Karl let his kids run with Charlie wherever they wanted to go. They had met long ago in South Africa, a meeting which Steinbach thought happened by coincidence. At a soccer match where Charlie just happened to be a coach.

But there were no coincidences in Charlie's life. Not anymore. Because Jimmy had it all scripted out and showed it to him on his telephone every single day.

It was Jimmy who had suggested that Charlie become Karl's "best friend." Oh, yeah, he had the "best friend" thing down pat.

Used it on Karl, along with some diamond deals.

Used it on Jack.

And it was Jimmy who told Charlie how to handle Alison Baines, too.

Yes, Jimmy and Charlie had worked it all out together. Karl was into diamonds, but he was also a drug smuggler: Sometimes he paid for his drugs with diamonds, and sometimes he paid for his diamonds with drugs. All things Charlie relayed to Alison/Maria, who told Jack. Beautiful Alison, the whore actress who didn't care what any of it meant as long as she could be part of a story of some kind—any kind—so as not to have to face the rest of her days knowing she was outside the main story and would never be a player. Never.

That was all that any of them wanted. To be a player in the story.

To not be gone like Jimmy (who was not, it must be remembered, gone at all).

And it was Roy/Charlie/Jimmy who supplied all the little leaks about Tim Andreen and his partner, Mr. Wink.

Maybe Jimmy even gave Mr. Winky his name. Why not?

Could have been that way.

His dead/not-so-dead son Jimmy who gave him the movies, which he then acted out in real life.

Yes, it was Jimmy, Jimmy, Jimmy who never would die. Or so C/R thought. Thought: "Death has not parted us. Death has not separated us. We are not alive and dead, we are one in the spirit, we are one in the life, we are one in the talent, Jimmy's immortal talent which I will carry out for him forever. Once we kill all

311

the people responsible for making him lose his body (but only his body, only his feet, hands, arms, head, neck, eyes . . . oh, how I miss his eyes, miss touching my son's thick hair), maybe, no surely, we will escape and there we will live (but where, didn't know yet, no signal from Jim yet, could his talent be out hunting for the right place even now, can his talent sail through the known world, through trees, without disturbing leaves, through the wheat, past the blinking cows, can his talent survive water, dive deep down and live among the coral, in a reef of sunfish) . . . and from there, wherever we live, myself and Jimmy's talent, we shall send our movies back to the world, astounding movies of Beyond the Dead. Movies which will show the world there is nothing to fear from death, that there is only failed promise, cut down in his youth . . ."

No, not that. There is only promise fulfilled in the land of the Not So Dead.

Except first there was a job to do . . . a job he had to do . . . now, and then talk to Jimmy again. (And why hadn't Jimmy been in touch on the cameras today? He didn't understand it.)

It had been such fun showing Jimmy the movies he'd made, back in the editing room.

Those were the Golden Hours, when Jimmy was literally there. So much so that Roy would ask him to come out on the "shoots" with him. But Jim couldn't do that. He had to stay behind, though Roy wasn't sure why. Maybe he used up his ability to appear if he stayed too long. Maybe he could appear in the flesh only when the movie was on. That could be it. There was that magical connection, the Hollywood Thing, that made it possible for Jimmy to show up in the editing room at Roy's house in the Palisades.

That was the mystical connection which only Jimmy understood.

Too far out for Roy.

312

But he understood, and was grateful, so grateful for the time they had together in the editing room.

Father and son working together.

Like it should have been in the real world.

Like it should have been except for the Feds and their deal.

Jimmy accepting the Academy Award.

Dinner at Spago.

All of it should have happened. To Roy and Faye and Jimmy.

For Jimmy The Immortal.

How he hated them all. He had lived on his hate/fuel for all these years. People said hate died over time, but this was yet another lie.

Hate was like a fine wine, aging, becoming deeper, more resonant.

He felt a stronger hatred for the Feds every year.

And now he was close. So close.

Finish off the last one, Billy Chase, then deal with Jack and his kid, a normal everyday kid, not gifted like Jimmy, not a friend of Spielberg, not an intern with a career people compared to Orson Welles (but would have been better even, because not a wastrel like fat Orson).

No, nothing really compared to his son Jim.

But here, here with hands, and eyes, and hair, and a smile, and a baseball, and a mouth which talked, and a hand which held Charlie's . . . and it killed him so that even though The Talent was still alive, that he could never touch, hug, kiss The Talent. Never hold his hand.

The brilliance of the kid. Using total immunity to get Karl out. But to also "play fair" with Jack. Yes, if Jack was smart enough (which he wasn't), he could have seen that the immunity scam was the same one that had gotten Jimmy killed.

Fair is fair, no? Billy Chase gets total immunity and Jimmy dies.

Karl gets total immunity and all the Feds die.

It was a game he and Jimmy played with them. To see if they were smart enough to nail them.

Which they weren't. The morons.

None of them saw it. They had been taken in by Karl, by the total-immunity scam.

And now Act Three of their movie. When Jimmy's movie, *Total Immunity*, ends in Total Fucking Disaster for the Feds.

Their greatest victory.

But also, Charlie was beginning to feel, their last victory.

And what would happen to Jimmy when they had avenged his murder? Would he be gone then?

Tell me you'll come back, Jimmy. Tell me you'll come back in your body so I can touch you and hug you again.

Charlie dragged Kevin out of the car (Kevin, the untalented, not like Jimmy. How could they kill Jimmy and not Kevin!) and carried him into the old boat factory and down the dark steps toward the boiler room.

And there they were, the two of them sitting there, waiting for him, all drugged out. Steinbach's brats.

Asleep. Yes, asleep and dirty, but alive.

All three of them, beautiful children, but alive. (Not like Jimmy.)

Alive, yes, for now, but not for long, not for much longer at all.

Charlie came out of the old factory in about an hour. It was dark outside, and he looked down at the rolling sea and felt suddenly at peace. He knew Jimmy was somewhere out there, too, watching things with him, maybe getting ready to make a transmission on his cell phone.

He started back up to the car, opened the door, and got inside. Then he backed up, turned around, and headed for the 405.

There was much to do now that his trap was laid. He had to get started immediately.

Get in touch with his brother, for one.

Important for everyone to stay focused now.

He pulled out onto the freeway and started north.

Then he noticed something and panic swept through him.

He'd left his coat in the factory. When he'd taken Kevin inside and tied him up with the others, he'd taken his coat off because it was stuffy down there.

And left it there.

Christ, there were probably credit-card bills in there from where he'd last gotten gas, or bought food from Ralph's. He had to go back. What an idiot he was to forget something that crucial. Nobody would come in, of course. But on the outside chance that someone did . . .

Jesus, he hoped Jimmy hadn't seen him. He didn't want his son to think of him as a fool and a clown.

He had to get off at the next exit, cross over, and come back down south. Jesus, what an idiot he was sometimes.

Forrester couldn't believe his own eyes.

His plan was to follow Charlie because he was sure Charlie would lead him to the money.

He was sure of it. Charlie had to be in on the stolen bank money. That's the only thing that made any sense.

So Forrester figured he would follow the clever bar owner and find out what kind of secret life he was leading.

He'd seen Charlie over at the Little League field, pulling out. He had one of the kids with him. Almost lost him as Charlie turned off, and must have stopped for a moment to drop the kid off. Forrester almost panicked then, but soon Charlie had come back on the road. Yeah, must have dropped the kid off because he wasn't sitting in the shotgun seat anymore.

Charlie had picked up the 405 and driven south.

Maybe Charlie might be headed for the beach house that the three of them bought with the stolen money from the bank job.

But Charlie didn't go to a beach house. Instead, he went to this crummy factory down in crummy San Pedro. And even though Forrester couldn't see everything from where he was parked—or Charlie Breen could have seen him—it looked as though he had taken something out of the trunk. No, not something. He'd just caught a glimpse of whatever it was as the door to the old factory closed, and it looked like a kid.

A kid in his trunk? The kid he had picked up? The kid he'd thought Charlie had dropped off.

Jesus, what were Harper, Hidalgo, and Breen into? Some kind of kid smuggling? Christ, if they were, this could be the greatest arrest in Bureau history. Way better than setting them up for the bank robbery.

Now he got out of his car and sneaked along the wet slats which ran alongside the factory walls.

He went up to the door, tried it. Of course, it was locked.

But there was a telephone pole alongside the building. Forrester climbed it quickly and jumped over to the old, sagging roof.

On top of the roof was an old window with two panes knocked out.

He crawled up to it, stuck his hands down inside, and opened it in a heartbeat.

He already had pictures in his mind as he climbed down to the top floor. He'd open a door somewhere and all these sex-slave kids would come pouring out, grateful to be saved from a life of captivity. Jesus, he'd go from being Bureau nerd to hero.

(And think of the movie deal, the parties at Spielberg's and Tarantino's!)

It was just a matter of finding them.

He reached for his revolver and made his way carefully through the old, dusty rooms.

Meanwhile, a block away, Charlie Breen pulled into an empty space right beside his building.

And looked at the car that was parked there already, a car which certainly hadn't been there when he left.

He took out his keys and grabbed a Mossberg 500 shotgun he had in the backseat. He also grabbed a 14-inch Maxam hunting knife he used for his occasional trips to the mountains.

Then Charlie walked up to the front door, put the key in the lock, and quietly turned it.

Downstairs, that's where the noise had come from. Downstairs. Little voices, whispers. Yes, Forrester thought. This is where they must keep them. Down here. In the filthy cellar.

He made his way down the steel steps, unable to see in the dark.

But the whispers were over in the far corner, though they'd stopped now. The poor bastards! They probably thought it was their captors coming back to whip their asses or something worse. Maybe Harper, Hidalgo, and Breen were using the kids as sex slaves.

"I'm coming, kids," Forrester thought. "I'll be there soon."

Charlie heard someone going down the steps below him. Christ, who could it be? Not the cops. That made no sense. If they had been tipped off that the kids were here, they'd come with a freaking platoon of guys.

317

No, had to be some kind of goof. Maybe another kid, or two kids looking for a place to screw.

Too bad for them. 'Cause this was the House of No Return. That was for sure.

You might walk in, but you sure as hell were going to be carried out.

Forrester wished he'd brought his flashlight.

He was stumbling over furniture. Making all kinds of noise.

"Hey," he finally whispered. "Anyone there?"

Silence.

"Seriously, I'm here to help. Anyone there?"

Another five seconds. Then . . .

"Over here. Help us."

"In the corner. By the boiler."

"Okay, I'm coming." His eyes were getting accustomed to the dark.

He made his way across the room. Heading for the kids. And now he saw them, tied up to the pipes on an old boiler. Jesus, what the hell was going on?

He looked down at them . . . dirty, great black bags under their eyes. Half starved. Drugged out.

What the fuck?

"Help us. We're tied up here."

He looked at the kid, who somehow seemed familiar.

He leaned over quickly and started untying the ropes.

Forrester was pleased with himself. He hadn't ever untied any ropes in his career before and was scared shitless that he had done it wrong now.

It proved that the other agents were wrong. He was still an ace of an agent, and he was about to catch some crooked creeps and God knows what the offer would be for the movie and book rights to his story.

As soon as he got these kids back to a shelter, he was going to call Spielberg and tell him all about his triumph.

As he trundled along in the dark—he should have brought in his flashlight—shepherding the kids toward the steel steps, he . . . Let's see . . . Colin Farrell would be good. And maybe—wait!—Clive Owen. He loved Clive. And also Daniel Craig.

How come all the cool actors were English or Irish guys?

Of course there was Brad Pitt, but Brad was getting a little old, and Clooney was definitely too old. He'd even let his hair go gray.

They were almost to the steps when Forrester heard the voice in the dark, somewhere behind him:

"Going somewhere?"

The kids jerked as one, as though they were still attached to the same harness. Forrester turned and looked into the darkness. In his hand was his .38.

"Breen? You're under arrest. FBI."

There was a brief pause, as if both sides were sizing one another up. Suddenly a hunting knife shot through the dark and landed in William Forrester's chest.

He made a gurgling sound and fell to the floor.

The kids screamed and both Kyle and Mike ran for the steps. Charlie Breen walked out of the darkness and aimed his gun at their backs.

"I think you better come down, boys," he said.

But the boys didn't stop running. He was left with no choice. He cocked his gun, aimed, and then was hit with a tackle from behind which caused his shots to go wild.

When he looked up, Kevin Harper was on top of him, pounding his face.

Still holding his pistol, Breen reached up and smashed Kevin in the head. The boy fell off him, blood spurting from his nose.

Charlie got up slowly, a pain in his back. The little bastard was as bad as his father. Both of Karl's boys were long gone.

They could be anywhere out on the docks. If he stayed around and tried to find them, he would be losing valuable time.

Fuck 'em both. They'd served their purpose. They were only day players in the movie, anyway.

The important thing was he still had Kevin.

He reached down and picked the dazed kid up by his shirt.

"You come with me, shithead," he said. "You make one move, you're dead."

They started up the steps, stumbled over the gurgling, dying Forrester, and then went the rest of the way to the car.

44

JACK PACED THE FLOOR at his house, which somehow didn't seem like his house at all now. Without Kevin, it was a cold, barren place. Nowhere to be. But then, without Kevin, every place was that same dead motel.

The phone rang and Jack's head jerked back as though someone had lashed his face with a whip.

"Harper," he said.

There was a laugh from the other end of the line.

"Harper," Charlie mimicked. "I like that, Jack. Firm, simple, like *you* were in control. Of course, it's all bullshit, because *we're* in control now, aren't we, Jackie?"

"We," Jack thought. That couldn't be a good sign. Who the hell was he talking about?

"Jack? You trying to diss me?"

"No way," Jack said. "You're in control, Charlie. There's no doubt about it. You have Kevin?"

"Yes, I do. You know, Jackie, it's a shame that the coach-and-player aspect of our relationship is finished. Because Kevin was getting quite good at going to the opposite field."

"Charlie, is he all right?"

"Just fine. Asleep right now, Jack."

"Charlie, I understand why you want revenge. But Kevin never hurt you. He loves and trusts you."

Charlie laughed again.

"Yeah, just like *we* trusted *you* to do the right thing, Jack. But you let that creep Chase kill my son, and then you gave him a whole new life."

Jack looked across the room where Oscar was working with the IT agents who were monitoring the call.

One of them raised his hand, showed two fingers.

Two more minutes and they'd have triangulated Charlie's location.

"Listen, Charlie, I know it was wrong. But it was my first assignment. I couldn't have talked Blakely out of it. I was more like a spectator than—"

"Bullshit," Charlie said. "That's bullshit. You were the best of them, Jack, even then. You could have done something. And afterward you could have made it impossible for Chase to get into Witness Protection, but you didn't do anything at all."

"I couldn't," Jack said. "That was the deal."

"My son's *life* was the fucking deal," Charlie said. "Now I'm going to tell you the *new* deal. You're going to give me Billy Chase. Once my brother has killed him, he's going to call me and then I'm going to tell you where Kevin is. If you or Oscar or any of your FBI buddies do anything to stop me, I'll slit Kevin's throat."

"Charlie, wait!" Jack said.

"And don't think you can stop my brother and make him lie to me. He won't give in, Jack. I'll expect the call by seven in the morning. You understand?"

322

Jack looked over at the agent, who shook his head.

"Yeah, sure, Charlie . . ."

He hung up.

"You get him?"

"No," the agent said. "General area. He's near the marina somewhere."

"The marina?" Jack said. "Jesus! He's got a boat out there. Let's get a helicopter out there now. And alert the Coast Guard."

But even as he said it, Jack felt that it was no use. Charlie wouldn't be dumb enough to use his own boat.

No, there was some kind of little trick he was playing, to make it sound as though he were in the Marina Del Rey. There were a million little tricks you could play with phones. Jack knew because he had used them all. You could route the phone through an operator at the marina and be standing in Los Feliz, if you knew the game, and clearly Charlie knew all about it. Still, they had to give the marina a shot.

Jack slumped onto the couch next to Julie, who grasped his hand.

"Baby," she said. "I'm so sorry. But I know we're going to get Kevin back."

"Of course we are," Jack said.

He smiled at her and turned away; he was right on the edge of madness. And nothing could be done about it until they saved his son.

45

THE DAY WAS DARK and wet as it usually is in Portland, Oregon. The rain came down in cold sheets, but it didn't seem to bother the small, furtive-looking man who walked alone by Eagle Creek in Benson State Park.

He wore a Trailblazers sweatshirt and, like most Portlanders, seemed to be impervious to the weather.

Only a rookie to the rainy, brooding countryside would wear a raincoat or carry an umbrella. And this man was not a rookie.

He'd lived in Portland for many years and could barely remember the earlier part of his life, the one in which he'd robbed banks with Adam Moore. He knew that some people might find it exciting, but to Eddie Larsen of Portland, Billy Chase barely existed anymore.

After all, wasn't that what the West was all about? Starting over, rebirthing yourself as the guys in AA (of which he'd been a member for twenty-five years now) called it.

Sure, that was it. Of course it was.

You made mistakes, and you moved on and learned from them and became a different person. A person with a kid, a lovely daughter named Rose, and a great wife, Martha, and you didn't spend your time looking back.

What was the profit in that?

He walked faster now, hoping, praying that the Feds were around him, protecting him.

Christ, he didn't want to die at the hands of a madman!

He'd worked so hard to break his old dope habits, wanted to stay healthy so he could see his daughter grow up and get married and maybe even have grandchildren.

Had to keep healthy.

Never even thought about the past until they came and told him that it was coming after him.

It was so unfair. He might get a bullet in his head or the lunatic from L.A. (and how he hated L.A. now that he was a good Portlander, with his sustainable garden and windmill-powered house. All those L.A. phonies with their emphasis on materialism. Ugh, how had he ever stood living there all those years?).

Where the fuck was he? Oh, yeah, the unfairness of it. Jesus, the loony might jump on his back from an overhanging tree that the Feds missed and stab him in the throat.

And for something he didn't even do!

Was it his fault that Billy Chase, the drug addict, held up a store and that a kid fell and hurt his head and died?

Well, yeah, technically, but couldn't anyone who wasn't a fucking lunatic see it was an accident? A freak thing?

Well, come on. Of course they could. They could even see that he, Billy Chase, was a victim himself. Wasn't he? Yeah, a victim of . . . the Mafia who sold drugs to kids, which was what he was when all this shit happened about ten million years ago. Anyone with half a social conscience could see that.

Anyone except this freakin' fanatic, this Roy Ayres. This guy couldn't get over it. What was his problem? Was he too sensitive or something?

Hell, couldn't Ayres see it was *another* guy who had killed his kid? No, that was wrong—not even killed him, just scared him.

Maybe that was what was wrong. Ayres and his family were just too fucking sensitive.

The sensitive little family.

Whining about his lost son all his life. Christ, people in other countries lose kids every day. How about Iraq? Lots of Iraq kids die in car bombings and shit every day, and do their parents walk around obsessing about it all the time? No, they get on with their lives. But he has to kill an overly sensitive guy's kid. Jesus!

The sensitive guy with the sensitive gun.

Couldn't anyone see how he'd changed? What a great guy he was now?

Fuck, couldn't Mr. Sensitive just have another kid? What the fuck was wrong with him anyway? You have a dick; stick it in another woman and presto, new baby! No . . . no . . . It was the L.A. thing, the sense of entitlement. They said the kid was a genius; that was why the guy couldn't get over losing him. But come on, *everybody* in fucking L.A. thought their kids were fucking geniuses. The assholes had Mr. Workingman, Bruce Springsteen, play at their school fund-raisers so the kids would grow up thinking they could be great, too, and their trendy parents made them do fucking calculus problems when they were one year old. And what did they grow up to be? Hack moviemakers who did dumb horror films, or else they turned into lame reality-TV producers named Barry and Mel. Not geniuses at all, but hustlers who sold cheap dogshit movies and didn't even care about global warming!

Like Eddie did.

He worried about it every day, and just because he'd had a

little accident a few years ago, he might die here. And leave his daughter, who *was* a genius and was being raised right . . .

He sure hoped the Feds were out there somewhere. Jesus, he felt like he might piss himself. Oh, man . . .

Walk faster, breathe in and out.

The world just wasn't fair. That was it.

He wondered if, when he died, he'd see the kid he maybe killed pointing at him and teasing him as he was sent via bullet train to hell.

Terry Ayres was dressed in a black hoodie and dark vinyl track pants. He waited next to a huge evergreen tree, though he didn't know the tree's name. Terry didn't know the name of any trees or plants. To him they were blotches of light and leaves, and bark. Names were too hard.

He spent most of his life watching movies and television and lived in a cloudy blur of action plots and tenth-rate sitcom dialogue. Random speeches bisected his thick skull, speeches from terrible, shitty sitcoms. He heard floating voices say, "Your mother's coming for the weekend. Oh, noooo! Hide the good jewelry." He didn't know where he'd heard this speech. Or what the original context was. In fact he wasn't big on "context" at all. It was just an isolated speech from some show he'd barely been conscious he was watching. Other speeches flew through his head, too. "Oh, no, it's fat Albert" was one he heard again and again. And "Get your mother-in-law out of here right now and don't twitch your nose, you cunt." He didn't know if that last one was real or he'd rewritten it.

Really, Terry thought sometimes, when he had brief moments of actual consciousness, there was no real Terry. He didn't exist. Not like other people, with a solid sense of . . . what did they call it? . . . "self." Nah, he was more like a cloud than a person.

The thought made him laugh, which was not what he was

327

supposed to do. Not out here in the rain. Not out here on this little hill looking down at the man in the sweatshirt with the Blazers written on it.

Terry wondered if the Blazers would be good this year.

Or if they would all get put in jail again.

The Portland Jailbreakers. Ha ha.

He shouldn't be thinking of that either.

He wished Roy was here with him. He liked to do things with Roy because Roy made him feel secure and happy. And competent.

Roy, for example, would know the names of the trees and would know exactly when was the best time to kill this shithead who himself killed Roy's son, Jimmy, who was going to put Terry in pictures.

It was true, Terry thought. He already had a movie picked out called *The Scar*, and Terry was going to play this heroic cop who gets a scar and then turns bad because prejudiced people laugh at him but then who gets some kind of redemption at the end and saves a kid. Or the world. One of them. Terry liked the world better than the kid. But Jimmy had told him the world might be too hard on their budget for the movie, which was two hundred grand.

Still, either way, it sounded great to Terry, who had even tried reading the script but gave up two pages in. Print on a page was like angry bees buzzing in his head. He was a Valley guy who liked to look at pictures, and hear people make statements about how they'd found their true calling. How they redeemed their lost lives.

Terry was a Redemption Junkie.

Stuff you saw on *Oprah*.

He'd found his, that was for sure. Doing jobs like this for his bro.

Thing is, Roy knew how to use him. And this was the way!

Like in a movie. He was the action hero, like Arnie before he became Senator . . . or was it Governor? Yeah, Governor.

Terry was a guy who really only lived for Big Scenes. Action stuff.

Like the night he pretended to run over Jack Harper and let Roy/Charlie "save Jack," which took any suspicion off Charlie.

Or the time he knocked Charlie in the head at Jack's house, which was so cool.

Like a movie. *Terminator* or *Die Hard*.

But this was the greatest role of all.

Shooting the guy that killed Jimmy The Genius.

Jimmy who had a million ideas for horror films and was going to be the next Steven Spielberg, was going to make *Scar*, in which he would play an action hero.

He ran through the whole plot of *Scar* again, imagining girls lining up outside of Mann's Chinese Theater, all of them down on their knees with their perfect collagen-lipped mouths open, ready to suck him off.

Yeah, there was no business like show business.

And now the guy was almost across the field and it was his job to cut him off, right there by the tree line (wonder what they were called . . . Jimmy would know if he wasn't dead).

The idea was to cut him off and to shoot him in the face.

Why in the face?

Because in his pocket Terry had a picture of the guy Billy Chase, and he had to be sure it was really him and not a decoy guy.

That's why. He had to remember that.

He loped down the hill with his Winchester in his hands. There it was: the perfect little hillside spot.

Chase would have to come through here.

And when he did . . . well, then, *blotto.*

Red-mist city, yessir!

329

And years of pain, missing being a star in Jimmy's movie *Scar* (in which he was the star, this cop guy with a scar who . . .).

He sat on a tree limb to steady the barrel and waited for Billy to come up the trail; waited, waited.

And then, out of nowhere, the trees around him seemed to be alive with what at first seemed like walking branches.

Holy shit!

Things—no, not things—people coming out of nowhere, and all of them with big guns trained on him.

Like he was Scar, and the cops were after him, but this time there was no redemption, no "saving the day" and no fucking parade.

They had him.

But he was smart for once—very smart—and gave up pronto, laying his rifle down on the ground and then falling down next to it on his knees, his hands clasped at the back of his head.

They had him. Shit! He'd really hoped he would get to shoot that guy Chase in the face. Wotta drag!

46

TERRY AYRES SAT ACROSS the interrogation table at the Portland Central Police Station from Oscar and Jack. Terry drank a Coke and, while they were hammering at him, he tried to trick them by thinking of product placement.

If this was *Scar* (the movie he was going to be in if Jimmy hadn't died and . . . blah blah blah), they would probably be getting a fee from Coca-Cola for showing their product on the screen—a fee he would never get a piece of because Jimmy was dead and these guys let the guy go who . . .

"Wake the fuck up!" Jack screamed, pounding the table so hard that the Coke spilled all over Terry's already-wet pants.

"Hey, watch it," Terry said, shaking.

Jack got up from the table and slapped Terry's face with the back of his hand. Terry fell off the chair onto the cold floor and looked back up at his tormentor.

"Hey, hey," Oscar said, jumping from his chair and grabbing Jack. "C'mon, partner. That's not the way."

Jack sat back down, breathing hard. Of course, it was their usual good-cop/bad-cop act, but this time, Oscar thought, Jack might have gone over the top. He was pretty sure that if he'd left Jack alone in here with Terry Ayres, the guy would come out a piece of meat.

Terry got back in his seat and took a sip of what was left of his Coke.

"You've had a pretty rough time," Oscar said.

"Not really," Terry said, looking straight ahead at Oscar, trying to avoid Jack's bullet gaze.

"Yeah, you have," Oscar said. "Looking over your sheet here, I see you been in and out of jail four times since you were first in juvy, when you were, what was it, twelve?"

"Yeah, so?" Terry said. He tried to set his jaw like a tough guy, but it hurt his ears.

"So, I see your dad abandoned the family. Mom died when you were ten. Means you had no one to look after you. No one to help you. 'Cept your brother, Roy."

"Yeah, that's right." Terry made his jaw even firmer, jutted it out like The Joker, but now his ears and his throat hurt. It was painful, being so tough.

"He's a guy you really depend on. Right? Guy you're loyal to?"

"Yeah," Terry said. "Which is why I'm never gonna give him up to you guys."

"You cocksucker!" Jack started across the table again, but Oscar grabbed him and shoved him back.

"Maybe you ought to go outside," Oscar said.

Jack's face was twisted in pain and fury.

He got up, walked by Terry Ayres, and went out the door. He walked around to the side entrance and went inside the observation corridor.

Two Portland Feds watched. They said nothing to Jack.

Inside the interrogation room, Oscar leaned across the table to get closer to Ayres.

"That's good, being loyal," he said, in a soft, kind voice.

Terry looked up at him with a puzzled grin. "You think so?"

"Yeah. Most of the time. But sometimes it can be stupid, too. See, so far we have nothing on your brother, but we've got you for attempted murder, and I imagine it won't be too hard to pin the other killings on you, too."

Terry Ayres bit his lower lip and blinked like a nervous bird.

"That's bullshit and you know it."

"Well, who else? It won't take a rocket scientist to see how this went. Roy wants revenge on people who killed his son, but he's too chickenshit to do it himself. However, luckily for him, he's got a very loyal but not-too-bright brother. He talks him into doing the killings, then sets him up to get caught."

Terry took a deep breath and blew it out, as if he was trying to blow away thirty-five years of stupidity.

"You're trying to trick me," he said. Just then an old TV voice floated through his head. It said, "The Rolli Mop. It's the only mop you'll ever need."

Oscar patted Terry's arm in a fatherly way.

"No, Terry, I'm trying to be straight with you. You're all set up, and if you don't call your brother by seven thirty, he's going to kill a kid. Apparently, that's all he has the balls to do. Slit an innocent kid's throat."

"No," Terry said. "That's not right."

"Yeah, it is," Oscar said. "Then after he kills a child, he's going to disappear. Which leaves you to take the rap as an accomplice to first-degree murder. How lenient do you think the jury is going to be toward you, Ter? I see you getting the lethal injection with or without him."

333

Terry looked like someone had lit his feet.

"But . . . but . . . You're asking me to give up my own brother."

"He gave *you* up," Oscar said.

"But they killed his son. Hey, James was a genius. He said I was a great natural actor."

"Focus," Oscar said. "What happened to his son was terrible, but it was an accident. You can use your acting skills now to help us bring in the right guy, and you won't end up on a steel gurney with poisons running through your arm."

Terry's straight tough-guy jaw began to quiver, and tears ran down his gaunt cheeks.

"All right," he said. "I'll call him and do what you want. Bring me the phone."

Oscar nodded and patted Terry on the head.

"Now you're playing it smart, kid," he said.

On the other side of the glass, Jack slumped forward, then started to breathe again.

47

JACK SAT AT a gray institutional desk, a cold coffee cup in his hand. Oscar leaned against the wall next to him, humming a song over and over.

"What the fuck are you singing?" Jack said.

"One of the great songs of my Mexican heritage," Oscar said.

"Which is?" Jack said.

"This Old Man." Oscar began to sing, "This old man, he plays three. He plays knickknack on my knee, with a knick knack paddy whack . . ."

"Jesus!" Jack said. "If you sing that fucking song one more time, I'm gonna slam my head into the wall."

"Promise?" Oscar teased.

Suddenly the phone rang and Jack's head jerked back. He let it ring once more, then picked it up.

"Harper," he said.

"Jackie," Charlie Breen said. "You did such fine work. Really, you ought to be commended. Jimmy tells me it was a walk in the park."

"That's right, Charlie. Billy Chase is dead and gone. Now tell me where I can find Kevin."

Charlie gave an odd little laugh on the other line.

"Why, right where you left him, Jack. In the old gym at Brentwood Park."

"Brentwood Park?" Jack tried to imagine the old gym. In his mind, the park ended beyond the right-field wall. But no, now he saw it: the battered old brick gym. A place that was there but invisible because no one ever used it anymore. How could he have not seen it?

"Look in the boys' locker room," Charlie said.

"He better be all right," Jack said.

"Oh, he's fine," Charlie said, as he ate a brisket sandwich he'd just bought from Carter's.

"Yeah, he's ready for a nice day on the field. I really am gonna miss coaching him, Jack. Going to miss all the kids. Maybe you can take over the reins, Jackie. I think you have a real talent for coaching."

Charlie wiped some of the barbecue sauce off his lip, and hung up.

Jack looked over at Oscar, who listened in on the second phone.

"They're already on it," he said.

"Fucking Brentwood!" Jack said. "Oh, man . . ."

He slumped on the desk, sweat pouring down his neck.

Within a half hour after the phone call from Portland, an LAPD SWAT team arrived at Brentwood Park, in three black, unmarked vans. They quickly broke into two columns, surrounding the gym from both the north and south exits.

One column of men kicked in the back door to the boys' locker room and, using their flash-lit rifles, headed inside.

The columns hurried down the aisles of old rusted lockers, kicking aside the old stools, which were still there.

The secondary group looked through the hallways and the basketball court.

Finally they searched through the girls' locker room, and five men went into the bowels of the old gym. They went into the furnace room, the janitor's bedroom, every nook and cranny in the gym basement.

All they found were about fifty rats scrambling through the hallways and a pile of old *Hustler* magazines.

Other than that, nothing.

No sign of Kevin Harper.

Jack and Oscar got the call five minutes after the search was completed.

Jack's face had become reddened and he felt a pressure in his temples, as if there was a hand inside his head, desperate fingers thrusting out.

His heart felt the same way and, as he sat at his desk with his head hanging, he suddenly understood the term "broken heart" for the first time.

He had always thought it was some kind of metaphor, but now he knew otherwise. He could feel his heart breaking. Cracking inside his chest like an ice floe breaking up.

Soon, he thought, it would crack open, but instead of water rushing out, it would be his own blood.

And yet, in the unbearable pain he felt without his son, there was some consolation in that. For if anything had happened to Kevin, he wouldn't want to go on living, anyway.

Now he felt a rough push on his back. He ignored it, not even sure if it was real or some phantom pain, commensurate with his agony. But there it was again, a kind of poking, which enraged him. He looked up, snarling.

"What the fuck is going on?"

He looked at Oscar's broad, strong face, his brown eyes wide open, determined.

"C'mon, man. This game ain't over yet. Get up off that chair."

"I can't," Jack said. "I can't . . ."

He wanted to say exactly what it was he couldn't do or think . . . but there was nothing else.

"You got to," Oscar said. "We're going to get Kevin back."

Jack gritted his teeth and imagined choking Charlie Breen to death, slowly, until his eyes popped out.

Oscar reached down. Jack took his large, powerful hand, and his partner pulled him to his feet.

48

IT WAS A DARK NIGHT at Benson State Park and the giant firs and cedars were illuminated by the brilliant moonlight. High up, only a few hundred yards away from Multnomah Falls, there was a home made out of logs and cedar shake. All the lights were off inside the place except one, a porch light shaped like an acorn.

A block away sat a simple panel truck with the words Department of Parks stenciled on the side.

Inside the truck, Charlie Breen, dressed like a khaki-clad forest ranger, sat looking at the acorn-shaped porch light and spoke to his fellow traveler, Martin J. Black, the real ranger who sat in the passenger seat, minus his clothes.

"Look at the acorn light. That's the kind of thing you get at Ikea," Charlie Breen said. "Can't you just see the happy family winding their way through Ikea on a Saturday afternoon? Happy little family with their happy kids, chatting about all the nifty furniture, and maybe thinking about the great deals on hot dogs and pizza they have as you leave the store with all your swell items. Can't you just picture that, Marty?"

Martin J. Black said nothing.

Charlie looked over at him and laughed.

"You're a quiet one, aren't you?" he said. "I read all about you forest rangers a long time ago in one of those Jack Kerouac books. The lonely sentinel high above the treetops in his manly lookout, kind of like a priest up there, communing with nature, watching out for fires, keeping all of nature safe. I admire that, Marty, I really do. But, unfortunately, you were also keeping a murderer safe. They thought they had me fooled, but, of course, I knew they'd catch my brother. And then I followed Billy Chase home."

Charlie/Roy (which one was he now, sometimes it was so hard to remember) laughed and stuck his flashlight in Martin J. Black's gaping neck wound. Blood coagulated on the bulb and made weird patterns on the windshield.

From the back of the truck there was a kicking noise, and Charlie got out and walked around to the back doors. He unlocked them and looked inside. Kevin Harper was hog-tied but had managed to slide himself over to the truck walls. He kicked the wall one last time as Charlie stepped inside and hit him in the side of the head with the flashlight, opening a wide gash.

"I told you not to make me come back here," he said. "Now let's keep it down back here, son, 'cause we're almost home."

He found his little parental joke amusing and began to chuckle to himself.

Now, he thought, it was time to finish this job.

He would go into the house and kill Billy Chase and anyone else he ran across. Well, wait . . . he still hadn't decided. Would he kill Billy first? No, he thought not. Best to kill Billy's daughter and make him watch. Of course . . . how could he have not thought of that?

Then he remembered. He had thought of it, but then forgotten it.

This short-term-memory thing had him worried. After he got done killing the Chase family, he'd have to get on a new diet regimen and see his doctor. Back in Munich.

A lot of this bad-memory shit, he thought, as he relocked the panel truck's doors, was due to the stress of having to plan this revenge over and over, reworking the script with Jimmy.

"But we're almost there now, Jimmy," he said to his son. "We are almost there."

He waited until he heard Jimmy's voice in his head. A soft whisper, like a boy who is going to sleep.

"Good job, Dad."

Roy felt a rush of satisfaction. It was always important to get Jimmy's approval. They'd made their film every step of the way, and now they'd finish it. He was glad Jimmy had decided to come with him on the final act of the production.

He stood there in the pleasant cover of dark for a minute and went over the story again:

First we kill the kids, then the wife. Then . . . The Big One. Billy himself.

On that one, he would have to get Jimmy's help.

He stopped and looked up at the moon.

And thought, for a second, that he saw handsome Jimmy coming down on a moonbeam, riding a trail of silver dust. His son coming, bright eyed, handsome, the genius. The filmmaker, not just some movie guy. The filmmaker.

The auteur.

That was going to be it.

The final scene in their movie.

The Big One.

Tonight was the night.

He reached into the backseat and picked up his camera.

49

IT TOOK HIM only seconds to cut the security lines, up on the side of the house. In another fifteen seconds, he'd opened the sliding door and was inside.

He walked through the living room, which he was surprised to find was very folksy. There were folksy Hummel figures—a whole shelf of them—cute little chubby kids all lovingly huddled together, just adorable; he couldn't wait to show Jimmy those.

"Look at these, Jimmy," he said. Billy Chase had terrible taste. Yet another reason to rid the world of him.

He took out his bone knife, the one with the polished shark-cartilage handle, and walked quickly up the stairs.

Stuck in his waistband was his .45.

He didn't intend to use the gun. There was no fun in that.

When the knife went into the man who'd killed Jimmy, he'd twist it and turn it, and make him squirm and beg.

Oh, yes, squirming and begging were essential.

He went down the hallway, thankful for the carpet, which muffled the sound of his footsteps.

He saw the master bedroom, and having gotten close enough to Billy Chase, after all these years, he suddenly forgot the whole plan again, the bit about taking out the daughter first.

He'd become blood-crazed and couldn't wait to go through with the whole ritual.

He just wanted Billy-boy on the end of his knife. All the rest was gravy.

He opened the master bedroom door and slipped inside. Trained his vid cam at the bed.

There—in the bed—was a figure. Waiting, lying there sleeping.

"It's Bill, Jimmy," he said inside his head. "It's the man who ended your life."

And in that moment, he forgot the whole deal about killing them one by one. It was Billy he wanted, it was Billy Jimmy wanted.

He moved forward and raised his knife. Balanced the cam on his shoulder.

"Hey, hey, hey, Billy-boy," he said, as he plunged the knife down toward his sleeping target. "How about this?"

He stuck the blade into the back of the sleeping figure.

He'd worked himself up to a fine rage, saliva flying from his mouth, and he raised the knife to plunge again, but then realized he'd been robbed.

Robbed of the essential pleasures of a scream from the victim and the even finer satisfaction of feeling the knife cut through tissue and bone, and perhaps a pink piece of lung.

He reached down and snapped back the covers.

Pillows! Pillows stacked up.

He heard himself give a meek little laugh, a whimper, and immediately felt a red blush spread over his face.

Then he turned and found Jack Harper behind him, a pistol in his hand.

"Hi, Charlie," Jack said.

"Jack," Charlie said, for a second unable to say anything else.

"That was good, Charlie," Jack said. "Your brother almost had us fooled with his 'breakdown' and his fake call to L.A., which you had forwarded to your cell phone in Portland. *Almost* worked. But after I thought about it a little, I realized you'd never let Terry kill Billy. It was too personal for that. It had to be *you*."

Charlie felt a sense of personal shame and failure, which led him to a rage-storm. He wanted to ram Jack's face with his head, smashing his nose. He wanted to bite into Jack's neck. But he suppressed his rage, stayed calm.

"You were very smart, Charlie. You kidnapped Karl's kids and held them hostage so he had to help you. But why all the drama?"

Charlie laughed.

"That was Jimmy's idea, Jack. After all, it's his film."

"Your son?"

Charlie nodded and gave a knowing little grin.

"Jimmy came up with it all. He tells me, and I carry it out. He loves big twisting stories where the hero is suckered in by his own confidence. We got you good, Jack. You gotta give us that."

"You and Jimmy," Jack repeated. And in spite of himself and all that Charlie had done, Jack began to feel a deep sorrow on his old friend's behalf.

"That's why the camera, Jackie. I've been filming it all—with Jimmy. When I finish with this, we'll have our masterpiece. By the way, you should know I decided not to kill you. You and Kevin get to live, for now, as long as you don't make any real trouble."

"Why, thank you, Charlie," Jack said. "That's kind of you."

"It wasn't my idea, Jack. It was Jimmy. He liked you and Kevin. He wouldn't go on with the film unless he had certain assurances."

"That's very nice of Jimmy, then," Jack said.

"Don't talk to me in that patronizing tone, Jack," Charlie said. "I know Jimmy's not here in a physical way, but his talent . . . you couldn't kill that. That's a spiritual thing. The talent stays alive because it comes from Jimmy's immortal soul."

He nodded as though he were reassuring himself that it was true.

"I know you're laughing at me. You think I'm nuts. But *you're* the one that doesn't understand. A guy like you has no understanding of the connection between me and my son."

"I'm sure I don't," Jack said.

"It's amazing," Charlie said. "For every one of you that died, Jimmy came more and more alive. Now I can see him, talk to him almost all the time. You're going to love the movie, Jack. After all, it was you and your pals who thought of the title."

"What is it?" Jack was interested despite himself.

"*Total Immunity,* of course," Charlie said. "You gave total immunity to Billy Chase. That's what got the whole project going."

"You're a sick man, Charlie," Jack said. "You gotta come with me. The premiere of *Total Immunity* is postponed indefinitely."

"I don't think so, Jack," Charlie said. "See, you're always one step behind me."

Charlie opened his left hand and showed Jack a tiny detonator.

"See what I have here, Jackie? Even if you pull the trigger, I can blow up the truck outside, the one with Kevin in the back."

Jack stared at him for ten seconds. Then:

"Okay," Jack said. "Go ahead, Charlie. Push it."

"You think I won't? It'll be a fair trade, Jack. Your son for mine."

"Push it!"

"All right, Jack. You asked for it. Look out the window."

He pushed the button. A second later, there was an explosion which rocked the house.

Jack looked down at the street, saw the flash. He felt numb inside.

"Now things can get right again," Charlie said. "I was going to kill you, Jack, but now I think it'll be much better to let you live. To suffer like I did for the rest of your life, knowing you couldn't protect your son. Finally, you and I will be dead even."

Jack smelled the smoke and saw the fire outside.

Then he smiled at Charlie Breen.

"I don't think so, Charlie. Take a look."

Charlie looked outside and saw two federal agents using hand extinguishers to put out the fire.

A few feet away from them, three other agents surrounded an untied Kevin Harper, whom Oscar covered with an Indian blanket.

Three local cops were walking toward the house, their guns drawn.

"You son of a bitch!" Charlie said.

In one smooth motion, Charlie threw the shark-handled knife into Jack's left side. The pain was blinding, but Jack managed to get off a shot which hit Charlie's right shoulder.

Ordinarily such a shot would push a man backward, but Charlie Breen was so pumped up with adrenaline and hate that he lunged forward, pulled the knife out of Jack's body and tried using it again, this time to cut Jack's throat.

Jack felt weak, dizzy, and knew that within seconds he'd be lying on the floor bleeding out.

He resorted to the oldest and most effective trick he knew in combat.

He kneed Charlie Breen in the groin.

Charlie groaned and fell back, but didn't go down. Instead, he picked up a chair and threw it at Jack, then turned, ran to the side window, and plunged through the glass.

Jack followed him, watched Charlie hit the parking-garage roof, then roll down it. He fell on the other side of a chain fence, which cordoned off the house from the trailhead in the dark woods.

All of the federal men and local cops were on the house side of the fence. If Charlie got into the forest, there was no telling where he might go.

Jack took the leap, rolled down the rooftop, jumped over the fence, and took off after him.

Jack saw Charlie disappear into the forest. There was no way the older man was going to outrun him.

But in front of him Jack saw two trails, both of them chewed up by hikers. It was impossible to tell which path Charlie Breen had taken.

Both of them led up to Multnomah Falls . . . and the deep forest beyond.

Jack decided on taking the less steep path, reasoning that Charlie would want to get as deep into the forest as possible in the shortest amount of time.

He ran up the path, his side leaking blood.

He touched his side as he ran and came away with a great gob of blood.

But there was no way he was going to stop.

The path stretched out in front of him, illuminated by moonlight, and he suddenly saw the two of them in his mind's eye, like cameo figures racing back in time, from the so-called civilized world into the primitive society of wild beasts, and giant lizards with great scales and sharp teeth.

347

He ran on, turned a corner at full speed, and barely stopped in time to avoid falling off a two-hundred-foot chasm.

On the other side of it stood Charlie, surrounded by mist.

"Coming, Jack?"

"You jumped this?" Jack said.

"Yep," Charlie said. He seemed to be reverting to his friendly, folksy coach persona. "You have to back up a bit there, then run like hell and leap. Bet you can't do it."

"How much?" Jack said, pointing his Glock .22 at Charlie's head.

"A hundred bucks," Charlie said. "I don't think you're motivated enough."

"But I don't have to jump," Jack said. "I can shoot you right here."

"No," Charlie said. "You can't, Jackie."

He opened his arms wide. It seemed to Jack that he was calling forth a mist from down at the base of the waterfall.

A waterfall, just to their right, which Jack hadn't even noticed.

He tried to sight Charlie through the mist, but the moon played tricks on the water, and suddenly Jack wasn't even sure if he'd spoken to Charlie at all.

He blinked, rubbed his eyes, tried to see, but Charlie seemed to have disappeared.

Then his voice came toward Jack, and in a canyon of moonlit water, it might have come from anywhere.

"You killed my son," Charlie said. "Were you ever sorry for it?"

"Yes, of course," Jack said, and he was. He felt—suddenly—as if it had happened just now, that he had been watching the boy and turned away, and Jimmy had fallen over the falls.

"You *should* pay for it," Charlie's deep, echoing voice said again, and it was the voice of somebody's idea of God, spoken from bushes, rocks, and dripping trees.

Jack said nothing. It occurred to him that in some universal

348

way Charlie had been right all along, that all of them deserved to die for wanting too much, for making a deal—not with Billy Chase, but with evil.

The devil, Jack thought, was always painted as huge, red-robed, with menacing horns and a pitchfork, but he seldom presented himself that way. If such a devil promised you endless riches, or a life of ease, anyone with half a brain would run in the opposite direction.

So he presented himself to you as a harmless small-time crook who could give you total immunity. Immunity from fear, immunity from death, immunity from robbery. A small, bright little bug of a man who could give you Adam Moore—the devil himself—on a platter.

You offered him immunity, and he offered you the same, and yea, there was joy and happiness in the kingdom.

Only one small, very bright boy had to pay. That was in the small print that none of them had bothered to read.

And now Jack knew that there was no immunity, there was no freedom—only deals which ground up a child, unhinged a decent man, killed police, and terrorized his own child, perhaps forever.

In the seductive moonlight, on the edge of the Multnomah Falls, it was Jack who was lost. He felt that it was his own cowardice that had set off this chain of events, his own timidity, trying to do well for his career when he knew what he was doing was wrong.

Could he have changed the way things turned out? He didn't know for sure. What killed him now was that he hadn't even tried. He had gone along with the others, even as he worried that it could somehow backfire.

And somehow, knowing that changed things. Now Jack knew that even if Charlie appeared out of the mist again, he couldn't just shoot him.

He had to jump, give Charlie a chance. He owed him that much for taking his son.

He backed up and breathed in deeply, then started running for the gorge and leaped off into the mist.

He flew, flew across, and looked down at the gaping slash of open air, the roaring water rising up to pull him down.

And then he was there, landed on the other side, and Charlie was rushing toward him, like a bear, a huge branch in his hand.

"You're going to fucking die, Jack."

He swung hard, and Jack felt the branch smash into his chest. He saw a flash of pain and fell backward, rolling toward the edge of the cliff. The world slowed to a crawl. He caught himself by grabbing a bush inches from the edge but now Charlie was coming at him again, this time with his leg kicking into Jack's head, screaming, "Here he comes, Jimmy. I've delivered them all to you, son."

Jack felt his head snap back, and then there was another stabbing pain as Charlie kicked him in the ribs.

Jack rolled even closer to the precipice. Charlie came closer, kicking out his foot again and again. Jack felt something in his ribs give way. He tried to get to his feet, but slipped. Then Jack waited, waited for Charlie's final blow. But as Charlie got set to deliver it, Jack slashed out with his own foot and caught Charlie off balance, mid-kick.

Charlie screamed a short, staccato burst, and fell over Jack, off the edge of the falls. He flailed wildly and grabbed Jack's right wrist.

Jack pulled with all his fading might.

But Charlie looked up at him and shook his head.

"I'm going to Jimmy now, Jackie," he said. And smiled in his warm way, like Charlie Breen always did. A warm, encompassing smile. And in spite of all Charlie had done, Jack felt as though he was looking at his own father.

"I'm sorry, Charlie," Jack said.

Charlie nodded twice, and then opened his hand.

Jack watched him go down, fast, giving out a yell, not a scream, more of a warrior's battle cry. He watched Charlie plunge into the roaring river seventy-five feet below. His body bounced off two big boulders, and then disappeared.

50

JACK STOOD with his arm around Kevin, who was still trembling. Around him, the other agents were cleaning up the mess.

Oscar walked over and patted Kevin on the head.

"I heard you were very brave. You saved the two Steinbach boys."

Kevin shrugged.

"I had to do something," he said.

"And you did," Oscar said. "Good boy!"

He turned to Jack.

"Down in the basement of The Deckhouse, he had a screen and an Avid editing machine. He was putting together the film of the murders."

Jack shook his head.

"All that time, he held that anger and fury. All that time."

"Yeah," Oscar said. "He made audiotapes, too. Only heard a couple of minutes. But apparently making the movie kept his son alive in his head. He'd talk, consult with him."

"Man!" Kevin said. "And all along I thought Charlie was like my uncle or something."

"Yeah," Oscar said. "Instead, he was *muy loco.*"

"I don't know," Jack said. "You know, when my dad died, I went out and bought old radio tapes."

"How come, Dad?"

"'Cause I missed him, and as a kid he listened to them with me. So there I am driving all around L.A. listening to old tapes with dead actors on them: Alan Ladd and William Conrad, and the whole time I'm feeling my dad sitting there next to me, commenting on them. At night I wrote a diary, too, putting all the things down that my dad used to say to me. I wrote stuff about camping trips we took, and how he used to come see me play lacrosse, and all of that stuff. This went on for almost two years. Your mother . . . she thought I was out of my head. Having conversations with a ghost about old radio shows in the car, writing for hours every night. She wanted me to go see a shrink."

"You do that, man?"

"No, Osc. I didn't. Eventually, one day I just didn't play the tapes, and soon after that I stopped writing. It was over. Not all of it, but enough so I could face the fact that he was really gone. What I'm saying is that Charlie or Roy . . . he didn't lose his dad, he lost his young son. And he didn't lose him through normal circumstances. He lost him because we fucked up. It took me two years to get over losing my dad, so maybe it's not that far out to think of him being destroyed by losing his son. Wanting revenge. Making the movie with 'his son.' It was his way of getting even and not facing his son's death. The whole fantastic plot was what occupied him, kept him in denial of his son's death."

Kevin shook his head.

"But I thought he really cared about me. I could have sworn he wasn't faking."

"He wasn't," Jack said. "He *did* care about you. But also, your presence made him enraged. That you should be alive, the son of the man he held responsible for his son's death."

"But you *weren't* responsible, Jack," Oscar said.

"Yes, I was. At least, partially."

Kevin looked at his father with a world of confusion, pain, and love on his face.

"Really, Dad?"

"Really," Jack said. "It's a long story, though, and we'll have to talk about it."

As he finished speaking, the retrieval team shone a light from the woods. The three of them looked over at the path and saw them bringing Charlie's body down on a portable gurney.

Charlie was covered with a white sheet. His right arm fell out to the side and dangled there.

Jack felt an intense pain in his chest and put his arm around his son.

"Funny thing," Jack said. "He was obsessed with the immunity deal. That's why he structured his whole revenge around it. It was like he was reminding us of it the whole time."

"Almost like he wanted us to catch him, bro," Oscar said.

"Yeah, and if we had," Jack said, "he would have probably come up with some deal to try and get himself immunity. Charlie knew a lot of people and, who knows, the way the world is now, he might have even thought he could really get it."

Kevin looked down at the stretcher as the team brought it through. The sheet had fallen off a little, and he could see part of Charlie's gray, waterlogged face, with a chunk taken out of his forehead where he'd hit the rocks.

"Well," he said. "He's got it now, Dad."

"What's that?" Jack said.

"Total immunity," Kevin said. "Nothing can hurt him again."

"That's right," Jack said as they turned away. "Total immunity. Let's go home, son."

He squeezed Kevin's shoulder as they walked together back toward the car.

ACKNOWLEDGMENTS

Thanks to Detective Frank Bolan (Retired) of the Wilshire Homicide Division. In addition to being a good pal, Frank explained to me all the ramifications of immunity cases, which got my imagination rolling. Frank, a born raconteur, and a legendary cop in the LAPD, is one of the many great people I met at Tom Bergin's Bar, including Chris Dolan, the writing and boxing bartender, who always brought me extra paper so I could almost keep up with Bolan's wild tales. Also best to Mike, Charlie, Lisa, and Rob.

At the FBI I got major help from Special Agent Laura Eimiller, who put me in touch with everyone I needed to know, and Special Agent Scott Garriola, who is not only a great agent, but also a hell of a storyteller.

Big kudos to my amazing agent Philip Spitzer, the master of not only the deal, but the world's greatest joke teller, and my Literary Manager Lukas Ortiz, one of the most amazing karaoke singers in the world, especially when it comes to Jim Morrison

357

impersonations. In Hollywood, my thanks to agent Joel Gotler, who loves to riff and plays blues harp to rival Sonny Boy Williamson.

Love and respect to Otto Penzler, my buddy for many years, and now, happily, my editor. Thanks to Lindsey Smith and Judith McQuown for their help in the editing process.

Thanks and big love to my wife, Celeste Wesson, and my sons, Robbie, Shannon, and Kevin. And special kudos to my mother, Shirley Kauffman, the true Queen of Baltimore.

And, finally, all my love to Jason and his family.